Flames Across the Susquehanna

by Glenn S. Banner

Published under the auspices of the
Columbia Historical Preservation Society
P. O. Box 578
Columbia, PA 17512

Illustrators

Cover art and chapter illustrations by Bot Roda, Lancaster, Pa.
"The Drummer Boy" dedication by Rosemary Robinson, Columbia, Pa.
"Crossed Flags" by Steve Weaver, Elizabethtown, Pa.

Brookshire Printing, Inc.
200 Hazel Street
Lancaster, PA 17603
717-392-1321

ISBN 1-880976-24-2

First Printing 1993
Second Printing 1993
Third Printing 1994
Fourth Printing 1997
Fifth Printing 1999
Sixth Printing 2003

FOREWORD

Students of Civil War history have long known of the significance of events which took place nearly a century and a half ago in and around the Susquehanna River towns of Wrightsville and Columbia, Pennsylvania. Historians have from time to time, written just briefly of the Underground Railroad in Columbia and the patriotic actions of the local citizenry when the Confederates arrived on the west shore of that bridge in June of 1863.

Ever since those historic happenings occurred, many have longed for a book which would chronicle the details of those dramatic incidents and, at the same time, present a story based on historical and sometimes fictional events and persons from that period. At last, there is such a book - a novel which appropriately tells the story; and it is especially fitting that ***Flames Across the Susquehanna*** is written by a former Columbian.

Author Glenn Banner carefully crafts a story which details in vibrant fashion many exciting happenings from those eventful years of 1862 and '63. Included are wonderful accounts of the highly secret workings of the Underground Railroad of Columbia under the watchful eyes of the Wright family. In addition, are found amusing and sometimes heart-rending tales of life in the 125th Pennsylvania Regiment as told from the eyes and mind of Joey Shelley, a teen-age drummer boy. Readers will readily take this lad into their hearts as they learn of his enormous courage, compassion, personal relationship with God, his love of family and dedication to his military compatriots. We can follow Joey from school days in York County to life on his father's farm near Accomac and his introduction into military life as a volunteer drummer boy. All the sounds and fury of battle are recorded as Joey finds his units engaged at Antietam and Fredericksburg, two of the bloodiest battles of the war. And finally we can read of Joey's return to civilian life only to witness one more momentous occurrence in the closing chapters.

As the title suggests, there are ***Flames Across the Susquehanna,*** and the author's powerful version of the events of that June day in 1863 make for memorable reading. There is much evidence of in-depth research by the author to bring to his readers many accounts not heretofore recorded.

One of the main reasons this novel is enjoyable reading is the author's concentration, not on the generals or the politicians of that era or on the military strategies employed, but instead on the ordinary people and soldiers of that day - the ones who bore the major burdens of that horrible struggle between the states. ***Flames Across the Susquehanna*** is a book for readers of all ages and one which reflects all of the ingredients of a good story.

Wayne Von Stetten

Principal *(Retired)*, Brandywine High School, Wilmington, Delaware
Awarded the Valley Forge Freedoms Foundation Educators Medal in 1973
Named Principal of the Year, 1971 and 1975
Selected as a Danforth Foundation Fellow in 1979
Inducted into the Pennsylvania Sports Hall of Fame, 1988
Member, Board of Directors, Columbia Historical Preservation Society

This ***140th Anniversary Special Edition*** *is dedicated to*
Dr. Claire F. Storm, *President of* ***Rivertownes PA USA,*** *for her tireless, constant efforts to carry to fruition all the events and ceremonies surrounding the reenactment of the bridge burning planned for June 28, 2003.*

Further kudos are extended to her husband ***Albert C. Storm, Sr.,*** *and her son* ***Albert C. Storm, Jr.,*** *as well as the following members of* ***Rivertownes*** *and the* *Events Committee* *who are similarly engrossed in this singular undertaking:*

Ginny Abendschein, *First Vice-President*
Fred Abendschein, *Secretary*
Lenny Droege, *Treasurer*

Don Lehman
Adam Mattern
Bob Schmidt

And . . . ***every*** *last individual involved with* ***Rivertownes*** *who has helped in any way to make our towns proud during this momentous occasion. I salute you all and thank you most sincerely on the behalf of every citizen of* ***Columbia, Wrightsville, and Marietta!!!***

This novel is further dedicated to the solemn memory of all teen-age drummer boys of the Civil War, both Confederate and Union.

PREFACE

This book was written primarily to point out the importance of a little-known event which took place on June 28, 1863, on the Susquehanna River in southeastern Pennsylvania. There are some historians of the era who were convinced that had it not happened, it is extremely likely that the battle of Gettysburg would never have been fought, and that the South, therefore, could have eventually swept to victory.

The main characters of the novel are fictional; but they become involved with persons who actually lived during the period, as well as with incidents which have been recorded in our country's history, several of them indelibly.

In writing this novel, the author has intentionally endeavored to make it "down-home and folksy," in keeping with the prevailing atmosphere of rural, small-town America during our country's first century of existence.

It will be important to keep in mind that the Civil War years were very likely the saddest era of our nation's history. Yet it was a time which clearly showed a strong love for God, country, and family, as well as a deep concern for others. These are four basic principles and ideals which, at one time, formed the very fiber of our nation but which have, unfortunately, begun to deteriorate rapidly, especially during the past half century. They will all be recaptured on these pages!

The Author

Chapter 1

The Storm

It was another bright morning in the spring of 1862; and brown-haired, brown-eyed Joe Shelley was seated at the kitchen table finishing his share of hotcakes that his mother had prepared for a family of five. Eight o'clock came around quickly; but this reliable, hard-working young man had already completed his morning farm chores. Joe considered most of his work around the farm to be routine except caring for Swift, his brother Dan's handsome, chestnut stallion. Joe had obtained permission to feed and help care for the animal in as many ways as a young lad of fifteen years was able to do.

Today was no exception. As he was finishing his breakfast, Joe had his mind on Swift. What a delight it would be to ride *him* to school rather than Becky, the family's faithful but slow-footed, dappled mare. Swift had been Dan's birthday present of not quite a year ago, and Joe could only hope that some day he would be as fortunate as his eighteen-year-old brother.

After gulping down his second glass of cool, fresh milk, Joe wiped his mouth on his shirt sleeve and shoved his chair from the table.

"Don't forget, Ma! I won't be home at noon," he reminded his mother, as he slid his lunch and schoolbooks from a cupboard shelf. Then he received his customary departing kiss on the cheek and headed for the door.

Joe had made arrangements to go exploring for more Indian relics today with his two friends, Dave and Ted. Their plans were to go during the noon hour, since the area they wished to search was not too distant from their one-room schoolhouse, nestled in the York County hills, overlooking the broad expanse of the Susquehanna River.

Joe vaulted over the porch railing; and as he raced down the stone path toward the stable, he could see the Wilson buckboard in the distance, as it neared the crest of a hill just north of the Shelley farm. Leaving for school in the wagon besides Mrs. Wilson and her own two youngsters, was Joe's fourteen-year-old sister Sarah.

On days when Becky wasn't needed for farm work, Joe preferred to ride her to school rather than yield to the bouncing transportation of the uncomfortable buckboard. He rode her despite his friends' taunts about her slow-footedness; but Joe comforted himself with the fact that only a handful of his schoolmates could claim a horse as their own, Dave and Ted among them.

Soon he was in the saddle headed for his rendezvous with his two pals, whom he would meet at the road leading to Accomac and the school. It was a clear, crisp morning with a light breeze caressing the trees that skirted the road; and only a few wispy clouds seemed to cling to the horizon, offering a pleasant contrast to the thunderstorms of the previous evening.

It promised to be a good day for the boys' jaunt through the low hills along the west shore of the Susquehanna at noon, and Joe had visions of uncovering a real find. The Susquehannock Indians had lived in this general area less than a century ago; and although the boys' collection of artifacts boasted numerous arrowheads and even a tomahawk, they yearned for some of the relics they knew could be unearthed if they were fortunate enough to stumble upon one of the ancient Indian villages or burial grounds one day.

As these thoughts raced through Joe's mind, he suddenly noticed that Dave and Ted had already reached the crossroads and were waiting for him. Dave was Joe's age, but Ted was a year older and had real artistic talent. He enjoyed drawing people, especially Indians, as well as Indian artifacts.

At that moment, Ted, his reddish hair flashing in the early morning sunlight, was waving his hat frantically as a signal for Joe to get Becky moving at a faster rate. Secretly, Joe hoped that his friends wouldn't want to race down the slope to the schoolhouse today; but he knew it was merely wishful thinking. The race was practically a daily event, and Becky always finished last!

"C'mon!" Dave yelled. "We've been waitin' nearly an hour!" he exaggerated.

Joe grinned. It was customary to poke fun at whoever was last to arrive, and this time it was his turn to take the good-natured banter.

"Yeah, if we don't get a move on, Mrs. Wilson's buckboard'll beat us to school; an' we'll be the laughin' stock o' York County!" Ted pretended to complain.

"Should we give you an' Becky a ten-length head start?" Dave chuckled.

Joe knew his friend was only joking. "No, thanks. We'll play fair an' square. Besides, Becky might be insulted an' leave you guys in a cloud o' dust."

This brought a howl of laughter from Ted, but in another moment they were on their way. For a short while it was nip and tuck, as first one and then another gained a slight advantage. But as usual, before long Becky began to lose ground; and Joe watched in helpless resignation as his chums began to move ahead, galloping down the gradual slope toward Accomac. In less than a minute the Wilson buckboard was in sight, and everyone in it was looking expectantly for the three boys. Actually, all their schoolmates had come to look forward to the event; and they lined the split-rail fence each day to watch eagerly for the boys to appear.

With dust and dirt clods flying, Dave and Ted passed the bouncing rig; and eventually Joe and Becky edged by, just before it reached the school yard. Joe's two buddies had such a close finish that at least a dozen of their school friends were engaged in a heated argument as to who had passed the gate first.

At last, satisfied to call it a draw, the boys dismounted; and then all three led their animals toward the pasture beside the school yard, where a friendly neighboring farmer allowed them to graze their horses.

As they returned to the yard, they were greeted by some of their cronies. One lad sang out tauntingly, "Why don't you give Becky to the Union Army, Joey? As slow as General McClellan moves, she'd fit right in!"

Joe laughed along with the others, realizing that although everyone joked about Becky, all of them were extremely fond of the gentle mare and often enjoyed riding her, especially the younger children.

Even before the boys rounded the front of the schoolhouse, they heard the sound of drum beats. "Sounds like Jeff Martin's wailin' the bejeepers outta his old, weather-beaten drum again," Dave remarked, shaking his head and smiling.

"Hi!" yelled nine-year-old Jeff when he saw Joe and his friends coming toward him. As far as Jeff was concerned, Joe was the greatest drummer in the world. Often he would stare in open-mouthed amazement while his idol tapped out the most unbelievable rhythms his young ears had ever heard.

"Hello, Jeffy!" Joe called. "Let me hear that beat again. I think you're catchin' on pretty good in such a short time. You must be practicin'!"

Smiling at this praise coming from his teacher, Jeff began rolling the drumsticks as well as his small hands could, trying desperately to keep the rhythm going the way Joe had recently shown him.

"That's pretty good, Jeff! Keep it up!" Joe encouraged him.

"Yeah, by this time next year you an' Joey'll be able to do a tricky duet together an' charge admission besides," said Dave, winking in Joe's direction.

"That's right, Jeff," Ted added. "An' in a couple o' more years you'll be so good that Joey'll be comin' to *you* for lessons."

Jeff blushed, deposited one hand in his pocket, stared at the ground and scribbled in the dust with his big toe. Then looking up sheepishly, he said, "Aw, shucks! You know I'll never be better'n Joey!"

Ted lifted the youngster and set him on the top porch step. After slipping the strap from around the lad's neck, he handed the drum and sticks to Joe. In a matter of seconds practically everyone on the school grounds gathered around, knowing very well what to expect.

"Make 'em roll, Joey!" Jeff pleaded.

"Yeah! C'mon, Joey!" chorused the others.

Drumming had been a tradition in the Shelley family for generations, and Joe's father had taught him to handle drumsticks even as a child. Ever since he was twelve he had been playing in a small band, along with his father, nearly every Saturday evening during the summers in the little community of Columbia just across the river.

Now, as everyone watched and listened, he began tapping a catchy cadence. Then as his fingers became accustomed to the feel of the sticks, he so nimbly rolled out a series of beats that it appeared as though he held a dozen sticks in each hand rather than one.

"Go! Go!" everyone was yelling, while they clapped rhythmically at the same time; but they were suddenly interrupted by another familiar sound, as Mr. Constein stood in the doorway ringing his ageless handbell.

"Aw, nuts! Just when Joey was gettin' warmed up!" Jeff grumbled, as everyone headed for the morning session of classes.

The hours seemed to drag endlessly for Joe; and several times, very uncharacteristically, his mind was not on his school work. His thoughts were shifting constantly from what he had been hearing recently concerning the progress of the war, and the boys' proposed noonday trip for Indian relics. But at last a sudden scuffle of feet interrupted his latest fit of daydreaming, and he discovered that everyone was leaving for lunch.

"C'mon, Lightning!" Dave cried as he scrambled past Joe's desk. "By the time you get ready to leave, it'll be time to come back!"

Even before Dave and Ted were off the porch steps, Joe put away his books and slate. Then, with his lunch packet in hand, he went dashing right past them. "Race you to the pasture!" he yelled.

A second invitation was unnecessary, but both boys knew they'd never catch him. Riding Becky, Joe came in dead last; but swimming or a foot race was another matter altogether. He crossed the plot and slithered through the rail fence well ahead of his two pals.

In a little while the boys rode to the main trail and were heading eastward toward the Susquehanna. When they came to a fork in the road, they chose the upstream trail, which quickly became so narrow that they were forced to travel single file. Dave led the way down a sharp incline and across a small creek. Then as they worked their way up the opposite bank, Joe happened to glance through some overhanging branches. Since leaving the school they had been chattering almost constantly about one thing or another, paying little attention to the sky. Now, above the hilltops to their left, it was becoming ominously black.

"Look at those clouds!" Joe exclaimed. "Maybe we'd better not try it today!"

"Just 'cause it's gettin' a little dark don't mean it'll rain for sure," Ted replied casually.

"Yeah. An' besides, we just had some thunderstorms early last evenin'," Dave recalled. "I doubt we'll get another one so soon."

"I hope you're right," Joe murmured. However, as they continued their ride near the riverside, he continued casting wary glances through the openings overhead.

Before long they arrived at Wildcat Falls, formed by a large creek that wended its way toward the Susquehanna. Dave turned in his saddle. "Let's try this spot again," he suggested. "We had some luck here the last time; remember?"

His comrades agreed and after tethering their horses, they walked toward the hillside, where the gentle, gurgling sounds of the gradually tumbling cascades were like soothing music to their ears. There they began scanning the ground closely, eating their lunch as they searched. From time to time, one of them would kneel or stoop to pick up an object; but in each case it was just another stone to be dejectedly cast aside. Cautiously, Joe slid down the creek embankment near the falls, where there was a rather large pool of calm water.

"Hey!" he shouted. "Here's a good spot! At least there's plenty o' stones."

Dave looked down from above him. "Yeah, there sure are. But that's prob'ly all you'll find. Stones!"

Despite his chum's opinion, Joe decided to give the objects at his feet a closer look. As he stooped, he squinted because of the sun's dazzlingly brilliant reflection in the creek; but at that very instant it suddenly disappeared. Lifting his head, he observed heavy, dark clouds moving to a point directly overhead, concealing the noonday sun. Standing bolt upright, he was about to inform his buddies, when Ted came dashing up the hillside waving his arms and yelling triumphantly.

"Look what I found!" he called.

Dave half slid, half ran down the hillside; and Joe scampered out of the creek in his haste to see why Ted was gesturing so enthusiastically. When their pal stretched out his hand, he was holding a shiny piece of brownish-white flint rock with an obviously unmistakable "vee" point.

"This is one o' the best arrowheads we've found yet!" Ted exclaimed. "Look how sharp an' jagged it is!"

"Where'd you find it?" Dave asked anxiously.

"Down there," Ted answered, pointing in the direction of a clump of brush only a few yards down the slope. "C'mon!"

The boys hadn't taken five running steps when they were stopped in their tracks by a sudden bolt of lightning and a near-deafening clap of thunder.

"Good grief!" Ted remarked, cringing and looking skyward at the same time. "There really is a storm comin' up, Joey! An' in a hurry!"

Then, just as they were hit by a sudden gust of wind that nearly took his hat off, he added, "You were right! We'd better get outta here!"

"But maybe there're more arrowheads down there!" protested Dave. "Who cares if we get a little wet?"

"If there are, we can get 'em some other time!" Joe barked. "This is gonna be anything but a spring shower. We'll come back!"

Convinced at last, Dave joined his pals leaping over rocks and small shrubs as they dashed toward their horses. Joe was first to reach the lower ground, where Becky was already prancing nervously. His left foot shot into the stirrup, and in another second he slid into the saddle.

"You two better go first," he called uneasily through the heavy winds that were already blowing lustily. "Becky an' I may hold you back if we take the lead."

The boys retraced the trail as rapidly as safety would permit. It was rocky, and countless tree roots stretched across it. To make matters worse, visibility was especially poor since the sun had ceased shining; and the blackness of the clouds, coupled with the dense overhanging tree branches, practically changed day into night. The wind was coming in even stronger gusts now, and a glance at the river showed that whitecaps were forming.

"Looks like we're in for it!" Ted moaned, ducking just in time to avoid being unsaddled by a low-hanging, wind-tossed limb.

Piercingly, another streak of lightning flashed across the sky, its brilliant whiteness filtering through the trees and momentarily illuminating their way. In the blink of an eye, a harsh clap of thunder echoed among the hillsides, frightening the mounts and causing the boys to cringe low in their saddles, almost hugging their horses' necks.

"Wow!" Dave gasped in an awe-filled tone. "You said it, Joey! This is gonna be a whopper!"

Speaking soothingly to their excited steeds, the boys finally regained the main trail. Immediately the horses leaped forward at full gallop just as raindrops began to fall, coming slowly at first; but suddenly, larger drops enveloped them in almost blinding, wind-blown torrents. Through the deluge they could barely see where they were headed; but fortunately, the horses instinctively held the trail.

Shortly, however, Becky lagged well behind the others; and before long Dave and Ted disappeared through the curtain of rain. Becky plodded cumbersomely along; and then, just as she reached the entrance to the school yard, the heavens unleashed still another hissing, crackling bolt of lightning which struck a huge oak tree standing near the edge of the trail. Accompanying the flash was a burst of ear-splitting thunder, startling both horse and rider. Almost instantly Joe heard the splintering of the aged tree's once sturdy

BOT RODA

trunk; then watched in horror as the heavy limbs and branches came hurtling directly toward them!

Whinnying fearfully, Becky reared and pawed the air while Joe tugged frantically at the reins, but all attempts to control her were in vain. Becky failed to respond; and within seconds the massive boughs collapsed upon them, hurling Joe violently from the saddle.

When Joe regained consciousness, his vision was somewhat blurred; and at first he didn't know where he was. Then, as his surroundings gradually came into focus, he realized he was lying on the schoolroom floor and looking into the face of his worried schoolmaster. Impulsively, he tried to bring himself to a sitting position; but a stinging throb along the right side of his head quickly changed his mind.

"Take it easy, Joey! You've been hurt pretty badly!" Mr. Constein cautioned. "Just lie still. As soon as the rain lets up, we'll get you to Doctor Taylor."

"You sure had us scared!" breathed Dave in an anxious tone.

"I'll say!" agreed Ted. "When the lightning hit that oak tree, it lit up everything! An' when we saw it fallin', we thought sure you were goners!"

"Oh, Becky!" Joe cried out, suddenly remembering what had happened. "Where is she? Is she all right?" he asked, trying to sit up again.

As Mr. Constein placed a restraining hand on him once more, Dave and Ted exchanged worried glances and looked to their schoolmaster for help.

When Joe noticed that everyone suddenly became quiet, he blurted, "What happened to . . ." But in his excitement his head began to throb even more painfully, and he was unable to finish. Losing his strength, he gradually slumped back to the floor as Dave and Ted slowly walked away.

"Both you and your horse are in a bad way," Mr. Constein began. "We pulled you out, but Becky was struck by one of the main limbs. She's still pinned down out there in the rain."

"Then we gotta help 'er!" And yet a third time Joe tried unsuccessfully to get up.

"We've sent for help, Joey," Mr. Constein assured him. "We don't have enough tools or strong arms and backs to move the limbs. While we were trying to free you, Sarah insisted that she take Dave's horse and ride home to get your father. And a few of the kids went to tell some of the other folks who live nearby. There'll be help here soon enough; so, please, just lie still."

Joe now had a sickening feeling in the pit of his stomach to go along with the throbbing pain in his head, both of which convinced him that he should accept his schoolmaster's advice. Raising his hand tentatively to investigate the painful area, he felt the makeshift bandages that had been wrapped around his scalp. They were damp to the touch; and as he lowered his hand, he saw that his fingertips were bloody.

"Here come some men in a rig!" Ted shouted, watching through a nearby window.

Mr. Constein left quickly; and in a matter of a few minutes, others arrived to offer their aid.

After the lightning had struck, the tree began to blaze; but fortunately, the rain came down in such a deluge that nature itself extinguished the flames of its own making. Now the lower portion of the jagged trunk stood smoldering, while the remainder of the tree lay across the trail. One large bough had struck the rail fence in front of the school, violently splintering two entire sections; and pieces of wooden rails, both large and small, were strewn throughout the area.

Becky, meanwhile, still lay helplessly pinned beneath one of the heaviest limbs of the tree. Pawing restlessly with one free hoof, she tried to move her head in a nearly futile effort to watch her rescuers.

"Let's get some o' those fence rails for levers!" shouted one of the men.

While they were going about the laborious task of freeing the animal, Joe's father and sister came riding down the muddy trail on Dave's horse, Beauty.

As the two rode toward the group, Mr. Constein hailed them. "Joey's inside. He regained consciousness, and I think he'll be all right as soon as we can get him to Doc Taylor. He'll get that wound closed." Then, nodding in Becky's direction, he added, "I'm afraid for her though!"

Without delay Mr. Shelley directed his course to the schoolroom; and after he was certain that Joe had been taken care of properly, he returned to the gathering outside. A half dozen men had managed to free Becky from the overburdening weight of the oak, but she was unable to rise to her feet. Mr. Shelley glanced inquiringly at Bob Loney, a neighbor and close friend, as well as the area's very reliable animal doctor.

Mr. Loney shook his head hopelessly. "That right hind leg is shattered!" he said.

Joe's father gazed forlornly at his faithful, dappled mare, now lying practically motionless. Whinnying softly, Becky lay her head on the ground, blinking painfully but still watching every move with mournful eyes, almost as though she realized her fate.

"Sarah, get inside, please," her father said firmly.

Moments later, after Sarah entered the schoolroom, closed the door and then leaned back upon it, Joe noticed her worried face.

"What's wrong?" he asked.

"Becky's hurt bad! I'm afraid . . ."

Her words were cut short by the piercing crack of a rifle shot. Joe winced, then fought to hold back his tears; but Sarah wept openly.

Shortly, Mr. Shelley strode into the room. "Let's go, son," he said, placing one strong arm around Joe's back and another under his knees. "The rain stopped."

"I think I can walk, Pa," Joe protested; but his father paid no attention. In a matter of seconds he whisked his son to Bob Loney's rig. Obligingly, one of the men took off his jacket and laid it on the flat boards, providing a dry covering where Joe could rest more comfortably. Quickly, Sarah jumped into the wagon, sat on her shawl behind him and cupped her brother's head in her hands to help the ride go more smoothly.

Mr. Loney clucked softly to his horse, heading for Doctor Taylor's home, less than ten minutes away. As the wagon passed through the gateway, Joe merely stared at the grayness of the sky, finding it difficult to swallow and impossible to talk.

It was more than an hour before they finally arrived home. When Mrs. Shelley heard the rig, she nervously rushed outside where her son's accumulation of bandages caused much concern.

The entire family expressed its gratitude to Mr. Loney, for their neighbor was well-known for helping others. Though Joe was only in his early teens, he had been entrusted with the knowledge that Mr. Loney was instrumental in helping many runaway slaves in their efforts to escape bondage, his home being used from time to time as a station along the Underground Railroad.

"I'm supposed to go to bed an' stay there till tomorrow, Ma. Doc Taylor's orders," Joe said after entering the house.

"Sounds like good advice, Joey," his mother admitted, concern in her voice. "But if you fall asleep, I'll be sure to have some warm supper when you wake. Dan's been away all day, and he probably won't get back till late. So I'll be keeping some supper warm for him too."

"Where'd he go?"

Mrs. Shelley sighed. Then, forcing a smile, she said, "He's gone to York for supplies . . ." There was an uncomfortable pause; and then she added, "And while he's there he plans to join the Union Army!"

"He does?" Joe asked.

Somewhat stunned by this unexpected news, he sauntered thoughtfully up the stairs to the room he shared with his older brother.

Early that evening, amid an uncommonly strained atmosphere, Dan and his father worked together unloading the supplies. When they finished, Mr. Shelley finally broke the silence.

"Your mother has some warm supper for you an' Joey. Afterwards I think we'd better have one of our family chats."

"Hasn't Joey eaten either?" Dan asked, surprised.

"No, that's one o' the things we'll be talkin' about, I suppose," his father informed him, stacking a bag of seed into a corner of the barn. "Your brother had a pretty bad accident today!"

Later, Mrs. Shelley took Joe's supper upstairs. Then, after Dan finished eating, he joined his parents and Sarah in the parlor, where the next quarter of an hour was devoted to the circumstances surrounding Joe's accident.

Rather shocked by this news, Dan shook his head. "We lost a horse, but at least we still have five in our family! We can be thankful for that!"

After turning to his father, he inquired, "How long did it take old Doc to close the cut, Pa?"

"'Bout half an hour. I couldn't even watch!" Mr. Shelley admitted. "But Joey hardly let out a whimper! He's got a lot o' spunk."

However, Mrs. Shelley had other concerns as well. Interrupting, she asked, "Now, how do you stand with the army, Dan?"

Her son shook his head once more. "I'm not sure, now that you told me about Joey," he answered, somewhat bewildered. "I planned to join the cavalry an' take Swift with me; but since Becky's lost, you'll need him more than I will."

Mrs. Shelley looked up from her spinning. "Swift's yours, Dan. Our gift to you. If you really want to take him with you, then that's what you should do."

"I know you feel that way, Ma," Dan acknowledged. "But I think I'd prefer to leave him here an' take my chances o' gettin' into the cavalry anyhow. It's just that I knew they'd be better if I had my own horse."

"Well, we appreciate your thoughtfulness, son," his father remarked. Then changing the subject, he asked, "But when will you leave?"

"I hoped it wouldn't be for at least two weeks yet, but I'm supposed to report next Thursday. That gives me eight days," Dan figured.

"They'll go fast," his father remarked. "An' I'd like you to know that if our positions were reversed, I'd've done the same, Dan. War's a terrible thing, but you know how your ma an' I feel. We've seen enough runaways to realize that a great injustice is bein' done!"

Nodding in agreement, Dan arose and strode toward the doorway. "Excuse me, please; but I'd like to talk to Joey a while if he's not asleep yet. I have an idea that may cheer him up a bit after what's happened today."

He ascended the steps and walked quietly to the room he shared with his kid brother. Gently pushing the door, he peered around it to see if Joe was awake.

"What's up?" Joe asked when he saw him, setting an empty dish on the table beside his bed.

Dan entered slowly, but for several moments he said absolutely nothing, simply staring at the multitude of bandages.

"I've just been told about your adventures this afternoon with Ted an' Dave," he said finally. "An' I can see by the looks o' things, you made one serious mistake."

"What's that?" Joe asked, knitting his brows.

"You shoulda had all those bandages put on *before* you got hit with that tree. You never woulda felt a thing!"

Dan's joking was just the medicine Joe needed. "Oh, don't make me laugh!" he pleaded. "It makes my head ache!"

"All right. Besides, I've got somethin' more serious to discuss with you," he said, sitting on the edge of the bed. Heaving a sigh, he continued. "I understand the family lost a good work animal today, an' that sorta puts a cramp in some o' my plans."

Joe lowered his gaze but said nothing. Then, as Dan told him of his decision to leave Swift at home, the older brother arose and paced a few steps from the bed. Turning to face Joe again, he asked, "Do you think you could take good care o' Swift for me till I come back?"

Joe could hardly believe his ears! He was so startled by the suddenness of the question, that he found himself practically speechless.

"Will I?" he finally yelped. "You bet I will! I'll take *real* good care of him, Dan! Heck, we're good friends already; an' it won't take long before he'll trust me the same way he trusts you. I know it won't!"

Dan received the very response he had expected. "Well don't forget," he said, pointing his finger at Joe. "Swift's just a youngster, an' needs *plenty* of exercise. Get him on the open road once in a while an' just let him go, 'cause he loves to run!"

The following Monday, as the buckboard bounced down the slope toward the school, Joe kept looking backward, expecting Dave and Ted to come thundering over the top of the knoll; but they never appeared. Then, once he arrived, he quickly became the center of attention; and Mr. Constein even came outdoors to greet him.

Jeff Martin couldn't take his eyes from the swath of bandages. "Gosh! Does it hurt, Joey?" he asked.

"Not anymore, Jeffy," Joe assured him.

"Well, then . . . you prob'ly feel good enough to play the drum, don't you?" chimed his idolizing admirer.

"I always feel good enough for that, Jeffy," Joe grinned; but before he had an opportunity to delight his friends with his favorite pastime, he heard the sound of hooves and turned to see Dave and Ted riding leisurely into the yard.

"What? No race today?" he inquired. "I expected to see you guys dashin' past our buckboard like you were goin' after the Rebs!"

"I guess we just didn't feel like racin'!" Ted offered somewhat dejectedly. "It ain't the same!" And he made no further remark, as he and Dave slowly walked their horses toward the pasture.

Joe had missed two days of school because of his accident, and he was happy to be back with his friends again. Even so, the day couldn't go quickly enough. When classes were finally finished, his mother came with the family wagon; and they stopped at Dr. Taylor's office on the way home. At last, when Joe left the company of the kindly physician, he felt much lighter, having traded his thick wrappings for a much smaller and more comfortable array of bandages.

The following day was an uneventful one at school; but after dismissal that afternoon, Joe called to Dave and Ted as they walked toward their horses. "How 'bout waitin' for me at the crossroads tomorrow?"

"All right. But why? You'll be in the buckboard, won't you?" Dave asked.

Avoiding the question completely, Joe replied, "Just wait for me, will you?" Then with a grin he turned and ran toward Mrs. Wilson's rig, while Dave and Ted exchanged puzzled glances.

As the Shelley brothers were completing some of their daily chores that evening, Joe asked permission to ride Swift to school the following morning. Not only did Dan give his consent, but he suggested that Joe saddle Swift and take him out that very evening.

"I'll finish your work," Dan insisted. "After all, he'll be yours for a while; an' you may as well get use' to one another."

Dan laughed inwardly, knowing what his brother had in mind for the next morning, since he had often heard Joe talk about the daily race. Then as his kid brother headed toward the stable, Dan called after him.

"By the way, since that cut's healed pretty good by now, fast ridin' won't hurt none. Let him gallop for a while. You know . . . Maybe . . . 'bout the distance from the crossroads to the school."

Joe turned and flashed a wide grin. "You think you're pretty smart, don't you?" Then he raced to the stable with Dan's laughter echoing in his ears.

Ten minutes later, Joe and Swift headed for the main road connecting Wrightsville to York. Once there, Joe rode leisurely for more than a mile toward the west; but when he noticed that there was very little daylight remaining, he decided to return home.

Leaning forward in the saddle, he patted the chestnut on his sleek, sturdy neck. Practically whispering, he said, "Hopefully, we'll be ridin' hard tomorrow, boy. Let's see how fast we can go back!"

Joe slapped his heels against Swift's flanks, and the response was immediate. With a sudden burst of awesome power, Swift sprang forward like a shot! Fortunately, Joe had a firm grip on the reins; for he was momentarily thrown off balance. Then, quickly regaining his equilibrium, he leaned forward, so thrilled by Swift's speed that he could hardly control his emotions!

The road was a succession of one gentle hill followed by another; and it seemed to Joe that Swift was hardly at the bottom of one rise before he was already at the top of the next, his sturdy hooves clapping the road like drum beats. Not until they reached the first home on the outskirts of Wrightsville, did Joe rein the stallion to a halt.

"You run like you're scared to death, boy!" he chanted, firmly patting the chestnut's neck several times. "Take it easy now, boy. I got a feelin' you'll get a chance to do plenty o' runnin' tomorrow."

As the sun was setting, Dan was about to walk onto the porch when Joe and Swift came down the lane and through the gate. "How'd it go?" he called.

"Great!" Joe laughed. "I bet I won't be able to sleep tonight. I can hardly wait till tomorrow!"

The next day, Joe thought the time to leave for school would never arrive; but finally his mother and Sarah left in the rig.

"Don't forget!" Joe yelled as they neared the gate. "If you see Ted an' Dave, tell 'em I'm on my way."

A few minutes later, Dan stood leaning against the stable door, watching Joe saddle Swift. "Good luck!" he said. "An' don't let him ride out from under you!"

Joe mounted Swift and waved, showing an anxious smile and hoping that nothing would go wrong to spoil his surprise. Then, a few minutes later, as Swift trotted around the final bend, Joe noticed that his friends were also just arriving. When they saw Joe astride Swift, they simply stared.

"Hey! What's this all about?" asked Dave at length.

"Ain't that your brother's horse?" Ted added, before Joe had a chance to answer.

"Yeah, but he'll be mine till Dan comes back some day. An' since this is the last day o' school, I asked him if I could ride Swift. Ain't he a beauty?"

"He sure is!" Dave said admiringly, leaning forward to stroke Swift's strong neck and flowing mane. "But let's go. It's gettin' late!"

As they casually rode along, they talked mostly about their plans for the summer; but finally, much to Joe's delight, Dave suggested a race.

"Hey! We gotta see if Swift can live up to his name!" he announced.

"Suits me," Ted agreed. "But maybe you'd better not do any fast ridin' yet, Joey."

Not wanting to appear too anxious, and yet almost being torn apart inwardly, Joe pretended to give Ted's advice careful consideration.

"Well . . . I *guess* it'll be all right," he drawled. "Doc Taylor even took the last o' the bandages off yesterday afternoon," he added,

running his hand through his hair.

"Well, what're we waitin' for then?" piped Dave.

First they brought their mounts to a complete stop. Then at Ted's signal, they galloped away. On previous occasions all three boys usually got off to a fairly even start, but not this time! Swift bolted forward and took the lead from the very outset; and Joe made certain he was prepared, leaning well forward as the air whipped through Swift's flying mane. In a few moments they cleared the crest of the hill and galloped down the slope in the traditional cloud of dust. Hazarding a glance over his shoulder and chuckling to himself, Joe saw that Dave and Ted were already nearly three lengths behind.

Seeing that the trail was clear, he realized that his mother's rig had already entered the schoolyard, where Sarah had probably informed everyone that there might be another race today; and Swift, responding to his chance to run, brought Joe across the imaginary finish line a full six lengths ahead of his companions.

For their friends in the yard, it was a treat to see Joe win for the first time ever; and a hearty, prolonged cheer, as well as several hats, went up from those who were lining the rail fence.

"Well! I guess we found out he can run!" Dave exclaimed, riding toward his friend.

"No doubt about it!" Ted remarked with an astonished expression on his face. "Looks like there's a new champion in the neighborhood!" he added, shaking his head in disbelief and patting Swift approvingly.

During the excitement of the race, Mrs. Shelley had been talking to Mr. Constein; and as the boys led their horses through the yard, she was climbing into the family rig.

Looking in their direction, she called, "We'll have plenty of things to take across the river to the Columbia Market on Saturdays this summer. Since you boys like to ride so much, maybe we'll have a job for all three of you sometimes."

"Just call on us," Ted replied. "We'll be glad to help if it's all right with our folks."

Before the boys left school that final day, they made plans to look for Indian relics once again. However, this time they decided to head for the Indian village and burial sites near Washington Boro, a tiny village on the other side of the river, just a few miles south of the long covered bridge which connected Wrightsville and Columbia.

Chapter 2

The Stranger

Several weeks had passed since the last day of school, during which the Shelley family was slowly adjusting to Dan's absence. It was Friday and everyone was helping with the preparations for the next day's marketing in Columbia. Joe was especially anxious for market day because Ted and Dave were going to accompany them, and he had received permission to spend part of the day with his companions searching for Indian relics in Washington Boro. However, his parents insisted that he come back early to help reload the wagon and then go to the Columbia park for the Saturday evening band concert.

Before the family was prepared to leave on Saturday morning, Ted and Dave rode into the yard.

Joe hailed them as he walked toward the rig with a basket of peas in one hand and a pail of beans in the other. "All set for the big day?" he asked.

"You bet! Can we help with anything?" Dave inquired.

"Ask Pa," Joe replied as he hurried toward the house. "He's in the barn. I still hafta finish breakfast," he called over his shoulder.

The boys helped with the final preparations; then Ted settled on the back porch with his sketching pad and stick of charcoal that he always carried in his saddlebag.

"Turn your head a little more this way," he directed Sarah, as she sat on the long porch swing. Quickly and skillfully, he began to draw her portrait, while they waited for Joe and his mother.

Approximately ten minutes afterwards, Mr. Shelley passed by.

Peering inquisitively over the young man's shoulder, he exclaimed, "Say, Ted, that's pretty good! You're gettin' to be quite an artist, young man! How'd you get started with that?"

"Thank you, sir," Ted replied. "I guess it's like my ma says: it's just a gift from God. After I look at someone for even just a few seconds, I can actually close my eyes and still picture every last detail of a face; an' I can remember it for months. But I drew this in a hurry. I can do better when I have more time," he added, as he handed it to Joe's grateful sister.

"You keep it, Sarah. Maybe I'll get a chance to fill in more details some other time," he said with a smile.

A few minutes later, Mr. Shelley came from the house carrying his own drum as well as Joe's, and placed them carefully in a corner of the wagon. "Well, I suppose we're just about set," he announced. "Hope you boys enjoy listenin' to the band tonight!"

At last it appeared that everyone was finally ready. Sarah and her parents clambered into the wagon, while the boys prepared to follow on horseback, their saddlebags packed full of various articles to be sold at the market place.

As they entered Wrightsville a short while later, they promptly began to descend the long slope leading to the Susquehanna River. Columbia and its surrounding hills were clearly visible across the wide stream; and the eye-catching view of one of the world's longest covered bridges lay before them, stretching for more than a mile.

Columbia was situated in a beautiful location and was actually considered at one time as a possible site for both the state and national capitals, Washington, D. C. being chosen by the narrow margin of just two votes! Columbians were rightfully proud of their very picturesque and busy little town. It had already become an important link of the Pennsylvania Canal System and was currently blossoming into a railroad center as well.

When they reached the bottom of the hill, they stopped to watch a single, horse-drawn train car rumble off the bridge.

"Sure looks funny seein' horses pull part of a train, don't it?" Dave observed.

"Well, if the locomotives came across, flyin' sparks could start the biggest bonfire you ever wanted to lay eyes on!" Ted remarked.

"Yeah! A wooden bridge *that* size might burn for a while!" Joe commented.

Mr. Shelley drove onto the ramp, and the rig soon disappeared into the semi-darkness. The boys, meanwhile, reined in their horses and gazed at the scene below them and to the south of the bridge.

The early morning sun glistened off the water and made them shade their eyes as they looked down upon the busy people just beginning their work day on the canal which skirted the wide river. The boys could see that several coal barges had come across from the Columbia side, on their way to Baltimore and other southern destinations.

Here was where the canal traffic crossed from one shore to the other; for along the south side of the bridge were two towpaths, one slightly above the other. While traffic was towed in one direction on the lower path, canal boats moving the opposite way could be pulled by horses or mules using the upper path.

"I'd sure like to take a trip on the canal sometime!" Ted wished, as they watched some mules amble onto the bridge towpath and begin to pull a low-slung barge toward Columbia.

"C'mon," Joe urged. "Let's get over to Columbia so we can watch 'em finish the trip over there."

The boys rode to the toll gate; and after depositing eighteen-and-a-half cents apiece with the attendant, they entered the bridge.

"Too bad you didn't walk today, Dave," Ted said jokingly to his companion. "You coulda crossed for six cents and saved a lotta money!"

"Not everybody's as cheap as you are, Ted!" his friend shot back, looking to get the final advantage in their usual battle of words.

To their left was a handrail which separated the roadbed from the walkway, and on their right was the separate section for train cars. The boards along the sides of the structure were spaced so that sufficient light could penetrate and allow travelers to see, though somewhat dimly.

A quarter of an hour later they rode off the bridge, then waited a short while before the slow-moving mules finally came along, pulling their burden toward the Columbia canal locks. As the animals came off the bridge towpath, they frightened some canvass-back ducks that were feeding in the waters where the canal joined the river; and their honking departure arrested the boys' attention momentarily. After Joe and his chums watched the canal boat complete its transit, they headed for Third and Locust Streets to help set up the Shelley's farm goods at the Columbia Market House.

Within a half hour, all the produce and Mrs. Shelley's hand-made articles were neatly arranged in an attractive display. Then, their work completed, the boys headed for Washington Boro.

As they rode toward the river trail, Joe suggested turning onto Second Street. "I'd like to go past the old Wright Mansion," he said. "There's just somethin' about the place I like. It's not out of our way."

"Why not?" said Ted agreeably.

As they approached the century-old, stone building with its wavy-glass windows, Joe asked, "Wanna hear somethin' that's liable to make you jealous?"

"What's that?" Dave asked.

"Pa says this was the first house built in Columbia, prob'ly as a kind o' fort. In those days there were nothin' but woods an' lots o' Indians around here, an' the Susquehannock would come right up to the doors an' windows an' trade with the Wrights."

"Jumpin' grasshoppers!" exclaimed Dave. "An' we gotta hunt an' dig for the stuff!"

Seeing the mansion put Joe in a pensive mood. Secretly, he knew what it was that really made him admire this old, stone home. His father had also told him that when it was constructed in the 1700's, it was believed that tunnels were dug as escape routes in the event of attack by the Indians; and this was probably the main reason why the mansion became one of Pennsylvania's most important stations of the Underground Railroad. Many runaway slaves had found a haven in this home owned by generations of Wrights, who were of strong Quaker ancestry and a very God-fearing people, openly hating slavery.

Actually, much of the *baggage*, as the slaves were frequently called, had found its way to the mansion via Wrightsville, which had gained its name from a descendant of this very same Wright family. Often the slaves had been brought across the covered bridge in the dead of night. Sometimes, however, if it was known that slaveholders or bounty hunters were in the vicinity and were watching the bridge closely, the runaways were often brought across the river by rowboat.

Joe knew that Bob Loney frequently had been involved in helping these people reach Columbia; and on more than one occasion, Joe's father had also volunteered his services when the slaves came in large numbers and extra help was needed. Since the beginning of the war, however, fewer and fewer runaways had been seen in the area; but nevertheless, one or two still straggled through from time to time.

It was said that the Wrights' methods of helping slaves escape were so uncanny, that anyone who pursued them to this area was completely baffled by the sudden disappearance of the slaves, just when he thought he was about to recover them. A well-known story was told that after losing track of some runaways in Columbia, one slaveholder had exclaimed: "There must be an underground railroad somewhere!" Supposedly, that was how the system received its now famous name.

Joe pulled on Swift's reins and stopped for a few moments to gaze at the house next door, where still another Wright descendant lived. He looked for signs of activity and hoped to see some member of the family around either of the homes, but no one was in sight.

Joe truly admired these people who had the courage to do what they thought was right, regardless of the danger involved. They had descended from a famous outspoken Quaker preacher, John Wright, who had actually given Lancaster County its name, taking it from his beloved Lancashire, England, where he was born. And after he had established a ferry across the river at this place in 1730, it was originally called Wright's Ferry in his honor. At one time his rafts ferried countless wagons across the Susquehanna, which helped immeasureably to expand the country both south and west; so very gradually, this proud little community of Columbia had been making a mark on its nation's rich history.

"Hey, Joey! Wake up!" he suddenly heard Dave calling.

"Yeah, you're really gettin' your money's worth out o' this place!" Ted remarked. "We'd better get movin'!"

"Sorry!" Joe apologized. "I just got carried away with my thoughts for a couple o' minutes."

Though Ted and Dave were his exceptionally close buddies, because of the necessity for extreme secrecy, Joe obeyed his parents and had never shared any of his knowledge about the Wrights with either of them, or with anyone else.

Soon the boys were along the river trail, where high hills rose sharply to their left; and the beautiful, wide stream flowed along calmly not too far from the other side of the trail.

"Think we'll have any luck today?" Ted asked, breaking the silence.

"You bet!" Dave answered, as he reached to skin the leaves from a honeysuckle branch that dangled limply from an embankment. "I got a feelin' we'll find so much today, we'll never hafta hunt again!" he added with an air of confidence.

"My, my! An' what else do you see in your wishin' well, pray tell?"

Joe asked, taking his turn to tease.

"All right, make fun o' me!" Dave retorted. "Just remember, when I get a hunch, it usually pays off!"

"Yeah, we know," chimed Ted. "Like that time last summer when we went fishin', an' you had a hunch you'd catch so many fish you wouldn't be able to carry 'em all home. Remember?" he asked. "Then Joey an' I caught thirteen between us, an' all you got were two wet feet an' a hungry gut!"

Dave laughed when he saw the tables were turned; but the customary banter went on unabated as their horses trotted along, keeping a good pace. Then, while hardly realizing it, they soon were entering the outskirts of Washington Boro.

Though it was a small village, it had once been an important lumbering center; and rafting on the river at this point had been quite common. However, for approximately the past decade, business had been on the decline, and the local people were turning to farming.

"Where do we go from here?" asked Dave.

"Well, if my pa's right," Ted drawled, "all we hafta do's locate the Shultz farm. Evidently the Indians must've had a village on their land years ago."

Just then, the boys saw a building that had a large sign above the door, indicating that they had arrived at Wertz's Hotel; and Joe went inside to ask for directions. In a few moments he returned with the information he was seeking. "It's not far," he called. "C'mon."

They urged their horses at a faster gait, anxious to reach their destination. After leaving the river trail, they traveled only a short distance before they saw a large, well-kept farmhouse.

"Maybe that's the place," Dave observed.

"Prob'ly so," Joe replied. "We'll find out in a minute."

As they neared the roadway leading to the house, they were greeted by a pair of barking beagles. At the end of the lane was a carriage house, connected to the farmhouse proper by a thick canopy of grape vines. On the steps of a side porch sat a rather shabbily-dressed man with an unruly shock of jet-black hair and a small mustache. It appeared as though he had met with a rather recent accident; for on his right cheek was a long, heavy, reddish scar which seemed not to be perfectly healed as yet.

"Handsome-lookin' cuss, ain't he?" whispered Dave. "Look at that scar!"

The man was devouring a plateful of eggs and bacon as though it were the first meal he had eaten in days. As the boys approached him, he glanced their way only briefly, concentrating heavily on his food.

Feeling certain that the man was a traveler or farm hand and not the proprietor himself, Joe asked, "Are the owners home?"

The stranger glared first at the boys, and then his gaze seemed to sweep from one horse to another. Finally, he looked back at Joe and simply nodded without speaking.

Joe dismounted, walked onto the porch and knocked at the door.

When it swung open, an elderly, gray-haired lady in a lavender dress smiled at him. "Land sakes!" she cried. "Sometimes we don't see anyone for weeks, an' today we get a whole flock o' visitors! Are you boys hungry too?"

Joe grinned. "No, thank you, ma'am; not yet anyhow. An' we've come supplied besides. We got plenty o' grub in our saddlebags."

Then coming to the point, he said, "We're lookin' for the Shultz homestead. Can you help us?"

"That shouldn't be too difficult," she informed him. "You're talkin' to one of 'em right now!"

"Are you the family that owns the land where the Indian relics can be found?" Ted asked excitedly.

"Land sakes! You too?" the lady chuckled pleasantly. "Such interest in old Indian junk I can't believe! But if that's what interests you, then you'd better talk to my husband. I don't know where he is, but I'll have him here in a jiffy," she announced confidently.

Then, walking briskly to the far end of the porch where an old, black skillet was hanging from a cord, she picked up a long, cast iron ladle and gave the pan three sharp raps.

"Wow!" exclaimed Dave as Beauty shied beneath him. "That's what I call a real ear-splitter!"

"That'll fetch him every time," the woman remarked; and as predicted, in less than ten seconds her husband came hastening around the far side of the barn, a friendly smile flashing across his tanned face.

"Howdy, boys," he called as he hurried toward them. "What can we do for you?"

"Good mornin', sir. My name's Joe an' these are my two sidekicks, Dave an' Ted."

The boys dismounted and reached to shake hands before Joe continued. "We came to ask you a favor, Mr. Shultz. The three of us are interested in collectin' Indian relics. Ted especially likes to use 'em for art work. An' since your farm's pretty well-known for the things that've been found on it, we were wonderin' if you'd allow us to look around an' maybe even do some diggin'."

"So . . . you're collectors, eh?" the man said slowly. Then after winking slyly in his wife's direction, he addressed the boys again, while he crossed his arms and stroked his chin as though he were in deep thought. "Well . . ." he drawled, "in the event you make any discoveries on our property . . . uh . . . what do you boys have to offer in return?"

Troubled by these unexpected words, the three looked at one another, beginning to feel slightly uncomfortable; for they hadn't given any thought whatsoever to such a development.

Mr. Shultz, meanwhile, strode slowly toward Swift and looked at him approvingly, running his hand across the stallion's left shoulder and patting the animal firmly.

"Mighty fine horse you got here," Mr. Shultz acknowledged, still gazing intently at Swift and nodding his head. "If you find anything o' *real* value . . . would you consider swappin' him?" he asked.

"Oh, no, sir! I couldn't do that!" Joe replied hastily. "In the first place Swift ain't mine; an' even if he was, I wouldn't trade him for all the Indian relics in the world!"

"Swift?" Mr. Shultz echoed immediately. "Now that's a right smart name! Is he *really* swift . . . or does he run like the water from my well pump? All in one spot!"

This brought a chuckle from the boys, but Dave sided with Joe. "I'll bet he's the fastest horse in these parts!" he stated emphatically.

"Yeah, I'll vouch for that!" Ted agreed. "We've raced already an' neither of us even finished close to him!"

Mr. Shultz put his hands on his hips. "Well, by the looks o' those nags, it's no wonder . . ."

"Oh, John, why don't you stop teasin' those boys?" his wife scolded.

The group cast a glance toward the porch to see Mrs. Shultz pouring another cup of coffee for the scar-faced man on the steps.

"Don't you boys pay him no attention a'tall," she said with a wave of her hand. "For some reason he likes to get everybody all worked up to a lather, just to see how far he can go! You're not the first ones who've come here lookin' for them confounded things, an' deep down inside he's only too glad you did! We don't get much company. Besides, if I know him like I think I do, he'll be down there helpin' you before the day's much older!"

Then turning to her husband, she added, "Now, John, why don't you let those boys get started? They're anxious!"

Mr. Shultz laughed, and clapping a burly arm around Joe's shoulder, he said, "All right, boys. You can put your horses in the carriage house or over there in the pasture," he offered, pointing to a nearby field. "Whichever you wish. Then I'll show you a couple o' likely spots down in the meadow."

The boys decided to stable their horses; and soon they were ready to follow the congenial farmer toward a plush pasture area, carrying the pick and two small spades they had brought along.

"Hold on, boys!" exclaimed Mr. Shultz, looking at them rather sternly. "Have you ever worked at an Indian site like this before?" he asked.

"Well . . . no . . . not really," Ted answered, puzzled by the look on the man's face.

"I thought so," Mr. Shultz observed. "You can't go diggin' with picks an' shovels! If you struck any pottery, you'd blast it to bits with tools like that!"

"Gosh! I guess you're right, sir!" Joe admitted. "We were just figurin' on gettin' down pretty deep, since we heard there were graves around here."

"Well, sometimes we do, but you can't get there with picks; that's a cinch! You come with me to the barn, an' I'll get you some smaller tools that're less likely to do any damage."

A few minutes later they were on their way once more, walking down a path that led from the Shultz's home, but equipped now with much smaller implements.

"There's where I uncovered a pair o' graves last August," Mr. Shultz announced, pointing with a small stick he had picked up. "I search from time to time, but I haven't had much luck lately."

Then with a sweep of his arm, he added, "Scrape the soil anyplace around here you'd like; but please, clear it *very* gently, usin' your fingers sometimes if you must. That's my only request."

"Yes, sir," the boys chorused.

"We'll be careful!" Joe added. "Thank you for warnin' us, Mr. Shultz."

"An' feel free to come to the house for a bite to eat around noon," their host called over his shoulder as he began walking away. "Just listen for the skillet!"

"Thanks anyhow, Mr. Shultz," Ted called. "But we've brought our own food along."

"Uh-oh!" Joe suddenly remembered. "I left mine in the saddlebag.

I'd better go back for it."

He walked a short distance with the gentleman farmer, but parted from him when Mr. Shultz headed toward the area where he had been working earlier. Then, as Joe turned the corner of the carriage house and was about to step inside, he came to an abrupt halt. The stranger who had been eating on the porch was tightening the cinch on Swift's saddle, and it appeared as though he actually intended to steal him! With his back toward Joe, he took Swift by the reins and began leading him stealthily through the broad doorway.

Joe was so astonished at the stranger's boldness, that at first he could only stare in disbelief! Then suddenly he blurted, "What's the idea, mister?"

Startled, the man spun around, threw a hurried glance at Joe and then quickly shot his foot into the stirrup. Without hesitating a moment, Joe made a desperate lunge, grasping him around the waist before he could complete his swing into the saddle. Joe's weight threw him off balance; and when Swift suddenly reared, the would-be horse thief fell backward, landing heavily on top of Joe.

Fortunately, Mrs. Shultz had opened the kitchen door and stepped onto the porch just in time to see Joe's headlong dive. With a cry of alarm she realized what was probably taking place. After scurrying to the end of the porch, she quickly grabbed the heavy ladle and began rapping the old skillet in groups of three steady raps, as fast and as loudly as she could.

Down in the meadow Dave and Ted were just beginning to survey the surroundings when they heard the sudden clamor.

"What's all the racket?" Dave wondered.

"Mrs. Shultz prob'ly wants her husband again," Ted guessed.

But when the clanging continued at such a loud, prolonged and rapid rate, Dave looked questioningly at Ted. "She must want him in a powerful hurry! Maybe there's somethin' wrong at the house. Let's go see!"

Dropping their implements, both boys bolted through the meadow and up the hillside.

Meanwhile, Joe learned quickly that a fifteen-year-old boy is no match for a grown man; especially a frustrated, desperate one. Joe tried frantically to hold onto the culprit; but in a fit of anger the man grabbed both of Joe's wrists, tore the lad loose, and then furiously gave him a vicious shove which sent him sprawling headlong into the grape arbor. However, as the man turned to escape in the direction of the main road, he wisely reconsidered; for Swift was right in front of him, rearing, pawing the air, snorting and whinnying loudly.

"Get him, Swift!" Joe yelled. Then, taking advantage of the opportunity, he sprang to his feet and made a second lunge at the man. He wasn't strong enough to bring his adversary to the ground, however; and once more the man tossed him roughly aside. At that precise moment, Dave and Ted came dashing around the corner of the carriage house just in time to see Joe go tumbling in the dust.

"He was tryin' to steal Swift!" Joe cried out when he saw his friends.

Again the man turned to whisk away, only to have Swift confront him threateningly a second time. When Dave and Ted saw their pal rush the stranger again, they didn't take time to ask any questions. Joe had hardly wrapped his arms around the man's waist before Ted crashed against his left leg, and Dave virtually sailed through the air with a chest-high, flying tackle. Joe staggered him, Ted's grasp began to topple him, and Dave's diving crash knocked him completely off balance, all four striking the ground almost simultaneously.

Dave was first to be thrown from the pile, followed seconds later by Joe. But before the man could free himself from Ted, both boys dived right back into the thick of the scrap still another time, while Mrs. Shultz kept up the steady three-pronged pounding on the skillet. To add to the confusion, in the midst of all this pandemonium, the two beagles suddenly shot onto the scene, spinning in circles and baying for all they were worth, while Swift kept prancing on his two hind legs, pawing the air and whinnying.

At last, furious with these pesky teen-agers, the man's right fist suddenly caught Ted on the side of his jaw with a stinging blow that sent him reeling to the edge of the driveway. Then, grasping the other two by the back of the neck and pushing them roughly, he freed himself once more and this time decided to head in the direction of the meadow.

However, he stopped dead in his tracks when he heard a deep-throated voice bellow, "Stay right where you are, mister!"

Pivoting, the stranger found himself staring down the barrel of Mr. Shultz's long rifle. Three teen-age boys he could handle, but this was another matter altogether; and resignedly, he did as he was told.

"Now, what in the name o' Sam Hill's goin' on here?" demanded Mr. Shultz.

"I saw the whole thing!" declared his wife, scrambling off the porch still clasping her ladle, and then shaking it directly in front of the

BOT
RODA

man's nose. "Of all the nerve! We give him a decent meal to fill his empty belly, an' he turns right around an' tries to steal a horse off our property! What do you think o' that?"

"I'm afraid she's right, sir!" Joe remarked. "When I came back from the meadow, he was saddlin' Swift in the carriage house. I was lucky I got here when I did!"

Then, looking at the stranger, the farmer asked, "Well . . . what do you have to say for yourself, mister?"

However, the scar-faced stranger merely stared at the ground and chose to say absolutely nothing.

Just then, hoof beats sounded on the lane. Riding toward them in a wagon was a burly, bewhiskered gentleman. Upon seeing the pointed rifle, he raised his eyebrows. "Not havin' any trouble are you, John?" he asked.

"I'm not, Abe; but this fellow made the biggest mistake o' his life when he tried to steal this young man's horse a few minutes ago. These three boys took after him like hornets in swarmin' season, but I'm afraid it was one o' the hornets that got stung!" he acknowledged, glancing toward Ted, who was still gingerly moving his jaw from side to side and holding it cautiously with his left hand.

"I'll be all right," Ted announced, when he could detect nothing other than some general soreness.

"Just take it easy!" Dave said in a comforting tone, placing his hand on his friend's shoulder. "An' don't worry if you can't chew none; I'll eat your lunch for you. It won't go to waste."

"The day you eat my lunch'll be the day the South wins the war!" insisted Ted.

Mr. Shultz chuckled in spite of the situation. "These boys are just like my own use' to be, Abe. No matter what's goin' on, teen-agers are always thinkin' o' their stomachs!"

Then, looking at the stranger once more, he quickly changed the subject and said rather sternly, "But we've got somethin' more serious to think about, boys. This man's evidently guilty of a serious crime an' should be turned over to the proper authorities to deal with accordin' to the law."

"Well . . . I was just headin' for Columbia, John," drawled the newcomer. "Stoppin' by jus' to see if there was anything I could bring back for you an' the Mrs. from market. I'd be glad to help take him to the constable at the town lock-up," he added, as he commenced to tie the man's hands with some strong cord that had been lying in the bed of his wagon.

"Well, thanks, Abe. That's right neighborly! The two of us oughta be able to handle that," Mr. Shultz acknowledged.

"Gosh, this is really all my fault!" Joe said apologetically. "An' when you get back, I'll gladly help finish your work, Mr. Shultz," he added.

Both Dave and Ted were quick to offer their help as well; and even though the farmer objected, the boys still insisted on lending a hand with his chores.

Then, remembering that Columbia's lock-up was in the cellar of the old market place, Joe said, "Sir, would you mind stoppin' in the market area an' tellin' my folks what happened? Just ask for the Shelley stand."

"Is that your family's counter?" Mrs. Shultz interrupted. "Land sakes! We've been buyin' rhubarb an' sassafras from you for years!"

"I'll stop in there gladly," Mr. Shultz replied. "An' maybe it'd be a good idea to get your pa to go along with us in case the constable needs him to press any charges against this man after I explain what went on. An' since it all happened on my property, I might hafta do some signin' myself," he admitted.

The Washington Boro farmer crawled onto the wagon, sat near the tailgate and laid his rifle across his legs. "We'll be sure to let your folks know you boys are all right," he called to Joe, as he and his friendly neighbor rode off, with the unsuccessful horse thief thoroughly tied and seated in the back.

Later, with all the excitement behind them, the boys were again surveying the meadow for prospective places to search. After discussing the matter for a while, they finally agreed to begin working in an area where Mr. Shultz evidently had previously begun to remove some soil. Then, working very carefully, they searched for more than an hour.

On one occasion, while Ted was taking a break from the hot, humid weather, he went to the carriage house for his artist's pad and charcoal stick which he kept in his saddlebags. After returning to the meadow, he sat near his friends and sketched a hasty drawing of them, making Dave's face appear as perspired and grimy as possible.

"There, Dave," he announced shortly afterwards, holding it so his companion could see. "That shows how hard you work!"

"Naturally! Now how 'bout helpin' out a while, Mr. Artist," Dave stated, flipping his trowel near Ted's feet. "It's my turn to set a spell. I'm gettin' blisters!" he exaggerated.

Within the course of two hours they changed their area of search several times. At length, it was Dave again who tossed his trowel knife-like into a small mound of dirt and flopped to the ground, pretending to be utterly exhausted.

"I don't think I can do this much longer!" he moaned, nestling into a soft patch of velvety grass and rubbing his wrists gingerly. "I didn't know it was gonna be this much work."

Joe snapped off the white head of a nearby clover and threw it at his reclining friend, managing to hit him directly on the tip of the nose. "Come on, loafer! You just took a break five minutes ago!" Joe pretended to complain. "Start workin' or I'll throw somethin' harder than clover!" he warned, reaching toward some stones which lay strewn nearby.

But Dave, knowing that his friend was simply heckling him, refused to budge from his comfortable spot. Joe was about to feint a throw when the jagged edge of the object in his hand suddenly caught his attention.

"Hey! For Pete's sake! Look!" he exclaimed.

Ted leaned over to stare into Joe's outstretched hand. "Well, if that ain't the limit!" he whined. "I was practically sittin' on it, an' you pick it up!"

"What is it?" Dave asked.

"An arrowhead!" Joe boasted, holding it closer.

At first Dave's expression was one of distrust; but finally he bowed to curiosity and slowly crawled over to inspect it more carefully. After taking one glance, he speedily picked up his trowel. "Now that makes me feel more like workin'!" he announced.

As they continued searching and periodically resting, they spent much of their time discussing the war, with Joe remarking on one occasion, "I wish I coulda gone along with my brother Dan!"

"You wouldn't be much help!" Dave laughed. "Everytime we go out shootin' rifles, the only thing we prove is that we can't hit the same spot twice."

"Well, I'll admit I'm anything but the world's champion marksman, but I could prob'ly do somethin' to help," Joe muttered as he skimmed a flat stone over the top of some waving meadow grass and into a clump of sumac trees.

After the boys took time to eat, Ted suggested choosing still another spot. But since their hands, wrists, back and knees were beginning to show signs of wear and tear, they decided that if nothing was uncovered within an hour, they would turn their attention to some of the Shultz's chores.

As time went by, they were becoming more discouraged with each trowelful of soil, and the countless false alarms which continually turned out to be nothing more than rocks. After a particularly drawn-out stretch of futile searching, Joe stopped for a few moments and looked up to see Mr. Shultz approaching.

"Any luck?" the farmer called.

"Just an arrowhead," Joe answered, reaching into his pocket and then displaying the one meager reward for their efforts.

"How'd you make out in town?" Ted wanted to know.

Mr. Shultz informed them that the stranger was in the hands of the local authorities, and that the constable had asked Joe's father to sign some papers in order to make the arrest legal, just as Mr. Shultz had surmised.

The farmer looked at Joe and said, "Your pa thinks it would be good if you're back around five-thirty, by the way; an' I promised him you'd be there."

"Thank you, sir, for all your trouble," Joe said gratefully. "We'll work a little while longer an' then give you a hand with some o' the things you woulda finished already if it hadn't been for us."

"Don't let that worry you, boys. The work'll get done in its own good time," he reassured them. "You stay at it till you find relics or blisters, whichever come first," he laughed, walking toward the barn.

"We already got the blisters!" Ted called after him, rubbing his palms together.

The boys bent to their task once more, continuing what was proving to be practically a frustratingly fruitless endeavor. However, a few minutes later, it was Ted who eventually struck something firm. As he continued to scrape carefully, he leaned forward to examine the object of his attention more closely.

Detecting Ted's sudden interest, Dave peered over his comrade's shoulder. "Hey! It looks like a piece o' pottery! Get it outta there!"

"That's what I'm tryin' to do!" Ted assured his excitable friend. "Control your emotions, will you? It looks as though it's pretty big."

"Be careful you don't break it!" Joe warned. Then looking at Dave, he said, "How 'bout gettin' Mr. Shultz?"

Dave muttered a few choice complaints under his breath as he turned to leave, but before long he came back with the farmer at his heels.

"Dave tells me you found somethin'," Mr. Shultz said, stooping to see what they were attempting to uncover.

"I think so," said Joe as he pointed at what appeared to be a smooth piece of earthenware, but still only partially visible. "We were workin' around it with our fingers while Dave went to find you, but we haven't accomplished much."

All three boys continued to remove the dirt cautiously with their fingers and the tools, and slowly the foursome saw what began to look more and more like a brownish-orange bowl or jar. Then at last, Ted freed it and held it for all to see; and as he gently rubbed away as much dirt from its surface as he could, they detected several intricate designs.

"Hey! Look at that!" Joe said admiringly, stepping closer. "If it was made by the Susquehannock, they were pretty good artists, Ted!"

Mr. Shultz congratulated the boys on their discovery and then insisted that if they intended to continue, to be extremely careful. "There's likely to be more pottery," he added. "An' what's more, if this is another grave site, you may even turn up some bone fragments."

"But why would there be pottery in a grave?" Dave asked, mystified.

"Because the Indians buried food with their dead. They believed it was necessary to take it with them to the Happy Hunting Ground," Mr. Shultz explained.

Joe cautiously took the bowl from Ted's hands and began to scrape away some of the solidly packed soil from the mouth of the vessel. After a few minutes the dirt suddenly crumbled, and Joe gradually turned the bowl upside down to pour some of the loose material into his hand. Quickly he turned his head.

"Phew!" he gasped, dropping it back into the bowl and setting it down. Hastily taking a few steps backward, he shut his eyes, made a face and said, "Good grief! Somethin' musta crawled in there an' died!"

"No!" laughed Mr. Shultz. "That's just what I was tellin' you about. There prob'ly was food in it. It wouldn't surprise me at all if you've hit another grave site. So please, be careful, boys!"

"Well, let's get started!" insisted Dave with renewed enthusiasm.

"But, Mr. Shultz," Joe said as he reached for his garden tool, "you'd better take that bowl up to the house so we don't break it."

"That's not a bad idea," the farmer said, cautiously picking up the reward of their labors and heading up the slope.

"At least we've finally found somethin' besides arrowheads!" Ted commented triumphantly, as they again set about their task. But though they worked diligently for nearly another hour, their efforts uncovered nothing more.

When they finally decided to stop, Dave sighed heavily. "You know, if this really is a grave, I'm just as glad we didn't find any bones. If I walked into our house with part of a skeleton, my ma would skin me alive!"

At that moment Mr. Shultz came walking down the path once more. Looking toward the sky he said, "That sun's tellin' me you boys better soon be on your way. I think it's time to call it a day, don't you? You've certainly had enough excitement around here to last a lifetime!"

When the boys agreed, he said, "Now don't you worry none about my work. Tomorrow's another day, an' I'll get it done. You three better head for the market."

"Well . . . if you insist, sir," Joe conceded reluctantly. "An' besides, me an' my pa hafta play in the band concert in the park tonight."

Then after pausing a few moments, he reached for the object in his pocket and added, "But, Mr. Shultz, you'd better decide what to do with the bowl an' this arrowhead. After all, it's like you said; we really found 'em on your property."

When Ted and Dave nodded their heads in agreement, the farmer thought for a moment. "Well, suppose I do with them the same as with almost all the other things we find around here. I'll have some people from Franklin an' Marshall Academy in Lancaster come an' get 'em. They have a number of Indian artifacts on display at their school, an' I'm sure they'll welcome these too."

"That sounds like a great idea to me!" piped Dave.

"An' what's more," their amiable new friend continued as they headed for the house, "I'll be sure to tell 'em who made the discovery. They always have some written material with their displays, an' I'll ask that they mention your names as the finders."

Feeling both proud and satisfied with their efforts, the boys shook his hand. Then, after giving their full names to the Shultzes and thanking them several times, the trio began their return trip. They were so excited with all that had happened, that they expended their energy galloping their horses nearly the entire distance to Columbia, where they arrived with plenty of time to spare.

As soon as Mrs. Shelley saw all the dust and grime her son had gathered during the day's escapades, she began brushing his clothes with her hand and even gave him a few stiff swats across the seat of his pants to help dispel much of what he had managed to accumulate.

"Ouch, Ma! Not so *hard!*" Joe complained, while his buddies were thoroughly enjoying the gentle thrashing he was undergoing.

"You might know you'd pick today to get all dirty!" his mother chided. "And you with a concert tonight! Now you march out to that horse trough and get cleaned up! You'll be a sight to behold in front of all those people tonight!"

"Aw, Ma! Me an' Pa are always way in the back anyhow. What difference does it make?" Joe replied in somewhat of an exasperated tone.

But suddenly catching a rather meaningful stare from his father, without saying another word, he turned and headed immediately to the horse trough to dutifully fulfill his mother's wishes.

Then he had to chuckle when she looked at his two friends and added sternly, "You too! Both of you! No food till your hands and faces shine! And get those ears clean!"

Then, within moments, the three boys were grinning sheepishly at one another's reflection in the watering trough, while they dispensed with all the Washington Boro topsoil they had managed to displace.

A few minutes later they were back in the market house where they had no trouble finding plenty of food to satisfy their hunger; and while everyone sat together and enjoyed supper, the boys shared excitedly all that had happened earlier in the day.

Then after reloading the wagon, they immediately headed up Locust Street to the community park area which graced the grounds of the Washington Institute building. As the evening hours approached, families from all over Columbia, as well as nearby farms and tiny villages, began to assemble in expectation of another Saturday evening band concert.

Although Joe was the youngest member of the ensemble, he already had been playing with the band for several years. During that time he had gained the respect of the older instrumentalists, as well as the people of the community in general, for his uncanny ability with the drum.

As they played that evening, Joe's attention was drawn several times to another teen-age boy, who stood close to a nearby tree and was doing his best to keep his eyes and ears on Joe and his father. All the while, he was attempting to drum along quietly to the cadences of the various numbers they were performing.

Dave, Ted, Sarah and her mother all enjoyed the nearly two-hour musical treat, as did the entire throng in attendance. The concert seemed the perfect way to end the week; and as Joe, his family and friends later returned to Wrightsville, the boys chattered constantly, reviewing the adventures of the day again and again.

Chapter 3

Caught in the Dark

Early the following Tuesday evening, Joe's father took the wagon to Wrightsville for some supplies and to check for mail. Meanwhile, his mother and sister were seated on the swing sewing some clothing, as Joe sat on the top step of the porch lightly practicing his drumming. However, when Mr. Shelley rode into the yard waving a letter, he attracted everyone's attention.

"It must be from Dan!" Sarah exclaimed.

After Mr. Shelley walked up the steps, he handed the letter to his wife, and at the same time extended a news sheet in Joe's direction. "There's somethin' in there that should interest you, Joey; but I got a feelin' it's not exactly good news!" he admitted.

The lad reached for the day-old issue of the *Columbia Spy*, and almost instantaneously saw an article which told of an escape from the town lock-up. When Joe read further, he learned that the fugitive was none other than the scar-faced man who had attempted to steal Swift.

"I wonder who he was?" Mr. Shelley mused. "He had no identification of any kind with him that day, an' he absolutely refused to give his name. As a matter of fact, he never said one word. He was a strange one!" he added, shaking his head in bewilderment.

"Well, I guess that'll save us the trouble o' havin' to attend the trial," Joe muttered. "I just hope he ran far enough away so I won't ever see him again; that's all!"

Meanwhile, Mrs. Shelley had set aside the socks she was darning and carefully opened Dan's letter. After adjusting her spectacles, she began to read aloud:

June 26, 1862

Dear Folks,

It's late and I'm tired, but I'll take time to write a few lines. When I first joined this regiment, everybody talked as though we would be in Richmond by this time and the war would be over. The past two days everyone's dreams turned to nightmares! We were at a little place called Oak Grove yesterday preparing to march toward Richmond. But before we could shake the sleep from our eyes, shells began exploding all around us. We spent most of the day retreating and trying to get our forces together again. By dusk we lost all the ground it took us a week to win.

But today was a day I'll never forget! We were camped outside a little town called Mechanicsville when we were roused out of our sleep before daylight. Our scouts learned that the Rebs were on the move again and might try the same thing as yesterday. This time we wanted to be ready for them. Our regiment was one of the first on the move and after about a half-hour march we saw them in a small valley below us. A regiment of New Yorkers were skirmishing with them and our captain planned to move our company down the hillside behind the Rebs. That was our biggest mistake! As we moved in behind them, gray coats by the thousands poured in from the other end of the valley and down the hills on both sides. Luckily our company was in the rear. With all the noise and confusion we didn't realize our danger.

But above the shooting and yelling I began to hear drum beats. Somehow our drummer boy heard the order to sound retreat. That boy saved my life today but his signal came too late for many of our men. I managed to get back up the hill and out of the trap along with about two dozen others. The rest didn't make it! I'll say a prayer for that drummer boy tonight.

I've got to get some sleep now. I'll write later and hope to have news of some victories. May God take care of all of you. I pray often.

With love,
Dan

When Mrs. Shelley stopped reading, there was a prolonged silence, each one deeply engrossed in his own thoughts. When Joe finally glanced up at his mother, her eyes were transfixed on the drumsticks that he was holding in his lap. Joe abruptly looked away, studying the hillsides and Mt. Pizgah to the distant south.

Then, fighting back her emotions, Mrs. Shelley replaced the letter in the envelope. "At least we know he's safe for another day!" she sighed.

"Remember how Dan use' to yell at Joey 'cause he's always drummin' so much?" Sarah asked. "It almost sounds funny for him to say he'll pray for a drummer boy! How 'bout it, Joey?"

Everyone glanced in Joe's direction; but he was staring into space, apparently lost in thought.

"Joey!" shouted Sarah. "Wake up! You're in another world!"

At the sound of his sister's shout, Joe was suddenly jolted back to reality. "What? Huh?" he stammered. "Were you talkin' to me?"

"Weren't you even listenin' to Ma while she read Dan's letter?" his sister chided.

"Sure! . . . I was just daydreamin' a while, I guess," he replied, somewhat embarrassed.

Mrs. Shelley cast a wary glance toward her husband. Then looking at her son, she asked, "What about, Joey?"

"Oh . . . nothin' much worth talkin' about, I suppose." Then, hastily excusing himself, he set his drum and sticks aside, slapped the dust from his pants and ambled down the steps.

"Where you goin'?" Sarah asked.

"Think I'll go hunt for some spearmint an' sassafras. I could stand somethin' good to drink if you an' Ma have time to make some."

"May I go along, Ma? All my work's done!" she pleaded.

Her mother smiled and nodded. "Yes, just be sure to get back before it's dark," she cautioned.

While Joe and his sister were walking down the lane, their parents watched from the porch. Finally, Mrs. Shelley broke the silence. "Are you thinking about the same thing I am?" she inquired.

"An' what might that be, dear?"

"Dan's letter and the way Joey reacted."

Her husband sighed; and then, slowly drawing out his reply, he said, "Yes . . . As a matter of fact . . . that's exactly what I was thinkin' about. I suspect that when Dan mentioned that drummer boy an' the part he played in his escape, it just may have gotten the wheels rollin' in Joey's mind."

Mrs. Shelley shook her head. "I wish I hadn't read that letter out loud!" she admitted frankly.

Mr. Shelley arose and walked slowly toward the porch steps. Then gradually turning, he said, "Lately Joey's been talkin' constantly to me about the war; an' though he hasn't said it in so many words, I can tell he wishes *he* was old enough to join the army too."

Then, before heading to the barn to finish some chores, he added, "My dear, this may not be of any comfort to you; but if I was Joey, I'd be thinkin' *very* seriously about bein' a drummer boy. I'm sure he remembers the stories I told him of his great-grandfather. Actually, the only thing that really surprises me is that he's never once mentioned it! God's given him an incredible talent with those hickory sticks! He surpassed my own ability long ago, an' even my father's!"

A severe mid-afternoon thunderstorm had left the fields quite wet; and as Joe and his sister strode along, Sarah said, "The dampness always makes it easier to pick up the odor of spearmint. We shouldn't have any trouble findin' some today."

Gradually they strolled in the direction of the York turnpike, where they had some favorite spots to find both sassafras and spearmint. Eventually, when they reached one of them, Joe began looking on one side of the road, while Sarah scanned the undergrowth on the other; and it wasn't long before their search was rewarded.

"Oh, there's spearmint over here; I can smell it!" declared Sarah.

Joe came running. As they started to break off some of the tender shoots, he gloated, "Boy! This is a good spot! There's enough here to last us all summer!"

"Not the way you drink it!" Sarah objected laughingly. "You just *know* we'll be huntin' for more before the week's out."

In a very short time, they stripped the stalks of some of their stems and leaves. When they had a sufficient amount, Joe said, "We've got plenty. Let's walk up the trail a piece. I know where we can get some sassafras for sure. There's a whole string o' trees an' saplings with lots o' roots at the bottom o' the next rise."

The sun was sinking by this time; and they knew that if they were to arrive home before dark, they soon would have to retrace their steps. But as they were descending the other side of the hill, Sarah pointed to a place in the road just a few yards ahead, where a deep rut ran almost the full width of the trail.

"Look at that gulley!" she exclaimed. "The afternoon storm must've done that!"

"Jiggers! That's pretty deep!" Joe observed, concern in his voice. "Maybe we'd better try to fill it with some loose stones. That could cause a bad accident!"

"But if we take time to do that, we might not be able to get some sassafras," Sarah pointed out.

"Maybe, an' maybe not; but somebody could get hurt here!" her brother warned.

"You're right, Joey," Sarah agreed. "C'mon; let's hurry! Maybe we'll still have time to do both. We can pile a lot o' stones in my skirt, as long as they're not too big."

But hardly had they headed for some beds of loose gravel along the roadside, when they heard a commotion on the trail in the direction of York. From their vantage point, they could see a wagon whose driver was cracking his whip, urging every last bit of speed from his horses that he could possibly muster.

"Here comes somebody now!" Sarah cried. "An' he's really movin'!"

"We gotta warn him about that rut!" Joe shouted; and dashing to the center of the road, he began waving his arms wildly in an effort to gain the man's attention.

As the rig drew rapidly nearer, he observed that the driver was a Negro, who suddenly threw his whip into the wagon bed and began waving his free arm from side to side, apparently indicating that he wanted Joe to get out of his way. The lad continued gesturing frantically, but the horses kept rushing relentlessly toward him.

"Joey! Watch out!" Sarah screamed.

When Joe realized that the man had no intention of stopping, in complete exasperation he leaped aside, aware that he had done all that he could to save the man and his animals from possible harm. As the loaded vehicle flashed by, he saw several boxes, bundles and packages jostling around inside the wagon, and then watched with alarm as the rig headed pell-mell, directly toward the deep washout in the roadbed.

Only when it was too late to avoid the danger, did the driver see with alarm what lay ahead of him. Within seconds the horses safely crossed the ditch, but the left front wheel took the full impact of the blow, causing the wagon to pitch, careen wildly, and then flip over on its side, the driver and the contents of the wagon scattering through the air in all directions.

Horrified, Joe and Sarah watched as the driver struck the ground

BOT RODA

viciously along the side of the trail, rolling over and over in the loose gravel.

However, despite all that was happening in the mere twinkling of an eye, something strange momentarily attracted Joe's attention. As one heavy crate thudded to the ground, a fairly large object was hurled from inside it, and went tumbling into the weeds. Joe thought his eyes were playing tricks on him! He could've sworn that bundle actually had arms and legs!

Although he was momentarily mystified by what he had just seen, his first impulse was to rush to the aid of the Negro driver, now lying motionless by the side of the trail. However, just as he reached the spot where the large box had struck the ground, he heard a rustling noise in the weeds. Turning, he simply stared awkwardly as a Negro boy about his own age attempted to stand up, but quickly sank to one knee, shaking his head in an effort to overcome his dizziness.

Swiftly Joe guessed why the driver had been in such a hurry. Springing to the boy's side, he looked quickly to see if he could detect any serious injuries. When it became apparent that he was merely badly shaken, Joe said, "Get down an' stay outta sight! We'd better see if we can help the driver!"

Joe rushed toward Sarah, who was already kneeling beside the man. "Is he hurt bad?" Joe asked.

"I'm afraid so!" Sarah replied fretfully. "I think he's unconscious!"

Her brother stooped, and taking the man gently by the shoulders, he rolled him gingerly onto his back. When they saw his bloody face, Sarah turned away, sickened at the sight of so many cuts, bruises and brush burns.

Upon looking carefully, Joe thought he barely recognized him to be Cato Jourdon, the man he had seen on two previous occasions when he visited Bob Loney's home, though Joe had never spoken with him. He learned from his father that Cato transported runaway slaves between York and Wrightsville, or between York and Columbia, if he knew he could safely carry his *baggage* across the long covered bridge.

"There was a Negro boy in the back o' that wagon, Sarah! He's in the weeds over there. He must be a runaway!" Joe said in a loud whisper.

He was just about to go unharness one of the horses and ride for help, but at that moment the man opened his eyes and began to mumble something.

Unable to distinguish what he was saying, Joe leaned closer. "What'd you say? Can you hear me?" Joe asked.

The old man's lips quivered, and Joe could see that he was making an exceedingly strained effort to speak. Placing his ear as close to him as he could, Joe heard him say in hardly more than a murmur: "The boy . . . Bounty hunters . . . They's aftuh him!" Then he lapsed into unconsciousness again.

At the sound of the words *bounty hunters*, a shiver ran down Joe's spine. Instantly, he cast an anxious glance toward York and then looked at Sarah. "Old Cato was prob'ly tryin' to get that boy to Bob Loney's or else to the Wright Mansion; one or the other. We'd better . . . "

But he didn't finish. Far in the distance he detected another cloud of dust rising from the York road. When Sarah saw the look of alarm on her brother's face, she turned her head to follow Joe's gaze. Looking into the sunset, they saw several riders coming from the direction of York; and they were in just as much of a hurry as Cato had been.

"I'll try to get that boy outta here!" Joe exclaimed, dashing toward the weeds. "If those men are who I think they are, he's in a peck o' trouble!"

Keeping low as he darted into the high weeds, he yelled, "You try to take care o' Cato; an' if those riders ask any questions about a slave boy, you don't know anything, understand?"

"Yes, Joey!" Sarah promised. "But if they catch you with him, you can get in a lotta trouble yourself!" she warned, suddenly on the verge of tears.

"That's just a chance I'll hafta take!" Joe shouted back; and wheeling farther into the brush, he grasped the boy by the arm. "Are you feelin' good enough to run?" he asked.

"Yas, suh. Ah can run like de wind when Ah's got to."

"Well, you got to!" Joe assured him. "Follow me!"

The riders were still some distance away; and fortunately, a long line of trees at the southern edge of the turnpike would block their view at least for a while. Without hesitating another second, Joe dashed madly southward from the road as fast as he could go, glad to see that although the boy was barefoot, he stayed right behind him.

Luckily, they were scurrying down a long, gradual slope, which seemed to help them run all the faster; and as they fled through what was evidently an old, abandoned pasture now overgrown with

high weeds and bushes, Joe had his eyes on a thicket nearly a hundred yards away.

Reaching their goal quickly, they leaped over some briars and into the woods, hoping that they hadn't been seen. Then, surrounded by the protective trees and underbrush, they turned to look back. By this time, the sun had nearly set; and the late afternoon shadows were turning darker with every passing moment.

"Good!" Joe said, half to himself and breathing hard as he scanned the skies. "It'll be dark soon!"

Meanwhile, along the York trail, Sarah was kneeling nervously by the roadside. Realizing that there was no home nearby to which she could run for help, she tore off part of the bottom of her petticoat and began to clean Cato Jourdon's injuries as well as she could. While she worked, the pounding of hoof beats became louder and louder.

In less than another minute, three men drew their horses to a halt and dismounted instantly. Two of them were bearded; and all three appeared to be nearly the same age - probably in their late forties or early fifties. Apparently they had been riding a long time; for their faces were sweaty and dirty, and their riding boots and clothing were covered with dust. In a few strides they were beside Sarah's crouching figure, looking over her shoulder.

"Do y'all think he's the one we'ah aftuh?" one of them asked gruffly.

"Prob'ly," another replied, taking Sarah roughly by the arm and pulling her to her feet.

"What happened heah? An' wheah's the othuh one?" he demanded, beginning to look around as though he expected to see someone else lying on the ground.

Sarah was too frightened to speak; and before she could say even one word, the man placed both hands on her shoulders and shook her.

"Ansuh me, sistuh!" he bellowed in his southern drawl. "Wheah's the othuh one, Ah said!"

"Wh-what other one?" Sarah stammered. "I was just comin' along the road huntin' tea leaves an' sassafras, when I saw this wagon overturn."

She reached down and picked up her spearmint leaves to show them to the man, in support of what she had just said.

But despite the evidence, he shook her once more and shrieked, "Don't y'all lie to me!"

Then one of his fellow riders called out, "Hold on, Cy! She's prob'ly tellin' the truth. Let's look around an' see if we can find some trace o' the boy."

When Sarah noticed that at least two of them had pistols strapped under their riding vests, she became even more frightened. Then in an effort to delay them, she asked, "Won't you help me get this man to a doctor? He's hurt bad!"

The men merely looked at one another and laughed, then started searching earnestly through the roadside brush.

When the wagon had overturned, the animals nearly broke away. Only a single strap kept each of them tethered to the wagon tongue, but they pawed the ground and snorted nervously from time to time. While the men were preoccupied with their search efforts, Sarah, working quietly, succeeded in unfastening one of the horses, scrambled onto the mare's back and hurriedly headed for home.

At the sound of the horse's hooves, one of the men turned quickly and yelled, "Hey! Wheah y'all goin'?"

"Let 'er go, Will. We gotta find that boy!" bellowed one of his companions.

For several minutes the three men rummaged through the scattered wagon goods and thoroughly probed the nearby shrubbery and high weeds.

"It's stahtin' to git dahk, men," said the man called Cy. "Ifn he was in this heah wagon an' ran, he might try an' find his way into the next town or prob'ly ovuh to Columbia. That's wheah they all go eventually; an' that means he may try crossin' that big bridge. Let's git on down theah!"

But as they turned to head for their horses, one of them suddenly halted. "Hey, y'all! Wait a minute!" he called. "Lookit them weeds ovuh yonduh. Ah didn't notice that befoah. It looks like somebody went right through theah!"

Then another pointed through the fields where the boys had run only minutes before, and said, "Yeah, an' ifn it was the boy, he musta gone in that direction!"

All during this time, Joe and the runaway had been watching anxiously, even from the time the three riders first halted; and a few moments later, Joe's hair bristled when he saw one of them roughly shake his sister. There was no doubt that they were disturbed; and when they began searching the weeds, Joe was certain that they were hunting for the boy. Then he saw Sarah mount one of Cato's horses and ride toward Wrightsville. However, when the men began to look and gesture toward the very thicket where the boys were secluded, a shiver of sudden fright ran down his spine.

It was then that Joe noticed for the first time, their tracks through the weeds, even a few yards right before their eyes.

"We must've left a trail the whole way, an' it looks like they've seen it!" he said, dismayed at his carelessness. "Let's get outta here! But lift your feet high. Let's not do it again!"

Hardly did the pair take even a few steps before the men were swinging into their saddles to follow the boys' trail toward the grove of trees. The two lads ran toward the southeast, skipping over rocks and brambles and dodging in and out among the trees, but always lifting their feet high whenever they were in tall grass or weeds. Moments later, when they came to the far end of the thicket, another broad clearing lay before them. It was still light enough for someone to be able to see them; and Joe knew that if they attempted to cross the large meadow, they might be easily spotted. Fretfully, he began looking for a hiding place. Then, an expression of half surprise and delight creased his face.

"Look how thick those honeysuckle vines grow around the trees here," he whispered. "C'mon. But be careful not to leave any more tracks!" he warned a second time, stepping gingerly as he moved.

Stalking slowly through the entanglement, they soon found themselves more than knee deep in vines; and at the base of several of the trees, the honeysuckle covered the trunks to a height that came nearly to the boys' shoulders.

"Crawl under the honeysuckle an' get as close to the trunk as you can," Joe directed, pointing to a nearby locust tree. "Then pull the vines around you as much as you can. Hurry!"

But the lad hesitated a moment. "Is y'all suah dis is a good place to hide?" he asked doubtfully.

"Don't worry," Joe assured him. "After you get in there, you may not even be able to find *yourself*! Now get movin'!"

In spite of the threat of the moment, the boy couldn't suppress a grin. "Dat sounds good 'nuf foh me!" he chuckled nervously, as he began to snake his way beneath the vines.

Joe moved stealthily toward another nearby tree which was similarly bedecked with honeysuckle, and in less than a minute both boys were completely out of sight. Half crouching and half sitting perfectly still inside their makeshift cocoons, the boys found that nature provided them with a most effective blanket of greenery.

At first, the only sounds that could be heard were those of rustling leaves; some whining, raucous locusts shrilling their undulating sounds through the early evening air; and the occasional twitter of a few birds settling down for the night. But the relative quietness didn't continue unbroken for long. Shortly, Joe could hear someone talking in the distance, though he couldn't distinguish what was being said.

Then a few moments later, came the sounds of crackling twigs. Moving the vines ever so slightly, he peered cautiously through the tiniest of openings. At first he saw nothing; but after hearing the sound of hoof beats, suddenly a horse and rider bolted out of the gathering darkness and through some underbrush not twenty yards away.

Moments later a second rider appeared, astride a shimmering, jet-black stallion. One of the men motioned with his hand. "Y'all look ovuh theah; Ah'll go this way."

As the one disappeared from view, the other headed directly toward the area where the boys lay hidden. Instinctively, Joe's eyes closed as he began to pray fervently for protection; and even as he was praying, the man's horse slowly picked its way among the trees and through the entwining honeysuckle, coming ever closer . . . and closer. Joe hardly dared to breathe.

At length, horse and rider moved behind him, disappearing from view; but by the sound of the animal's hooves, he knew their pursuer was only yards or perhaps even just a few feet away. Joe was sure his heart was going to leap right out of his shirt, as he lay with his head close to the tree. He became fearful that the horse might actually trample his right leg or foot, which were stretched out to one side under the vines. Then there was an aggravatingly long silence, one which made Joe worry that perhaps the man had guessed where they were hiding.

Then, at that precise, agonizing moment, something else suddenly commanded his attention. At first he thought the vines were merely rubbing against him; but a continual tingling sensation left him with little doubt that some tiny insect had chosen that extremely critical moment to take a tantalizing tour of his right ear!

As the wee creature moved along its slow but ticklish meanderings, Joe tried desperately to keep from either screaming in anguish or laughing hysterically. But realizing that either course of action would lead to their discovery, he bit his lower lip and chose to suffer through the most comical torture he had ever thought possible.

Fortunately, he didn't have to endure his suffering too long; for the rider, evidently convinced that no one was near, suddenly yelled to his companions, "Let's go, men; it's almost dahk."

In a moment all three were within a short distance of the boys, and Joe thought he overheard one of them suggest that they ride for Columbia.

Then, as soon as they disappeared, Joe wasted no time in emerging from his hiding place, slapping at his ear in an effort to rid himself of his relentless tormentor. At the same time, the Negro lad leaped from his honeysuckle haven, sputtering for all he was worth!

"What's wrong?" Joe asked, completely mystified by the boy's peculiar behavior.

"Dat's de las' time Ah hides in honeysuckle!" the boy declared emphatically.

"Why? What happened?" Joe asked, somewhat astonished by his remark.

"Well, suh," he began to explain, "Ah done peep tru de vines an' seen mah mastuh! An' lihk de fool dat Ah is, Ah jus' lay deah agapin' wif mah mouf wide open . . . an' a bug crawl in!"

Joe quickly clamped a hand over his mouth to keep from laughing out loud. "An' I thought I was in a bad fix with one in my ear!" he said in a loud whisper, endeavoring to stifle a fit of giggling.

Then, struggling to regain his composure, he stood perfectly still for several moments, listening intently to be certain the men had left. When he heard nothing out of the ordinary, he pronounced in a low voice, "We'd better get movin' so we can take advantage o' the little bit o' twilight we have left."

As they stepped into the clearing, Joe finally had time to introduce himself. "My name's Joe, but everybody calls me Joey. Joey Shelley. What's yours?"

"Mah whole name's Nathaniel Winslow Brown, but mos' folks jus' calls me Nat," he replied, stepping carefully to skirt the edge of a narrow creek bed.

"Well, we prob'ly have a long hike ahead of us, Nat; so let's be careful walkin' in the dark. The last thing we need is an overturned ankle!"

As they moved cautiously through the onrushing night, Nat asked, "Wheah's we'all headed?"

Joe would've gone directly to Bob Loney's home, but he had heard his father mention that he went to Philadelphia just two days earlier; and he was afraid that he may not have returned.

"Did your driver happen to mention where he was takin' you?" Joe finally replied rather thoughtfully.

"Yas, suh . . . but Ah done fohgits de name," Nat admitted ruefully.

"Do you remember the name of Loney or Wright?" Joe suggested.

Nat thought carefully for a few moments. "No, suh, Ah don'," he said apologetically, wagging his head.

"How 'bout . . . Columbia?" Joe asked hopefully.

"Dat's right! Dat's de place! Dey say dat once a slave gets to Columbia, he's as good as free!" Nat said enthusiastically.

"Well, I wouldn't go quite that far," Joe cautioned. "But the way the Wrights operate things, it's a pretty good bet that you *will* be free before long. An' we're gonna head for their place right now."

Nat looked at Joe somewhat quizzically. "But don' we'all hab to cross a ribbuh? Mr. Jourdon done said somethin' 'bout a *big* bridge," Nat recalled.

"Yeah, an' that's what's got me worried!" Joe admitted. "When those men rode away, I thought I heard one of 'em say somethin' 'bout goin' to Columbia."

Soon the boys completed their trek across the pasture and were following the downhill course of a creek through another section of woods. Although the trees often completely obstructed their view, from time to time they could glimpse the reflections of distant lights on the smooth surface of the Susquehanna.

"Over there's Columbia, Nat," Joe informed him on one occasion, pointing to the opposite shore; and as Nat stared into the distance, he found himself wishing that they were already there.

By this time, total darkness had enveloped them; and during their nocturnal meanderings, they attracted the undivided attention of numerous dogs along the southern outskirts of Wrightsville. At one point of their journey through the woods, Nat became the owner of a wet leg, soaked to the knee when he slipped into the creek. But at last, at the foot of the hills, they reached a roadbed running parallel to the canal, just as a three-quarter moon blossomed forth in all its silvery brightness, helping them to see more clearly.

The boys could discern several canal barges tied up for the night, and hear the subdued snorting and pawing of the horses and mules that were tethered in several locations nearby. Joe listened carefully but was happy he could hear no voices. If anyone was on any of the barges, he was hoping they were all below deck.

While they were standing along the trail beside some fairly tall bushes, Joe gazed intently to his left toward the bridge entrance, which was not too far away. His secret fear was that possibly it might be guarded by one or even all three of Nat's pursuers.

Finally, gathering his courage, he said to Nat, "You stay here till I walk to the bridge to see if it's safe. Somebody could be up there . . . just waitin' in the dark!"

Moments later, as he approached the huge structure, he gradually slowed his pace, trying to appear as unruffled as he possibly could. Then, neither seeing nor hearing anyone, he finally stopped completely, approximately a hundred feet from the entrance, continually watching and listening intently for signs of any kind of activity. Joe could tell that he was frightened when he realized he could actually sense the throbbing of his heart beats even in his neck!

After feeling satisfied that he wasn't being observed, he sauntered casually up the sloping ramp. Stepping onto the main part of the bridge, he rested his hands on the toll gate and simply stared into the inky blackness, still listening with all the intensity he could possibly muster, for more than a minute. Finally, convinced that all was clear, he turned around and stepped directly into a pair of outstretched arms!

Chapter 4

A Desperate Leap

Instantaneously a frightened, involuntary gasp leaped from Joe's throat; and within seconds he felt as though his heart would explode! For as big as the man was, he had come from behind him as silently as a cat. As Joe's heart continued to pound at an alarming rate, he twisted in an effort to escape; but he realized that any attempt to struggle would be in vain. Those arms were like two bands of steel.

The moon was fairly bright; but the man's broad-brimmed hat cast a shadow, hiding his face. Joe, on the other hand, was standing in the edge of the shadow of the bridge.

"Let me go!" Joe finally shrieked; and although he didn't expect it, he was totally surprised when the man actually relaxed his grip, though he still grasped Joe's elbow firmly with his hand.

"What ah y'all doin' here?" came a gruff voice.

Angry now, though still rather frightened, Joe said stammeringly, "I . . . uh . . . was just . . . lookin' for someone," he said as off-handedly as he could under the circumstances. "Now, *please* ! Take your hands off me!"

"Jus' . . . take it easy, sonny boy! Guess Ah should apologize, but Ah thought y'all was somebody else. Ah been lookin' foah a boy 'bout yoah size, an' Ah . . . 'spected him to cross this heah bridge. I mistook y'all foah him in the dahk, that's all," he explained. And then, looking at Joe quizzically, he pressed him further. "Who was y'all lookin' foah anyway at this tahm o' night, sonny?"

Joe was absolutely certain that this was one of the three men who had been chasing Nat, and he had no intentions of striking up a conversation. As he felt the man's hold relax almost completely on his arm, he never took a moment to answer the man's question. Instead, mustering all his strength, he quickly tore himself loose and bolted down the ramp, once again running for all he was worth!

Taken totally by surprise, the stranger's natural impulse was to give chase; but after taking merely a few strides, he stopped dead in his tracks. Earlier, the lad had been no match for his strength; but it took only a moment for him to realize that now he would be no equal for the teen-ager's speed, as Joe quickly melted into the darkness along the road that skirted the railroad and the canal.

Within less than a minute, Joe came rushing toward Nat.

"Is somebody chasin' y'all?" Nat asked wide-eyed, staring in the direction of the bridge.

Not even taking time to answer, Joe grabbed Nat by the arm and whispered loudly, "Head for the trees again!"

The pair scrambled through the darkness and didn't stop until they reached a more secluded spot farther back in the woods. When Joe thought they retreated far enough, he signaled for Nat to wait, then turned to listen, hoping desperately that they weren't being followed. After a prolonged silence, he began to feel safe again.

"Phew! That was scary, Nat!" Joe sighed, breathing heavily. "I sure am glad I didn't take you with me up to that bridge!" he said gratefully, sitting down in an effort to catch his breath once more.

The runaway sprawled beside him; and after Joe told him what had happened, Nat slowly began to chuckle.

Joe was dumbfounded! "What's so funny?" he wondered. "I thought I was a goner for sure, an' you start laughin'!"

"Dat's not what Ah's laughin' 'bout, Joey," Nat replied, breaking into another fit of giggling. Then, after finally getting control of himself, he said, "So . . . he done thought y'all was a dahky, lihk me, eh?" And he started laughing still another time.

Then, beginning to see the humor in the situation himself, Joe began to chuckle right along with Nat.

"Well . . . y'all's got to admit . . . sittin' heah in de shadows, y'all's eveh' bit as black as Ah is! No wonduh he mistaked y'all foh me! Why . . . eben de whites o' yoh eyes is black, Joey!"

Then it was Joe's turn to laugh. But gradually he became thoughtful for a few moments before saying, "You know, Nat . . . I got a feelin' there's prob'ly a real message in what you just said. Bet Pastor Jackson could make a pretty good sermon outta that!"

He paused a moment and then gave Nat a friendly punch on the upper arm. "But it wasn't so dad-blamed comical when I was up there on that bridge a while ago; you can bet on that too!" he said.

Nat just giggled one more time and then returned the friendly punch.

The boys sat in complete silence for a while, Joe's mind racing a mile a minute; but he failed to come up with an answer to their problem. Finally he said, "I'm stumped, Nat! I just can't seem to figure out a way to get you to Colum . . ."

Then, snapping his fingers, he interrupted himself. "I got it! Why didn't I think o' that in the first place, for Pete's sake? Good grief!"

"Think o' what?" Nat asked, sounding hopeful.

"The canal an' the towpath!" Joe exclaimed, as though his very words were self-explanatory.

"Canal? . . . Towpath?" Nat repeated, but without comprehending.

"Yeah!" All we gotta do is get down to the canal. C'mon!" Joe announced, suddenly regaining his confidence.

Within a matter of minutes they returned to their earlier hiding place along the trail. When they couldn't see or hear anyone, they bent over as low as they could and crossed the road, as well as the Baltimore and Susquehanna Railroad tracks which ran south out of Wrightsville. Then, breaking through more weeds and shrubbery, they soon came to the edge of the towpath.

Again they carefully watched and listened for signs of people around the barges, or of anyone who might possibly be lurking somewhere in the darkness. When the situation seemed to be safe, they cautiously moved along, Joe noticing to his surprise that the horses and mules that were tied up at various places paid them very little attention and, fortunately, remained exceptionally quiet.

When they came to an area where there was very little to seclude them, Joe signaled for Nat to get down low; and the two of them began crawling on their hands and knees. Nearly fifty yards in front of them the boys could distinguish the outline of the long bridge stretching over the Susquehanna; and as they crept along the towpath, the only sound they could detect was the eerie

hooting of an owl, perched in a nearby tree.

"I wish he'd keep quiet!" Joe whispered. "Owls give me the creeps!"

"Ah don' 'zactly caeh foh dat kind o' singin' eithuh!" Nat remarked. "Mah pappy use' to say dat weah dey's owls, dey's witches!"

Joe chuckled inwardly. "There's a couple o' things worse than witches hangin' around here, Nat; an' I know where at least one of 'em is. I just wish I knew where the other two are!"

This fact put Joe on the defensive, for the men might have the towpath entrance guarded also; or possibly they were watching the Wright Mansion itself. Whatever the case may be, he knew he'd have to keep his wits about him.

As they moved along, Joe had his eyes focused intently on the towpath entrance of the bridge, hoping above all else that it had been left unguarded. Finally, they reached the place near the bridge where the canal joined the river. Here they crawled off the towpath and took refuge behind the thick foliage of a full-grown lilac bush.

Pointing, Joe whispered, "Up there to the left is the main entrance where the wagons, train cars an' people ridin' horseback enter the bridge. That's where that man grabbed me. Prob'ly he's still there. But see where this towpath goes? Right up alongside, an' it hooks onto the outside o' the bridge way out there. D'you see where I mean? The towpath entrance is about two hundred feet away from that other one. So keep your fingers crossed they don't have this one guarded too!"

Taking Joe's words literally, Nat rapidly crossed four fingers on each hand, and even his thumbs for good measure!

Then, preparing for the worst, Joe told Nat how he could reach either the Shelley farm, or the Loney's, in case something went wrong. When he was sure Nat understood, he again directed him to wait behind the lilac bush while Joe went on alone.

Slowly, he began crawling along the embankment, his eyes moving constantly from the towpath entrance to the main passageway and back again. When he was within several yards of his destination, he stopped. As he listened carefully, he glanced upward and saw that some clouds were beginning to appear, but the moon continued casting its whitish glow.

With still no trees or shrubs to conceal him, he felt uncomfortably exposed by the light of the moon. Then, after pausing for what seemed to be several minutes, he mustered all his determination and continued crawling. At any moment he expected someone to rush at him from along the towpath itself or from some other likely hiding place near the walls at the base of the main entrance to the bridge.

It was then that he realized that his heart was pounding so forcefully that he could feel its palpatations even in his eardrums, and his breathing had become so heavy that he hardly recognized his body as his own.

He paused yet another time and stared toward the pitch blackness of the path entryway, his senses braced to take instant flight. A shiver ran down his spine, as he wondered if his system could stand another shock like the one he had experienced less than a half hour earlier.

The outer wall of the towpath section was only about a yard high to allow for the passage of ropes from horses or mules to barges below. However, roofing extended over the short wall and cast a foreboding shadow upon the path itself. Joe could see nothing but blackness, even as his mind began imagining all kinds of dangers.

A horrible sensation began to tighten his throat, almost as though someone were actually choking him; and his mouth was like cotton. Then, almost as though someone were tapping him on the shoulder as a reminder, Joe recalled what his parents had always taught him; and closing his eyes he prayed simply, "Father! Help!"

And within moments, even to his own surprise, with ever-quickening pulse he suddenly found himself walking boldly directly up the slope. Within seconds he was swallowed by the blackness, fully expecting someone to catch hold of him again; but although he subconsciously braced his body for just such an encounter . . . it never came! Then, suddenly recalling what had happened earlier, he quickly spun around and looked back . . . but this time no one was there!

Breathing the deepest sigh of relief of his young life, he paused a few moments to allow his highly distressed senses to regroup and return to normal. As though a great weight had been taken from his shoulders, he felt himself heaving yet another long, relaxing sigh of relief, finding it hard to believe how really frightened he had been!

Beneath him, for just a few moments, he watched the peacefully flowing, glistening waters of the Susquehanna and the moon's incredibly beautiful, shimmering reflection, all of which seemed to be totally in direct contrast to the tremendous inner turmoil he had just been experiencing. Then, after taking a moment for a short prayer of thanksgiving, he headed quickly back along the path to find Nat, who was awaiting his return with much anxiety.

A few minutes later, they were striding hurriedly along the bridge towpath, one behind the other. By this time they were sensing a strong inner urgency to reach their destination; and they moved quickly, hardly saying a word. When they were nearly a hundred yards from the opposite shore, Joe glanced toward the southeast. He knew the Wright Mansion was not much more than a quarter of a mile from the foot of the bridge, and he prayed that someone would be there to help them.

Then a sudden thought occurred to him, and he stopped abruptly. "Nat!" he whispered as he turned to face him. "Can you swim?"

Nat closed one eye, set his hands on his hips, and simply stared quizzically at Joe's silhouette.

"Well, can you?" Joe persisted.

"Yas, suh. Lihk a fish. But why does y'all aks me dat now? Why didn' y'all aks me dat when we was on de udduh side o' de ribbuh? We's already 'cross de ribbuh now!"

"Not yet we ain't!" Joe pointed out. "Not by a *long* shot! An' I been thinkin' . . . If somethin' happens that we can't get off the bridge, I'd sooner jump an' swim for shore rather than try to run the whole way back to Wrightsville again."

"*Jump!*" Nat exclaimed, his eyes practically bulging from his head.

"Shhhhh!" Joe cautioned, quickly clamping his hand across Nat's lips. "Not so loud! Somebody could hear us!"

In another second Nat was leaning over the short wall and staring wide-eyed at the Susquehanna flowing beneath them. "Oh, say y'all don' mean dat, Joey!" he begged. "Ah don' mind swimmin' lihk a fish . . . but flyin' lihk a big bihrd ain't foh me, nohow!"

"I'm not sayin' we'll *have* to jump!" Joe said, disturbed by Nat's reaction. "But if worse comes to worse, we may be *forced* to! We're not far from shore!"

"Oh, Ah don' caeh how *fah* Ah's got to swim! But Lawdy me, it's jus' de trip from heah to deah dat Ah don' lihk!" Nat whined, pointing timidly toward the water, many yards below.

Although Nat's negative response upset Joe, with a resigned shrug of his shoulders he said, "Well . . . c'mon. We're almost at the end o' the line. Let's just hope we don't run into any more trouble the rest o' the way!"

The blackness of the tops of the trees along the shoreline silhouetted against a starry background, and the street lamps along Front Street and at the railroad station, indicated that they were nearing the end of the bridge. However, the boys could barely distinguish the towpath exit.

Joe reached back and put his hand on Nat's chest in an effort to slow his friend's anxious pace. Then, putting his hand on his shoulder and pressing down hard as a signal for Nat to crouch, they began creeping along, staying as low as they could. Everything seemed exceptionally quiet, and Joe hoped it would remain that way.

Suddenly, the flare of a tiny flame cut through the darkness like a knife, the boys' hearts fairly leaping to their throats! Instinctively, they backed off a few steps. Glowing almost torch-like in the solid blackness, the small flame, flickering gently, revealed a man sitting at the exit ramp of the towpath, resting his back against the wall and casually lighting a pipeful of tobacco. Fortunately for the boys, he was totally engrossed with the flame, puffing strenuously on his pipe in an effort to light it; for Joe thought that he could possibly have seen them had he glanced in their direction.

After the match was tossed aside, the red glow of the lighted tobacco was all that the boys could see from time to time, as the man puffed lazily on his pipe.

Meanwhile, the boys hardly breathed. During this forced delay in their journey, Joe was planning a retreat toward deeper water where he knew that he would have to convince the runaway to jump. Reaching out with his hand, he nudged Nat gently as a signal to turn back; but as the lad pivoted, he lost his balance and fell against the boards with a sudden thud.

Looking fearfully over his shoulder toward the exit, Joe could barely distinguish the man's dim outline, as he slowly assumed a standing position. Although he couldn't determine for certain, it appeared at first that the man was merely looking in their direction. But then, realizing that he was actually walking slowly toward them, Joe didn't hesitate a moment.

"Run!" he said in a loud whisper. "He heard us!"

Needing no further encouragement whatsoever, swiftly Nat was in full stride, with Joe right behind him.

"Hey! Come back heah!" yelled the man.

But the boys paid no attention. Their only thought was to run as fast as their legs could carry them!

Their pursuer, believing it was only the runaway boy scurrying through the darkness, turned and called toward shore at the top of his voice. "He's runnin' back across the bridge, Cy! Ride to the othuh side an' head him off!"

By this time the pair already had run quite a distance, but Joe overheard the man's words and grabbed Nat by the shoulders in an effort to bring him to a stop.

"Did you hear that, Nat?" he asked. "We don't have a *chance* if we run back to Wrightsville! We *gotta* jump!" he insisted.

Again Nat stared fearfully over the side. But time was quickly running out as they could hear the man's hurrying footsteps in the dark, coming closer and closer! With sudden resolution Joe leaped onto the boarding and grabbed the runaway by the upper part of his left arm.

"C'mon, Nat!" he practically screamed, tugging at him despairingly. "We gotta jump! Don't you understand?" he shouted.

Nat looked first at Joe; then he hurriedly glanced successively at the water, back to Wrightsville, and finally toward the man who was now just a few yards away. Finally, grabbing Joe's left arm, he threw caution to the winds and scrambled onto the railing with him.

Never giving him even a second to change his mind, Joe seized his left arm firmly with both hands. Then leaning outward, he flexed his knees and pushed with all the strength his legs could provide, carrying Nat with him into the thinness of the air.

It was a plunge of nearly twenty-five feet, and in a matter of seconds they struck the water feet first with a resounding splash. Moments later, when they bobbed to the surface, Joe clutched Nat by the arm once more.

"You all right, Nat?" he asked as he began treading water.

"Yas, suh," Nat sputtered, while trying to empty some of the water he had nearly swallowed. "But Ah done hit bottom!"

Relieved that they were safe at least for the moment, Joe glanced upward; but because of the darkness, he was unable to see the one who was chasing them.

When the man had reached the spot from where the boys leaped, momentarily he actually considered jumping after them. However, after placing one foot on the boards and seeing that the water was a long way below him, he suddenly changed his mind. Now he was standing in the shadows peering at the dark waters,

BOT
RODA

surprised at having learned that there were two boys instead of one. He watched for a while to see if he could spot them, but it was too dark. Then, still determined to catch the runaway slave, he began to hurry back along the towpath toward Columbia, hoping he could see them coming ashore.

By this time Joe was sorry he had worn his shoes when he and Sarah set out in search of spearmint and sassafras earlier in the evening; for usually he went barefoot on most summer days. Now, after much tugging and an inadvertent mouthful of water, he managed to remove them. Since they were well worn by this time, it wasn't too painful simply to release them and let them slip to a watery resting place.

Then, side by side, the boys set out in earnest for the shore. However, they didn't swim far before they realized that the current was too swift to make much headway; for they were gradually being swept downstream. When they began to tire, Joe suggested that they try to rest by treading water; but when he lowered his feet, he was surprised to find that he could touch bottom, though they were still quite a distance from shore.

"Hey! A sandbar!" he exclaimed.

"It shoh feels good to rest a while!" Nat declared as he settled his feet. "But it feels moh like a pebble bahr dan a san' bahr," he remarked, his toes cautiously surveying the many river stones beneath him.

"Well, we can't be too particular at a time like this," Joe chided. "At least we can take a breather."

Even though the boys had their feet planted firmly on solid footing, they could still feel the current pushing strongly against them, forcing them to brace themselves and lean upstream in order to keep their balance.

Joe remained concerned about the man on the bridge. "Nat," he said after a few moments, "what would *you* do if you were that man up there?"

Nat pondered a while. "Why, Ah b'lieb Ah'd run lickety-split foh de ribbuh bank an' see if Ah could lay eyes on two boys a-swimmin' foh de shoh."

"That's exactly what I had in mind," Joe acknowledged. "But let's take our chances an' head for shore now, before those other two men get here to give this one a hand. We'll have more of a chance gettin' away from one man than from three. What d'you think?"

"Ah's ready!" Nat answered.

Joe pointed toward shore. "See the outline o' the tops o' that grove o' trees?" he asked.

"Yas, suh."

The Wright's orchard has to be just behind them, an' the mansion's right in back o' the orchard. If that man sees us an' we hafta run for it, then head in that direction. With all the trees an' bushes, we can prob'ly find some place to hide an' . . ."

Joe broke off speaking when they suddenly found themselves drenched in darkness. Looking skyward he said, "Look up there!"

The moon had suddenly become almost totally obscured by a heavy cloud.

"That couldn't've happened at a better time!" Joe said gratefully. "Let's go. But try to swim as quiet as you can."

Once more as the boys headed for the river bank, the current continued to force them downstream; so that by the time they approached the shore, they were near the very trees Joe had indicated earlier.

For a short time, the moon reappeared fairly brightly, but fortunately it was soon hidden again. Joe, who was a short distance ahead of Nat, stopped kicking in order to feel cautiously with his feet for the river bottom. On the first attempt he failed; but after a few more strokes, his toes touched a squishy, oozing mud.

Soon they stood together in water up to their shoulders, listening intently. Despite the fact that it had been a rather warm summer day, the water was cool; and the only sound Joe could hear was Nat's chattering teeth.

"You all right?" he asked his new-found friend.

"Yas, suh. Ah guess so," Nat replied. "Ah jus' don' know ifn Ah's cold . . . o' jus' plain scaehed to death! Ifn mah mastuh catches me . . . dis' be de end o' Nathaniel Brown!"

Joe wrapped his arm around Nat's shoulders and gave him a reassuring hug. "Hang on, Nat! We've come a long way, an' we ain't quittin' now!" he said with firm resolution.

The air was so still that not even the trees and bushes stirred along the shore. Feeling satisfied that no one was near, they waded cautiously toward the bank. But just as they were about to step out of the water, they heard shrubbery moving, followed by the sound of footsteps scrambling across a stony surface.

"Someone's comin'!" Joe whispered. "Get down in the water,

an' don't let much more'n your nose stick out!"

Whoever was coming toward them was moving at a rather fast rate, even though it was doubtful that he could see properly; and before Joe was completely submerged, the person stumbled and fell. Joe heard a deep mumbling voice, as though someone was muttering something to himself; and then silence reigned. Lying with only a part of his head above the surface, a few moments later Joe again detected the rustle of some bushes and then saw the blurred figure of a man stop and peer fixedly toward the river. Fortunately, he stayed for only a few seconds and then continued stumbling and mumbling through the night.

Joe nudged Nat, who had been completely submerged for quite a while. As the Negro lad cleared the surface with a heavy gasp for breath, Joe said, "Let's go, before he decides to turn around an' come back!"

Staying close together, they waded ashore as quietly as possible. After walking gingerly over a stony embankment, they gently moved the branches of shrubbery with their hands as they passed, being almost cat-like in their quietness. Soon the rough, jagged ground gave way to an almost sandy loam; and they were able to forge ahead more quickly. Joe stealthily led the way across the deserted river road and then among more trees and bushes, warily searching for the railroad track which he knew lay between them and the Wright Mansion orchard. When they eventually came to a clearing, he felt stones beneath his feet again.

"Careful!" he cautioned. "There's prob'ly a railroad tra . . ."

But a sudden mournful groan told him that he had spoken too late.

"Oh, mah toe!" Nat moaned, as though this were unquestionably his last day to walk the face of the earth. He had stubbed his foot on one of the railroad ties lying directly in their path.

"Mah, oh mah!" he whined, falling first to one knee and then rolling over on his back and holding his foot. "Ifn Ah'd knowed runnin' away was gonna mean upset wagons, swallerin' bugs, jumpin' off bridges, swimmin' ribbuhs, an' stompin' mah toes off in de dahk, b'lieb me, Ah'da stayed right weah Ah was! Oh, Lawdy me!"

Caught somewhere between laughing and crying, Joe merely said as comfortingly as he could, "Well, c'mon, Nat! See if you can manage just a short distance more." Then, helping him to his feet, he added,

"We're only a couple o' minutes away. You can't give up now!"

At length, Nat's foot gradually began to feel human again; and they crossed the tracks as guardedly as they could, without any further calamities. Moments later, stooping to avoid some low-hanging branches, they stole unseen into the Wright orchard. At long last, after what seemed an incredible adventure, the mansion stood before them . . . cloaked in total darkness!

Joe's heart sank like a lead weight! "Oh, no!" he muttered. "Somebody's just gotta be home after a night like this!"

"Maybe dey's in bed!" Nat said, his teeth still chattering.

"I hope you're right!" Joe answered, as he began looking for a good hiding place. Noticing the shadows of some thick shrubbery at the north corner of the house, he said, "I'll see if I can rouse somebody, but you'd better hide. We don't know if any o' those men are around here or not. You get lost in those bushes while I see if anybody's home."

As Nat obediently scurried to the relative safety of the shrubs, Joe walked carefully in the opposite direction and moved quietly around the southern side of the long, stone building, hopeful that he would catch a glimmer of light from somewhere within the bowels of the old mansion. Then, while groping through the darkness, he bumped directly into the housing that surrounded the well, and cringed when he crashed the wooden bucket against the inside of the wall and then down into the water with a loud splash!

Thoroughly disgusted with himself, he quickly squatted as low as he could in the corner formed by the well, where it joined the outside of the mansion itself. Again he felt his heart pounding heavily as he could do no more than listen, to determine if the noise had attracted anyone's attention, either inside or outside the home.

When several minutes passed and he could detect nothing, he heaved yet another sigh of relief, regained control of his nervous system and slowly emerged from his hiding place. Cautiously, he passed the well and turned the front corner of the ivy-covered homestead. There his spirits soared, for near the northern end of the front of the mansion, he noticed a dim light at an upstairs window; but even before he could take another step, it suddenly disappeared!

Exasperated by these quirks of fate which seemed to be uniting against his every effort, Joe decided to wait a few moments; but when the light failed to reappear, he determined to knock at the front door itself. Walking between the two pillars that guarded the Second Street entrance, he searched the door for a knocker. But when his hand came upon such a ponderous object that he was certain it could summon anyone within a hundred yards, he resolved not to risk making too much noise. Instead, he rapped with his bare knuckles and then waited.

As he stood on the flat stone porch, he realized for the first time that he was actually shivering. While on the move, he hadn't been very mindful of his wet clothing. Now, however, not only did he feel cold; but his shirt and trousers were clinging most uncomfortably to his body.

When there was no answer, he became somewhat impatient and knocked louder. Minutes passed which dragged like hours of hard labor; and as he waited, the moon came out again, almost directly overhead. Instinctively Joe stepped back against one of the pillars in order to hide himself as best he could. Still there was no answer.

Then another idea occurred to him. He stepped off the porch and began feeling the ground in search of some tiny stones, but unsuccessfully. Recalling that he must have tread upon nearly a thousand of them during the course of their flight from Wrightsville, he was virtually disgusted with not being able to find just a few now that he really needed some! Then, remembering that the street was not too far from where he stood, he hastily walked to the edge of the property and soon easily gathered a handful of fairly small pebbles.

Scurrying back to a spot beneath one of the upstairs windows, he took a few of the smallest pebbles in his collection and tossed them underhanded toward his target. As they rattled like heavy rain drops upon the panes, Joe cringed and gritted his teeth, hoping desperately not to hear the sickening, tinkling noise of broken glass.

When a few minutes passed with still no results, he determined to repeat his performance at a different window. Palming a few more pebbles, he let them fly; and again they rattled upon the panes before raining down through the ivy and eventually dropping to the ground near his feet.

Staring upward, he waited again. Slowly the back of his neck was beginning to complain; and with this new discomfort, the many frustrations and succession of events of the evening were beginning to take their toll, even on this teenager's unusually high level of patience. At long last, with staunch determination to summon the attention of whoever was at home, even if it meant breaking a window, he selected three of the largest stones he had. Slowly, he swung back his hand to let loose this third barrage, when suddenly, he felt two strong hands clamp his arm like a vice!

Chapter 5

The Stationmaster

Joe quickly spun around to face whoever had grabbed him, and at the same time he instinctively pulled away in an attempt to escape. However, those strong hands refused to let go; and the ominous, deep-throated growl of what sounded like a fairly large dog, let him know that he had better not attempt anything foolish.

"Could I ask what you're doing here?" came a question out of the dark.

Immediately Joe was certain that the voice did not belong to either of the two men he had encountered at the bridge earlier in the evening. But did it belong to the third one? Although he hadn't detected any type of southern accent, and not knowing how he should possibly answer, he merely stammered, "I . . . uh . . . Well . . . you see . . ."

By the same token, the sound of Joe's voice, confused though he may have seemed, let the man in the darkness know that he was evidently dealing with a rather frightened teen-ager.

Then the man spoke again. "What I want to know is . . . why are you throwing stones at my sisters' home?" he asked.

Joe was so relieved to hear these words, that his knees almost gave way beneath him! Finally, gathering himself together, he asked hopefully, "You mean . . . you're Mister Wright?"

"Yes, I am," the man admitted. "My two sisters live here, and my family and I live right next door. When I heard noises through my open window, I came over here to see what was going on."

Joe again heard the deep growls of the man's dog and then felt his warm muzzle actually touch his leg, causing goose bumps to momentarily course up and down his spine.

The man waited a moment before speaking again. "Now I'd like to know who *you* are and what you're doing here. What do you *mean* by disturbing people in the middle of the night, young man?"

"Well, sir . . . my name's Joe Shelley, an' . . ."

"Shelley?" Mr. Wright interrupted. "I don't recognize the name."

Joe realized by the sound of Mr. Wright's voice that he was rather upset. Then he remembered the password which his father had used at the Loney's home, and which other people engaged in Underground Railroad activities in this part of the country employed.

"I'm sure you don't know *me,* Mr. Wright." Then he paused for a few seconds before adding, "But you *do* know . . . *William Penn,* don't you?"

Instantly, Mr. Wright released Joe's arm. "Oh, young man! Forgive me!" he said in a most apologetic tone of voice. "It's just that . . . well . . . we haven't had anyone stop by here for many weeks."

At that moment the upstairs window was at last thrown open, and Joe heard a woman calling.

"Is that you, William?" she asked. "It sounds like your voice."

"Yes, Mary. Quickly! Come down and open the door! We have a guest from *William Penn,* my dear!" he called quietly, though somewhat excitedly.

After sending his dog back to the other home, Mr. Wright placed his arm around Joe's shoulder and led him toward the small front porch. "Why . . . you're soaking wet, young man!" he said, somewhat astonished. "And you're shivering besides!"

"Yes, sir. It's a real long story, but first . . ."

Joe was interrupted when the top half of the old Dutch door swung open with a slight creaking sound. A middle-aged lady, clutching a rather stylish robe tightly about her, smiled and extended a candle toward the pair.

Mr. Wright seemed to look in every direction for a few moments and then at Joe. Raising his eyebrows, he asked, "Is . . . anyone *else* with you?"

"Yes, sir. Out back," Joe informed him.

Tilting his head slightly, Mr. Wright stared questioningly into Joe's eyes. "*Baggage?*" he asked, almost as though he half expected a negative reply.

"Yes, sir," came the somewhat surprising answer.

"How many?" asked Miss Wright, instantly blowing out her candle.

"Only one, ma'am. A boy . . . 'bout my own age, I reckon. He's hidin' out back."

"And *you* brought him *yourself*?" Mr. Wright whispered, hardly imagining it to be possible.

"That's right, sir. By way o' the river," Joe said a little sheepishly. "That's why I'm soakin' wet!"

After the kindly lady opened the lower half of the door, Mr. Wright led Joe inside and quickly bolted both halves. Hastily, Miss Wright relit the candle and looked at the soaked, shivering lad from head to toe.

"What have *you* been up to?" Miss Wright inquired, quite concerned and shaking her head in bewilderment.

"Please, ma'am! It really is an awfully long story, but don't you think we'd better get Nat?" Joe pleaded. "I know he's just as cold an' wet as I am."

Mr. Wright nodded in agreement. "Yes, by all means! Where's he hiding?"

"He's in the bushes right up at that corner o' the house," Joe informed them, pointing toward the northwest section of the mansion.

However, at that moment, a second woman, probably in her middle twenties, came down the stairs. "Do we have *baggage*, and can I help with anything?" she asked in a concerned tone of voice.

"Yes, Susan," Mr. Wright answered as he headed for the back door. "We've got two soaking wet boys on our hands. Get enough clothing for the two of them out of the trunk in the back bedroom, please."

Then looking at Joe he asked, "And when was the last time you ate anything, young man?"

"I had supper around . . . five-thirty," Joe recalled, surprised that he hadn't thought much about it. "I guess I've been so busy runnin' an' swimmin', I haven't even had time to think o' food. An' really, I'm not too hungry; but I have no idea when the last time was that Nat had anything to eat. I just ran into him a couple o' hours ago over on the other side o' Wrightsville, an' we've been high-tailin' it ever since!"

Mr. Wright looked at his sister Mary. "I guess you know what you can be doing while we bring this boy inside," he said with a disturbed look in his eye.

While Mary Wright headed for the kitchen, Joe's host reached for a coverlet on a nearby couch. "You'd better wrap this around you for the time being," he suggested.

"We really didn't plan on goin' swimmin'," Joe offered with a grin. "It just sorta turned out that way," he murmured out loud, as he thankfully draped the coverlet, shawl-like over his shoulders.

Mr. Wright reached for a second one to give to Nat, and then led Joe through a hallway toward the rear door. There he set the candle on a broad window sill, for it took both hands to throw the bolts on the double sections of the cumbersome door.

"Oh, Mr. Wright!" Joe suddenly remembered. "Nat's master an' two other men've been chasin' us!"

An expression of concern quickly swept across the stationmaster's face. "They're probably a pair of cut-throat bounty hunters!" Mr. Wright remarked. "The scum of the earth, as far as I'm concerned!" he added, his voice laden with scorn. Then, reflecting for a few moments, he leaned over and blew out the candle.

"I think we saw one of 'em down by the river when we waded ashore," Joe informed him. "We managed to slip past him though, but right now I have no idea where any of 'em might be."

"Well then, let's not waste any more time," Mr. Wright decided, speaking in a low voice, as he opened the door and peered out cautiously.

The two figures slithered quietly into the yard and moments later, returned with the cold and shivering runaway. Mr. Wright then rebolted the Dutch doors and made certain that the curtains at the hall window were fully drawn, before relighting his candle.

"Oh, dis has got to be heaven!" Nat said, wide-eyed, glancing in all directions, while constantly rubbing the warm coverlet against his trembling body.

"Well . . . maybe just a taste, Nat," Mr. Wright smiled. "Follow me, boys," he directed.

With the aid of the flickering light, they ascended a plushly-carpeted, winding staircase. Just as they reached the top, Susan Wright approached them with an armload of clothing.

"These things may not fit perfectly, but they'll be warm and dry," she said pleasantly, extending them toward the boys. "Lots of neighbors and friends contribute things just for occasions like this," she informed them.

After the boys thanked her, she looked at her brother William and said, "Just bring their wet things down to the kitchen."

"Good idea," Mr. Wright answered. "I think Mary's preparing something for them to eat right now; so she probably has a fire already started."

At the mention of food, Nat's eyes reminded Joe of two banjos. "Y'all mean . . . y'all's gonna feed us too?" he asked in disbelief.

Mr. Wright laughed. "Over the years we've managed to fill a few hundred empty bellies, Nat. Yours won't be the first; believe me," the gentleman assured him. "My sister Mary has a pretty big pantry!"

As Nat's teeth continued to chatter, the trio moved away from the top of the staircase and entered a rather spacious room containing a large, four-poster, canopy bed and some other fine furniture. Along the northern wall was a fireplace with accompanying andirons, a bellows, and a large copper pot filled with firewood. On either side of the fireplace was an exceptionally long closet, built directly into the wall.

After asking Joe to light the candles on the mantelpiece, Mr. Wright told the boys to get out of their wet clothing. "Just dry yourselves with those coverlets; that won't do them any harm. Then put on the clothing Susan gave you. I'll be back shortly," he added, leaving the room.

The boys did as Mr. Wright had directed, and before long he returned with some rather elegant robes and two pairs of slippers. "Put these on for a little while if you wish," he said. "It's been a fairly warm day, and I expect you'll be back to normal in no time at all."

After pulling the robes tightly about themselves and tying the sash, the boys grinned at one another; for the garments practically swallowed them alive.

"They're a little big," Joe laughed, "but at least they're dry!"

After Mr. Wright recorded Nat's name in a ledger, which he furtively returned to a hidden compartment at the rear of an upper book shelf, he spoke to the youngster. "You'll spend the night in this room, Nat; but by tomorrow evening, I expect to have you on your way to the next station."

This brought a quick grin from Nat, whose teeth had finally stopped chattering, the change in clothing already beginning to take its desired effect.

Mr. Wright paused a few seconds before taking on a very serious tone of voice. "Now . . . listen carefully. I'll tell you what to do in case we receive any . . . univited guests, shall we say."

He opened a closet door right beside the fireplace in order that the boys could look inside. As they watched, he pressed heavily against a side panel, located directly behind the fireplace, forcing it to move inward. The light from his candle flickered from a sudden draft, but revealed a secret passageway where a ladder was attached to the wall.

"Holy catfish!" said Joe, with a sudden look of surprise.

"If anything unexpected happens, you climb down that ladder, Nat," Mr. Wright explained, pointing to the evenly placed slats nailed to two long wooden runners against the wall. "It leads all the way to the basement. As soon as you get to the bottom, you'll find plenty of matches and candles on the floor right beside the ladder. And you'll also see there's lots of space down there; even several places to sleep in case you'd have to stay for a long time."

Nat's eyes opened wide. "Sufferin' ghosts an' goblins! Ah nevah see a house like dis befoh!" he said, shaking his head in disbelief.

Mr. Wright laughed to himself and simply nodded his head in agreement. "Actually, Nat, when you get down there, you'll be directly behind the basement fireplace; so if anyone does go to our basement to search, they'll never see you."

"I've heard stories about secret tunnels," Joe said. "Are they true, sir?"

"Oh, yes indeed!" Mr. Wright acknowledged, as he let the panel swing back into its former position before shutting the closet door as well.

However, without elaborating, he turned again to Nat. "Now, young man, for the next few days you're probably going to be doing a great deal of traveling; so I'd advise you to get as much rest as you possibly can. One of my sisters'll bring you some food very shortly; and we'll want you to eat right here, in case our evening gets interrupted by any unwanted callers. But as soon as you've finished eating, you'd better get to bed. Understand?"

"Yas, suh, an' thank y'all vehry much, suh, foh ahl yo' help!" Nat said in an extremely grateful tone of voice. "An' . . . well . . . Ah's tahed, but dis day hab been sooo full o' eggcitement . . . Ah don' think Ah'll sleep foh a week, suh!"

Mr. Wright chuckled. "Well, some food'll help settle things

down a bit, I'm sure," he said sympathetically. "Now just remember what to do if anything strange happens," he reminded the boy, pointing toward the closet door.

"Ah will, suh," Nat assured his benefactor.

As Mr. Wright was about to turn and leave the room, he gathered the wet clothing, looked at Joe and said, "You can come along downstairs. I'm sure Mary'll have something for you to eat too. Then we'll decide what to do in your case."

"I'll be down in just a few minutes, sir," Joe assured him.

As the door closed, Nat turned slowly and looked steadfastly at Joe, simply staring into his eyes for a long time. Joe couldn't tell if he was worried or just engaged in deep thought. After several moments of complete silence, Joe was surprised to see Nat's eyes gradually filling with tears.

Feeling somewhat embarrassed, Joe extended his hand toward the Negro lad. "Goodbye, Nat," he said, detecting a sudden huskiness beginning to crowd his throat. "After all we've been through, I just know I'll never, ever, forget *this* day!"

Nat clasped Joe's outstretched hand with both of his, just as full-fledged tears began to trickle down both cheeks, all his pent-up emotions finally beginning to catch up with him. Slowly his gaze dropped, and he looked toward the floor for a few moments, swallowing hard. Starting to shake his head slightly, he said, "Ahl mah life . . . white folks has treated me mean . . . mean . . . mean! Mighty mean!"

Then, unhurriedly, he raised his head and looked again, deeply, into Joe's eyes, tears still gliding softly down his face. "But in jus' . . . one evenin' . . . y'all has done wiped out . . . ahl the hate in mah heahrt! An' Ah . . . will nevuh, evuh, fohget . . . Joey Shelley!"

Joe felt Nat release the grip on his hand; but instantly, he found himself being clasped in the strongest, most heart-rending bear hug he had ever experienced!

"De sad thing 'bout ahl dis is . . . dat Ah can nevuh pay y'all back foh what y'all's done foh me!" he said, a tone of profound, heartfelt remorse in his voice. "But Ah truly thanks you, Joey, from de bottom o' mah heahrt!" Nat sobbed, resting his chin on his friend's shoulder, his tears now falling down the back of Joe's robe, as the grateful runaway held him tightly in his arms.

"You're welcome, Nat!" Joe answered consolingly, emphasizing his words with several gentle pats on the runaway's back, even as he fought mightily to restrain tears of his own.

Then, laughing lightly as he spoke, he added, "I just *know* . . . there was a *very special* reason why God made me thirsty for spearmint and sassafras today!"

Nat took a sudden step backward, wiped some of the tears from his face, and looked at Joe rather quizzically, evidently expecting some kind of explanation.

Joe chuckled even more when he saw the expression on his face. "I guess . . . you really wouldn't understand that, Nat," he smiled. "But hopefully, some day you will. You see, I don't believe things *just happen!* There's no doubt in my mind that He sent my sister an' me out to that road *today,* of all days!"

Then, when his eyes fell upon the Bible that was lying on the table beside the four-poster, Joe pointed to it and said, "See that book?"

"Yas, suh," Nat replied as he gazed toward it.

"Well . . . if it wasn't for the Bible, I prob'ly never woulda done what I did tonight," Joe said emphatically.

"Does y'all really mean dat?" Nat asked almost unbelievingly. "Y'all risked yoah own neck foh me, jus' 'cause o' what's in dat book?"

Joe nodded his head several times before saying, "Without a doubt, Nat."

The runaway shut one eye and thought for a few moments; then looked from the Bible . . . to Joe . . . and back again. Finally, Nat looked him square in the eye and said in a very decisive tone of voice, "Den some day, Ah's gonna learn how to read . . . an' Ah's gonna read dat book!"

Joe grinned. He thought for a few moments and then remarked, "A while ago you said you could never pay me back, Nat. Remember?" Joe asked.

"Yas, suh."

"Well . . . you can," Joe said, staring at him with a rather determined look in his eye.

"How's dat?" Nat asked, slightly bewildered.

"Well . . . I've got a favor to ask." Joe paused a few moments, and then said, "We don't know where you're headed; but some day I hope you find a really happy home, with somebody to love you the way I know my folks love me. An' when you do, you find a good church, an' learn all you can about the Bible. Will you promise me that?"

Nat smiled. Then thrusting out his hand, he said, "I'll shake yo' hand on it, Joey!"

Then, after sealing their pact, Joe turned to leave. "Goodbye, Nat!" he said in slightly more than a choked whisper. "An' you can bet I'll be prayin' for you *mighty hard* . . . for a *long* time to come!"

Somewhat later, Joe sat at the kitchen table enjoying some of Mary Wright's wholesome cooking. Sue, in the meantime, had wrung out the wet clothes and strung them on a makeshift line stretched close to the kitchen fireplace, and had just brought Nat's tray and dishes downstairs.

Joe had already discarded his robe; and just as he finished eating, Mr. Wright came walking into the kitchen. The boy glanced at the fire and said, "I've never seen so many fireplaces! Practically every room has one," he observed.

"Yes," Mary interjected. "We have three upstairs and three on the first floor, but you should see the one in the basement!" she added, as she cleared the table and smiled mysteriously at her brother.

"Yes, you mentioned it upstairs, Mr. Wright. Is it different from the others?" Joe inquired.

"Well, come along and I'll show you," Mr. Wright answered with a glint in his eye.

Mary and Susan took that moment to bid Joe a good night; and after he thanked them for their help and the delicious food, he followed Mr. Wright to the cellar, flip-flopping down the narrow steps in his over-sized slippers.

Soon they were walking toward the northern end of the mansion, where Mr. Wright's candle illuminated still another fireplace which, as far as Joe could determine, appeared to be nothing out of the ordinary. He began scanning the wall for closets; for he remembered that his host had said that the ladder in Nat's room ran all the way to the basement, and he thought that perhaps a similar situation existed on this level.

Not seeing any closets, however, he asked, "Is there a way to go through the wall down here like you can upstairs?"

"Yes," Mr. Wright nodded. "But don't you notice anything strange about the fireplace?" he questioned his young acquaintance.

"Not really . . . 'cept it's a *lot* bigger . . . and . . . it's pretty clean," Joe observed. "But then I'm sure you don't use it much."

"Ah, but it's been used a great deal during these many years," Mr.

Wright insisted. "However! Not for the same reason that the others are used," he added. "Watch!"

Then taking a heavy poker, he placed it against the back of the fireplace and pushed firmly. To Joe's surprise, it moved! He felt a sudden strong draft of air rush about his feet and legs, as the rear section of the fireplace swung straight back and upward.

"Good grief!" Joe exclaimed, uttering one of his favorite expressions.

Chuckling at the look on Joe's face, Mr. Wright said, "Here, take this candle and crawl inside. There's plenty of room."

Joe eagerly followed his suggestion, but the air moving through the opening almost extinguished the flame. Shielding it with his hand, Joe crawled to the back of the fireplace and peered inside.

"Why, there's the ladder you showed us upstairs." And then, spying a sealed doorway, he asked, "Is this where the tunnel starts?"

"Yes," nodded Mr. Wright from a crouching position. "But it's no longer used. As a matter of fact, at one time there were two tunnels leading from this basement."

"Really?"

"Yes, back in the mid-seventeen hundreds, for several years there was only one other home in the area, about a quarter of a mile north of here. It's still there today, on the hill not too far from the bridge entrance. It's called Mount Bethel and was built by the Blunston family."

"Yeah, I see it every time we come to Columbia," Joe remarked.

"Well, that's where the tunnel used to go that's sealed up inside this fireplace. You see, when this home was built, there were still many Susquehannock living in these parts; and the Wrights and the Blunstons had tunnels dug so their families could escape any Indian attacks."

"But what about the other tunnel?" Joe asked. "Where was that one?"

"Well, it ran directly west toward the river, and started over there," Mr. Wright said, pointing toward a section of the wall that had obviously been sealed up along the south-west corner of the basement. "In case it was necessary to flee both homes, they could escape easily, because that tunnel had a hidden exit down towards the river," Mr. Wright explained.

"Boy! That must've taken a heap o' diggin'!" Joe admitted, crawling from the fireplace.

"I rather imagine they didn't finish it all in one day!" chuckled Mr. Wright, as he swung the fireplace wall back to its original position. "The tunnels made this home a natural place for an Underground Railroad station, wouldn't you say?"

"An' it really is underground!" Joe added, nodding his head emphatically.

"Well, when slaves first started coming here, my folks said the tunnel to the river was used many, many times. In the past half century or so, hundreds of slaves have passed through this mansion; and often they were brought across the river by rowboat in the early days and then came through the river tunnel. Then they brought them right through that wall over there, had them crawl through this fireplace, and hid them in the room behind it."

Joe just shook his head in wonder.

Mr. Wright became extremely pensive for a few moments. Heaving a prolonged sigh, he too shook his head and added with a touch of mournfulness in his voice, "But then the railroad came, and some of our land was needed to lay tracks to the bridge. Eventually the rumbling of the trains collapsed that tunnel, and its entrances had to be sealed."

"But at least you still manage to hide people here an' move 'em to the next station, *with* or without tunnels," Joe reminded him, admiring the courage and determination of Mr. Wright and his two sisters.

"Yes, we never know when the next frightened and suffering runaway will appear; just like you with Nat this evening," he admitted.

Then, looking sternly into Joe's eyes, he asked, "Why can't everyone see that God loves *these* people too? My great-grandfather, John Wright, was a Quaker preacher, and at times, a missionary to the Susquehannock. And I *know* that for his great love of God, and concern for those whose skin is *red*, he would want us to help these *black* folk gain their freedom from bondage!"

He made this last statement with such deep feeling, that Joe easily understood why the Wrights and their ancestors had run the risk of operating this station for so many years.

In the parlor not long afterwards, Mr. Wright sat on an old settee. "I know it's late," he said; "and right now your parents are probably very worried about you, Joe. But with those men being in the area, I think the best thing to do is to keep you here for the night and then get you home in the daylight hours. What do you think?"

"I just know my ma's gonna be fit to be tied!" Joe admitted. "But still, I'm sure you're right, sir. An' besides, I've had enough problems for one day! I don't think I'd wanna head home right now an' prob'ly ask for more!"

"Well, then," said Mr. Wright, settling back and making himself more comfortable. "Why not tell me about this boy, and how you got him here tonight?"

Joe leaned back in his chair, kicked off his slippers and commenced his story. "It all started on the other side o' Wrightsville, not far from our farm. Cato Jourdon came . . ."

"Cato Jourdon!" Mr. Wright interrupted spiritedly. "Was the boy with *him*?"

"Yes, sir," Joe replied, and then informed him of the events surrounding Cato's accident.

"That's too bad!" sighed Mr. Wright, when Joe finished with the details concerning the Negro driver. "Cato has brought countless slaves here. I do hope he's all right!"

Then, continuing with his story, Joe spent nearly the next half hour describing the various harrowing adventures of the evening.

When he finished, Mr. Wright remarked, "You boys really had a time of it, didn't you? But tell me, how did you know the mansion was a station for runaways?"

"Well, sir, on several occasions my father has helped Mr. Loney bring slaves across the river by rowboat."

"Yes, I know Bob Loney well. He's been here many times, and I've even visited his home," Mr. Wright interjected.

"Well, since he an' my pa are real good friends, I've known 'bout the Underground Railroad for at least two years. Twice slaves came through our property when they were lost, an' me an' my older brother helped Pa take 'em to the Loney home. That's how I learned about the password, by the way. Pa told me they were usually delivered to you after that, but I've never told *anyone*. Honest!"

"I'm certain of that, Joe," Mr. Wright assured him with a nod. "Actually, then, it's quite possible I've met your father already, though I don't recall of ever being introduced to him. Of course, quite a few men have been here on several nights when slaves came in; but often very few words are spoken."

Their attention was distracted by a grandfather's clock, as it began striking the hour of midnight.

"Jumpin' grasshoppers! I didn't think it was *that* late!" Joe exclaimed.

"Yes, time flies on a night like this," said the stationmaster, as he arose and headed for the kitchen. "Let me check your clothing; perhaps it's dry by now."

As the man left the room, Joe's eyes were drawn to a news sheet lying on a nearby table. Casually, he reached for it and found it to be a copy of the *Lancaster Intelligencer.* He was scanning the important topics on the front page by the light of a flickering candle, when suddenly one article especially arrested his attention. After reading it closely, he looked up thoughtfully for a few moments. However, his ponderings were disturbed when Mr. Wright re-entered the room.

The gentleman was just about to speak when Joe held out the *Intelligencer* and asked, "Mr. Wright, have you finished with today's news?"

"Why, yes; I read it late this afternoon, as a matter of fact. My sisters and I share it, but I'm sure they've read it by this time too. Would you like to have it?" he inquired.

"Well, there's an article here that interests me very much. Could I have it?" Joe wondered.

"By all means, young man. Take the entire sheet," Mr. Wright insisted. "Mary already has a complete stack of them in her library collection, and she certainly won't miss just one."

As Joe folded the news sheet, Mr. Wright remarked, "I'm afraid your clothing's still quite damp, but hopefully by tomorrow morning . . . "

Mr. Wright's words were suddenly interrupted by the sharp pounding of the front door knocker!

Joe snapped to his feet in an instant and stared at Mr. Wright. "Those men!" he whispered fearfully.

"Possibly . . . though I can't think how they'd know," Mr. Wright reasoned. "But quick! We can't take any chances. Get the clothing from the kitchen and warn Nat! Then you get in the bed upstairs; there's no telling what may happen. In case there are any questions, as far as you're concerned, you're the son of a friend from Wrightsville just visiting for a spell. Understand?"

Joe nodded but didn't hesitate a second. Snatching a candle, he dashed for their clothing and then clambered barefooted up the steps, while Mr. Wright simply stalled for time, waiting in the parlor. Hardly had Joe reached the top of the steps before a second knock was heard, both louder and longer.

When Joe burst through the bedroom door, Nat sat up briskly in the bed, still fully clothed; for he hadn't been able to sleep.

"Get down in the basement!" Joe cried. "Somebody's knockin' at the door!"

Nat needed no coaxing; but as he scurried toward the closet, Joe called after him. "Take your robe! It's cool down there! An' here; take all our wet clothes too. Just pitch 'em down right beside the ladder," he directed, pushing hard to move the wall panel inward.

Nat tossed the clothing through the opening; then Joe held the candle close to the ladder as the excitable runaway began his hurried descent. Seconds later, after Joe saw Nat strike another flame far below, he closed both the panel and the closet door. After setting his candlestick on the mantel and extinguishing its light, he went on tip-toe toward the hallway door. Holding it slightly ajar, he listened intently and heard Mr. Wright finally throwing one of the bolts of the front entryway.

Soon Joe detected the mumbling of voices but was too far away to determine any words from the conversation. Next there was a period of silence followed by the sound of the second bolt, and moments later, the doors closing and the bolts noisily locked into position once more. Then Joe's heart began to accelerate when he heard the padded footsteps of people coming up the spiral staircase!

Within seconds he tumbled into the bed and pulled the light coverlet up to his ears. Shutting his eyes, he pretended to be sleeping soundly.

First the door creaked slightly, and then some floor boards groaned near him under the weight of heavy steps. Through the thinness of his eyelids, Joe knew someone was approaching him with a candle. Then a hand grasped him firmly by the shoulder and shook him!

Chapter 6

The Call for Drummers

"Pa!" Joe shouted in total shock when he opened his eyes. "You're the *last* person I expected to see!"

Quickly, he jumped from the bed and dashed to the passageway to call Nat.

After much shuffling and scuffling, the Negro lad finally reappeared. He was somewhat comically bedecked, with all the damp clothing draped around his shoulders and neck; and the robe he was wearing, dragged along the floor.

Looking at Joe with a somewhat bewildered expression, he asked, "Is dis de beginnin' of a new advenchuh . . . oh jus' paht o' de ole one?"

Joe laughed. "Well, the clock just struck midnight not long ago, Nat; so I guess this is a new one."

"I suppose this is the one Sarah was tellin' me about," Mr. Shelley surmised.

Then as Joe made the introductions, Nat shook hands shyly before carefully draping the clothing over a bedside chair. He took off the robe; and at last, looking as though the adventures of the day were finally beginning to wear him down, he sat with a heavy sigh on the edge of the bed. Suddenly looking extremely fatigued, he sprawled on his stomach and caressed the thick pillow. Mr. Wright drew the coverlet over him as Joe put his hand on Nat's shoulder and bid him a final farewell. Then, picking up his damp clothing, he turned to accompany his father and Mr. Wright down the stairs.

Upon returning to the parlor, he tucked Mr. Wright's *Intelligencer* under his arm and was preparing to leave, when he remembered the injured Negro driver.

"Pa, do you know anything about Mr. Jourdon?" he asked.

"Yes, we got him to Doc Taylor; but he was still unconscious when I left. Doc said he probably has a severe concussion."

Mr. Wright was saddened by this news, but he managed a smile as he reached to shake hands with Mr. Shelley. Then, turning to Joe he spoke quite seriously.

"Young man, few adults would've attempted to do what you did tonight; and even fewer would've succeeded as you did. You've got a good head on your shoulders," he affirmed. And then, tapping his index finger on Joe's chest, he added, "And what's probably even more important . . . a real heart for others!"

Upon hearing these words, Mr. Shelley put his arm around Joe's shoulders; and unable to conceal the gleam in his eyes, he said, "Thank you, Mr. Wright. His mother an' I are pretty proud o' this young man!"

"Well, considering the circumstances, it took a good deal of courage to get that boy here tonight," Mr. Wright conceded.

"Thank you, sir," Joe answered, somewhat embarrassed by the sudden praise being heaped upon him.

Then quickly changing the subject, he said, "An' I'll bring your clothes back the very next time we come over to market; so hopefully, I'll be seein' you again real soon."

Before departing, Mr. Shelley inquired, "Will you be safe till this *baggage* is taken care of?"

Mr. Wright smiled. "The Lord has taken care of us all these years, and He won't let us down now. We'll be fine, and there's no need to worry."

After shaking hands again, Joe and his father took leave of the dedicated stationmaster. Then, when they reached the street, Joe was surprised to see Swift tied to the hitching post, and four men in a wagon, all carrying muskets.

"Say! You came prepared, Pa!" Joe remarked.

"Listen, son, after hearin' Sarah's story, I didn't know what to expect. She told me about the three men on horseback an' said they had guns. I figured I might need to do some fast ridin'; so I brought Swift!" he said emphatically.

"I'm sorry if I had you worried, Pa; but I just *had* to help Nat!"

His father turned agilely and placed both hands on his son's shoulders. "Listen, Joey. I don't question your decision for even *one* moment; an' right now there's not a prouder father anywhere on the face o' this earth!" Mr. Shelley assured him. "What's done is done; an' accordin' to Mr. Wright, it couldn't've been done better," he remarked, shooting his foot into the stirrup and sliding into the saddle.

Elated at his father's words, Joe turned to greet the men, all of whom were neighbors, and then grabbed his father's arm and swung up behind him to ride tandem on Swift.

They hadn't ridden far when Joe asked, "What happens to the slaves after they leave the Wright mansion, Pa? Do you know?"

"I've been told they have a clever way o' sendin' 'em to Christiana, or all the way to Philadelphia with no trouble at all," his father responded.

"What do they do?" Joe wanted to know.

"Well, Nat may go by wagon to Bird-in-Hand or Strasburg, an' then to Christiana; or, if what I've heard is true, Nat could find himself along the railroad tomorrow night bein' hidden on a train. There's a special car that Mr. Wright uses, with a false end to it, sorta like a double wall. The slaves just crawl in between the two walls where there's room enough to sit, stand, or even lie down."

Joe shook his head again in amazement. "The Wrights sure have some good ways o' hidin' people!" he said, admiring their ingenuity.

In a short while they reached the familiar wooden bridge, and Joe couldn't help wondering what had happened to the three men who were chasing them. But as far as he was concerned, he wouldn't be disappointed if he never saw them again!

Before Swift and the other horses plodded boldly through the main portal of the framework, John Cartright, the wagoner, lit a lantern which barely cast enough light to see just a few yards ahead. Then, while they recrossed the amazing structure that had provided Joe with such an unforgettable experience earlier in the evening, he informed his father of nearly every detail of his adventures with Nat.

It was during the very early hours of the morning when they arrived at the Shelley farm, where both Joe and his father warmly thanked their neighbors before they departed for their homes.

A light from the parlor window indicated that at least one other member of the family probably had not gone to bed as yet.

"Looks as though I've caused a change in the Shelley sleepin' habits, Pa," Joe observed, pointing to the light in the window, as they led Swift toward the stable.

"Not only the Shelleys, but your neighbors an' Doc Taylor too," his father reminded him. "It took quite a while to get old Cato to Doc's place, an' I stayed there as long as I could to help. Then because of all that Sarah told me, I was afraid you might be in more trouble than you bargained for. So I rounded up the neighbors, an' we scoured the woods on the south side o' Wrightsville well into the night."

"Did you ever see anything o' the three men?" Joe asked, loosening the cinch around Swift's midsection.

"No, but Bob Loney was really concerned about 'em! He just arrived home from Philadelphia right before I got to his house; an' he didn't wanna leave for fear you'd show up there. Then when the rest of us couldn't find you anywhere, I had an idea you mighta tried to take that boy to Columbia. That's when I decided to cross the river an' head for the Wright Mansion."

They finished bedding down Swift and walked toward the house; but even before they reached the porch, they heard the sound of hoof beats. Someone dismounted in the darkness, hitched his horse, and came hurrying up the path.

"Who is it?" Mr. Shelley called out.

"Bob Loney," came the answer.

"No need to worry, Bob! Joey's right here with me."

"Yeah, I know," Mr. Loney replied. "I just met some o' the men down the road a piece, an' they told me you found him."

Then turning to Joe he asked, "What in thunder've you been doin', boy? When you didn't reach my place by midnight, I thought I'd better help search!"

Before Joe had a chance to answer, his father interrupted. "Come inside, Bob; an' I'll try to tell you all about it. But I want Joey to get to bed. This one evenin' has been more like a month. He needs some rest!"

As Joe opened the front door, his mother, who had dozed off in her favorite rocker, quickly opened her eyes and ran toward him with an exclamation of surprise and relief.

"I'm all right, Ma. Nothin' to worry about," Joe assured her, trying to sound as casual as he could.

"Nothing to worry about!" she harped. "*Well*... not *now,* I suppose!"

After a concerned hug and a much more tender kiss than usual, she held him at arms' length. Then, touching the wet clothing he was carrying, she exclaimed, "Why are these clothes wet? And where'd you get those things you're wearing? Where've you been, Joey?"

Joe and his father looked at one another and laughed. "Would you like me to answer 'em one at a time or all together, Ma?" Joe inquired with a grin.

Then turning to his father, he said, "Looks like I'll hafta put this story in writin', Pa; or I'll be tellin' it the rest o' my life!"

"Very likely you'll be sharin' it with your grandchildren one day, son; so you may as well get use' to it," his father laughed.

Joe took a deep breath, looked squarely into his mother's eyes and said teasingly, "Ma, it was such a beautiful moonlit night, I just couldn't resist goin' for a swim. As a matter o' fact, I made one o' the *greatest* cannon ball dives o' my life; an' the water was fine! You shoulda gone along!"

"All right!" laughed his father, swatting him on the seat of his pants. "Put your wet clothes out in the kitchen, hike up those stairs, an' get some sleep. It's been a long day!"

Still laughing at his mother's somewhat bewildered expression, Joe bid everyone a good night; but as he stepped through the kitchen doorway, he remembered the news sheet. Pulling the folded paper from inside his shirt, he held it for all to see and placed it on a cupboard shelf.

"Please, don't throw this away," he cautioned. "I'd like to talk to you about it tomorrow."

When Joe awoke the following morning, he could tell by the brightness of his room that he had slept late. He dressed quickly, for he was anxious to speak to his parents about the news article. However, the more he thought about it, the less eager he became; and slowly his anxiousness began to turn to concern, and then even to worry.

When he was completely dressed, he simply sank to the edge of his bed, fearful of going down to breakfast and saying what was on his mind. Then, remembering what his parents themselves had always instilled in him, he slid to his knees by the side of his bed and prayed for several minutes.

After he was finished, he sat on the bed a second time and became completely absorbed in thoughts about the preceding evening, and then about his brother Dan, and the war over slavery. At length, gathering his courage, he slapped his thighs, sprang to his feet and resolutely strode toward the door, determined to take his stand.

As he descended the stairs, he heard the kitchen door slam. Craning his neck to look over the bannister, he saw his father come through the kitchen door with an armload of vegetables and a freshly cleaned chicken. Mr. Shelley glanced at Joe but said nothing before going on with his work.

His mother, who was kneading dough on a large pie board, looked up for a moment, but strangely, failed even to bid a good morning. Joe looked at her quizzically, as she turned her back to him and reached into a nearby cupboard for some seasoning. His father, continuing his own strange silence, disappeared into the cellar and soon returned with a pitcher of fresh milk.

Mystified by his parents' uncustomary quietness, Joe slowly took his usual seat at the table. He felt as though ordinary circumstances would've made it difficult for him to say the words he wished to speak, but this turn of events was almost certain to make the situation even worse. He was about to postpone the little speech he had been so carefully planning, when his father suddenly sat in the chair next to him and leaned his arms on the table.

Looking very seriously at Joe, he said point blank, "You'd like to be a drummer boy, wouldn't you, son?"

Astonished, Joe simply stared at him. But when he turned to look at his mother, her eyes refused to meet his, as she went about preparing his breakfast, almost as though she were completely unaware of what was being said.

Looking back to his father, he asked, "How'd you know I was thinkin' about . . . "

However, before he could finish, his eyes focused upon the spot where he had laid the news sheet during the very early hours of the morning; but it was no longer on the cupboard shelf.

"Were you readin' the *Lancaster Intelligencer* that Mr. Wright gave me last night?" he asked.

Mr. Shelley nodded. "Yes," he admitted. "I saw Governor Curtin's message, as well as the article about the army needin' drummer boys. But I didn't need to read 'em to know what you had in mind. I sensed it most especially last evenin', after Ma read Dan's letter."

Before starting to eat his breakfast, Joe bowed his head. But instead of his usual prayer of thanksgiving, he found himself praying that his parents would somehow understand all the churning and anxiety that had been passing through his mind. He opened his eyes and slowly began to drink his milk. After he set the cup on the table, he waited silently a few moments before speaking.

"I know it's bad enough now that Dan's gone," he began; "but if it's at all possible to do without my help too, then . . . yes . . . I'd like to become a drummer boy. If you've read that article, you *know* they need drummers bad! *Any* age!"

"That's true enough, Joey, I'm sure," Mr. Shelley agreed. "An' I'm also certain you'd make a good one. No question about that!"

His father paused for a few seconds, and then added, "But the news article sure makes it sound as though that kind o' life offers nothin' but parades an' adventure, an' we know first hand from Dan's letter just how far that is from the truth. It'll be anything but goin' to a picnic!"

Throughout the time that Joe was eating breakfast, the two of them thoroughly discussed the matter. However, though his mother remained in the kitchen, not once did she contribute even one word to the conversation. At length, Joe and Mr. Shelley seemed to have nothing more to say.

Then, carrying his breakfast dishes toward the sink, Joe looked at his mother. "You haven't said anything at all, Ma," Joe observed. "Usually when we talk things over, all of us say what we have on our minds."

Mrs. Shelley stopped rolling her dough and simply stared solemnly at her son. Then returning to her task once more and fixing her eyes on her pie board, she spoke in a somewhat quavering voice. "After Bob Loney left last night, your father discovered the news articles; and we guessed what was on your mind. We talked about it then; and as far as I'm concerned, I've already said everything I have to say on the matter."

In the uneasy silence that followed, Joe glanced from one parent to the other, not knowing what else he could say.

Finally, his mother spoke again. "Your pa seems to think . . . that if this is what you *really want* . . . then he'll give you his permission."

Joe could hardly contain himself! "Does she mean that, Pa?" he asked, almost unable to believe what he had heard.

Slowly, Mr. Shelley began nodding his head with just a bare trace of a rather forced smile. "Yes, son . . . if you're *sure* that's what you *really* should do. But . . . I hope you've prayed about it! I know I did almost all last night!"

"Oh, yes, Pa! I really have! Twice already this mornin'!" he assured him.

However, Joe's happiness was to be short-lived. Looking at his mother again, he asked, "But how about you, Ma? I wouldn't leave home unless I had *your* permission too."

His mother quickly set her roller aside, turned her back to both of them and lifted her apron to her face, shaking her head all the while. "Joey . . . I can't *believe* that *any* mother would allow her fifteen-year-old son to go off to war!"

She heaved a heavy sigh before she turned to look at him, her eyes filling with tears. "If you do this thing . . . it's your father's responsibility . . . not mine!" she concluded, turning yet another time to lean distraughtly on the cupboard behind her.

There was another prolonged silence. Then Joe quietly set his dishes in the dry sink and walked somberly toward the door. He paused for a few seconds, took a deep breath and said, "Ma . . . you an' Pa have two sons," he reminded her. "Do you remember what Dan wrote about the drummer boy in his company?"

His mother thought for only a moment before nodding, still holding the apron to her face.

"Well . . . I got a feelin' that drummer boy was prob'ly 'bout my own age. Maybe a little older . . . or maybe even a little *younger*! Who knows? But regardless o' how old he was, we can be glad he was there!" Joe continued, feeling his voice becoming slightly husky. "If *his* parents hadn't allowed him to be a drummer boy . . . you an' Pa might have only *one* son right now instead o' two!"

Then opening the door, he stepped onto the porch and ambled slowly toward the stable. With his mind in turmoil, he led some of the animals to the pasture and then began to curry Swift. As he was brushing the animal's strong back, he was surprised to see a shadow appear on the sun-drenched floor near the huge doors. Gazing over top of Swift, he saw his mother standing in the doorway. Though her face still bore traces of a worried expression, it was no longer streaked with tears. Joe stopped what he was doing, managed a half smile, but said nothing as he began brushing Swift's mane.

His mother walked slowly around the stallion; and after coming to Joe's side, they looked at one another. Mrs. Shelley paused for a few moments and stared deeply into her son's brown eyes. Suddenly she reached out with both arms and drew him close to her.

Joe was well aware of the feelings she must have been experiencing: concerns and worries which only a mother could bear. Demonstrating a maturity for someone far beyond his age, he was certain that this was definitely a time for absolutely no words at all.

After a few moments, she stepped back and placed her hands on his shoulders. He was taller than she was now, and she had to look up slightly to be able to gaze directly into his eyes.

"I'm sorry, Joey!" she apologized. "I was being selfish, wasn't I?"

Joe was thoughtful for a few moments before closing his eyes momentarily and shaking his head. "I don't think so," he said calmly. "What can I say? You're my Ma! I know you love me, an' you only want what's best for me! I'm only fifteen, but I figured *that* out *long* ago!"

His mother smiled. "Well, after you reminded me about Dan's drummer boy . . . I realized that a lot of feelings were racing through my heart and mind . . . and selfishness was one of them," she admitted. "But darn it, Joey, you're one wonderful son! And it's just that . . . well . . . " she stammered, "I've sort of gotten attached to you after having you around for fifteen years; that's all!" And she began to laugh and cry at the same time.

"Almost sixteen," Joe reminded her in a whisper, realizing that his mother was trying to do all she could to make him feel better.

"Yes," she acknowledged, "the years are flying; and what happened last night certainly proved you're no longer a boy. You've become a fine young man right before our eyes!"

She paused a few moments, and with a catch in her throat she heaved a long sigh. Then, hugging him again, she rested her chin on his shoulder and said as courageously as she could, "Since your father has said you may become a drummer boy, it's my duty to agree with him. Besides," she added, stepping back and looking into his eyes once more, "he's the one who'll miss your work around here; and how he'll manage without *both* his sons, I'll never know!"

Then it was Joe's turn to hug his mother tightly; and as they held one another close, he said, "Thanks, Ma! That's really an answer to prayer, you know; an' I promise to be *real* careful, wherever I am!"

Full of motherly pride, Mrs. Shelley stepped back again and looked at her son admiringly. "Many boys are goin' off to war now," she admitted, wiping the tear stains from her face. "So I guess all the neighbors'll just have to help one another more than ever; that's all."

Suddenly beaming, Joe blurted, "Boy, just wait'll Dave an' Ted hear about this! Is it all right if I ride over to tell 'em?" he asked.

"Well, the news article says you should write to Harrisburg. Don't you think you'd better do that first?" she suggested.

"I'll write just as soon as I get back," he promised as he began saddling Swift. "I should be home before noon. An' tell Pa I'll work till after sunset to finish the chores."

Minutes later he passed through the main gate; but as he was about to ride onto the north trail, a rig stopped right in front of him. The black driver signaled and Joe stopped to see what the stranger wanted.

"I'm lookin' for a gentleman by the name o' Robert Loney. Could you tell me how I could reach his home?" he inquired.

"Yes, sir. I'm headin' in that direction myself," Joe informed him. "I'll go with you most o' the way if you wish."

The gentleman smiled while nodding gratefully. Joe nudged Swift onto the trail and rode beside the stranger. After a few casual remarks about the weather, he introduced himself.

The man acknowledged the introduction and said, "My name's William Goodrich. I'm from York."

In a flash the name caught Joe's attention, since he thought he recognized it as one which he had heard his father mention in dealings with the Underground Railroad. Wondering if there was any connection between this man and the events of the preceding evening, he asked in a slightly mysterious tone, "Are you sure . . . Mr. Loney's the man you're *really* lookin' for?"

The question obviously perplexed Mr. Goodrich. "Why, certainly!" he exclaimed in a surprised voice. "Why would I ask you where the man's home is if I didn't wanna see him?"

Joe pretended to be almost disinterested, as he replied in a rather sing-song tone of voice, "Oh . . . I just thought that possibly . . . you were really lookin' for a man by the name of . . ." Then he looked rather slyly at Mr. Goodrich out of the corner of his eyes, before he said: "Jourdon?"

Taken completely off guard, the man gave a sharp tug on the reins, bringing his horse to a sudden standstill. "What'd you say?" he asked, even though he had heard Joe's remarks perfectly well.

Obligingly, Joe repeated his words, while Swift pawed the roadbed nervously, obviously anxious to be running.

"Just . . . how do *you* know this man . . . Jourdon?" Mr. Goodrich wanted to know.

But rather than give a reply, Joe thought for a few moments before saying, "Maybe before I answer, sir, I really oughta ask *you* about *another* name." He paused a few moments, and then said, "I'll give you the *first* name; you give me the *last.*"

The man simply gazed at Joe very intently, wondering what was going through this teen-ager's apparently very sharp mind.

Joe said, "The first name just happens to be the same as yours." Then he paused a moment before he said: "William."

A look of disbelief crossed Mr. Goodrich's face. Joe could see that he was really thinking carefully before he answered. Then after a rather lengthy interval, he responded in what was an almost questioning tone of voice.

"*Penn*?" the gentleman said rather inquiringly, raising his eyebrows and looking askance at Joe.

Joe smiled, reached out a friendly hand and remarked, "I thought so."

Mr. Goodrich returned the smile, accepted Joe's handshake and then just shook his head in stunned amazement. Snappily he asked, "How old are you, young man?"

"Just fifteen, sir; but I've managed to get involved with the Underground Railroad a couple o' times. And especially with Cato Jourdon just last evening."

"Last evening?" Mr. Goodrich echoed, raising his eyebrows once more. "Tell me about it. That's why I'm here! To the best of our knowledge, he didn't return home; an' no one knows where he is!"

But Joe paused a moment before asking a question of his own. "Does Mr. Jourdon ever do any work for you, sir?"

Mr. Goodrich pondered for a few moments, casting wary glances toward this youngster who evidently knew much more than one would normally imagine.

Finally he answered. "Yes . . . At times."

"Hauling . . . *baggage* ?" Joe questioned further.

The man's eyebrows raised still a third time, and he looked about him once or twice to make certain no one was drawing near. Seeing that the road was bare of travelers, he said, "Yes . . . Hauling *baggage*."

Then you really *are* looking for Cato, aren't you?" Joe inquired.

"That's right, but I thought Bob Loney would know where he is, if anyone would. That's why I was goin' there," Mr. Goodrich replied.

"Mr. Loney knows where he is all right, an' so do I. But I'll tell you, sir . . . I'm afraid he's in pretty bad condition!" Joe informed him.

Within less than ten minutes, Joe led his new acquaintance into the vacant waiting room at old Doc Taylor's home. After entering, he spryly knocked on the door that led to the room where the doctor saw his patients. Joe stood quietly for what seemed to be an exceedingly long time without knocking again, for he knew Dr. Taylor well. He was an elderly gentleman who was no longer capable of going anywhere in a hurry. However, despite his lack of agility, few doctors could match his skills.

Finally, Joe heard the unmistakable shuffle of the doctor's feet. Stepping back, he watched expectantly for the door to swing open; and as it did, Dr. Taylor characteristically lowered his chin to his chest and peered for several moments over the top of his spectacles.

"Well, young man," he finally muttered in his bass voice, knitting his eyebrows and looking at Joe through half-closed eyes. "What kind of escapade are you involved in now?" he inquired, breaking into just a hint of a smile, which let Joe know he was teasing in his usual good-natured way.

"Good mornin', Doctor," Joe said respectfully. "This is Mr. William Goodrich from York. He's lookin' for Cato Jourdon. May he see him?" he asked quietly.

The doctor kept his chin on his chest and continued peering over the top of his glasses, looking first at Joe and then at Mr. Goodrich.

"Well . . ." he drawled, "he's not much to look at right now, but the gentleman may come in if he'd like," he said in his typical matter-of-fact manner.

"I'll hafta leave you now, Mr. Goodrich, since I'm on my way to visit some friends," Joe said, shaking the man's hand.

However, at that moment Bob Loney appeared in the same doorway, standing directly behind Dr. Taylor. "Did I hear Joey Shelley's voice?" he inquired; and then, surprised at seeing Mr. Goodrich as well, he said, "Will! I didn't expect to see *you* here! I was gonna head for your place this afternoon."

"Well actually, I was lookin' for *your* home when I happened to bump into this young man along the road; an' he's been makin' my head spin ever since I met him!" Mr. Goodrich admitted with a smile.

"Well, you've met a really fine young man, an' thanks to him . . . "

"Excuse me, please," Joe interrupted, suspecting that some embarrassing praise might be coming. "I really must leave," he said.

But before departing, he turned to Dr. Taylor once more and asked, "Is Cato gonna be all right, Doc?"

"I think so," the physician affirmed with a nod of his head. "He had a bad night of it, but I'm sure the critical hours are over. He's lucky your pa got him here as quick as he did."

"Well, I'm sure *you* had a *little* somethin' to do with it too," Joe countered knowingly, as he turned to leave. "Goodbye, everyone."

Twenty minutes later he arrived at Dave's home, surprised to learn that Ted was there as well. He told them the exciting news about his intentions of becoming a drummer boy; and although they were sorry to hear that he would be leaving home and school, they shared in his excitement.

While he was with them, he obtained his friends' promises to stop at the Shelley farm from time to time to ride Swift. Joe still wished to keep his own pledge to Dan, and he knew Dave and Ted would gladly take care of Swift's need for exercise. However, to his special delight, both his friends offered to help around the Shelley farm now that he would be gone.

When he returned home, he told his parents about meeting Mr. Goodrich, and also informed them of Dr. Taylor's optimism concerning Cato Jourdon's recovery.

"Well, that's good news!" his father commented.

"Yeah, an' I guess you really won't be too surprised to hear that Dave an' Ted both said they'll be over to ride Swift from time to time; an' they'll also help with the chores in any way they can. So it looks like you'll lose one an' gain two. How's that for a bargain?" he asked, throwing an arm around his mother's shoulder.

"Well, I suppose that's what neighbors are for," Mrs. Shelley remarked. "You've got two really good friends, Joey. You'll miss them!"

After eating the noon meal, Joe wrote his letter volunteering as a drummer boy and then rode directly to Wrightsville to mail it.

For the next week he practiced drumming almost endlessly between chores, and anxiously rode into town often to check the mail. Once, there was a letter from Dan; but ten days passed before he finally received a letter bearing a Harrisburg postmark.

It was an official-looking envelope with a blue eagle stamped in the center near the top. As Joe walked from the store which also served as the town post office, his fingers shook with excitement as he nervously opened the letter and fumbled for its contents. Reading the enclosed orders quickly, he learned that he was to report to Camp Curtin in Harrisburg on the fifth of August.

The ride home was like a race with the wind. Seeing his father near the barn, he called, "I hafta be in Harrisburg a week from Monday, Pa!"

"Well, they didn't waste much time, now did they?" Mr. Shelley remarked with a shake of his head. "I guess they really do need drummers!"

The time passed quickly. Joe spent his last Saturday helping his family at the Market House in Columbia, and in the evening he played his final band concert in the park alongside his father. Twice Mr. Shelley caught Joe's attention and motioned toward the same young teen-ager who often stood among some trees in the park, endeavoring to tap out the same rhythms on his drum that Joe and his father were playing during several of the numbers. Joe could see him only from a distance; and while the band was enjoying a short intermission, he decided to speak with him. Unfortunately, however, the lad disappeared into the crowd; and Joe saw him no more during the remainder of the concert.

As the final number of the festivities that evening, since this would be Joe's last performance, the bandmaster insisted that he and his father play one of their favorite arrangements, which featured the drums. Joe was especially proud to accompany his father to the front of the platform; and when they finished their sparkling number, which included many kinds of highly precisioned beats and cadences, they received a rousing ovation from the hundreds of people assembled in the park. Then, before the father and son team could walk away, every member of the band came to wish Joe luck and to bid him farewell.

The day before he was to leave, he attended church as usual with his family. After the morning worship service, Pastor Jackson suggested that the Shelleys spend a few minutes with him. He chatted in an extremely positive manner for quite a while, and then prayed with

RODA

such reassuring words that the entire family later headed for the farm, feeling tremendously uplifted and at last completely at peace with Joe's decision to leave home.

After the family enjoyed a magnificent Sunday dinner, Joe decided to share the afternoon with Ted and Dave, while taking Swift for one last ride. He spent the time with his friends riding aimlessly over the rolling hillsides of eastern York County. Usually the trio chattered constantly, but this day they were rather uncharacteristically quiet; and while they sat in almost total silence on a hillside overlooking the beautiful Susquehanna, Ted labored with extreme care over an exceptionally detailed portrait of Joe.

As he was completing the final touches, Dave sat close beside his redheaded friend. "Hey! That's the best one you've ever done, Ted!" he remarked. "When're you gonna start makin' a livin' doin' this?"

Ted held it so Joe could see his own likeness. "What d'you think? Does it look like you?" he asked.

Joe nodded his approval and smiled, though somewhat embarrassed by Ted's extraordinary piece of art work. "That's really good, Ted! Thanks!" he said, extremely grateful for what his friend had done on his behalf.

"I'll get my pa to help me make a frame for it, an' we'll give it to your folks. That way they'll still have you *hangin' around the house*, even if it is only on paper," he laughed. "An' we'll be able to see how much you change by the time you get back," Ted added, carefully placing the portrait inside a special pouch in his saddlebag.

"Yeah! Who knows?" piped Dave. "Maybe by that time you'll be wearin' a beard!" he laughed.

"I kinda doubt that," Joe grinned, stroking his chin. "It's only a six-month enlistment, you know."

"Of course, if the war lasts long enough, Dave an' me may be in uniform one day too," Ted added wistfully.

Then, after bidding some difficult farewells, Joe returned home to spend his final evening with his family.

Chapter 7

A New Companion

On Monday morning everyone arose early, but breakfast was an unusually quiet affair. At last Mr. Shelley said as he arose from the table, "Well, son, I suppose we'd better be on our way."

Joe swallowed hard as he felt his mother place her hand on his. Looking at her as she sat beside him, he saw a smile, though he knew she was unhappy.

After she arose from the table, his mother opened a cupboard drawer and lifted out a brand new Bible.

"Here's something special we bought for you, Joey," she smiled. Then, handing it to her son, she added, "I hope you'll find time to read something from it every day."

"I will, Ma," he promised her somberly. "And thanks . . . bushels!" he said in a slightly choked voice, before kissing her and placing their thoughtful gift carefully in his satchel.

Before long they had Swift hitched to the wagon. Mr. Shelley tossed Joe's satchel gently into the back of the rig, everyone climbed aboard and slowly they headed for the railroad station in Columbia.

After they arrived, Joe took some time to stay close to Swift for a few special moments, before giving him several strong pats on his sleek neck. "Goodbye, boy; I'm sure gonna miss you!" he whispered.

Then after grabbing his satchel, he walked with his mother and Sarah to the window where his father was showing Joe's orders to the stationmaster. As they waited, Joe noticed another boy nearly his own age seated in the far, darkest corner of the waiting room area, talking with a man who Joe thought was probably the lad's father.

The half-hour wait for the train may have been the fastest thirty minutes of Joe's life; for it seemed like no time at all before they heard its engine approaching from Philadelphia.

Joe's mother seized his arm. "Goodbye, Joey. Keep your chin up," she advised. "The first few days'll be the hardest for all of us. And remember . . . there's Someone who has said that He'll always be with you. That means no matter *what* happens . . . or *where* you are. And He's only a prayer away. Don't ever forget Him, and you'll see how well everything goes."

"I'll remember, Ma," Joe assured her.

After kissing his mother and Sarah, Joe turned and extended a firm hand toward his father.

"Goodbye, son. Our country's bein' torn apart by this war, an' you may be seein' some mighty miserable things; so keep in mind what Ma said. An' you're gonna meet a lotta people in the next few months. Some of 'em you may not even like to be around. So pick your friends carefully," he added. "Hopefully, you'll find someone like Dave or Ted. Now get on with it, an' do the kind o' job that'll make us proud, as I'm sure you will."

"I'll do my best, Pa," Joe answered, feeling a churning sensation in his throat.

And then, for the first time in several years, his father gave him a strong, prolonged embrace. Joe felt a sudden emptiness in the pit of his stomach; and when he felt tears beginning to cloud his eyes, he quickly turned to board the train. But as he did, he accidentally bumped into the boy he had seen in the waiting room, just as he and the man who was with him were about to board the car immediately following the one Joe had selected.

"Excuse me!" Joe apologized.

The blonde-haired boy merely stared at Joe for a few seconds. Then looking at the man who was accompanying him, he remarked, "Thunder an' tarnation, Pa! Look who it is!" Then, flashing a broad grin, he turned to Joe and said, "Not headin' for another concert, are you?"

But before Joe could respond or determine what had caused the remark, the boy beamed another smile and stepped quickly aboard the coach, his father right at his heels.

Joe merely looked back at his family in bewilderment, shrugged his shoulders and then scurried aboard to find a seat at an open window a few yards from where they were standing.

"Goodbye, Joey!" Sarah called, as the train jerked from its standing position. "Don't forget to write!"

"I won't!" he promised as he began to wave goodbye, a sudden nervousness weaving its way through his entire body. He stuck his head from the window; and despite the belches of heavy smoke, he waved several more times before his family was finally out of sight.

Then, slowly, he slumped back and simply stared at the empty seat in front of him, his mind in sudden turmoil. He caught himself questioning whether all this was really happening to him; not knowing if it was reality, a dream . . . or a nightmare! For several moments he caught himself wondering if he was making the biggest mistake of his life!

As the train began to head north and leave Columbia, Joe slid to the other side of the coach, where he could look directly across the broad Susquehanna. As he gazed through the window, he caught one final glimpse of the long, majestic covered bridge which connected the two small but unforgettable towns that were so much a part of his life.

His mind quickly flashed back to his incredible experiences with Nat, and he couldn't help wondering where the runaway might be even at that very moment. Almost automatically, upon thinking of him, he kept his promise to the lad and remembered him in a prayer for his safety. Then as he opened his eyes and glanced once more at the bridge, little did he realize that before even another year would pass, that very same long, wooden structure would provide him with still another unbelievably nerve-racking adventure!

The train moved slowly and made frequent stops, many of which seemed almost endless to Joe. As the time passed, he found himself becoming more and more anxious about whatever may lie ahead of him on this uncertain occasion; and he often found himself fidgeting uncharacteristically nervously in his seat. To make matters even more difficult, after several stops along the way, many more travelers now crowded his coach; but except for a few tiny children, they were all adults and mostly men. Joe felt somewhat apprehensive about attempting to strike up a conversation with any of these total strangers, one of whom now sat beside him and others even directly facing him; and this rather uneasy situation tended to make the trip seem even longer than it was.

BOT RODA

Gradually, he found himself wishing he had gotten on the same car with the boy he had bumped into at the station in Columbia. Perhaps he could've at least satisfied his curiosity about the strange remark he had made.

He passed some of the time nibbling half-heartedly on the lunch his mother had sent along; and then, at last, sometime near mid-afternoon, the train reached Harrisburg.

With the excitement of the arrival at his destination, Joe forgot completely about the boy; and much to his delight, even as he was descending from the train, he saw a long line of wagons and accompanying military personnel.

A corporal was shouting for all volunteers who were heading for Camp Curtin, directing them to stow their gear in one of the wagons and load themselves into the others that were standing nearby.

Eventually, when it appeared that there were no more stragglers, the convoy began the long, uncomfortably bumpy and dusty trip to the camp. Joe began to look hopefully for someone his own age, but unsuccessfully. Most of the men sat quietly, since almost no one knew anyone else; and when some of them did speak, Joe simply listened to them converse, mostly about the progress of the war.

Finally, they approached the main gate of the camp, where a sentry stepped smartly from a small building. Realizing that it was a train of new volunteers, he motioned for the drivers to enter. Within a few minutes they stopped in front of a row of long buildings, where everyone climbed out of the wagons.

Several officers were telling the men to form lines in groups of ten; but before Joe even had time to step into one of them, he felt a hand on his shoulder. Turning about, he found himself gazing into the face of a stern-looking sergeant.

"You don't look old enough to be a volunteer!" he said gruffly.

"I'm a volunteer, sir," Joe informed him, "but not as a soldier. I'm here to be a drummer boy."

"Oh," the sergeant nodded. "Do you have any papers?"

Joe scrambled through his satchel; and after fumbling nervously through his belongings, he finally produced the envelope he had received in the mail. The sergeant quickly scanned its contents, then stepped back a short distance. After calling a corporal to his side, he squinted somewhat under the bright sun and pointed toward a small group of buildings.

"Orderly, take this boy down to the Special Assignments Building," he commanded.

Joe had to hustle to keep up with the corporal's long strides, and in a matter of minutes he was standing in front of a rather rickety structure that obviously had seen better times. As they were about to enter, another sergeant bustled through the doorway, nearly bumping into them. Side-stepping quickly, Joe got out of his way just in time to avoid three other men who were following hurriedly in the sergeant's footsteps. Each had a bundle slung over his shoulder, and all three were scurrying to keep pace with the fast-moving sergeant. Since they were dressed in civilian clothes, Joe was sure they were raw recruits, heading for their first introduction to army life.

Joe stared after the foursome a few moments, then looked at the corporal, who nodded his head in the direction of the door. Once inside, he waited for more than an hour before a company clerk finally checked his orders, only to inform him that he had arrived too late in the day to be processed, and would have to wait until the following morning. Then, after placing Joe's orders in a desk, the clerk took him to still another building. There the soldier obtained bedding for him and showed him his sleeping quarters for the night. Finally, before leaving, he told Joe where to get his evening meal, as well as what he was to do the next day after reveille.

At first, Joe felt strange being in such a large room all by himself. There were at least twenty empty, wooden bunks available; and none of them was covered with any kind of bedding. Joe selected one that looked decently stable; and as soon as he finished making up his crude sleeping space, he struck out in the direction of the nearest mess tent, where he ate with some men who had just finished sentry duty. The food wasn't like home cooking, but there was plenty available; and when he left the table, he felt as though he had done justice to his first army meal.

As he strolled from the huge tent, his attention was drawn to an enormous field which stretched even farther than the corn field back home. Except for a few trees off to one side, it was almost completely surrounded by hundreds of tents. Joe smiled to himself. Something was telling him that he would become well acquainted with that field before too long, for evidently this was where the men marched. It reminded him of a gigantic dust bowl; and even as he gazed upon it, he was intrigued as the late afternoon breezes kicked up tiny "tornadoes" that seemed to appear and disappear, almost as though someone were stirring the field with a gigantic, invisible spoon.

There were no trees on the field itself, and evidently thousands of marching feet had long ago killed almost all the grass. Now, there were mere traces of it only around the borders. Joe felt warm even after the heat of the day had passed, and he was certain that the marching grounds would be uncomfortably hot during these long August afternoons.

He began looking in other directions and was especially awed by the many cannon clustered here and there in small groups. As he meandered among the sea of tents, numerous soldiers walked past him. Noticing the way they looked at him, and reading their thoughts, he knew they were wondering what somebody his age was doing there. Beginning to feel conspicuous, he subconsciously threw back his shoulders and jutted out his chest, in an effort to bring himself to his tallest height as he walked along.

After returning to the building where he was to sleep, he lay down with the back of his head resting in his hands. Staring blankly at the ceiling, his thoughts turned sharply homeward; but before he could become engrossed in his daydreams and possibly lapse into any kind of homesickness, he heard a door slam.

As he turned his head sideways, his eyes suddenly fell upon a most welcome sight. Joe could hardly believe his eyes! Strolling toward the bunks with a black valise in his hand, was the very same boy he had seen at the Columbia Railroad Station; and now that he had time to look more carefully, it was obvious that he was actually younger than Joe. After springing to his feet, he practically ran toward him.

The lad looked at Joe in amazement. "Thunder an' tarnation!" he remarked. "So this is where you were headin'! If I'da known that, you coulda rode with me an' my pa!"

"Practically the whole way up here, I was wishin' I'da done just that! The trip got a little boring," Joe admitted with a wry face.

The boy set his bag on the floor and said, "You don't know me from Adam, but I been watchin' you an' your pa play in the concerts in Columbia for the last two summers."

"You have?" Joe said, somewhat surprised.

"Yeah! . . . You're sorta my heroes, I guess. I use' to bring my drum practically every Saturday night an' try to keep up with the two o' you, but I always managed to get lost somewhere along the line," he confessed.

"You mean you're the one we would see standin' off in the distance an' drummin' along with us?" Joe asked, smiling from ear to ear.

"Yep! That's me!" he replied with an impish grin.

"Well, I'm glad I finally get to meet you!" Joe laughed. "I went lookin' for you durin' the intermission just this past Saturday night, but you disappeared in an awful big hurry!"

Then extending his hand in greeting, he said, "My name's Joe, but most everybody calls me Joey. Joey Shelley. What's yours?"

"Jonathan Cooper," the boy answered as they shook hands. "But everybody calls me Jon, an' I *hate* to be called Jonny! So I'll call you Joe, if you don't mind. I only live a block from the park in Columbia, on Walnut Street; an' I think you're from Wrightsville, ain't you?"

"Yeah. How about that? We live right across the river from one another, an' we hafta come all the way to Harrisburg to meet for the first time!" Then, pointing to a bunk near his own, Joe said, "Why don't you take this one next to mine?"

Jon flashed a ready smile as he sat on the edge of the crude, wooden bunk; for he too was feeling better at having met someone nearly his own age.

"Did you eat?" Joe asked.

"Yeah. With my pa in a big tent up the road a piece. Then they sent me down here an' took him somewhere else. I don't know when I'll see him again!" Jon said with a concerned look.

By his tone of voice, Joe figured the blonde-headed lad was in a somewhat dejected mood and decided not to press the conversation. "Just sit there an' take it easy," he advised. "I'll try to get you somethin' soft to sleep on."

He headed for a closet that was marked *supplies;* and when he returned, he found Jon stretched out on the wooden planks, his eyes already closed. Shaking him lightly, Joe said, "Here, lay this bedroll on those boards. It oughta be a little more comfortable anyhow."

"Thanks," Jon replied. Then after he was situated again, he said, "I'm sure you're here to be a drummer boy too, ain't you?"

Joe grinned, nodding his head. "You bet!" he answered with obvious delight. "With the two of *us* bangin' the sticks, this war's *bound* to be over soon!"

Jon laughed and shot out his right hand again. "Shake!" he said.

But as they clasped each other's hand, neither boy realized even for a moment, that this would be the beginning of an extremely exceptional companionship.

"How old are you?" Jon asked.

"Fifteen," Joe answered. "How 'bout you?"

"I'll soon be fifteen. Next month," Jon added.

"How'd you get your folks to let you be a drummer boy?" Joe inquired, recalling his initial difficulties with his mother.

"Well," Jon began, "my ma's dead nearly a year now, an' my pa just joined the army. He's gonna train right here; an' when Governor Curtin asked for drummer boys a couple o' weeks ago, Pa wrote to Harrisburg an' got permission for me to be a drummer in whatever regiment he gets assigned to. That way we'll always be together."

"Sounds like a pretty good idea," Joe admitted, nodding his head.

Jon paused for a few moments. Then in almost a whisper, he continued. "The problem is . . . I'm not the best drummer in the world," he confessed. "But mostly, I'm just glad to get outta school!" he added with a wide grin. "No more *book* learnin'! Yahoo!" he shouted, as he punched the air and brought a chuckle from Joe.

The boys spent the next half hour getting better acquainted; and eventually, Joe suggested taking another walk through the camp while they talked. Then at dusk they returned to their bunks, where Joe took advantage of the final remnants of daylight to read his first passage from the new Bible he had received. Then, as complete darkness fell, the boys settled down to their first night of sleep away from home.

The next morning they reported for processing. When their physical examinations were finished and all the proper paperwork was completed, they were directed to report to Captain Colter, the head musician, to begin their six-month enlistment. As they crossed the huge drilling area on their way to the captain's quarters, they heard the sound of a drum and saw a company of men march onto the field. The boys watched them move forward, to the flank, about face, and halt, all to the sound of the drum.

"Thunder an' tarnation! Do you think we'll hafta do that?" Jon asked. "Listen to all the different beats he plays!"

"He's a lot older than we are, Jon; an' he's prob'ly had a lot more experience," Joe assured him. "But don't worry; what we don't know, we'll learn. Let's go."

Jon scurried to keep pace with Joe, and a few minutes later they were standing somewhat nervously in front of a large tent. They could hear someone moving around inside it; but since neither boy knew exactly what to do, they stood for a few moments simply looking somewhat sheepishly at one another.

Grinning, Jon finally asked, "How do you go 'bout knockin' on a tent anyhow?"

When Joe started to laugh, a tall officer swung the tent flap aside, staring first at one boy and then the other.

Being the older of the two, Joe felt it was his duty to speak. "Sir, we were sent here from . . . "

"You don't hafta tell me," the officer interrupted. "I know who sent you." A broad grin swept across his face as he set his hands on his hips. "You're prob'ly Shelley . . . an' this must be Cooper," he said as he glanced in Jon's direction.

"Thunder an' tarnation! That's right! How'd you know?" Jon inquired.

"Oh, I know more'n most people give me credit for," the officer laughed. "But there's a war goin' on, an' we don't have a minute to lose. Follow me!"

As they walked, the captain glanced at Joe. "I won't joke with you, young man; fifteen years of age is too young for anyone to go off to war." And after pausing a moment, he added, "An' comin' into the army at the age of fourteen's absolutely ridiculous!"

This comment he directed to Jon. And then he admitted, "But it's a cinch we can't get enough grown men who know how to drum; an' generally, what men we do get, we need for fightin'. So I've gotta do everything I can to make good drummers outta you."

"We'll do our best, sir," Joe asserted.

"After watchin' the drummer on that field, I'm not so sure I'll be o' much use," Jon remarked dolefully. But with a determined look on his face, he added, "I'll learn though, if it's the last thing I do!"

"That's the spirit!" the captain commented, suddenly stopping. Looking at Jon, he said, "Hold out your hands!"

The young Columbian stretched them forth, wondering what was happening.

"All right!" the Captain remarked. "Eight fingers and two

thumbs! That's all the equipment that's necessary. I pronounce you eligible to become a drummer boy!"

Joe laughed at the bewildered expression on Jon's face; and nimbly the pair scampered after the captain who was already entering the main supply building. There the boys were informed that they'd have to wait a full day until uniforms could be made to fit them. However, they did receive fatigue caps called kepis, canteens, bedrolls and ponchos, a camp candle-stick, and much other equipment. Jon was especially intrigued by an implement which served as a combination knife, fork, and spoon.

After they reccived their complete issue, the captain helped them pack their haversacks. "I guess you've got everything now but one important little item," he remarked.

The boys followed him to another supply area where more than a dozen snare drums were hanging from hooks. "There you are, boys," he indicated with a wave of his hand. "Pick any one you like."

Setting their haversacks and equipment on a nearby table, they hurried to look at the drums. Joe gingerly removed a beautiful ashwood snare from its hook, flicking its vellum head with a brisk movement of his fingertips.

"Here. Try these hickories on 'er," suggested the captain, handing him a shiny pair of new drumsticks.

Joe rolled them gently between his fingers for a few moments to get the feel of them. Then he glanced toward Jon, who quickly returned a sly grin. Joe hesitated a moment, then started slowly with some single and double strokes; but as he began to get the feel of the sticks, he moved into some fancy flams and ruffs. Captain Colter nodded approvingly, casting a surprised look in Jon's direction. When Joe switched to some ratamacues and some even more highly precisioned paradiddles, Jon's eyes nearly bulged in disbelief. Then, after gradually increasing the speed of his strokes, Joe finished with a snappy roll.

"Say! Where'd you learn all that?" asked Captain Colter, beaming his obvious satisfaction.

"I guess it just runs in the family, sir. I learned from my pa, an' he learned from his. An' my great-grandfather was a drummer durin' the Revolution!" Joe said, a touch of family pride in his voice.

"Well, that's impressive to say the least! I'm glad you're keepin' up the family tradition!" the captain remarked.

Then, turning his attention to the Columbian, he asked, "How 'bout you, Jon? See a drum you'd like?"

"Well . . ." Jon drawled, "after listenin' to Joe . . . I'm not sure I wanna go through with this!"

Joe looked at the instruments again. "Say, some o' these are made o' rosewood, ain't they?" he observed.

"That's right, an' that one has silver on the sides for tuning instead o' leather like the ashwood drum you just played," the captain informed him.

Joe slipped one off its hook and draped the strap around Jon's shoulders. "Here. Take the sticks an' let's see what it sounds like, Jon," he said.

The slender blonde gave his new friend a wry look before tapping out some single and double strokes. "That's just about the only thing I can play without makin' too many mistakes," he said apologetically when he finished.

"Don't let that worry you!" Captain Colter consoled him. "Just last week I started workin' with three men who never even touched a drum in their entire lives! This army's at a point where we can't afford to be particular. If people volunteer, we'll teach 'em!" he declared.

Each of the boys finally selected a drum that pleased him, and later they set up their tent next to Captain Colter's. Then when they were prepared to leave for their first session on the drums, they were surprised when the captain told them to bring only their sticks. The boys cast wondering glances at one another before picking up their hickories and following the head musician. Before long they were standing among a group of approximately a dozen other drummers, all older, ranging in age from their early twenties to the late forties. Like the boys, each one was carrying sticks but no drum.

"Men, I'd like you to meet our two newest drummers," Captain Colter called out, as he stood between Joe and Jon. "And . . . as you can plainly see . . . both of 'em are seasoned veterans!"

This brought a few chuckles from the group, but a number of the men stepped forward to introduce themselves and shake hands.

"All right, we're late gettin' started this mornin'; so let's get at it," the captain urged. Then directing his attention to a lanky orderly standing nearby, he called, "Conerly, bring those boards over here!"

The men quickly formed three groups before sitting Indian fashion in straight lines under the few trees that were near the drill field. Joe and Jon joined three other drummers, resting one of the long boards across all their knees. Joe guessed impulsively what was about

to happen. The captain was going to have them drum on the boards!

In this manner they began learning the beats which would carry orders to the foot soldiers. For nearly a half hour they practiced only the single and double drag before they were finally given a break to stand up and stretch, but Jon's legs were so numb that he could hardly rise to his feet.

"What's wrong?" Joe asked.

"Oh, my legs!" Jon grunted. "They went to sleep!" he moaned.

Grasping his outstretched hand, Joe pulled him to a standing position; and Jon began to limp and make faces as though he had been mortally wounded, bringing hearty laughs from the others.

"What's wrong, young'un? Can't take sittin' down, eh?" chortled one of the oldest drummers. "Wait'll yer out marchin' on that there grinder; you'll soon wish you was sittin' back here in the shade again! How 'bout it, fellers?" he asked, spitting a stream of tobacco juice that quickly coagulated some nearby dust.

The others laughed and cast a few more good-natured remarks, but they hardly had time to relax their fingers and stretch their legs, before Captain Colter had them drumming once more. They spent the remainder of the morning working on fundamental drum beats, and it wasn't long before everyone was aware of Joe's talents. To no one's surprise, the captain soon had him helping the others. At first he felt somewhat out of place giving instructions to older men; but when their questions and enthusiasm showed that they were more than willing to learn from him, he relaxed and found his unexpected role as instructor to be an enjoyable experience. He especially spent much time with Jon, whose determination and keen sense of rhythm made him a surprisingly fast learner.

At long last, there was a break for the noon meal; and after the boys returned to their tent, an orderly informed Joe that he was to report to Captain Colter. He stepped quickly to the officer's large Sibley tent, where the captain told him to be seated on the stool beside his desk.

"Joe, you're an excellent drummer! Almost without delay I could assign you to one o' the companies bein' formed here at Camp Curtin, but more new drummers'll join our group even by tomorrow."

He paused to light his pipe before continuing. "So I suppose you can guess what I've got in mind for you, can't you?"

"I'm not sure, sir," Joe admitted, somewhat puzzled.

"Well, I'd like you to help me work on the fundamentals with these men. The only thing you can't handle at the moment are the actual signals used on the parade grounds or on the battlefield, an' it certainly won't take you long to learn those! That'll only be a couple hours' work for you. So I'll keep you here for a week or so before assigning you to a company."

"That's fine with me, sir. Whatever you say, I'll be glad to do," Joe replied.

"Good! Then it's settled," said the captain, rising to his feet as Joe did likewise. "With Governor Curtin's request for more men, we'll have plenty o' regiments formin' here durin' the next month, I'm sure; so we won't have any trouble placin' you with one of 'em when the time comes. You've got a great attitude, young man. Hang on to it wherever you go!"

"Thank you, sir. I will!"

"Now, one other thing," the captain said, looking very intently at Joe. "Any parents worth their salt are gonna be very worried about a son your age who's servin' in the army far from home." Then tapping his index finger on the center of Joe's chest, he said, "I want you to make me a promise."

"What's that, sir?"

"Every week, you be sure to write 'em a letter an' just hand it to me. I'll make sure it gets mailed," he said with a note of real concern.

"Thank you, sir. I was plannin' to write as often as I can," Joe assured him.

"Good!" Then, pointing toward the exit area, the captain said, "Now, you an' Jon are supposed to report to the clothing center."

A short while later, the two boys were doing their best to hide their excitement as they walked into the building where they were to be measured. When the rather elderly tailor finished, he hung his measuring tape around his neck, stood back and shook his head objectionably.

"Boys your age have no business bein' fitted for army uniforms!" he grunted. "But stop by here tomorrow after the evenin' meal, an' maybe they'll be ready by then."

As they paced their way back to their tent, Jon was mumbling under his breath. "Thunder an' tarnation! Here I was hopin' we could get our uniforms today!"

"Well, I guess it does take more'n just a couple o' minutes, Jon," Joe consoled him. "After all, I guess they don't exactly have a flock of our sizes already made up."

Much of the afternoon was spent in the same manner as the morning hours. However, some of the men didn't report for practice, since it was necessary for them to drill with their own companies. On the other hand, a few different drummers came on the scene who weren't present earlier in the day.

As the hours slipped by, Joe could detect some improvement as they tapped out their beats on the long boards; and a smile creased his face as he especially noted Jon's obvious progress.

"Nice goin', Jon!" he commented on one occasion, after his companion completed a series of single and double strokes topped with some flams that Joe had taught him. "I knew you'd catch on in a hurry! Just remember, keep your elbows out so you get most o' the force from your shoulders, not from your hands. That's the trick to it!"

"Yes, sir!" grinned Jon, firing a snappy, mock salute.

They broke the monotony by periods of marching, as they learned some of the simpler parade commands; but finally, it was time to call a halt to their long day of developing the very basic fundamentals of military drumming.

Early in the evening, time was set aside for various types of recreation. Joe and Jon watched some of the men engage in wrestling matches, and they actually participated in some relay races; but as soon as the sun was about to set, they returned to their tent. However, just a few minutes later, Captain Colter requested that they accompany him to watch and listen carefully, as some drummers and buglers sounded tattoo and brought an end to the day's activities.

That night the boys talked for a long while as they lay in the dark. Their first full day of army life had been a busy one, which made Joe happy; for he was sure he would have a difficult time keeping his thoughts off home and riding Swift. As he stretched out on his bedroll, he couldn't help being amazed by the fair-haired package of enthusiasm who lay beside him. Jon was only fourteen and had gone through the day as though he had been born in the army! Then, realizing that his young friend had finally dropped off to sleep, he recalled his mother's parting advice; and words of comforting prayer were soon echoing through his mind, as he too, fell asleep.

The following day the boys could hardly wait for drills to

finish, in order that they could eat supper and head for the clothing center. Then, during the early evening hours, when they finally donned their uniforms for the first time, it marked one of the proudest moments of their lives.

"Thunder an' tarnation! Everything's a perfect fit!" Jon beamed, as he glanced from himself to Joe and back again.

"Boy, I'll say! You did a *great* job, sir!" Joe remarked, complimenting the tailor, who stood nearby with a noticeable twinkle in his eye, thoroughly enjoying the antics of this pair of excited teen-agers.

"Well, I figured these uniforms would be somethin' special for you two young'uns; so I gave 'em a little extra time. I'll admit I'd sooner be makin' uniforms for grown men, but Cap'n Colter tells me we need drummers pretty bad. So, I did the best I could," he added, as he brushed some lint from the back of Joe's jacket.

Then, stepping back for one last professional look, he remarked, "Well . . . if I do say so myself . . . you look right sharp!"

After sincerely thanking him for his efforts, the boys headed directly to Captain Colter's tent to show off their brand new uniforms. As they stood before him, he checked them from kepi to boots, slowly nodding his approval.

"Now you'll *really* feel like playin' those drums!" he announced. "An' if you take good care o' those new outfits, they'll last a long time. Keep 'em well-brushed; an' I'll get one o' the men to show you how to take good care o' all that leather."

During the course of the next ten days, Camp Curtin became more and more crowded, as new volunteers arrived day after day. By this time also, the drummers graduated from the boards to the use of their instruments. The almost unending practice was beginning to reap excellent results; and by now they had nearly mastered quite a number of the basic cadences and drum signals that were required of them, for marching and battle situations as well.

Then one morning, following their final practice session, Captain Colter took them out of the hot sun and into the welcome shade of the trees that skirted one end of the dusty marching field. After he praised them for their efforts and continued progress, he fumbled in a shirt pocket and drew out a folded sheet of paper. From it he read ten names, Joe's and Jon's among them. He dismissed the other drummers, and then spoke seriously to the ten who remained.

"Most o' you've been here for only two weeks," he began; "others not even that long. There's no question that several of you are far from accomplished drummers; but as I keep sayin', this war won't wait! You've all been detailed to the 125th Pennsylvania Regiment which leaves here tomorrow, an' I've been assigned to go with you as head musician."

The men greeted this news heartily, but the boys were especially happy, Jon leaping into the air and giving a yell that could be heard practically throughout the camp.

"All right, Cooper!" barked the captain. "Save some o' that energy for the drums! You'll be needin' it!"

The others laughed at the impish youngster, but Jon was too happy to be embarrassed. And secretly, although neither boy expressed his feelings in words, they were both over-joyed that they had been assigned to the same regiment; for they walked back to their tent, their arms around one another's shoulders and extremely happy about their assignment.

After a fitful night's sleep, the boys packed their haversacks soon after dawn and struck their tent. Then they spent much of their time waiting impatiently, their drums dangling at their sides. Every few minutes Jon softly practiced his drumming, fearful that he was certain to lose his rhythm and throw his entire company out of step when the regiment marched to the railroad station.

Joe laughed, though he too was somewhat anxious. "Take it easy, Jon! If you lose the beat, just listen to the drummer ahead of you, or watch the men's feet in front of you," he advised.

"Yeah, but what if I get Company A?" Jon muttered. "Then there won't *be* anyone in front o' me!"

"Well, even if you do, you know all the beats used for parade. So relax!" Joe said in a confident tone of voice, trying to calm his friend's jitters.

As the boys would soon learn, things go slowly in the army. It seemed to take forever to strike tents and load the wagons with what seemed to be an endless array of military equipment; and as they were beginning to expect, the boys themselves were pressed into service to give a helping hand with all kinds of work details.

Eventually, it wasn't until after the noon meal that the drummers finally reported to Captain Colter. Joe was surprised to learn that he had been assigned to Company A, and delighted that Jon was to follow with Company B. Excitedly they checked one another's equipment. Each one had his bedroll wrapped inside a rubber blanket, or poncho, and fastened securely across the back of his shoulders. One pair of straps secured the haversack directly below the poncho, and still another strap supported the drum. Then, as they finished getting themselves organized, in the distance they heard columns of soldiers marching onto the huge drill field.

"There they come, men!" Captain Colter declared. "See how sluggish they march? Well, we're gonna put a stop to that right away! We'll parade onto that field with those drums clappin' such a rhythm, they'll feel like marchin' from here to Virginia an' back again! You got that?"

He paused and glared into their faces. "Well, don't forget it!" he barked.

Joe thought that if he could beat the drums only one-tenth as well as his heart was beating right then, he'd have no trouble at all. He looked at Jon out of the corner of his eyes and saw him looking right back, almost white with nervousness.

"Hey, Jon!" Joe whispered. "This is what we came for, ain't it? I can't wait!"

"Thunder an' tarnation! I wish I had your gumption!" Jon muttered.

"The companies form in alphabetical order," the captain announced. "Company A's at the far end o' the field. When you get in front o' the company you've been assigned to, stop marchin' an' do a right-face; but *keep drummin'*! I'll give the signal when you're to stop. Any questions?"

No one spoke. They knew their job. They were to make these soldiers *feel* like soldiers. Slowly all ten of them walked to the edge of the field, their drums slapping softly against their thighs. By this time the entire regiment had formed and was standing at parade rest. To Joe's right and immediately in front of the awaiting regiment was an empty reviewing stand. When he noticed a group of officers and two civilians walking toward it, he looked inquiringly at Captain Colter.

"Those are the regimental officers. Colonel Higgins is in command," the captain said in answer to Joe's unspoken question.

"But who are the men in civilian clothes, sir?" Joe asked.

"The one in the dark blue suit is Governor Curtin, an' I believe the other one's a congressman from Washington."

As soon as the group took its place on the reviewing stand, the captain said, "All right, men; this is it! Shelley, get us started with the right cadence. And don't forget, everybody; *keep drummin'*!"

Joe tapped out two measures before the others joined him. A smile crossed the captain's face, as the quality of the drumming was just what he had hoped it would be. He shot a quick glance at the governor and the others of his group and saw them stare approvingly at his file of generally inexperienced but extremely determined drummers.

They were an impressive sight as they struck out one by one in perfect step, flaring their beats rhythmically. Then, as they marched down the field with absolute precision, each drummer stopped and pivoted in front of his respective company and faced the reviewing stand, still drumming for all he was worth. At length, Jon reached Company B and came to a halt, all four feet, eleven inches of him still concentrating upon putting every last ounce of effort into his cadence. Then, as Joe approached his own company, he smiled to himself when he looked at the men's shoes; for even though they were standing at attention now, he noticed that many of them could hardly keep their feet still.

By the time Joe came to a halt and made a right-face, Captain Colter was already at the reviewing stand; and when the officer slapped his hand to his thigh, all drumming ceased simultaneously.

The regiment spent the next half hour listening to short speeches by Colonel Higgins and the governor. A slight breeze gently wafted the color-bearers' company pennants and served the double purpose of relieving the men from the heat of the day, as well as bringing the speakers' encouraging words to their ears. Then, the speeches finally ended, the signal was given to begin the long march to the Harrisburg Northern Central Railway Station. The Pennsylvania 125th Regiment was headed for war.

Chapter 8

A Picket's Challenge

When Joe began drumming the *Common Time March*, Jon and the other drummers picked it up vigorously. With Lieutenant Stewart and the rest of Company A's officers leading the way, Joe and the color-bearer followed closely behind them. Nearly a thousand men, freshly equipped with Springfield-rifled muskets, marched snappily toward the main road, beginning a long but enthusiastic and highly anticipated journey to Virginia.

Citizens of Harrisburg lined the streets to watch, wave flags and bunting, and cheer them as they marched, making it an inspiring and exciting occasion for both the military personnel and civilians as well. Once, Joe tapped out a burl and staccato, while his company made a turn at an intersection. Marking time as he pivoted, he turned his head to catch a fleeting grin from Jon, whose company followed right on his heels. Joe smiled to himself as it appeared that Jon was having the time of his life!

With all the men, equipment and wagons involved, it was already early evening by the time the entire regiment boarded the train. There, Jon was finally reunited with his father, who was also assigned to Company B; and the lad promptly introduced him to Joe.

"I sure am glad Jon met you!" Mr. Cooper said, shaking Joe's hand. "It'll make it a whole lot easier with someone nearly his own age hangin' around."

"Yeah, I sorta noticed that myself a couple o' times," Joe grinned, as he playfully dug an elbow into Jon's unprotected rib cage. "We hit it off right from the start!"

The trio spent several hours sharing common knowledge about Columbia and Wrightsville and generally becoming better acquainted, all of which helped the time pass more quickly under rather severely crowded conditions. However, as the hours wore on toward midnight and later, they began to nod from time to time and snatch short stretches of sleep, resting their heads on one another's shoulders.

After an uncomfortable, extremely long ride, due mostly to frequent stops along the way, they finally arrived in Baltimore just before daybreak the next morning. There the regimental cooks set up a mess area right in the city streets. After a hasty breakfast, they marched to the B & O Railroad Station several blocks away, where they boarded still another train. This time they were bound for Washington; and by noon they were at Capitol Hill, quartered in a large warehouse, where Joe was happy to learn that Chaplain Stewart had made arrangements for late Sunday worship.

Before the service began, Joe found time to write a letter to his family and handed it to Captain Colter. Then, when the men began to assemble for worship right within the warehouse itself, he took his Bible and sat on the floor with Jon and his father, who confessed that it was the first time they had ever been to church.

With all the turmoil and inner concern Joe was feeling ever since they had left Harrisburg, the hour of worship had a welcome calming effect. He especially enjoyed the music that Captain Colter led, accompanied by several of the musicians from the regimental band. It was inspiring to hear almost a thousand strong male voices singing many well-known hymns, as the warehouse walls reverberated with a beautiful blend of hundreds of tenor, baritone and bass voices. Joe found himself wishing his family could be sharing these special moments with him, even as he lapsed into prayer for them.

But his own petitions were suddenly interrupted by Chaplain Stewart, as the officer began his prayer for the regiment. Suddenly, goose bumps swarmed over Joe's arms and back, as the chaplain began to ask for protection during battle, which could be only days or even hours away!

As Joe listened to the chaplain's words, the extreme reality of just such a circumstance began for the first time to make a highly indelible impression upon him; and impulsively, though his eyes remained closed, he found himself placing his arm on Jon's shoulder, who very quickly was becoming as close to him as a kid brother.

After the exceedingly somber service, the 125th bedded down anywhere that space could be found; and totally fatigued from their long travels, two York and Lancaster County drummer boys were asleep within moments.

The following morning the regiment was assigned to the First Division of the Twelfth Army Corps and prepared to march into Virginia. While the sun gleamed brilliantly, Joe's drum set the pace as his unit moved like a giant serpent from Pennsylvania Avenue and crossed the bridge spanning the Potomac. At the end of an hour of constant marching, the supply wagons were on hand to provide tents almost as soon as the men broke ranks.

Although Joe and Jon had been assigned to different companies, Captain Colter quickly realized how much their companionship meant to one another; and he made arrangements for them to share the same tent, which they again set up adjacent to his, just as they had done at Camp Curtin.

By the end of the day, the 125th was encamped in a large field near Hunter's Chapel and Fort Richardson, with the defense of Washington as its assignment. Other regiments also streamed into the area even after dusk, so that by the following morning, the area looked like a sprawling city of tents.

After breakfast everyone began drilling more in earnest than ever. While some units had target and bayonet practice or marched to the nearby forts to work with heavy artillery, Captain Colter called his drummers together. They could sound cadences for such things as general assembly, reveille, tattoo, and common marching, as well as various battle signals; but they needed to learn many more important drum calls which were necessary for a fighting unit to function properly.

When they were grouped for their practice session, the captain spoke seriously. "There's no tellin' how long we'll be camped in this field. We might be here two weeks or even a month. Then again, we may be sent to the front lines tomorrow. We just don't know!" he said, kicking a stone through the dust. Then pounding his fist into his hand he added, "Now, we've got to learn every beat that's used on the field o' combat an' master 'em quickly! There'll be times when officers won't be able to shout commands for fear the enemy'll hear 'em too. An' in that case, you drummers hafta relay their orders to the foot soldiers!"

Stepping forward he picked up Joe's drum and sticks. "Today we'll work on beats that signal advance, trail arms, double-quick, and charge bayonets."

After taking a few minutes to demonstrate one of the beats, he let the drummers proceed. Joe learned quickly, and soon he was helping some of the others who also never had battle experience. As soon as they became fairly adept at handling the proper combination of beats that distinguished one set of signals from the others, the captain would call them out, hoping the drummers would respond with the proper beat or series of beats. At first there was some expected confusion; but eventually, with much repetitious practice, the captain reached a point where he could no longer trip up anyone. Obviously pleased with their ability to assimilate quickly what they were learning, he discovered he could teach them even an extra pair of signals before the morning session ended.

When they finished, the captain led the two boys to the fires where Manny Welles was in charge of preparing the noon meal. Borrowing Jon's drum this time, the captain said, "Now listen closely. Here's one beat you've gotta learn at all costs. It's the mess call. An' it goes by the name o' *Roast Beef.*"

The captain hardly finished the drum call before men were coming on the run from all directions, and in a matter of minutes nearly the entire regiment was assembled in front of the company fires.

Wide-eyed, Jon looked at the captain and blurted, "Thunder an' tarnation! If all our drum calls get results like that, we'll have the sharpest regiment in the brigade!"

"You can bet on it!" laughed the captain. "An' before the week's out, I'll teach you *Peas on a Trencher* too."

"*Peas on a Trencher*?" Joe echoed, mystified.

"Yep! That's the call for breakfast! C'mon; let's eat."

During the course of the next week, the boys learned countless drum calls and practiced constantly with both fifers and buglers. At other times they were detailed to Dr. Feay, the head surgeon, learning to help take care of some of the routine chores at the camp hospital.

From time to time Jon spent an hour or more with his father

when both were free from their various duties; and often Joe accompanied them, especially in the evenings when all kinds of camp activities would take place. It wasn't long before Mr. Cooper was feeling as though he had a pair of sons in the regiment instead of just one, because the two lads had become practically inseparable.

Nearly every day after the noon meal, there was mail call. Joe had been receiving a letter almost weekly from his family, and quite naturally he was always happy whenever there was an envelope addressed to him. Each day when mail arrived, he would listen with anticipation, hoping the company clerk would call out his name.

On the other hand, Jon had no close living relatives aside from his father; and consequently, he never heard his name at mail call. For Jon it simply wasn't the happiest moment of the day. However, whenever Joe would receive news from home, Jon would always ask him to read out loud, since he enjoyed hearing anything about the Columbia and Wrightsville area, even if it wasn't addressed to him.

One day at mail call Joe had a special treat. He knew there was a letter for him when he heard the clerk yell out, "Where's our mascot?" It was a word that both Joe and Jon were growing accustomed to hearing, because the men were beginning to really "take a shine" to their two teen-age drummers.

The men quickly opened a path for Joe, and before long he was happily clutching his letter from home. Then, after elbowing his way back to the perimeter of the struggling, anxiously-waiting men, he walked with Jon to their tent to open the envelope.

As had become his custom, he read it aloud for Jon's benefit, and was glad to hear that things were going well at home. But after he came to the end of the letter and his mother's signature, he was surprised to see that there was still one more page. It was a special note signed by Dave and Ted, who had come to the Shelley farm one day to help his father, and ride Swift. While they were there, Joe's mother had insisted that they take a few minutes to write to him.

"Now that'll sure make the day go better!" Joe exclaimed after he finished. But as he folded the papers and was tucking them inside the envelope, he couldn't miss seeing Jon's somewhat crestfallen expression.

"Yeah. It must be great to hear from family an' friends!" Jon remarked, as he rolled over on his back, cupped the nape of his neck in his hands and stared blankly toward the top of the tent.

Joe looked thoughtfully at his friend for several moments, his concern for him beginning to set his thinking processes into motion; and before long his naturally active mind was already turning over a few budding ideas.

One day at noon the regiment received orders to move to nearby Fort Barnard, and it was late by the time the men were settled in their new surroundings. Near the time for the evening meal, a dismal drizzle began to fall, and the boys had to drape their ponchos about themselves to keep the vellum heads dry and tight, as they sounded what turned out to be a rather muffled *Roast Beef.*

The next morning Joe and Jon were called to Colonel Higgins' quarters. As they stood respectfully at attention before him, the colonel asked, "Do you boys know anything about horses?"

Guessing almost impetuously what was probably on the officer's mind, Joe was quick to respond. "I've kept care o' horses ever since I can remember, sir. An' if you'd like us to look after yours, I can teach Jon what to do in a hurry! I *love* horses!"

The colonel smiled when he saw how quickly Joe had sized up the situation. "Have you ever had a horse o' your own?" he asked.

Joe shook his head. "No, sir, not really; but I'll get my wish one day. When my brother volunteered an' left home, he gave me his horse Swift to take care of till the war's over; an' for me that was the toughest part about leavin' home! I really miss ridin' him, but I know I'll have a horse just like him sometime!"

"Well, I've got a mare I'm right proud of; an' it sounds like I came across the right people to take care of 'er. There's lots of animals in the corral area for the men to look out for; so I'm sure they'll be glad to have you boys work with mine. An' if the pair of you would like to help out in any other way at the corral, just check with whoever's in charge down there an' tell 'em I sent you."

"We'll be glad to, sir," Joe assured him, happy to be able to work with animals once more.

Then before the boys left, they were also given the responsibility of helping to sound reveille, tattoo, and taps, making their day a long one; for they would be among the first to rise, and the last to return to their tents at night.

During the first days at Fort Barnard, battle-worn troops arrived, their morale low because of their defeat at the second battle at Bull Run. After receiving this disappointing news, drilling was stepped up; and the drummers spent more and more time with their companies. At first, the men merely sat and listened, as the drummers sounded the various beats. The next step was to march or maneuver, responding to the drum calls without spoken commands.

On one occasion Company A went to the far end of the huge drilling area. Marching close to his sergeant, Joe sounded the calls given to him in a low voice. In the beginning quite a few of the men became easily disoriented; but gradually, with the constant practice, the entire company began to get the knack of it. At length, after more than two hours of concentrated drill, with the exception of a mere two or three individuals, the company was responding both quickly and correctly.

Since Joe had been working steadily with only the fifers, buglers and other drummers, he had little opportunity to learn to know these infantrymen, whose confidence and appreciation he was gaining more and more with each passing day.

It was when a break was called and he was becoming acquainted with some of the men, that he noticed one of the soldiers constantly glaring at him. At first Joe thought nothing of it; but when he glanced at the infantryman a second and then a third time, only to see that practically his every move was still being closely watched, Joe became somewhat puzzled. Once, he returned the gaze for a few seconds and thought momentarily that there was something about the man that was vaguely familiar; but yet he felt certain he didn't remember him from anywhere in particular.

However, eventually the sergeant ordered the men to fall into ranks again; and by the time drills were at last halted for the day, Joe had completely forgotten about the incident.

The boys returned to their sleeping quarters with intentions of leaving at once to feed and curry the colonel's horse and then reporting to Dr. Feay. However, Captain Colter called them to his tent before they could leave for the regimental corral. They settled themselves on some camp chairs and waited patiently, while the captain lighted a pipeful of tobacco.

First he inquired as to the success of their drills with the men; and after he was assured that all had gone exceptionally well, he took his pipe from between his lips. Looking rather thoughtful, he pointed the stem of his pipe directly at the boys and asked, "How would the two o' you like to help me organize a special marchin' unit? I'd like to have a group of our finest men do precision marchin' an' handlin' o' their weapons."

"Sounds interesting," Joe admitted, nodding his head.

"Such a team could accomplish two things," the captain continued. "First of all, it would help make good use of some o' the men's spare time; an' secondly, it would train 'em to an even higher degree for certain battle situations. An' since all the other drummers are old enough to bear arms in actual fightin', I thought I'd ask you boys to be the drummers for the unit. What do you say? How 'bout it?"

"I'm sure I'd really like that, sir!" Joe responded enthusiastically.

But when the two of them turned their eyes toward Jon, it was obvious that the blonde-haired youngster was somewhat reluctant.

Finally shaking his head slowly, he said in an apologetic tone of voice, "I really don't think I'm good enough to handle that, sir. You'd better let Joe do it alone."

"Listen, Jon," piped Joe. "Remember that first day we walked across the field up at Camp Curtin?"

Jon nodded, having a sixth sense for what was probably coming.

"We promised ourselves we'd learn everything we possibly could, didn't we?" Joe pointed out.

Jon crossed and uncrossed his legs as he squirmed on the camp chair. "Yeah . . . but this is different," he mumbled. "Cap'n Colter wants to make a special kind o' squad outta only the best men; so he should have just his best drummer too!"

Captain Colter interrupted. "Jon . . . one day you're gonna be an excellent drummer! Why we've only been workin' with you for less than a month, an' already you've shown a great deal o' progress!"

For a while there was a silence which seemed an eternity to the blonde youngster. Then, with his head down and his eyes peering warily from under his white eyebrows, he looked first at one of his hecklers and then at the other, as his typical, patented grin slowly began to creep across his face.

"Well . . . all right," he sighed. "But thunder an' tarnation, while we're drillin', if Joe gives the signal for *trail arms* an' I get mixed up an' drum for a flank movement, don't blame me if somebody gets jabbed in the seat o' the pants with a bayonet!"

Joe burst out laughing. "I knew he wouldn't refuse, cap'n!"

"All right," the officer chuckled, "I'll see that all the men hear about it, an' we'll begin as soon as I can get things organized. That'll be all."

The boys headed for the corral where they took care of the colonel's mare and helped the handlers with some of their routine chores. Next, they directed their course for the hospital area and worked for nearly an hour with Dr. Feay, making preparations for the next morning's sick call.

Later, after a hasty supper, they decided to find a far away spot where they could practice drumming without bothering anyone else, or being hindered themselves. They walked through the gate, crossed the drilling area in front of the fort, and soon found themselves winding their way through a fairly heavily wooded area.

"Hope we can find at least a small clearing where we can practice," Joe said, half to himself.

"As many trees as there are around here, somethin' tells me it woulda been better to practice right on the drill field," Jon mumbled, side-stepping over the trunk of a fallen tree.

They were in the woods less than five minutes, when suddenly a soldier stepped from behind some bushes with his rifle held in front of his chest. "That's far enough!" he ordered. "Don't move!"

The boys came to an immediate halt. It was one of their own pickets; and when he came closer, Joe noticed that it was the same soldier who had been staring at him earlier in the day. Again he felt extremely uncomfortable as those piercing, dark eyes seemed to look straight through him.

"No one's allowed this far from the fort!" he snapped.

"We weren't tryin' to leave the area," Jon attempted to explain. "We're just lookin' for a small clearin' where we can practice drummin'; that's all."

"We didn't know we were so close to the picket line," Joe added hastily.

At that moment a second sentry came noisily through the underbrush just as the first one bellowed, "Well turn around an' head back to the fort, before you get yourselves in trouble!" And as he spoke, he grasped Joe roughly by the upper left arm and gave him a push that sent him reeling backward into some heavy underbrush, almost knocking him off his feet.

Joe quickly regained his balance, and the boys promptly retreated; for they knew no one was permitted beyond the picket

BOT RODA

line. However, before they were out of earshot, they overheard a remark from the second sentry.

"You were pretty rough on 'em, weren't you, Slade?" he said. "They're only our drummer boys!"

But his fellow picket replied in a surly voice, "I *hate* that kid!"

When Joe overheard these words, he stopped instantly and looked straight at Jon, not believing his ears! Looking back over his shoulder he was absolutely puzzled by the soldier's last comment, wondering what he could possibly have done to cause *that* remark. Then he shot still another quizzical look at Jon, who simply shrugged his shoulders and accompanied that gesture by an expression that seemed to say: "Now what was that all about?"

As Joe continued walking in silence, Jon lumbered along grumbling about the soldier's gruff treatment.

After a short while, Joe stopped for a moment to remove some burrs which were clinging to his uniform. Still steeped in consternation, he looked at Jon and asked, "Ever see that soldier anywhere before?"

Jon leaned against a tree, twisting his face in deep thought. "Nope . . . Can't say as I have," he drawled, shaking his head.

Joe frowned. "First I saw him starin' at me earlier today, an' now I didn't exactly care for the way he shoved me!"

He reflected for a few moments. "When I saw him this mornin', I thought maybe there was somethin' that seems familiar about him, but I can't put my finger on the time or place."

"An' we didn't have any problems with anyone at Camp Curtin . . . or on the way down here, did we?" Jon questioned.

"Not that I can recall," Joe mused, completely mystified by the strange circumstances.

He continued to walk along slowly, shaking his head. "Oh, I give up!" he commented finally. "He's prob'ly just someone who likes to show his authority while he's on picket duty. C'mon; it's gettin' late an' we still got a lotta drummin' to do."

Quickening their pace, they soon found their way back to the drill field where Jon spotted some huge but rather flat rocks along one edge of the open area. "Why can't we climb up there and practice?" he inquired.

"See any pickets?" Joe grinned.

Jon put his right hand to the visor of his kepi and exaggeratedly peered in all directions, Indian fashion. Then with as serious an expression as he could muster, he reported, "Sir, I see neither friend nor foe. Shall we risk it?"

"To the cliffs, drummer!" Joe nodded, pointing the way.

Moments later, when they were perched upon one of the highest rocks, they began practicing their rolls. "You're soundin' better all the time," Joe commented presently. "But the finish needs to be sharper. At the end it's two strokes down with the upper hand, then two with the lower. Watch."

Joe needed only a few moments to demonstrate what he meant. "Now, you try it."

Jon took a turn, making a few mistakes at first, but then playing it perfectly nearly a dozen times.

"You're gettin' there," Joe commented. "Now let's try it together."

After going over the beat time and again, Joe finally felt satisfied. "Now," he said, "there's one more thing you've really gotta learn."

"*What now?*" Jon demanded, pretending to appear disgusted. "Seems every time you teach me somethin', you say I still have only *one more thing* to learn. I don't think you can count!"

"Oh, quit gripin'! No one ever learns it all anyhow," Joe chided, but realizing all the while that Jon was anxious to learn everything he could.

"All right, Mr. Drumsticks, what's this *one more thing* I need to learn?" Jon asked, trying to hide his real curiosity about what was coming next.

"I'll show you somethin' my pa taught me," Joe said, a touch of family pride in his voice. "First, pick any three beats you'd like, an' play 'em one right after the other."

Jon shut one eye, obviously engrossed in deep thought for several moments; but when that famous Cooper grin slowly started to come on the scene once more, Joe began to wonder what was going through his friend's impish mind.

Finally, Jon appeared ready. "All set?" he asked.

"Any time you are," his companion answered.

"Well, first . . . you hafta sorta get this picture in your mind," Jon said, trying to sound as dramatic as he could. "There's an infantry man . . . an' he's chasin' a steer with his rifle."

Cocking his head to one side, Joe simply stared, totally puzzled. "Good grief, Jon! What in Sam Hill's that got to do with your three drum beats?" he wanted to know.

"All right . . . first . . . I'll play *Advance* . . . then . . . *Charge*

Bayonets . . . an' then . . . *Roast Beef* ! . . . Get it?" Jon asked, opening his eyes as wide as they would go and grinning like a bear.

At first, Joe simply stared at him and absolutely refused to even smile. But finally, unable to hold back any longer, he just burst out laughing. "Jon! You're a nut!" he blurted. "All right! I got the picture," Joe chuckled. "Now let's hear the beats."

Jon tapped the series in reasonable fashion, one right after the other, just as Joe had requested.

When he finished, Joe said, "Now . . . *if* you don't mind . . . I'll chase the very same steer. But listen carefully," he added, with a glint in his eye.

Jon accompanied still another of his grins with a wave of his hand and a slight bow. "I'm all ears! I can *hardly* wait, maestro!" he taunted.

Joe proceeded to play the same three signals; and as he did, Jon's grin was suddenly replaced by an expression of admiration.

"Hey! I never really noticed you playin' like *that* before! But maybe I never listened close enough," he admitted. "You were changin' the strength o' the beats, goin' from loud to soft. Do that again; I like it!"

Joe repeated the identical drum calls, again giving them the very noticeably different touch that he had added the first time. When he stopped, Jon crossed his arms and nodded admiringly. "Thunder an' tarnation! I really like that sound! It just goes *up* an' *down* . . . almost like a wave," he added, motioning with his hand as he spoke.

"My pa worked with me for a long time before I caught on to it; but once you get the hang of it, it starts to just come naturally. Pa says it's the trick to really good drummin' - different timing and different strengths."

Jon turned his head at a different angle and gazed at his companion out of the corner of his eyes for a few moments. "Bet you'll make a drummer outta me yet!" he confessed.

"You really are gettin' there, Jon. An' in a hurry! It's already time to learn some o' the fine points," Joe complimented his friend.

After practicing nearly an hour, the boys finally ambled back to the fort under a beautiful reddish-purple sunset. However, little did they realize that before long, the quiet peacefulness under those skies . . . would suddenly be shattered!

They were tired by the time they sounded tattoo and taps; but later, after reading his Bible, Joe found it difficult to close his eyes and sleep. A vivid picture of the soldier on picket duty continually flashed before his mind's eye, and the brusk shove into the underbrush kept haunting him, along with the words: *"I hate that kid!"*

After a rather fitful night of much tossing and turning, Joe felt sluggish on the drill field the next morning, where he purposely avoided any contact whatever with the soldier who had given him trouble the previous evening. At the first opportunity, however, he asked Sergeant Abbott who the man was.

"His name's King," the sergeant answered. "Slade King. He's not only the best shot in the company, but so far he's the only man who can get off three shots in less than a minute. And nobody can touch him when it comes to shootin' targets!"

Joe milled the name over in his mind, but he couldn't associate it with anyone he ever knew. Finally, thoroughly convinced that he had been unnecessarily concerned, he returned to the drills with a more relaxed mind.

Before dismissal, Sergeant Abbott took the entire company to the edge of the field where the trees blocked the warm rays of the late August sun. They had hardly stretched out in the shade when Joe saw Captain Colter approaching. Soon he was standing before them, informing the men of his plan to organize a drilling unit to perform at special events, such as brigade inspections, when visiting dignitaries were frequently present. Although many of the men either laughed outright or grumbled under their breath at the mere thought of drilling voluntarily in addition to what was already required of them, nearly a dozen indicated that they would be interested.

That evening, approximately seventy-five candidates from the entire regiment assembled on the drill field, where for more than an hour the captain watched carefully, as the men marched in small groups and responded to the boys' drum calls.

"Some of 'em still don't know their left from their right, an' a few others have slow reflexes," the captain confided with the boys after their first session was finished.

"Will you keep all of 'em?" Jon asked.

"Oh, no! I'd like to have a group of exactly thirty-two, if it's possible," replied the captain. "That's the number that'll work best for the kind o' drills I have in mind, and I want only the sharpest men we have."

The following morning the boys learned that it was pay day; and while they stood waiting anxiously for their money, they chatted with Jon's father. Eventually, Joe and Jon each received five dollars and walked away from the pay line as though they had struck it rich!

"Thunder an' tarnation! This is the most money I ever had at one time!" Jon remarked; but he quickly handed it to his father. "Here, you keep it, Pa. Money makes me nervous!"

Joe slipped his pay into his pocket and said, "I'll ask Cap'n Colter to keep mine, but I bet the sutlers' wagons'll get most o' the men's money," he surmised, motioning to one of the nearby civilian wagons that followed the regiments almost everywhere they went, carrying various kinds of goods and food items.

The next few days were extremely routine, with practically everyone now beginning to grumble about the constant drills, picket and fatigue duty, and other assignments. One morning, however, Joe noticed that the complaints were louder than usual.

"I tell you I didn't lose it!" he heard one man bellow. "I say someone *stole* it!"

"Yeah!" agreed Slade King. "It's no accident that so much pay's disappeared into thin air!"

"What's goin' on here?" interrupted Sergeant Abbott as he suddenly broke into the group. "That's a pretty serious charge!"

Once the sergeant walked onto the scene, the men's voices became somewhat calmer; and after they informed him of the circumstances, he promised to carry their complaints to the company officers.

Within half an hour a special inspection was called for the companies in which pay had disappeared; and it became rather evident that a thief was operating in their midst, much to the chagrin of more than a dozen men, including several from Joe's company, and Jon's father as well.

While the enlisted men waited restlessly in the drill field area, a rather large contingent of regimental officers and sergeants made a thorough search among the tents in an unsuccessful effort to locate the missing money. Then, after warning the men to be more careful with their pay in the future, Colonel Higgins dismissed them with a cautioning word that if a thief were found, he would be dealt with severely.

"That makes me mad!" Jon said, kicking the dust as he walked away with his father and Joe. "I worked that whole month for nothin'!"

"It's mostly my own fault," Mr. Cooper admitted, upset with himself because of his carelessness. "I shoulda made sure I always had it with me. But if someone did steal it, he'll slip up one day; an' somebody'll nail him! You wait an' see."

Although August gave way to September, there seemed to be absolutely no relief from the hot weather. The early days of the new month raced by quickly; and with the passing of time, there was less talk about the thefts and more about the war. The men were becoming restless after hearing so much talk from other units returning from the front, and they were getting anxious for some action themselves.

Joe and Jon were kept busy drilling in the mornings; working at the hospital, caring for the colonel's mount, and helping at the corral during the afternoons; drumming with Captain Colter's special unit later in the day; and sounding the mess calls, reveille, tattoo and taps.

Then on September 6th, just after the evening meal, it happened. When orderlies began racing through the fort seeking their officers, everyone realized that something unusual was in the wind. Joe and Jon were right beside Captain Colter, when a corporal gave him the news that the regiment had received orders to move out.

Hardly did they hear the orderly's words, when buglers' calls began piercing the air. In just a few fleeting minutes the boys were among the first to strike their tent. Shortly afterwards they had their haversacks and bedrolls made up, ready to be cast into the waiting wagons, since the regiment had been commanded to march light.

"We must be goin' pretty far!" Joe remarked excitedly after tossing his equipment to one of the men stationed atop a wagon. "Otherwise we'd prob'ly hafta carry these things ourselves!"

"Wonder where we're headed?" Jon questioned, as they hurriedly picked up their instruments and sticks and ran to assemble with the other drummers.

It was the same question that appeared to be on nearly everyone's mind, but none of the enlisted men knew the answer. Manny Welles asked everyone in sight, while he busily tried to cook rations and stow gear at the same time; but all he received in return were shrugged shoulders and bewildered looks.

"Just don't forget to bring the food, Manny!" shouted Jon's father, as he dashed by the mess area in search of his son.

Moments later he found Jon engaged in an animated conversation with Joe and some of the other drummers. Rushing up to him, he grasped him by both shoulders and stared into his sparkling blue eyes for a few moments. Then gripping his slight young frame even more tightly, he said in a very serious tone, "Remember, Jon. No matter what happens, be brave! An' do your job the best you can!"

Then turning to Joe, he added, "You too, buddy-boy! An' keep an eye out for one another!"

Before either boy could say a word, he rushed off through the swarming maze of soldiers, who were scampering from all directions to form their companies.

At that moment, two infantrymen came running from different areas and in their haste bumped heavily into one another, one of them sprawling face down in the dust right in front of the boys. From the impact, the man's rifle slid across the ground a few feet from where he lay. Quickly, Joe bent over to pick it up; and when he turned to hand it to the soldier, he found himself looking straight into the face of Slade King.

"Gimme that, you brat!" he said bruskly; and with a swipe of his hand he jerked the rifle from Joe's grasp. Then as Jon and Joe exchanged wondering glances, he sped toward the middle of the company.

However, the boys didn't have time to dwell on the situation, because at that moment the last of the drummers arrived just as Captain Colter rushed up to them. Even though the buglers already had been blaring their clarion calls for some time, he ordered the drummers to sound *Assembly* and to keep repeating it. Joe was amazed at how quickly the regiment formed! Excitement was running high; and with the drum and bugle calls sounding incessantly, the men of the 125th sensed the urgency of the moment. Joe was even more certain of it when Colonel Higgins reined in his chestnut mare right beside them and ordered Captain Colter to move the regiment quickly once it was on the open road.

"You heard him, men!" barked the captain as the colonel galloped away. "We'll start with *Common Time*, but be listenin' for the order to switch to the *Daddy-Mammy*. Shelley'll almost always get the signal first, an' he'll pass it along to the rest of you. So take a break in your drummin' every once in a while an' be sure to pick up whatever you hear the drummer in front o' you playin'. An' keep listenin' to your officers!"

At that moment a trio of scouts raced past them, sod flying from beneath their horses' hooves. At the same time, Lieutenant Stewart came riding at full gallop from the corral, heading directly toward the drummers. "Move out!" he shouted with a wave of his hand, as he sped past them to lead the way.

Joe's sticks responded energetically, as the other drummers scampered to join their own companies farther back in the closely-formed column. Joe stepped out hastily with the company color-bearer at his side; but it was only minutes later when Lieutenant Stewart wheeled in his saddle and barked, "Speed up that cadence, Shelley!"

Without hesitation Joe closed off the *Common Time March* with a roll and moved right into the *Daddy-Mammy*, a snappy beat which the captain had taught them just that week. Despite the rhythmic sound of his company's quickening, marching feet, Joe heard Jon pick up the beat from right behind them. Their companies moved out to its cadence as though they were headed for the most important event of their lives; and if the whispered rumors circulating among them were true, Joe thought that perhaps it would *be . . . just that!*

Chapter 9

An Unexpected Invitation

The sun had already set, and Joe was wondering how long they would be marching into the night. Soon, riders came from the rear with torches, taking their places beside the lieutenant to help show the way. Still there was no indication as to where they were headed; but Joe kept a close eye on the heavens, picking out the constellations with which he was familiar. He could see both the Big Dipper and the North Star and knew the regiment was headed westward.

As they marched, he drummed steadily, resting only briefly from time to time to shake the stiffness from his fingers. During those moments he could hear dogs howling along the way, as the drums and stamping feet disturbed their slumbers.

After nearly another hour of marching, Lieutenant Stewart and the torchbearers came to a halt at a crossroads, Colonel Higgins coming forward to join them. They unfolded a map near the light of a flame; and when the colonel was apparently satisfied as to their location, he ordered the column to continue its advance after a brief rest. However, to Joe's surprise, they took the trail leading north. Perhaps they weren't going to engage the Confederates after all, he thought.

Within another half hour, they reached a small town where the citizens, roused by their dogs, flocked outdoors to see what was causing so much excitement. Shortly, the 125th passed through the hamlet and crossed a bridge spanning a rather wide stream. Joe wasn't certain, but he thought it might be the Potomac; and if that were true, they would be marching into Maryland. Instantly, a mental picture of the state flashed into his mind. Pennsylvania was not too far to the north, and his native York County was right at the Pennsylvania-Maryland border. Joe's heart sank with the thought that possibly they were moving north, because the Rebels were planning to invade his own state!

It seemed to be hours later when they finally heard the welcome order to bed down. Joe estimated that it must be nearly two o'clock in the morning, and suddenly he realized how tired he was! As soon as he heard the order to break ranks, he dragged himself wearily to the rear of his company and hailed Jon.

Fortunately, the supply wagons were not long in arriving; and soon the boys were casting their bedrolls in a field of clover beneath a starry sky. As they crawled inside their bedding, they overheard some remarks that startled them.

"Someone said the Johnny Rebs are halfway through Maryland on their way to Pennsylvania!" one soldier commented, as he prepared to kindle a fire.

"Yeah, an' they say they've got us out-numbered two to one besides!" replied another.

In the dim glare of some freshly-lighted fires, the boys looked at one another in surprise. "Sure hope those rumors ain't got a word o' truth in 'em!" Jon muttered.

Joe lay on his back, staring at the glistening heavens. "So do I! It'd be ridiculous to come all the way to Virginia just to turn around an' march the whole way back to Pennsylvania again!"

"Thunder an' tarnation! Don't talk like that!" Jon moaned. "My feet are on fire! I musta tramped on every stone in the *road* since we left Fort Barnard! If we hafta march all day tomorrow, I'm gonna look for the biggest guy in the company an' get him to take me piggyback!"

"If I know you like I think I do, you'll have enough energy by tomorrow mornin' to run, let alone walk!" Joe snickered. "Now hush up an' let's get some sleep!"

Joe awakened to the sounds of loud talking the next morning; and when he saw that the men were up and about, he practically leaped from his bedroll. He and Jon hadn't sounded reveille!

He was about to shake his buddy when he heard Captain Colter's voice. "Let him sleep a while yet, Joe. It was a long night, an' we don't hafta move out yet. It won't take him long to get ready."

Joe turned somewhat sheepishly to face the officer. It was the first time the boys missed reveille since it had been assigned to them. "Why didn't the orderly wake us, sir?"

"I told him to let you sleep," the captain informed him. "I figured you'd be mighty tired; so I took care of it myself this mornin'. An' you two must've been worn to a frazzle, 'cause you never heard a thing!"

Joe blushed, slightly embarrassed by the situation. While he rolled his bedding, Manny Welles brought him a pair of biscuits and some hot coffee from the mess area that had been set up just a short distance away.

"Here you are, Jonny. Not the best thing in the world fer a growin' boy, but we can't be choosey," he remarked with a practically toothless smile.

Joe returned his grin. "Thanks, Manny, but I'm Joe; he's Jonny. Remember?" he asked, as he pointed toward his sleeping comrade.

"Oh, I always git the two o' yer mixed up a might. Yer both such short snorts," he chortled.

Joe chuckled to himself; but feeling really hungry and especially grateful for the biscuits, he promptly bit into one.

"Boy! Thanks, Manny!" he called, as the cook headed back to his wagon. "That hits the spot!"

Wheeling around, Manny faced him once more, quickly putting his finger to his lips. "Shhhhh! Not so dad-gummed loud!" he said in a hoarse whisper. "Wanna git me in trouble? I hadda give hardtack to the rest o' the outfit!"

Then looking around to see that no one would overhear, he added, "I saved some o' yestiday's biscuits jus' fer you an' young Joey there."

"He's Jon!" Joe corrected, with a slightly exasperated roll of his eyes.

Manny simply shrugged his shoulders. Then after displaying another of his semi-hideous grins, he shuffled off to his fires once more.

Shaking his head and laughing to himself again, Joe finished his breakfast and arranged his gear. Finally, he decided to awaken Jon. His companion yawned and stretched, sat up, rubbed his eyes and looked around squintingly.

"'Bout time you wake up! I hadda take care o' reveille all by myself this mornin'!" Joe said, endeavoring to keep a serious face.

"Good! That's what buddies are for," Jon countered, still half asleep. "An' if we start marchin' again, do me another favor," he said, as he lay back in his bedroll once more and pulled the blanket over his head.

"What's that?"

"Just roll me right up inside my poncho, an' throw me in the wagon too!" came the muffled reply.

Instantly, Joe leaped to the head of Jon's bedroll, reached under his friend's armpits and dragged him out bodily. "Let's go, Sleepy!" he barked. "Manny saved you some biscuits for breakfast; an' if you don't get a move on, somebody else is gonna get 'em!"

In ten seconds flat, young Jon was standing in front of Manny, looking into the cook's eyes like an undernourished puppy.

"Now . . . jus' what might be on *your* mind, young'un?" Manny asked, hands on his hips, but knowing full well that Joe had told him what to expect.

By this time Jon was already wetting his lips, salivating at just the mere thought of Manny's delicious corn biscuits.

"Oh . . . I just thought you might have somethin' *sorta special* for a poor, starvin' li'l kid!" Jon answered, trying to look as forlorn and neglected as he possibly could.

Then Manny's gargling giggle gurgled gleefully from his throat. He slapped his thigh and said, "By cracky! Now look what I jus' *happen* to have over here!"

Almost as though he were going to perform some amazing feat of magic, he very gently lifted a skillet that was lying upside down on one of his mess tables. When Jon saw the objects of his quest, his eyes lit up like embers! Quickly he reached for them; but then just as suddenly, drew back his hand and snapped it behind his back. Closing one eye, he slowly looked up at his benefactor and whispered, "How many can I have?"

"Well . . . " Manny drawled, stroking his chin. "Three . . . ifn you take anothern for your pal Jon."

"You got a deal, Manny! Thanks! But he's Joe. I'm Jon!" the lad reminded him.

"Dad-blame it! Yer both short; yer both got short names an' they

both start the same way! No wonder I git the two o' yer mixed up!" the grandfatherly cook complained.

"Don't worry, Manny!" Jon consoled him. "Actually, we don't care *what* you call us, just so's you call us in time to eat!" Jon said with his customary grin. "Unless . . . all's you got is hard tack, o' course," he added quickly.

"All right, young'un; now skeedaddle!" Manny wheezed, as he playfully thumped the lad on the seat of his pants with a long-handled ladle.

After thanking the cook again, Jon seized his treasure and ran back to the sleeping area, where he promptly handed Joe his share of what had been successfully sequestered.

When Manny turned to resume his camp chores, he realized that Captain Colter was standing nearby watching him, and obviously had seen and overheard everything that transpired.

Smiling broadly, Manny blinked a few times, shook his head and said, "Them boys sure do put a *little* bit o' *kick* in this here outfit, now don't they, cap'n?"

The officer smiled and nodded. "You betcha, Manny. Things won't get too boring with them around. You can count on it!"

As things developed, there was more marching that morning; but by nine o'clock the regiment reached the outskirts of a town called Rockville, and halted in a grove lying next to a church. Camp was established well before noon; and the boys were detailed to Dr. Feay, helping him to process all kinds of medical supplies.

"I don't like the looks o' this!" Joe murmured, while they were cutting and rolling bandage wrappings.

"Where'd they get it all?" Jon sighed, as he looked at the work which lay before them. "Did you ever see so much quinine in all your born days?" he asked, looking around him in wonder.

"Well, if we meet the Rebs, our boys ain't gonna be sittin' down to play backgammon an' checkers with 'em. You can bet on that! It looks like Dr. Feay's gettin' prepared for some real hard times!"

"Do you really think we're headed for a battle?" Jon muttered, a certain amount of doubtfulness trailing through his voice.

"Well, Cap'n Colter said we're to report for heavy drills this afternoon; an' with all the rumors goin' 'round, chances o' seein' some real action sure look pretty good, I'd say."

That afternoon the regimental officers informed the men that the Confederates had indeed begun an invasion of the north, and consequently drills were more concentrated than ever. Once, during a break, as Joe stretched out in the grass beside his drum, his mind began churning. Suddenly he was no longer certain how he felt about the possibility of being engaged in combat, and his father's warning that he wasn't going to a picnic, echoed through his mind.

Later, after supper, the boys received permission not to pitch their tent, since it was such a hot day. As Joe sat reading his Bible to Jon near the place where they planned to sleep for the night, Captain Colter approached them. "You boys haven't had much time to yourselves ever since we left Harrisburg," he admitted.

Then reaching into his pocket, he pulled out a coin. Flipping it to Joe, he said, "Some o' the men've been given permission to go into Rockville till dusk. Why don't you boys do the same an' see what you can buy that's better to eat than hardtack an' beans?"

"Thunder an' tarnation!" yelped Jon. "That sounds like fun!"

The boys chorused their thanks and left in search of Jon's father to see if he could accompany them. However, when they learned he had drawn picket duty for the early evening hours, they decided to join the many other uniformed figures striding in the direction of Rockville, situated just a short distance away.

The boys roamed through the town looking for anything which might capture their interest. Wherever they went, however, because of their ages, it seemed that *they* were more or less the center of attraction.

"Why's everybody starin' at us like that?" Jon whispered, after two women under a parasol had taken a step backward and simply glared at them in disbelief.

"What d'ya mean, starin' at *us*?" Joe taunted. "They're lookin' at *you*! They think you're General McClellan! They're all sayin' to themselves: <Hey! There's little Mac!>"

Jon smiled his most sickening smile, then attempted to land a playful kick on his tormentor's shins; but Joe anticipated the move and was quick to dodge the point of Jon's boot.

"Hey! There's a general store!" he exclaimed, slyly changing the subject. "Let's see what they got!"

The boys raced across the street and skipped up the three wooden steps leading to the door. Once inside, they were amazed at the variety of products that were stacked haphazardly over practically every square foot of floor space. At least half a dozen soldiers were milling around inside the establishment, along with several of the local townspeople.

Joe and Jon meandered through the various aisles scrutinizing the multitude of merchandise. Near the main counter they could hear some of the military men grumbling dejectedly because the owner had already sold the last of his tobacco supply. Joe recognized a few, though he didn't know their names. One of them, he remembered, was a trouble-maker as well as a poor marcher, and had often gotten into trouble with Sergeant Abbott.

However, at that moment, Jon saw some glass jars standing on a shelf along a side wall. Jabbing an elbow into Joe's left arm, he pointed. "Look over there!" he said, opening his eyes almost to their widest.

Joe turned to see quite a variety of candy in almost every color of the rainbow. "Hmm! Can't tell you the last time I had some o' that!" he remarked.

They walked around a tall display of all kinds of kitchenware and were gazing wistfully at the stick and horehound candy jars, when Joe happened to notice Slade King standing near the back of the store, inspecting some articles on a shelf. Not wanting to have his evening spoiled by another unsavory encounter with the soldier, Joe promptly got Jon's attention. After pointing toward King, he motioned for his friend to stand with him behind the display of kitchen implements, where they had less chance of being seen.

The boys waited patiently while the other infantrymen were engaged in conversation with the owner at the front counter, hoping all the while that King would soon leave the store.

Just then, an extremely fashionably-dressed young lady approached the main counter, made a purchase, and then walked elegantly out the door to a waiting carriage.

"That'll be a good find for some lucky man!" the storekeeper remarked to the group of men in front of him, as he watched her step gracefully into the carriage.

"And why do you say that?" one of the men inquired.

"She comes from a very well-to-do family just outside Rockville. You prob'ly came right past her home on the way to town. Her father could *buy* Maryland if he wanted it!" he exaggerated, but his tone of voice indicating that the man was obviously quite wealthy.

One of the men nodded his head. "Yeah," he recalled. "I did

see a rather nice home on the way here. Had a lot o' ivy around it, if I remember rightly."

"That's the one. Wilson Miller's place," the clerk continued, as he dusted some small articles with his apron. "That family has owned almost all the land on the west side o' Rockville since before the Revolutionary War."

At length the men bought several articles and were ready to leave, Joe heaving a sigh of relief when they called to Slade King, who hurried from the back of the store and followed them through the doorway.

Not long afterwards, the boys eventually attracted the attention of the storekeeper and made their own purchase. Soon, they were on their way back to camp enjoying some of the sweets they had bought, while a few extra pieces were stored in a pocket for future reference. Joe was savoring a stick of sassafras candy, which automatically reminded him of sassafras tea, and quite naturally, of home.

It was all he needed to set his thoughts on his family; and as they wound their way back to camp, even though Jon kept chattering to him from time to time, Joe was hardly aware of what his friend was saying. His mind was almost a hundred miles away; and he had to fight against some sudden attacks of homesickness, as a bird's-eye-view of Wrightsville, Columbia and the long, wooden bridge flashed through his mind. Yet again that vision stirred up thoughts of Nat, and Joe wondered where he could be. Safe, hopefully; and he remembered to pray for the runaway, even as he strolled along the dusty Maryland road.

After tattoo and roll call, Joe and Jon lay awake, gazing at the stars and talking in low tones; but even after Jon's breathing indicated that he had fallen asleep, Joe tossed about, for some reason unable to find slumber. The wind whispered lightly as it wrestled its way through the trees, creating an atmosphere which seemed entirely too peaceful for war to be so close.

As was typical of this time of night, thoughts of his family again pierced his mind; and he took that as a sign that he should be praying for them. But hardly had he begun, when he was disturbed by the sharp snap of a twig. Curious, he raised himself on one elbow and stared in the direction from which the sound had come. After a brief silence, he heard the slight rustling of some bushes. Peering intently into the night, with the help of the dim glow of a nearby campfire, he thought he could distinguish the outline of a figure creeping away from the sleeping forms clustered around him. Then, deciding that it was very likely one of the pickets going on duty, he lay back to resume his prayers and eventually fall asleep.

The next morning Joe was awakened early, for it was still dark when an orderly told him in a loud whisper that it was time for reveille. He grabbed Jon lightly by the chin and gave his head a shake, but his friend pretended to remain asleep. When Joe shook him a second time, he almost lost one of his fingers when Jon playfully bit him.

"C'mon! Get outta that sack!" Joe bellowed, shaking his stinging finger. "We've got some drums to roll!"

Soon they started reveille, and other drummers throughout the grove picked up their beat. A bugler added his blaring notes; and before long the darkened camp was filled with the sounds of activity, most of it caused by all the usual grumblings that accompany disturbed sleep.

The boys prepared themselves hurriedly; and after returning their bedrolls and haversacks to one of the wagons, they stayed close to Captain Colter, awaiting his instructions.

As dawn began to break, Joe was watching Colonel Higgins and some of the company officers riding toward them, when his attention was momentarily attracted by the sound of a carriage rattling along the narrow roadway that wound crookedly through the grove. An officer on horseback was riding in front of it; and when he saw Colonel Higgins, he signaled the coachman to stop.

The major saluted sharply. "Colonel, this gentleman wishes to speak with you, sir."

It was then that Joe took a close look at the people in the carriage. He didn't recognize the elderly man, but the woman was the same young lady he had seen in the store at Rockville the previous evening. The man had evidently met with some sort of mishap, for he was wearing what appeared to be a rather heavy, fresh bandage around his scalp. Stepping slowly from the carriage, the elderly gentleman supported himself by clinging firmly to one of the wheels, as Colonel Higgins rode toward him.

"Is there something I can do for you, sir?" the commander inquired.

"I believe so!" the man answered somewhat gruffly. "Last night I was not only robbed by one of your men, but beaten as well!"

"Are you certain it was one of mine?" the colonel asked doubtfully. "I was informed that every man was present or accounted for at roll call early last evening."

"That may be true; but I don't know of any other force in the area, and the thief was definitely wearing a Federal uniform. He had a heavy three or four-inch scar on his right cheek. I'd know him anywhere! You *must* have someone who answers that description!" the man demanded.

"What color hair did he have?" the colonel asked.

"Why . . . I believe it was . . . brown." Then he thought for a moment. "Or was it black?" he mumbled, half to himself. "Oh, I don't know! But he had this ugly scar!" he said, placing his finger on his right cheek as he spoke.

"Was it an officer or an enlisted man?" the colonel questioned further.

"Why . . . uh . . . I didn't notice. The only thing that attracted my attention about him was that fresh scar! He must've been wounded in a recent battle!" the man insisted, almost shouting his words.

"Well, sir, our regiment is yet to engage the enemy, even for the first time. Do you remember any markings on his sleeves, or on the shoulders, or even on his kepi? Or could you estimate his age?" Colonel Higgins continued to inquire.

"Thirty . . . well, maybe forty . . . Oh, I'm not certain of that either!" the man bellowed; and unable to provide any further descriptive information, he simply kept making more remarks about the scar, all the while slowly tracing with his index finger along his own right cheek for emphasis.

Finally, the colonel shrugged his shoulders and said with a certain air of resignation, "Well, anyone with a scar like *that* shouldn't be hard to find, if he's a member of *our* regiment."

Then, turning to an aide who was standing nearby, he directed, "Send word to all the company officers; I want any man who answers that description brought to my tent at once!"

Promptly the aide sent three orderlies scurrying to carry out the colonel's directions. At the same time, Captain Colter turned and walked away. Joe was about to follow, when he happened to notice Slade King and some of his friends sitting along the other side of the road. King was calmly sewing his jacket and smiling to himself. For a moment he looked up to watch the gentleman and his daughter drive away in their carriage, following the colonel through the grove. However, when King turned his head and saw Joe looking at him, the smile disappeared abruptly.

"What're you starin' at?" he sneered.

Fortunately Joe didn't need to answer, for at that instant Captain Colter called for his drummers; and Joe spun on his heels and ran. They sounded *Assembly* and within another fifteen minutes, the regiment departed from Rockville.

As they marched, the incident of the robbery and beating preyed upon Joe's mind for quite a while, especially the man's comments concerning a scar-faced assailant. He had never noticed any man in the regiment with a heavy scar; but momentarily, he reflected on his own tussle with the stranger at the Shultz farm several weeks earlier, and the heavy scar on *that* man's face. But after dismissing it as a mere coincidence, the movement of the regiment soon occupied all his thoughts.

They had been out of Rockville less than an hour, when he noted an encampment about a quarter of a mile in the distance. As they neared the site, a married couple and their teen-age son came out of their farmhouse and stood just inside the split-rail fence close to the trail. Meanwhile, groups of soldiers began to huddle along the roadside, also watching as the 125th approached. Nearly a hundred men in uniform were milling about, talking and laughing; but because of his drumming, Joe was unable to hear anything they were saying or to determine why they were laughing.

When the signal came to halt, Joe topped off his cadence with a sharp flam, standing almost directly in front of the family of three, where he unexpectedly caught a polite smile from the mother. Joe returned her smile; and while watching them out of the corner of his eye, he was certain by the way she was speaking to her husband and looking at Joe from time to time, that she must be talking about *him.*

There were just a few moments of almost total silence, but then a mocking voice suddenly rang out from among the men along the roadside.

"Lookit them *purty* blue britches an' coats, boys! Now ain't they just *too fine* for words?"

"My, my!" taunted another. "Now they *are grand*, ain't they? Sooo purty an' *clean!* Now if that don't beat all!"

When Joe detected the Tenth Maine regimental flag waving from a color-bearer's staff, and then saw the pennant of the Fifth Connecticut as well, he realized that these rather tattered-looking New Englanders surely had seen previous action and were giving the untried 125th the "old razz."

Then, looking toward Joe, one veteran in ragged clothing squealed in a rather high-pitched voice, "Hey, sonny! Didja bring yer mother along to hold yer hand?"

As he finished his words, he punctuated them by spitting a heavy stream of tobacco juice that landed close enough to Joe, so that it splashed on his boots and part way up one pant leg.

It was the biggest mistake of that soldier's life! Joe hardly had time to blink an eye before he saw one of the men from the front rank of Company A come sailing directly at the veteran soldier, and with a resounding right fist to his jaw, sent him sprawling through the dust, tobacco juice spurting in all directions.

"Lay off our drummer boy!" the husky, tow-headed young man from Company A growled. "He's not only our mascot but the best drummer in this here army! You wanna get smart with somebody, pick on someone your own size! Like me!" he bristled, as the surprised soldier from the Connecticut 5th lay on his back, too stunned either to answer or get to his feet, and tobacco juice dribbling across both cheeks and down his chin.

"And me!" bellowed someone right behind the tow-headed soldier.

"And me!" chorused still others, as almost the entire company began to break ranks and huddle proudly around their young drummer, staring down not only the man lying on the ground, but everyone else in the immediate vicinity as well.

At that moment Lieutenant Stewart came riding briskly toward them. "Get back into formation!" he shouted. "Nobody gave orders to break ranks! What's goin' on here?"

Just as suddenly as the fracas had started, it was followed equally as quickly by utter silence. Nobody said a word. The men from Company A slowly returned to their places, but all the while glaring menacingly over their shoulders, and never for

even one moment taking their eyes off the veteran soldiers standing by the side of the road.

Lieutenant Stewart watched, mystified, as the New Englander sluggishly began to pick himself up from the dust, gingerly rubbing his aching jaw and cleaning the tobacco juice from his face with one hand, while returning his cap to its proper position with the other.

"I wanna *know* what's goin' *on* here!" Lieutenant Stewart repeated sternly, glaring at the men in the front ranks of Company A.

Still, there was complete silence.

Finally, another of the men from the Connecticut regiment gradually swaggered forward, placed the butt of his rifle on the roadbed and leaned on the upright barrel. "Well, lieutenant . . . as I saw it . . . it was sorta like this." And gazing straight up into the sky, he pointed heavenward. "The littlest black cloud you ever did see come over . . . real quick like, you know . . . an' *rained* right on your drummer boy here. An' would you believe it? At that *very same* instant . . . a bolt o' lightnin' come outta nowhere and nailed poor Sammy here, right square in the jaw!"

Lieutenant Stewart noticed several stifled snickers, accompanied by a few nodding heads, numerous broad grins, and two or three outright guffaws!

"That's right, lieutenant, sir!" came another voice out of the crowd. "We was *all* standin' *right* here; an' that's just *exactly* what happened! We seen it *all*, didn't we, fellers?"

"Amen, brother! I seen it hit!" commented yet another New Englander.

"Yes indeedy!" affirmed still another rather seedy-looking witness.

The lieutenant looked at Joe, who quickly turned his head straight forward, scared to death he was going to start laughing out loud. Then, seeing the stains on Joe's pant leg and noticing the veteran infantryman still trying to rub the tobacco juice off his face with the back of his sleeve, the lieutenant's sharp mind quickly began sizing up the situation. Realizing he was on the receiving end of an "enlisted men's run-around," he decided not to press the issue any further.

"All right!" he shouted. "Let's break it up! You men get to your own regiments!" he directed the veteran soldiers, as he tugged the reins and spun his horse about.

Gradually the New Englanders walked away, meandering toward their own camp site. As they were departing, Lieutenant

Stewart looked at the men of Company A, his eyes roving slowly from man to man.

Finally, he leaned forward in his saddle and said, "Remember to save some o' that . . . *lightnin'* . . . for when we hit the Rebs!"

After hearing a somewhat muffled chorus of deep-throated laughter, Lieutenant Stewart was about to ride away. However, the woman standing by the fence caught his attention with a wave of her hand. Joe watched as the officer rode toward the split rails, removed his hat and began talking with the lady and her husband. The couple spoke in low tones, and once the woman pointed toward Joe. He couldn't hear the conversation; but when Lieutenant Stewart turned in his saddle and smiled in Joe's direction, he heard him say aloud: "Yes, ma'am. We really have two of 'em, you know. There's another one a little younger with company B. Could you handle a pair of 'em, by chance?"

Joe saw the husband and wife look at one another, smile and nod in agreement. Then, before the lieutenant turned away, he said, "I'll speak with my commandin' officer, folks, and let you know. Thank you for your kindness!"

Riding toward Joe, he smiled broadly. "Looks like somebody's taken a shine to you an' young Jon!" he said. "If we camp here, see me as soon as we get things organized, but don't bother to set up your tent."

Puzzled, Joe glanced again at the family of three and caught several more smiles.

Suddenly, the boy came running along, climbed onto the fence and sat on the top rail. "Howdy!" he called. "Where're you from?"

"Pennsylvania," Joe replied. "York County. We're almost neighbors, I guess."

"That officer says you an' the other drummer boy can spend the weekend with us, if your regiment camps an' don't move out. He's gonna see if he can get permission," the boy informed him.

Joe was stunned! Then it was *his* turn to flash a broad smile. By this time the boy's parents had walked closer.

"Thank you for the invitation, ma'am . . . sir," he added, looking toward the husband. "It seems like a year since I've been inside a house! I hope we don't keep marchin'!"

"Well, when I saw you, I thought o' Tommy here. If he was away from home, I'd want somebody lookin' out for *him* now an' then!" the mother confessed, putting her arm around her son.

Just then, the regiment was directed to break ranks and await orders. Joe ran to tell Jon the good news and quickly brought him to the fence, where they all introduced themselves. Then, hoping for the best, the two boys hurried to the area where the 125th was to set up camp.

As they hustled along, Joe grabbed the arm of Dan Hicks, the infantryman who had flattened the tobacco-chewing New Englander.

"Thanks for the bolt o' lightning!" Joe laughed, as he passed the husky Pennsylvanian.

"My pleasure!" Dan chuckled. "Enjoyed it immensely, if I must say so myself!"

While the boys were helping Doctor Feay unload hospital supplies, word began to circulate through the area that the regiment had just been assigned to General Mansfield's command. And it wasn't long before the story of the tobacco juice began to circulate throughout the entire regiment. Everyone quickly learned all the details, including the officers. During a pre-noon staff meeting, when Colonel Higgins himself heard of it, he nearly doubled over with laughter.

"The Rebs better be careful they never touch our two kids, or this war might be over in another twenty-four hours!" he roared, clapping his hand to his thigh.

During the meeting, Lieutenant Stewart learned that the regiment wouldn't be marching until further orders, and he relayed to Colonel Higgins and Captain Colter the invitation that the boys had received.

"That's fantastic!" the captain remarked. "Colonel, I think it'd be great for those two kids to get a little home life for a day or two. They've been workin' like beavers!"

"I agree!" replied the colonel. "Besides, they'll just be across the road. Permission granted!"

Several minutes later, both Captain Colter and Lieutenant Stewart found the boys helping an aide put up the captain's tent. As they were tying the last of the cords, Captain Colter gave them the good news that they were excused until reveille on Monday morning. The boys were nearly delirious at the thought of a welcome break in routine!

"By the way," Lieutenant Stewart said. "Mrs. Murphy insisted that you bring along every article of clothing you own. So I got a feelin' I know at least one thing she has in mind!"

"An' just stow all your other gear in my tent," Captain Colter offered. "Hopefully, we won't get orders to pull outta here in a hurry; but if we do, we know right where you are. Now go have a good time!"

After thanking both officers, it took the boys only a few minutes to follow their orders and then walk hurriedly among the men as the regiment continued to set up camp. Within a matter of minutes they found Jon's father and informed him of their good fortune.

"Now that's right neighborly o' them folks!" Mr. Cooper remarked. Then looking at Jon especially, he said, "Don't forget to tell 'em your pa sends his thanks. And mind your manners . . . *both* of you," he added, looking in Joe's direction as well.

"We will, sir," Joe assured him. "Don't worry."

They quickly crossed the field and hurried to the other side of the road, where they saw young Tom Murphy riding the railing on the front porch, watching for them. When he saw the boys approaching, he yelled something into the house and then ran to meet them.

Moments later, Mrs. Murphy stepped through the doorway, clutching a large basket in her hands. The three boys walked briskly toward the house, her son flanked by his two new friends.

"Looks like you got permission!" she called.

"Yes, ma'am," the boys replied in unison, though feeling somewhat embarrassed carrying their extra underclothing and socks wrapped up in several rather soiled shirts.

"Well, good! I see you brought your things with you. An' the idea o' that man spittin' filthy tobacco juice on that nice uniform! We've got plenty o' extra clothes in here you can wear. So, Tom, you show 'em where to change clothes, an' both o' you get out o' those uniforms. I'll get all your clothes washed right now."

Joe laughed. "You sound just like my ma, ma'am! I feel right at home already!"

"Well, that's not all that's gettin' washed!" she remarked. Then, looking at them with a motherly eye, she asked very pointedly, "An' just when *was* the last time either o' *you* had a good washin'?"

Joe and Jon looked at one another even more embarrassed than before. "Well . . . uh . . . I guess it's been a spell, ma'am, now that you mention it," Jon admitted, getting a little flushed in the cheeks.

"Well, tonight you're gonna get a good Saturday night *bath*; you can be sure o' that! Now get those things changed, put all your dirty clothes in this basket, an' then you can go with Tom to help his pa with some o' the chores out back. Gotta earn your keep, you know!" she said with a quick nod of her head. Then after handing the basket to Tom, she spun on her heels and headed for the kitchen.

Joe and Jon just looked at one another for a few moments, and then laughed out loud.

"That's my ma!" Tom said. "*Straight* an' *to . . . the . . . point!* But there ain't *nothin'* she won't do for *no* body!" Then, looking at his new friends with a smile of his own, he added emphatically, "An' just wait'll you taste *her* cookin'!"

"Thunder an' tarnation! *Home* cookin' 'stead o' hard tack! I can't wait!" Jon exclaimed, his eyes widening to match his grin.

Within a short time the boys were decked out in civilian clothing, and gladly went with Tom to help his father around the barn and in the small apple orchard, located on the hills not too far from the house. They enjoyed a light but delicious meal in the early afternoon, and then helped again with even more chores. Later, at Mr. Murphy's insistence, they went back to the camp and informed Colonel Higgins that he and Lieutenant Stewart could keep their horses in the farmer's stable, if they weren't in special need of them for the weekend.

"That's fine with me," the colonel agreed happily. "An' I guess you really wouldn't mind if I told you to take Princess out for a little *exercise* , would you?" he asked coyly, all the while looking at them out of the corner of his eye. "After all, if you're gonna have a horse o' your own one day, you'd better keep in practice!"

"Oh, we'd be *glad* to do *that,* sir!" Joe replied with a ready smile. "But we won't go far."

A few minutes later they also had Lieutenant Stewart's mount in hand. Jon had never ridden a horse before, and Joe helped him swing into the saddle for the first time. Then, as the Columbian rode slowly with his companion alongside, they both waved at some of the men and exchanged a few jibes with them as they passed by, since nearly everyone made some kind of remark about their "fancy new uniforms."

The Murphys had several horses of their own, and the three boys spent more than an hour riding around the farm area. By the time they returned to the house, Mrs. Murphy had prepared a sumptuous roast duck supper with all the trimmings.

As they sat at the table and Mrs. Murphy kept bringing more and more tantalizing food to set before them, Joe's and Jon's eyes began to rove from one dish to another, to Mrs. Murphy, to one another, and back again to the piping-hot food.

Finally, Joe said in an extremely grateful tone of voice, "Ma'am . . . I think this is the most thankful I've ever been for a meal in all my life! May I please say grace?"

"You certainly may, young man!" she replied, casting a smile in her husband's direction.

By the way the boys ate, and through their many comments about the food and hospitality, their host family knew that their invitation to these two young drummer boys was highly appreciated.

After the meal, everyone helped with washing the dishes, emptying wash water, drawing other water for baths, and getting a roaring fire started outdoors. When the water was hot, they carried the same wooden tub that was used for washing the clothes, to the shed that stood beside the stable. Then, after much drawing, carrying and heating of water, the little building became the Saturday night bath house.

Later in the evening, as they sat and chatted by candlelight, Jon was content mostly to sit practically motionless in the family rocking chair. "Thunder an' tarnation!" he remarked on one occasion. "I ain't felt this clean since the day I fell in the crick! I'm scared to move for fear o' gettin' dirty all over again!"

Then, all of a sudden he stopped rocking, sat especially erect, and began sniffing the air strongly, before looking at Joe out of the corner of his eye and flashing his famous Cooper grin.

Jon's antics didn't slip Mrs. Murphy's eye, and she began to laugh as she got up from her spinning wheel.

"Yes, I guess you know what you're smellin', Jon. We didn't have you pickin' apples today just for the fun of it! I've got five big apple dumplin's in that oven, an' they oughta be just about done!" Mrs. Murphy announced.

Needless to say, the boys really enjoyed that very special treat. "I sure am glad you waited till now to bring these outta the oven!" Joe said. "I could never've handled it at supper time!"

"Yeah, I'm so full I can only breathe outta one lung at a time!" Jon admitted, his eyes bulging almost as much as his stomach. "This is better'n a whole month's pay!"

They all sat and chatted for nearly another hour, but after a while Joe noticed that Jon's head began to nod. Looking quickly at the Murphys, he realized that they also had observed his companion's weariness.

"I guess we're not such good company!" Joe whispered apologetically. "But really, it seems like we've practically marched clear around the world the past couple o' days! I guess we're pretty tired!"

"It's really the other way around," Mrs. Murphy replied, a sudden catch in her voice as she arose and walked toward Jon. Then, stroking the lad's blonde hair lightly, she added, "You're the *best* company we've *ever* had; an' if it was up to me, you'd never leave this house and march off to war! I'd sooner keep you *forever* than see that happen!" she said with tears coming into her voice.

"Well, you boys are gonna sleep in Tommy's bed," Mr. Murphy interrupted quickly, slipping an arm around his wife's waist. "He'll sleep in the hay mow. He's done that a hundred times; it's plenty comfortable out there. So let's get a good night's sleep, an' we'll head for church in the mornin'. How's that?"

"Perfect!" said Joe. "We ain't been indoors for a church service since we left Washington!"

Sunday morning found them gathered with a small congregation less than a mile from the Murphy farm, and then they enjoyed an unforgettable meal of chicken and dumplings in the early afternoon. By this time the boys decided that Tommy had told them only half the truth when he informed them about his mother's good cooking.

The three boys spent several hours riding through the countryside before Joe and Jon sat down to appreciate supper and the evening hours with the Murphys. It had become a very special weekend, which they were disappointed to see finally draw to a close.

Mr. Murphy called them the following morning before he left to do a few early chores; but shortly afterwards, they were all gathered around the table once more, savoring yet another hearty breakfast. It was the first meal that was relatively quiet. The boys were in an extremely pensive mood, sadly realizing that it was already time to depart. Then, when they heard reveille being sounded in the nearby camps all around them, they reluctantly got up to leave.

"I'll bring the horses around to the front gate," Mr. Murphy said as he headed for the door.

"Thank you, sir," Joe responded. "I'm sure the colonel and the lieutenant really appreciate what you've done, an' I know Jon an' I had a great time with all of you. Thanks so much for everything!"

After Jon added his own gratitude as well as his father's, the boys gathered their freshly washed clothing and walked toward the door, feeling especially comfortable in their spanking-clean uniforms. Afterwards, at the front gate, everyone shook hands to bid a final farewell.

"I'm gonna send your name an' address to my folks," Joe said. "I just know you'll hear from 'em!"

"Thanks again for all the food, an' especially for makin' our uniforms look like new again!" Jon added, as Joe took the reins from Mr. Murphy's hands.

The boys began heading across the road toward the encampment, when suddenly Jon stopped, turned, and looked back. Then after thrusting his clothing into Joe's arms, he dashed back to the gate at full stride and threw his arms around a rather startled Mrs. Murphy.

Looking up at her with tear-filled eyes, he said, "Thanks for givin' me a Ma again, even if it was just for two days! I'll never forget you!"

Then, after kissing her on the cheek, he turned and ran after Joe, as Mrs. Murphy discovered in an instant that she was shedding some tears of her own.

Chapter 10

Repairing the "Cracker Line"

Later that morning, the regiment broke camp; and the boys helped sound *Assembly* along the road, almost directly in front of the Murphy homestead. It wasn't long before they saw Tom and his parents walking toward the split-rail fence, and at that moment Mr. Cooper came rushing from out of the ranks of Company B to express his thanks to them. After he returned, the family huddled together until the order was given for the regiment to advance; and then they waved a final farewell, as first Joe and then Jon marched past.

The next few days were spent in troop movements and more drills. The constant marching was beginning to become monotonous, and hope of ever encountering the Rebel army was practically abandoned. However, the boys' biggest disappointment was that Captain Colter was unable to find much time to work with the drilling unit.

One day, shortly after noon, the mail wagon pulled up to the mess area. Jon stood alongside his pal waiting to see if Joe would receive any mail, when he suddenly thought he heard his own name being called in the distance. Joe was so engrossed in listening to the clerk handling Company A's mail, that he heard nothing out of the ordinary.

"Jon Cooper!" bellowed one of the soldiers, as everyone from Company B began looking for their mascot.

"Where's our drummer boy?" someone else shouted.

"Here!" Jon finally blurted, shocked beyond words and elbowing his way toward company B's clerk, who was waving an envelope and still calling his name.

"Thunder an' tarnation!" Jon shouted. "Did I really get a letter?"

"We didn't think you knew anyone who could write, Jonny boy," taunted one of the men from his company, bringing a round of laughs.

Jon stopped dead in his tracks, raised both fists into a fighting position and stared at his heckler as if to say: <I'm gonna knock you flat!>

His impish antics brought even more laughter; but before he had time to teach the villain a lesson, somebody pushed him toward the front, even while his letter was being passed toward him.

When he was finally clutching it in his hand, he called out, "Hey, Joe! Look!"

Then he suddenly stopped and checked carefully for his name, to make certain there was no mistake. Shaking his head in wonder, but finally convinced it was his very own, he waved it as though he had just struck gold, and dashed toward his comrade.

"Look what I got!" he screamed. "Somebody wrote to me! I don't believe it!"

"Who's it from?" Joe asked, trying to seem as surprised as possible. "Open it up!"

The envelope had no return address, and Jon began to tear it open just as Joe finally heard his own name being called.

"Wait a minute, Jon! I got one too!" Joe shouted, scrambling in the direction of the wagon.

Within minutes they were both secluded in their tent, seated cross-legged on the blankets. Joe laid his own letter aside for the moment and couldn't take his eyes off Jon's expression. The mischievous blonde was ecstatic!

"Three pages!" he suddenly exclaimed, beaming his broadest smile as he removed the contents from the envelope. Then, after glancing quickly at the last page to check the signature, he dropped both hands to his lap and sat staring at Joe in disbelief.

"Well . . . who's it from?" Joe asked, still trying to be coy.

"It's from your sister Sarah!" he said, almost in a daze; and he fell straight back onto his shoulders. "I got a letter from a girl!" he shrieked toward the top of the tent. Then, sitting bolt upright, he began to read it.

Joe watched him as he read nearly the entire first page to

himself. "Well . . . ain't you gonna read it out loud? You always make me read mine to *you,*" Joe reminded him.

"Yeah, but yours is always from your *mother.* This is different! This is from a *girl* !" Jon said emphatically.

"Well, she's *only* my *sister,* for Pete's sake!" Joe said as though he were complaining, but really was only teasing his friend.

At that moment Captain Colter stepped inside their tent and handed Joe a second envelope. "Here," he said. "You left too soon. You got two letters today!"

Joe thanked the captain; and as Jon continued reading silently, obviously treasuring every moment of his time, Joe began reading his own letter with the earliest date. He hadn't heard from his family in quite a while; and since the regiment had been on the march for several days, evidently the mail was just beginning to catch up to them.

Joe completed reading his first letter; but before he began the second, he glanced toward Jon, who was still reading intently. Then when he concluded his second one, and Jon continued to be utterly absorbed in the pages he was holding, he asked in disbelief, "Didn't you finish that yet?"

Jon slowly turned his head and looked at Joe in total consternation. "What d'ya mean, finish it?" he asked, not believing his ears. "This is the fourth time I read it!" he exclaimed.

Joe just shook his head in amazement. When he had written earlier and suggested that Sarah send Jon a letter, he never would've believed it would mean so much to him. And as he sat and watched his buddy simply devouring, and practically memorizing every word, it would be a scene that he would recall many times in the years ahead.

The weather remained warm with hardly a sign of approaching autumn. With the exception of one miserable, rainy night spent in a field near Damascus, Maryland, the weather seemed made to order.

On a warm mid-September morning, the long lines of men were again tramping northward; and from Joe's point on the road, he could see marching columns for nearly a mile ahead of him. Suddenly, he noticed the officers on horseback raising their hands and shouting for silence. Gradually the companies came to a hushed standstill, and Joe found himself actually holding his breath. He thought he heard thunder, but the sky was perfectly clear.

"Cannon! Cannon!" the men began whispering loudly among themselves.

In the distance Joe could see the lines of the preceding regiment beginning to move at a much faster pace; and shortly, at a signal from Lieutenant Stewart, his own drum picked up the *Double Quick*, Jon speedily passing it along. Marching rapidly, the blue-clad units headed in the direction of the cannonading. Then, as they forded the Monocacy River, the sight of thick, white smoke increased the general excitement.

Joe held his drum high above his head, but the water kept getting deeper. Suddenly, Dan Hicks, the burly, tow-headed infantryman who had come to Joe's defense in front of the Murphy's home, swung him easily to his shoulders. Spontaneously, Joe turned his head to see how Jon was managing, and laughed to himself when he saw one of the biggest men of Company B swing the blonde-haired lad to his shoulders as though he were just another haversack; and Jon never lost a drum beat! As the men splashed their way across the ford, both boys kept drumming heartily from their lofty perches, while the men laughed and cheered them on.

Upon reaching the top of a hilly ridge running along the west bank of the Monocacy, they saw that fighting was taking place along the sides of some mountains ahead of them. However, to everyone's disappointment, they were brought to an abrupt halt.

The men began complaining harshly among themselves, wondering why they had stopped with action so close at hand. Some stamped the ground in disgust, fidgeted and grumbled, but all to no avail; and still a more crushing blow to their pride was yet to come. When they finally began moving again, they headed north, *away* from the sounds of battle. But as they marched, they continually glanced over their left shoulders, bitterly observing the billowy puffs of smoke.

By noontime they came to the outskirts of a town from which the Confederates had recently retreated. Here the men continued grumbling as they established their camp in the surrounding fields.

"There were a couple o' days when we sat around an' did almost nothin'!" one infantryman whined, sitting down disgustedly. "If we'da been on the move, we coulda caught the Johnny Rebs right here!"

"That's what I say!" agreed another.

"Why don't you guys just shut up?" Slade King snapped. "You

gripe when we march, an' you gripe when we don't march! You're never satisfied!" he bellowed, angrily kicking an empty coffee pot and sending it rattling through the dust and the tall grass.

However, the men were in a complaining mood; and to make matters worse, the *cracker line* was broken, which was the name that Manny Welles had given to the supply line. During the past week, the movement of artillery and men had closed practically all roads to the wagons that carried their food; and consequently, the men soon learned that the company cooks had little or nothing to offer them.

Soon a call came for volunteers to go to nearby homes and farms in quest of food; but even though Joe and Jon made themselves available to accompany the detail, their raised hands were ignored.

Captain Colter happened to approach just as Company B's sergeant selected Jon's father as the last man. Seeing the boys turn away somewhat dejectedly, the captain whispered to the sergeant, "Why not take the boys along? Who'd be able to refuse 'em without lettin' his conscience bother him?"

The look on the sergeant's face was somewhat less than enthusiastic; but after a shrug of his shoulders, he called after them. "Hey, boys! C'mon back! Hop in that wagon. You're goin' shoppin'!"

Jubilant, Joe and Jon raced one another to the second wagon and scrambled onto the back. Captain Colter himself decided to jump up between them; and Mr. Cooper sat beside Jon, happy for the opportunity to be able to spend some time with his son. Together, the foursome dangled their legs over the opened end gate, as the pair of canvas-covered supply wagons began to bump their way toward the town of Frederick.

"Cap'n Colter, sir," said Joe, after they had been riding a short while. "There's somethin' I've been wantin' to ask you."

"What's that, Joe?"

"I been wonderin'. Do you remember the man an' his daughter who rode up in the carriage just before we left Rockville last week?"

"Yes," the captain nodded. "Why do you ask?"

"Did you hear whether they found the man with the scar on his face?"

"No, they didn't. As a matter of fact, I was wonderin' about that myself just yesterday; an' I asked one o' Colonel Higgins' aides about it. Apparently, no one in our regiment answers the description the man gave. What made you ask?" the captain inquired.

"Well . . . I saw the man's daughter at the general store in Rockville the day you gave Jon an' me some money to go find somethin' to eat; remember? An' since we're out lookin' for somethin' to eat again, I guess that just sorta reminded me."

Jon leaned forward to peer quizzically around the captain. "When did you see a lady in the store?" he asked. "I don't remember seein' 'er, an' I was with you the whole time!"

Joe laughed. "You're only fourteen, little boy. While you were lookin' at the candy, I was lookin' somewhere else!"

Jon leaned over farther in an attempt to reach around the captain and take a playful swipe at his pal, but lost his balance, and would've fallen off the wagon had his father not grabbed him by his belt.

Just then the wagon came to a halt, and shortly the sergeant walked to the rear and called the names of three of the men.

"Let's see how generous this farmer is," the sergeant remarked, as they stooped to pass under a thorny rose trellis arching the front gate.

When they returned a few minutes later, however, they were carrying a small sack of flour and exactly ten green apples.

"Well . . . it's a start!" the sergeant frowned, when he saw the captain's disappointed expression.

After a short ride, the wagons stopped at a second house; but this time the captain decided to take matters into his own hand. Calling to Jon's father, he said, "Cooper, you an' I'll take the boys this time an' see what we can do."

With his hands on his hips and a stony glare in his eyes, the sergeant stared after them as they walked to the rear of the house. They were gone nearly a quarter of an hour; and when they finally reappeared, each was toting a large basket filled with apples, tomatoes and other fruits and vegetables. Although the sergeant was glad to see the food, he was obviously annoyed by their success.

"You just need the right touch, sergeant," the captain said, somehow restraining a smile.

"Beggin' the cap'n's pardon, sir; but that don't mean the rest of us couldn't've gotten just as much!" the sergeant grumbled.

He was about to return to the front of the wagon, when a woman's voice came from the front porch. "Oh, Major!" she called. "Would you please send those two boys back here again?"

Nearly everyone chuckled at the captain's sudden promotion in rank, but Joe and Jon didn't waste a moment. Like a pair of greyhounds they dashed under the trellis and raced each other to the porch. The men watched as the boys followed the woman inside, then grinned a few moments later when they came bursting across the front yard carrying four massive pumpkins.

As the men and boys waved in appreciation, Captain Colter glanced slyly at the sergeant and said, "Next farm, please, driver."

When they arrived at a fairly large country place not too far down the road, the captain was about to insist that his group do the job again; but he quickly determined that the sergeant's pride evidently had been dealt a rather severe blow. Therefore, saying nothing, he simply indicated with a wave of his hand that the sergeant should go ahead.

Again three men went with him; but this time they returned completely empty-handed, the sergeant refusing even to look at the captain as he passed the rear of the wagon and hastened toward the driver's seat.

"Uh . . . just a moment, please," the officer called.

The sergeant spun about and peered around the left rear of the wagon. "Yes, sir?" he said inquiringly.

"The boys . . . are thirsty, sergeant . . . They'd like a drink o' water," Captain Colter informed him.

As the sergeant frowned at what he considered to be a totally unwarranted delay, Joe looked at the captain in complete surprise.

"No, I'm not, sir!" he said, puzzled.

"Neither am I!" Jon exclaimed. "Sir, you just watched us drink nearly a pitcherful o' meadow tea in that lady's kitchen back at the last farmhouse!"

"But I say you're *thirsty!*" the captain repeated, looking from one to the other, squarely in the eye.

Joe thought he'd try again. "Cap'n, I'm really not the least bit . . ."

"Drummer Shelley!" the captain interrupted, slowly emphasizing both words and placing his hands on his hips. "Need I remind you that I'm your commandin' officer? An' if I say you're thirsty . . . then *you're* thirsty, young man!"

Joe looked at Jon, and Jon stared back, accompanied by a shrug of his shoulders and an expression that indicated beyond a shadow of doubt that the captain had suddenly gone *daffy!*

Then, clutching his left hand to his throat, Jon fired a salute and said as dramatically as he could, "Yes, sir; I believe you're right, sir! I'm just . . . dyin' o' thirst!"

"Good!" the captain countered. "Just as I thought! Now the two o' you walk around to the back door o' that farmhouse, an' ask those good people if they could spare a drink o' water."

However, Joe thought carefully for a moment before leaving. Then looking at the captain rather questioningly, he inquired, "Shouldn't we ask 'em for anything *else,* sir?"

"Oh, no!" the captain responded hastily. "The sergeant an' his men've already done that! All you want is a drink o' water to quench your *unbearable* thirst! Now . . . go!" the captain ordered, pointing toward the farmhouse and winking on the sly at Jon's father.

The boys were too dumbfounded even to talk to one another as they approached the rear of the home. Joe rapped, and moments later a woman opened the door.

She hardly peered through the doorway before Joe asked, "Ma'am, could you spare a drink o' water, please?"

It was evident that the woman was somewhat taken aback by the two teen-agers dressed in Federal uniforms. "Merciful sakes! Don't tell me the two o' *you* are in the army! Why, you're hardly old enough to leave your mothers' apron strings!"

Jon looked at Joe as if to say: <Oh, no! Not this again!> But Joe flashed her a quick smile and answered, "We're in the army, ma'am; but we don't do any fightin'. We're drummer boys for the 125th Pennsylvania," he said proudly.

The woman took a step back, folded her arms and was silent for a few seconds, slowly tapping her foot on the floor. Then, gradually nodding her head as if to grant her personal permission for the boys to remain with the regiment, she stepped aside and invited them to enter the kitchen. Still looking at them and shaking her head as though she couldn't believe her eyes, she reached for two cups.

"Are you boys with the men who were here just a few minutes ago?" she asked, as she ladled water from a bucket in the dry sink.

"Yes, ma'am," Jon responded, after sipping exceedingly slowly from the cup of water she had handed him.

"Why were they askin' for *food*? Merciful sakes! Don't the army feed you people?" she asked in a half-surprised tone of voice.

"Well, you see, ma'am," Joe began to explain, "we've been marchin' for a *long* time, an' with so many soldiers on the roads, our supply wagons haven't been able to keep up with us; so we don't have any food!"

"Heavens to Betsy! Now when was the last time you boys had a cooked meal?" she wanted to know.

"Well, Jon an' I were lucky because a family back east a ways sorta kidnaped us for a little while an' really treated us royal. But the men've had only hardtack an' odds an' ends now for days! No real meals for quite a while that I can remember," Joe admitted.

"Not since we left Fort Barnard, near Washington, anyhow," Jon added. "An' I guess that's over a week ago!"

A look of exasperation crossed the woman's face, and she began looking around the kitchen. Then she stalked toward a door and opened it.

"Henry!" she called. "Bring a basket o' them tomatoes an' apples up from the cellar. We got some hungry boys up here!"

Then turning to Joe and Jon, she said, "We had some pretty good crops this year. The Lord's treated us *real* good! You can go along with my husband to the barn an' get some dried corn, an' I got a feelin' he'll have some bacon an' ham down in the smokehouse besides," she added with a nod of her head.

"Thank you, ma'am!" said Joe, his eyes lighting up as he set his empty cup on the table.

But snatching it instantaneously, the lady exclaimed, "My lands, you can drink more'n that! After marchin' all *that* distance, you oughta have a terrible thirst!" And before Joe had an opportunity to refuse, she thrust a second full cup of water into his hands.

"You too, young'un," she added, snatching Jon's half-empty cup right from between his hands.

"No, thank . . ."

"Nonsense!" she interrupted, topping the cup off with another ladleful of water. "I know a pair o' thirsty boys when I see 'em! Heaven knows, I raised three o' my own!"

Seconds later, Jon's eyes crossed as he found himself clutching another cup of water, wondering almost painfully if his system could hold even another drop! As Joe dutifully downed his cupful, the woman's husband appeared from the cellar and set a large basket of beautiful, wine-red apples on the floor. After smiling amiably at the boys, he turned and retreated down the steps to fetch some tomatoes as well.

Coyly keeping his eye on everyone, Jon took these moments of distraction to hide his full cup behind a huge brown jar on the kitchen table; and in a little while the boys were scrambling behind the elderly farmer, on their way to the barn.

Fifteen minutes later, the look on the sergeant's face was worth

BOT RODA

the touch of an artist's brush; and Captain Colter could hardly keep from laughing out loud. As the boys struggled toward the wagon carrying their heavy load, Jon's father and the other volunteers ran to help them and gather up other baskets of food as well.

Then, whistling happily, the captain returned with his two winsome drummer boys to the house, where he wholeheartedly thanked the gracious farmer and his wife. Then, after hoisting to his shoulder still another basket piled high with an assortment of foods, he gathered a shank of smoked ham in the crook of his left arm and began once again to whistle one of his favorite tunes, as he disappeared around the corner of the house and headed for the wagon.

Before the boys could pick up the final basket of tomatoes, the kindly woman placed a small package inside their coat pocket and put her arms around their shoulders. "There's some o' my famous molasses cakes especially for the two o' you," she whispered.

Pleasantly surprised, the boys smiled their thanks and were about to leave, when the woman turned and reached for a cup that sat on the porch railing. Extending it toward Jon, she said, "Here, sonny, you forgot to finish your drink! I found it when I got the molasses cakes outta the jar on the table!"

Almost collapsing at the mere sight of it, Jon reluctantly took the cup in his hands and looked to Joe for help, his eyes almost bulging from his head.

But when Joe saw the expression on his friend's face, he was totally unable to control himself and simply doubled over in an absolute fit of laughter!

For several moments, Jon shot the world's most somber "death stare" directly at his nearly hysterical buddy, while the farmer and his wife merely exchanged blank stares. Finally, unable to escape the agony of the circumstances that faced him, Jon's eyes took one complete circuit of their respective sockets, before he took a deep breath and gulped down the contents of the now utterly despised, tin cup.

Moments later, as they made their way toward the wagon, carrying the basket between them, Jon whispered, "I feel more like I'm in the navy than the army!"

"Why?" Joe asked.

"I feel like I'm floatin'!" Jon moaned, rolling his eyes once more and placing his free hand over his stomach.

When everything had been stowed inside the wagons, the sergeant's eyes happened to meet the captain's point-blank stare. Raising his arms in surrender, he said in complete resignation, "All right! All right! From now on *they* go for the food!" he announced.

After Jon hopped off the wagon at the next farmhouse, he paused a few moments. Then, characteristically closing one eye and looking somewhat forlornly at Captain Colter, he begged, "Please, sir! Don't say we're thirsty again! One more sip an' I just *know* I'll explode!"

With the sounds of laughter ringing through the air, the boys and two soldiers began another successful quest for food from the generous Marylanders.

Late in the afternoon as they returned to camp, both wagons were completely filled with all kinds of smoked meats, flour, pumpkins, fresh fruits and vegetables, and even a fair quantity of freshly baked bread and preserved foods in all kinds of jars and other containers. The boys sat in front beside the sergeant; while the others trudged happily alongside, carrying even more food and waving merrily to the shouting men who awaited them.

When Manny Welles set his wondering eyes on the abundantly loaded wagons, he picked up one of his skillets and began thumping it with a long-handled ladle, while marching up and down in front of his mess tables forming a one-man parade and shouting, "We'll eat tonight, boys! We'll eat tonight!"

When everyone at camp learned that Joe and Jon were especially responsible for the success of the trip, the men hoisted the boys onto some strong shoulders and paraded them among the tents. Just as they arrived in front of the mess area, and before they could escape, Manny shrilled at the top of his voice, "Git the blankets, boys, an' give 'em a ride they'll *never* fergit!"

Several blankets seemed to come out of thin air; and the men quickly stretched out two of them, setting Joe in one and Jon in the other. Within moments the boys were flying high into the air, as the men kept tossing them skyward, laughing and cheering uproariously. When the boys were finally released, they walked happily, though somewhat dizzily, to their camping site, their arms around one another's shoulders and tucking away still more treasured memories of their careers as drummer boys.

After the evening meal, the men in the special drilling unit practiced some precision handling of their rifles and listened while Joe and Jon sounded the various signals they all needed to memorize in a proper order; but Captain Colter kept their marching to an absolute minimum, since they had done so much of it in recent days. The head musician and the boys were becoming impressed with the men's ability to manipulate their rifles, even twirling them, and passing them back and forth between themselves with more and more speed and accuracy.

Much later that evening, as the boys lay near a campfire, they noticed that more men than usual were absent because of picket duty; and the ever-present fiddlers and banjo players weren't to be heard. Uncustomarily, no groups were singing around the campfires; and even very few of the men were playing cards or checkers, two of the most favorite evening pastimes. Though the men of the 125th were outwardly discouraged because of the military decisions made earlier in the day, nearly everywhere small groups talked more excitedly than ever about the prospects of battle.

The boys lay on their bedrolls, nibbling the small molasses cakes they had received earlier in the afternoon, while taking in all the bits of conversation they could overhear. Eventually tattoo, roll call, and taps slipped by; and a pair of extremely weary drummer boys found that sleep came rather easily despite the excitement.

Because Chaplain Stewart realized that the possibilities of going into battle were becoming more and more evident, he had asked for permission to hold a special service at sunrise the next morning. While he was in the midst of delivering a short message, the hundreds of men who were seated around him gradually became distracted by noticeably slow and extremely doleful drum beats approaching the area. Closer and closer they came, until the men's attention became so completely diverted that the chaplain simply ceased speaking altogether.

Then, along the nearby road came a short procession of just two drummers, one Union and one Confederate, followed closely by a Union rider bearing the Federal flag and two Rebel cavalrymen, one carrying the Stars and Bars and the other a flag of truce. Behind them were three open wagons, each bearing four crude caskets.

First one man in the gathering along the hillside arose to salute,

then several, and finally every man attending the service stood and snapped his right hand to his forehead. They watched in complete silence until the small procession disappeared from their view, and the mournful drum beats faded to mere murmurs in the distance.

Before they sat down again, first Joe and Jon exchanged several seconds of silent, rather disturbed, eye-to-eye contact; then Jon looked at his father, who slipped his arm around his son's waist and drew him close for a few moments.

The impromptu service was a very short one; and as soon as it ended, Joe said, "Mr. Cooper, would you an' Jon do me a favor?"

"Sure. What do you have in mind, Joe?" Jon's father replied.

"Just . . . come along with me a couple o' minutes, will you?" he asked, almost pleadingly.

Then stepping between them, Joe interlaced his arms around their elbows and headed straight for Chaplain Stewart, who, Joe had recently learned, was Lieutenant Stewart's cousin.

"Sir!" he called, as the clergyman was about to step into his tent.

Chaplain Stewart turned and smiled as he instantly recognized the two drummer boys who were beginning to mean so much to the entire regiment. "Yes, what can I do for you?" he asked.

"Well, sir," Joe began, "Jon an' his pa never went to church till that Sunday in the warehouse when we arrived in Washington, remember? But everytime you've held a service, they've been comin' along with me ever since that day."

"That's good to hear!" the chaplain smiled, as he extended a hand to greet Jon and his father.

"Well, sir . . . " Joe paused a moment. Then, not knowing exactly how to put his thoughts into the proper words, he simply said, "Well . . . the situation bein' what it is, sir . . . I thought it might be a good idea for you to have a sort of . . . well . . . personal chat with 'em, if you know what I mean. Even before the regiment sets out this mornin', if you have time, sir."

The chaplain smiled. "I know *exactly* what you mean, young man; and I'll *take* the time!" he said, taking his Bible from under his arm and motioning toward his tent.

But as Jon and his father stepped inside, Joe excused himself. "I think maybe . . . I better wait out here, sir, if you don't mind," he added.

The chaplain nodded his head understandingly, lifted the flap of his tent and stepped inside.

Meanwhile, Joe ambled away from the tent area and sat down

on the thick, protruding roots of a stately nearby tree. The procession of caskets, probably containing the bodies of men who were born and raised in nearby towns and villages, had made his heart heavy and put him in an extremely somber mood. For a few moments he simply stared at the chaplain's tent, before briefly lifting his eyes heavenward. Then, lowering his head and closing his eyes, he began to pray earnestly for Jon and his father, and then for his own family, his friends, and Nat.

Eventually, his prayers were interrupted by the sound of footsteps. Glancing up, he saw Jon and his father walking toward him, their arms around one another. As Chaplain Stewart stood a few yards behind them at the entrance to his tent, he caught Joe's attention, and accompanied a broad smile with a reassuring nod of his head.

Immediately, Joe heaved a grateful sigh and beamed a grin of his own.

"Thanks for takin' us to the chaplain, Joe," Mr. Cooper said very solemnly. "He opened up a whole new life to us, an' that just took away all the fear of possibly goin' into battle!" he added, a strong tone of confidence in his voice.

"Yeah! Thanks, Joe!" Jon said, agreeing with his father. "Inside, I've been gettin' more scared every day; an' that sure helped a lot!"

Less than an hour later, the morning became an extremely trying one. Marching men filled the roads once more, each carrying enough rations to last several days, as well as forty to eighty rounds of ammunition. After the untested 125th's brigade was ordered to move out, the men spent an agonizing, upsetting and heart-rending two hours, standing in the streets of Frederick, Maryland, waiting for other more-seasoned troops to move ahead of them. Enlisted men and officers alike were visibly angered at being left in the rear, pride and anxiety for action gnawing at them from within.

Eventually, however, they were heading in the direction of some high hills to the west. Somewhat encouraged, Joe drummed more enthusiastically than ever, and the men appeared to march with gusto to the rataplan of the *Daddy-Mammy*. Unquestionably, they were keyed up; and their tenseness became more apparent when orders were passed along to eat their rations on the move.

Then, late in the afternoon, as they were marching among the hills, once more they could hear the unmistakable clamor of cannon in the distance. This time there was no halt. Instead, officers shouted for the drummers to speed up their cadence at once; and as they marched out of a wooded area, Joe noticed thick smoke rising from the mountain passes far to the north.

Gradually, however, the day's marching began to have its telling effects. Not only were Joe's hands tired, but his feet and legs were almost numb. Nevertheless, the marching continued even after dusk; and his miseries increased when their brigade was forced to cross a swiftly moving creek in the semi-darkness. There he slipped on some moss-covered rocks and fell forward into the chilly waters, managing desperately to keep his drum from getting wet. Later, he was relieved to hear the order to cease drumming; but marching in chilling, drenched clothing did little to raise his spirits.

Finally, they were brought to a halt near the base of a mountain, where they moved to the edge of the road in order to allow some wagons to pass. Although the men were glad for the rest, most of them grumbled because they thought they were being ordered to wait, so that more units would be able to move ahead of them. This time, however, they came from the opposite direction; and the wagons turned out to be ambulances for removing the dead and wounded from the battle areas.

As the cumbersome vehicles slowly jostled past, no longer were there voices of complaint; and even though everyone was practically numb with fatigue, not one man sat down. An unexplainable force from deep within compelled them to remain on their feet, as they stared intently, almost reverently, at the burdened wagons. Joe watched their lanterns dancing crazily to and fro, a cold shiver running down his spine, as he heard some of the wounded cry out in pain.

Soon they were marching again, pausing from time to time to allow still more wagons to pass, while the sounds of cannon continued to echo through the valleys before them.

Then, although rather muffled at first, another sound began to reach their ears - music! By the melodies, it was evident that a Confederate band was lending moral support to its fighting men; and, as if in answer, a few of the 125th's fifers began to play *Marching Along.* Amazingly, the music seemed to take the drudgery out of the men's steps; and Joe began drumming along with the fifers. Moments later he smiled, as he realized Jon was marching right beside him; and the two of them lent the other musicians their support.

It wasn't until nearly three o'clock in the morning when the long-awaited halt was finally called. The boys had their bedrolls and blankets spread quickly; and the last thing Joe remembered was Slade King stumbling through the darkness, fuming about having been assigned picket duty.

It seemed to Joe that he had not been sleeping even five minutes before someone awakened him. The first thing he noticed was his clothing, folded neatly beside him. Manny had prepared a fire and dried everything for him in his usual grandfatherly fashion. His two drummer boys had become the apples of his eye.

A crystal clear blue sky was looking down at Joe, and he had to squint as the sun streamed through the leaves of the trees around him. Reveille was later than usual, but the officers barked constantly at the men to keep them moving; and consequently, they soon were on their way once more.

The sounds of battle had faded; and yet again the men were disappointed that others had seen action, while the 125th did nothing but march, march, march!

Within an hour the truth of the situation became only too real. After entering a mountain pass, they came upon an open area where countless dead Union soldiers lay strewn upon the ground. Detachments of men were removing the slain from the fields and placing them in waiting wagons. Farther on, they passed a stone wall, behind which lay hundreds of mortally wounded Confederates who would never again raise a weapon to their shoulders in the act of rebellion. Suddenly sickened by all thoughts of war, Joe marched along, drumming only from mere force of habit.

They passed through land torn by the recent battle, where cannon and damaged gun limbers were overturned along the sides of the road; but after having missed still another battle, the men moved listlessly. Regardless as to how the drummers slammed their beats, they seemed completely unable to rally the men's spirits.

Then, sometime before noon, Joe heard a faint clamor from the rear, which gradually transformed itself into a roar, as for some unexplained reason the men began shouting and cheering jubilantly! Everyone, enlisted men and officers alike, turned in an effort to determine the cause of the commotion. Coming from the southeast and riding toward them, was a group on horseback; and as they passed Jon and Company B, the men of the 125th were yelling at the top of their lungs!

"It's General McClellan!" someone shouted.

"Little Mac!" and other cheers gushed forth as the galloping horses dashed by. Some of the infantrymen waved their kepis as they called, and others put theirs on the tips of their rifles and held them in the air as they yelled. And when the general, in the lead, took off his own hat and waved it as he dashed past on his black stallion, the men roared their delight!

Two minutes later, the entire brigade was stepping along toward Boonsboro with renewed vigor. Then, before they reached the town, Joe set his eyes upon Confederate soldiers once more. However, as members of a party seeking the body of one of their generals, they were traveling and searching somberly under a flag of truce.

The hurried march through Boonsboro was an unforgettable one. Dead horses were scattered along the streets, and a number of homes were badly damaged as a result of a Federal cavalry skirmish with a Confederate patrol earlier in the day. Passing through the small town, the brigade turned off the Hagerstown road and headed southwest. Late in the day they set up camp, while thundering cannon again echoed through the hillsides ahead of them.

The following morning there were rumors that the 125th would finally engage the enemy, but once more the only sounds of battle came from artillery divisions somewhere in the distance. Since there were no orders to march for the first time in several days, the men had an opportunity to rest their weary feet.

Joe and Jon had little chance for a break, however. Dr. Feay managed to keep them extremely busy for the greater part of the day, aiding with the latest arrival of medical supplies. They also helped pitch hospital tents and searched for straw, fuel, and water. Then, as their final task, they were given the grim chore of helping to prepare headboards for grave markers.

After taps that evening, it appeared that they would at last get a good night's rest; but they had not been asleep even a half hour when Captain Colter shook them.

"Let's go, boys!" he called. "Get those drums! We just got orders to move out; this is it!"

Chapter 11

Under Fire

By midnight the regiment was on the move with instructions not to speak above a whisper, and to arrange their equipment in such a manner as to prevent it from rattling in any way. Since the drums were to be silent also, Captain Colter ordered Joe and Jon to ride in one of the wagons; and before long they crossed a stream which their driver said was probably the Antietam Creek. About an hour later, the regiment set up camp as noiselessly as possible. However, because of scattered firing, it was almost impossible to sleep.

Neither drums nor bugles sounded reveille when dawn began to erase the darkness. It was a quiet, ominous awakening that seemed even to forecast danger. A light drizzle had fallen during the early morning hours; but the gray, misty skies were now showing signs of clearing.

Joe and Jon were having breakfast under Manny's watchful eye, when completely without warning, the roar of nearby Federal cannon threatened to shatter their eardrums! Neither boy ever finished eating, for in a few moments officers were racing here and there, shouting for the buglers and drummers to sound *Assembly.* Almost miraculously the regiment somehow managed to form, even though the company clerks were unable to take roll call because of the near-deafening noise of the constantly roaring guns. Within minutes, however, the exceedingly anxious125th Pennsylvania was the first unit of the Twelfth Corps ready to advance. Then, with Colonel Higgins leading the way, they began moving in the direction of the battlefield, Joe and Jon beating their drums sharply, nearly keeping pace with the pounding of their hearts!

Soon the other regiments were behind them, tramping through the dampness across alternate areas of open field and stands of timber, only dimly lighted by the breaking dawn. Since frequent orders to halt were passed along in the wooded areas, it took nearly an hour to reach the field of battle. Intermittently, exploding cannon balls landed around the corps as it proceeded; but they suffered no direct hits. As they approached one section of woods, Joe watched with concern as Union wounded straggled toward them, away from the battle area.

Later, as they were about to leave the protection of still another wooded area, Joe gazed in awe at the tremendous struggle going on before them. The land sloped gently downward; and a few hundred yards distant, Union forces were firing toward their gray-clad enemy at the far end of the field. To the left, some small farm buildings were burning furiously, belching tall columns of black smoke.

When he looked again toward the battlefield, he saw a lone rider racing toward them, lashing his reins from side to side in a frenzied effort to urge more speed from his mount. Coming to a halt directly in front of Joe and Company A, he called out instantly, "Who's in command here?"

"I am!" responded General Mansfield himself, as he came riding out of some nearby brush immediately to Joe's left.

The rider saluted and spoke quickly. "General Hooker's in the field just ahead, sir, an' requests assistance at once!"

Taking a folded paper which he was carrying inside one of his gloves, he handed it to the commander.

After reading it hastily, the general looked directly at Joe and ordered, "Drummer! *Double Quick*! An' when we attack, keep that long roll goin'!"

"Yes, sir!" Joe answered, snapping a smart salute.

Then the officer reeled in his saddle and waved his arm in a forward motion, as Joe simultaneously thrust his arms, hands and nimble fingers into action.

With a piercing yell, shouted almost in unison, the 125th emerged from the woods and descended the slope, their ravening hunger for action climaxed at long last! Soon, they were rushing through a small orchard where enemy artillery fire became more severe with each running step, sending showers of dirt upon them.

Then, suddenly, they were face to face with the enemy! At first there were only a few of them: a thin line of skirmishers who were momentarily separated from the main body of Confederates. Seeing they were out-numbered, they turned and fled for the security of some nearby woods, Company A pursuing them, as Joe drummed at Sergeant Abbott's heels.

At one point, amid the confusion and exchanges of volleys, Company B surged ahead. The entire regiment had nearly covered the two hundred yards separating them from the woods, when enemy muskets began to bark from the trees and brush lying directly ahead.

An infantryman running beside Jon, suddenly screamed, dropped his weapon and fell to his knees. For a few seconds he clasped his hands to his blood-spattered face, then reeled and collapsed convulsingly upon his back.

Jon stopped and simply stared helplessly at the fallen rifleman, while others rushed past. Then, feeling a momentary tug at his arm, he turned to see Joe.

"C'mon, Jon!" he shouted. "There's nothin' we can do for him! Hurry, or you'll lose your company!"

Shaking himself from his temporary daze, Jon turned and dashed forward to regain his position just as Company B reached the woods. Movement was slower among the trees and undergrowth; and in the distance, the Confederates in retreat were scurrying to keep ahead of the larger Union forces following doggedly in their tracks. Shortly, the regiment came to a large corn field, where Lieutenant Stewart finally called a halt.

Trying to catch his breath, Joe sat with his back to a tree, gazing at the field. A close look revealed scores of lifeless blue and gray forms lying half hidden among the trampled stalks. Evidently the corn field had been a bloody arena earlier in the morning, and Joe wished above all else that it wouldn't have to be entered again. However, even at that very instant, on their left flank, he caught a glimpse of Federal troops trampling through the underbrush and moving cautiously into the corn field. He saw a color-bearer carrying the flag of the 46th Pennsylvania and felt relieved that the 125th hadn't been ordered to advance first. He watched as they rushed in crouching positions from the woods, their muskets ready.

During the lull that followed, Joe realized he was thirsty and reached for his canteen. But just as he gulped his first thirst-quenching swallow from the container, he was suddenly jolted by the concussion of an exploding cannon ball, which landed less than a hundred feet from where he was sitting. In an instant he was behind the tree, flat on his stomach. Then came another, and still another. At the same time, the corn field became a constant roar of blood-curdling Rebel yells and musket fire. Evidently the Confederates had been hoping that an unsuspecting Union force would once more enter the field.

Then Joe had the fright of a lifetime! His right hand detected a soaking dampness along his side. Fearful that he had been injured by the first explosion without realizing it, he looked, half expecting to see a blood-stained coat; but he sighed with relief when he saw his still uncapped canteen lying over a protruding tree root and slowly gurgling its contents upon him.

With still another sigh, he capped it quickly. But at the same time he glanced toward the field where he saw a saber cut a menacing swath through the air above the corn, and off to the right he saw rifle butts being swung like clubs. He swallowed hard when he realized that his own regiment could have been sent there, and now the heavy artillery fire made it impossible for anyone to go to the aid of the 46th.

Joe lay for a long time with his left arm covering his head, while cannon balls and canister seemed to pound the earth endlessly, even as his heart felt like it would burst right through his chest!

Then, amid all the uproar and bedlam, his mother's parting words at the Columbia Railroad Station slowly eased through his mind: <There's Someone who has said He'll always be with you.>

Then, in spite of his chaotic situation, Joe slowly smiled to himself and mentally repeated those words several times, before lapsing into prayer for protection. And not surprisingly, within moments his jangled nerves and extreme anxiety gradually began to settle down. The incredible beating of his heart also slowed its pace, his alert mind cleared, and he found peace, even in the midst of the most terrifying moments of his life.

After nearly half an hour, the bombardment finally ceased. Joe noticed that the sounds of musketry in the corn field weren't as heavy as before, but still the fighting continued there.

At that moment, this time somewhere off to his right, another drummer sounded *Advance;* and rushing from the woods came the 128th Pennsylvania Volunteers, easily recognizable by their white haversacks glistening in the morning sun.

As the 128th disappeared among the remaining stalks, Joe heard hoof beats behind him. Rolling onto his left side, he peered over the top of his drum and saw General Mansfield, stopping for a moment to gaze across the corn tassels. Then, clucking to his steed, he glided toward the section of the field where the 128th had so recently disappeared. Ominously, there seemed to be a momentary lull in the fighting. Suddenly, a lone shot rang out; and at practically the same instant, the general clutched at his throat and slowly toppled from his saddle.

Instinctively Joe leaped to his feet in an effort to rush forward, when a strong hand firmly grasped his shoulder and pushed him vigorously back to the ground.

"Stay where you are, Shelley!" came Sergeant Abbott's stern voice.

Obediently Joe watched as the sergeant and three other men raced to the general's side. Carefully they carried him on some muskets to the shelter of the woods and laid him on his back, while two others hurried in quest of a litter. Shortly, they carried their commanding officer on a blanket to the rear; and Joe never saw him again.

Within minutes someone else evidently had assumed command, for now the 125th was ordered to take the death-laden corn field. At the sight of the utter carnage now piled in heaps before his very eyes, Joe felt a sudden, uncontrollable nervousness churning in his abdomen, as he tapped *Advance* and stepped forward cautiously. They had gone less than twenty yards when Lieutenant Stewart ordered him to signal a left flank movement, directing the regiment southward. Joe kept his eyes constantly on the ground, since so many soldiers of both armies lay in the field that it was difficult to walk without treading upon them, their agonizing looks of death sending a giddying sickness streaming throughout his mid-section.

At any moment he expected to hear the same rousing Rebel yells that had greeted the 46th; but slowly they picked their way through the field, failing to encounter any enemy gunfire whatsoever. It was evident that the southern end of the field had seen no action, for there the stalks remained in perfect rows.

When they halted at the edge of the field, a group of officers gathered. Joe could hear them discussing the situation as they surveyed the open fields before them, where hundreds of slain and wounded had already fallen.

Few trees dotted the landscape, but there were countless formations of rock jutting from the ground at all angles; and a lone white

church lay in the distance, embraced by a stand of trees. In front of it Joe barely distinguished some gray-uniformed men milling about a solitary cannon, evidently preparing for any assault which might come their way.

At that moment Lieutenant Stewart shouted, "*Double Quick!*"

Joe responded promptly and the regiment dashed among the furrows toward a Union battery which had recently begun firing at the enemy positions near the white building. Almost spontaneously a roar belched from the Confederate gun in front of the church, as well as from others on the hills to the northwest. As whistling canister and cannon balls rained among them, everyone fell flat, some in shrieking pain. From the cries of the men around him, Joe knew that some had been seriously wounded and others possibly killed outright. As a natural reaction, he balanced his drum on the ridge of a furrow and let it rest partly on his head, in order to take advantage of what little protection it offered.

Suddenly his thoughts turned to Jon. Although he hadn't seen him either enter or leave the corn field, he was almost certain that Company B had been directly behind or beside his own.

After nearly fifteen minutes of constant bombardment, the ground and the air finally stopped throbbing. Joe raised his head to look for Sergeant Abbott, but all the figures lying on the ground appeared to look alike. Then, surprisingly, as men started racing past without any given signals whatsoever, among this general confusion, Joe scrambled to his feet and began looking on both sides and to the rear for Jon. Not only couldn't he see his companion, but neither could he see signs of even one drummer anywhere. However, as he turned to join the others in their mad rush forward, he finally caught a fleeting glimpse of his friend about fifty yards ahead of him, flying pell-mell toward a distant roadbed, where he leaped over a split-rail fence and an embankment and quickly disappeared from sight, his drum sailing right behind him.

At that very moment heavy artillery began to blaze still another time. Disappointed at having lost his own chance to get across the open field, he dived again for the soft earth and then crawled forward and lay behind a massive outcrop of grayish-white rock.

There, rather well protected for the moment, he winced at the hissing screams of musket balls, grapeshot and canister, as he waited hopefully for another opportunity to escape. When he finally scampered from the field nearly a half hour later, he found Jon waiting anxiously amid some of the few trees bordering the field.

They hardly had a moment to speak to one another before Lieutenant Stewart called and set them to the task of helping the companies regroup. As they drummed their signals, Joe noted that the Union battery had silenced the Confederate gun near the church, and a long-awaited peacefulness gradually floated across the countryside.

Soon the companies were re-formed and on their way, this time setting their course toward the woods beyond the church. However, their first objective was a pike which ran in front of the timbered area. As they neared a fence bordering the road, some Confederates began firing from behind the countless, mortally-wounded men dressed in both blue and gray, who lay singly, or piled in heaps, all along the railings. Some of the dead were spread-eagled across the rails, evidently killed in their attempt to escape the bloody battlefield.

Charging relentlessly, the 125th quickly drove the men in butternut and gray toward the woods, advancing with such ease that victory seemed certain. As the last of the Rebels disappeared among the trees, the regiment came to a halt just beyond the pike. Company G advanced as skirmishers toward the woods, while Jon and his company were ordered in the direction of the church. Joe watched as his comrade and his sergeant led Company B back toward the pike, heading ultimately for the small white building. However, just as the remainder of the regiment prepared to follow the skirmish line, heavy enemy artillery fire began to stream into the area from the fields far to the northwest; and musket balls struck the dust like raindrops on the surface of a lake, sending everyone scurrying for the protection of the rocks.

The rear section of Company B had not yet cleared the pike, when seemingly out of nowhere came three horses at full speed, each pulling a Union cannon. Joe watched horrified as one of the gun limbers hit a crater in the road, careened wildly, upset, and then flew with all its force directly into the last row of men in Company B, who never had a chance to get out of its way! Joe shut his eyes in both disgust and agony, shaking his head in disbelief, as his abdominal muscles and heart wrenched violently within him!

But hardly had this occurred, before he realized that a wave of Confederate soldiers, who had been hiding in another woods a few hundred yards away, were swarming toward them! Hurriedly

Company G's skirmishers fell back to strengthen the fire coming from the main body of the regiment. Much to Joe's relief, the marksmanship of the 125th proved to be extremely deadly, slowing the Confederate advance considerably. Joe saw Slade King fire confidently and watch his target stumble to the turf; but then, when his musket became fouled, he was forced to pound his ramrod home with a rock in order to reload.

At that moment Joe heard drum signals, and turned to see Jon and Company B returning from the church area to lend their aid, the men scurrying for protective positions among the outcrops. Joe yelled for Jon when he was within earshot; and the two of them crept behind a natural embankment, resting against one of the countless rocks which seemed to be everywhere. A group of perhaps twenty men sought the same refuge, while Lieutenant Stewart shouted orders.

They drove back the first wave of Confederates; but hardly were they repulsed before a second charge came streaming across the fields, filling the air with gut-wrenching Rebel yells. As the men stood to fire over the ridge of their natural protective fortress, Joe peered cautiously over a rock in order to watch the progress of the battle. It was then that the movement of some men just yards away, along the sunken pike area, caught his eye; and he turned to see them crouch over those who had been struck by the gun limber only a few minutes previously. Suddenly, Joe closed his eyes in agony, when he realized that one of them was Jon's father!

He fleetingly looked at Jon, whose attention was arrested for the moment by some debris he was attempting to empty from one of his boots.

Fortunately, at that moment Joe felt a tug at his elbow and turned to see a bewhiskered man resting on one knee. Joe recognized him as one of the regimental fifers, too old to fight, but ageless when it was a question of patriotism.

"C'mon, sonny," he pleaded, fingering his fife. "These boys need a little encouragement. Let's give 'em some fightin' music!"

It was the perfect opportunity to keep Jon from possibly looking in the direction of the pike. Joe nodded to the old-timer and said, "Go ahead; you start. Me an' Jon'll pick it up."

With a nod of his head, the bewhiskered fifer rose to his feet, his nimble fingers beginning to pour forth *Red, White, and Blue* with as

BOT
RODA

much enthusiasm as he could muster from his aging lungs.

Quickly, Joe and Jon combined their musical talents with his; and even without realizing it, their stirring efforts served not only to inspire the men around them, but to take their minds from the incredible danger as well.

At one point, while Lieutenant Stewart was reloading his pistol, he caught Joe's eye and nodded his head in approval. "Keep playin', men!" he urged. "It not only gives us somethin' to fight for, but it gives me the goose bumps besides!"

With the fife and drums ringing in their ears, the 125th broke this second wave of grays, though it was evident that even more Confederate reinforcements were being hurled against them. Later, a third attack nearly overran them but failed to continue its drive, bringing a welcome break in the action.

Just as the fifer and the boys struck up *Rally 'Round the Flag*, out of the corner of his eye Joe saw some men carrying Jon's father back toward the corn field and the rear lines. At the same time Union reinforcements came from the direction of the pike. However, their numbers were few; and lack of ammunition made it evident that if another attack came, they probably couldn't withstand it.

While the men looked in vain for others to join them, they took advantage of this momentary lull in the battle to reload, as well as to wash the dust from their severely parched throats by gulping quaffs of refreshing water from their canteens.

For nearly five minutes, except for the sounds of fife and drum, there was practically complete silence. Then, with another chorus of high-pitched Rebel yells, the Confederates sprang a massive fourth attack.

Hearing the lieutenant relay the order to fall back, the boys tapped *Retreat* even as they began to run, racing to the fence they had so recently scaled. Joe saw Slade King vault the obstacle, turn and fire; but he had no time to reload, for the Confederates were practically screaming down their necks!

However, as they rushed across the open field, Joe saw a welcome sight! In front of them was a Federal artillery unit, swinging field pieces into position. Two officers were galloping toward the regiment, urging the 125th to re-form its lines behind the cannon, since they were aimed low and couldn't be discharged until the infantrymen were out of the line of fire.

With the Federals retreating before them, the Confederates failed to see the heavy guns, already generously primed with canister and grapeshot. Then, as the 125th dashed past the field pieces, the grays suddenly found themselves staring point blank down the barrels of more than a dozen cannon. Joe turned in time to see an artillery officer swoop the point of his sword to the ground as a signal to fire, and then closed his eyes in horror after he witnessed the gallant Confederate lines being torn almost completely to shreds by the screaming fusillade of pellets and shrapnel, hurtling through the air with incredible force!

After the smoke lifted, he gazed across the field, where now less than a third of the enemy was swarming in hasty retreat toward the woods, leaving scores of dead and writhing wounded. Both boys sank to their knees, too winded and terrified to utter a word!

Very slowly, the men of the 125th began to catch their breath and regain their composure, many of them yelling both their encouragement and gratitude to the artillerymen who unquestionably had just saved their lives. But although they had been forced to retreat, they were justifiably proud of the fact that no other Federal unit had penetrated the Confederate lines so deeply, untried in battle though their regiment may have been.

At length, the remaining officers sounded forth the call to regroup the companies; and only then did they learn that two of the regiment's drummers had been killed and two others seriously wounded.

As they sounded the rataplan for *Assembly,* Joe kept watching Jon carefully as his pal was obviously craning his neck to scan the troops of Company B, hoping to catch a glimpse of his father. As soon as the signal was given to cease drumming, Jon began to rush here and there among the men, asking excitedly if anyone had seen him.

Joe scurried to his friend's side and threw his arm around his shoulders. "I think your pa's hurt, Jon; I saw some men carryin' him to the rear, but I didn't wanna tell you till now. We had enough problems on our minds!"

For several moments, Jon simply stared blankly into Joe's eyes, unable to speak, his face suddenly turning pale as he gradually sank to one knee. Joe quickly knelt beside him, one arm still around him.

"I'm sure he's alive, Jon! Or they wouldn't've taken him back like they did! He's prob'ly at the hospital area right now, an' you *know* Doctor Feay'll take *real* good care of him!" Joe said, trying to encourage his buddy as much as possible.

Slowly Jon lifted his head and looked again into his friend's eyes. "I hope you're right!" he responded, choking back tears and sighing heavily with each breath.

A half hour later, the regiment, now baptized in battle, retired wearily in the direction from which it had attacked many hours earlier, though battered and depleted of many of its troops.

After finally reaching a wooded haven, they halted in order that some could attend the slightly wounded as best they could; and others were detailed to the Sanitation Corps to help remove the hundreds of dead and severely wounded from the surrounding fields. Although the fighting was over for the 125th, they could tell by the sounds of heavy bombardment to the south, that the struggle was far from ended.

Later, as the battle-worn regiment eventually came into sight of the main encampment, Joe saw their head musician rushing toward them.

The officer spoke first to Lieutenant Stewart. "Drummer Cooper's father's badly injured, lieutenant; an' he wants to see his boy!"

"By all means! Take him with you!" the lieutenant replied instantly. Then turning, he yelled, "Break ranks!"

Captain Colter took Joe by the arm and said, "This'll be tough for Jon! You'd better come along!"

When they turned to head for Company B, Jon was already running toward them. The captain reached out, put his arm around his young shoulders and said, "Come along quick, Jon. Your pa wants to see you!"

Jon shot a concerned look at Joe before they tucked their drums under their arms and began to trot with Captain Colter toward the hospital area. When they arrived, Doctor Feay was scurrying about, shouting orders in all directions; but as soon as he saw the captain and the boys, he stopped what he was doing and led them to a nearby wagon that served as an ambulance.

Looking straight at Jon he said, "Your father's hurt bad, son! We'll have to send him to a hospital in Frederick right away. Don't take long because every minute counts!"

Quickly the three of them stepped to the wagonload of wounded, where Jon's father was lying at the rear gate, his head resting on a bed of straw. One look at his face showed that he was obviously enduring great stress. Nevertheless, he forced a smile.

"Looks like . . . I'm gonna have a pair o' bad legs for a spell, son," he whispered loudly, speaking through clenched teeth.

Jon instinctively looked toward the lower part of his father's body; but Mr. Cooper had made certain that his legs were covered with a blanket, not wanting his son to see the full extent of his injuries.

Perspiring profusely and gasping in short breaths, Mr. Cooper grimaced with pain and said, "Cap'n Colter, sir . . . you're practically like a father to him already . . . so I'd like to ask you . . . to keep lookin' out for him while I'm gone . . . Will you, please?"

"Of course, I will!" the captain assured him. "You don't need to worry about that for a moment!" he added, soberly accepting the responsibility that was being conferred upon him.

Then looking again at his son, but pointing weakly toward Joe, Mr. Cooper said, "An' this guy . . . has to be the greatest big brother . . . anybody could ever ask for!" He managed another smile. "You keep stickin' close to him, Jon . . . An' both o' you . . . keep bein' the best drummer boys in the whole army . . . like you showed today!"

At that moment, Doctor Feay interrupted. "I'm sorry, but we just can't wait any longer!" Then looking at the driver he called, "Get this wagon to a hospital in Frederick as fast as you can possibly get there!"

Jon and his father quickly embraced for a few seconds before the wagon had a chance to move. Then, as the forward motion of the ambulance thrust them apart, Jon's arms fell limply by his side; and he wept, feeling utterly lost and helpless, as the wagon began the long journey.

As Joe's eyes also began to fill with tears, he looked to one side in time to see Doctor Feay catch Captain Colter's attention; and as the surgeon slowly shook his head hopelessly, Joe's heart sank!

The captain and Joe stood on either side of the youthful drummer, the officer's arm around his shoulders and Joe's around his waist. As they watched the wagon gradually disappear from view, all three were completely at a loss for words.

At last, as the ambulance finally drove out of sight, Captain Colter spoke. "Well . . . as your substitute father, I can tell you in an instant that the best way to get your mind off your troubles, is to get it occupied with other things. So both of you get some food in your stomachs, an' then go see how you can help out around here any way you can. An' those are orders!" he said, but casting a half-smile in their direction.

"Yes, sir," Joe replied in a somewhat uncharacteristically subdued tone of voice. Then, looking at Jon, he wiped away his tears, managed a smile and said, "C'mon, darn it! I always wanted a little brother to pal around with anyhow!"

Slowly, the impish Cooper grin forced its way across Jon's face, beginning to help dissipate more tears that he had been trying so hard to restrain.

The two of them headed straight for Manny, who spoiled them as best he could, especially after seeing that they had returned safe and sound.

Soon the boys were back in the fields, wending their way among the dead horses and damaged artillery wagons. They labored all afternoon, helping to bury the dead and escorting the wounded to the hospital area; and then, far into the early evening hours, they worked side by side with Captain Colter, helping Doctor Feay.

It was during this time that they heard a rumor that President Lincoln had come to meet with General McClellan. Joe and Jon kept on the alert, hoping to see him; but unfortunately, their seemingly never-ending work kept them from catching even a glimpse of him.

It was after midnight when the doctor saw how fatigued the boys were. "Captain, I think these two young men deserve a hard-earned rest!" he observed, motioning in their direction.

The captain looked at them and nodded in agreement. "Yes, sir; an' I'd just like to say that I've heard all kinds o' comments from Lieutenant Stewart right on down to the sergeants and the enlisted men. They're all talkin' about the way you two handled everything out there today. You musta really done a job! I'm proud of you!" he said, reaching to give them each an extremely firm handshake.

Somewhat embarrassed but obviously encouraged by the captain's remarks, the boys thanked him and decided to head for their sleeping area. As soon as Jon stepped outside the huge tent, before Joe could follow him, Captain Colter seized his elbow and whispered, "This has been a really tough day for Jon! Keep an eye on him!"

"I will, sir!" Joe assured him. "An' don't worry! There's Someone else keepin' an eye on us too!" he added, looking upward.

The captain smiled and nodded. "You've got a lotta things goin' for you, young man; an' that's one o' the most important!"

It was sometime during the very early morning hours when the boys finally found an unoccupied place in the damp grass to unroll their bedding.

"I sure wish we coulda seen the president, don't you?" Jon remarked, as he spread his poncho on the ground, but speaking more in an effort to try to get his mind off his father than for any other reason.

"Yeah," Joe replied, "but who knows? Maybe we'll get a chance to see him some other time."

The odor of gunpowder continued to pervade the air, and the stars near the horizon were dimmed by the heavy haze that continued to cling stubbornly near some distant treetops. As the boys lay unusually quiet side by side, simply staring at the heavens, gradually the horrors of the most difficult day of their young lives began to flash through their minds; and they found sleep to be completely impossible despite their total weariness.

Joe could tell that his friend was especially restless. He was about to ask him a question, when he realized that the emotion-packed day had evidently caught up with Jon; and he knew by the slight sounds he was making, that he was actually trying desperately to keep from crying.

"Are you all right, Jon?" he whispered at last.

"I . . . guess so," he answered haltingly, but with obviously tear-choked words. "Thunder . . . an' tarnation! What an incredible day!" And then, unable to hold back his tears, he began to cry outright.

"Go ahead, buddy; just let 'em rip!" Joe said, his own voice becoming husky. "It's nothin' to be ashamed of. I got a few tears inside me that are just bustin' to come out too!"

They were both silent for a few minutes, simply allowing their drained emotions to run their natural course, tears gently flowing out of the corners of their eyes from time to time.

Finally, Jon confided, "Every time I close my eyes . . . I see my pa!"

"I guess that's the most natural thing in the world," Joe assured him. "That only proves how much he means to you, Jon! But he'll be all right; I just know it! They'll take *real* good care of him at Frederick. You'll see," he remarked, trying to encourage him once more.

Then after another period of silence, Jon spoke again. "Joe?" he whispered in an inquiring tone of voice.

"Yeah?"

"I guess . . . " But his voice broke again before he continued. "I guess . . . I'm really gonna need . . . a big brother!"

Joe sat up slightly, leaned on one elbow and peered through the darkness toward his buddy. "Well . . . I'll tell you somethin', Jon. I got a big brother. Had one all my life. An' the whole time I was growin' up, whenever things got tough or seemed to go wrong . . . at night I'd just go climb in his bed, he'd wrap his big arms around me, an' just pray . . . pray till we both fell asleep in the arms o' the Lord."

And even as he spoke, Joe reached out with both hands, pulled Jon's bedroll right up against his own, slowly extended his arms to wrap them around his "little brother," and began to pray as fervently as he ever did in his life!

Chapter 12

An Unexpected Guest

The following day a truce was called for the purpose of interring the dead. Again the boys helped with the grim task, working side by side with burying details from Confederate divisions as well as with civilians from nearby Sharpsburg.

On Friday morning, however, there was an early reveille, since it was expected that the struggle would be resumed. A chilly fog made the task of assembly a miserable one, and the boys were wondering if they had sufficient stamina to make it through another day of battle. Then, just before the officers were prepared to give orders to march, a messenger brought information that the enemy had retreated across the Potomac during the night.

The men received the news with mixed emotions. Some were elated and declared the battle a victory. Others were dejected, for they were looking forward to settling some scores from Wednesday's encounter.

After burying some Confederate soldiers who had been left in the fields, the regiment, as part of the Twelfth Corps, advanced to the town of Sharpsburg. Of all the marches Joe had made thus far, this one was the most unpleasant. The carcasses of the many horses killed in the battle had been set afire, making breathing almost unbearable; and Joe found himself actually holding his breath for long periods in an effort to escape the stench.

Then later, as they passed through Sharpsburg, dead or wounded Confederate soldiers lay on the lawn or porch of nearly every home.

The battle at Antietam Creek had been a costly one for both armies.

After marching the entire day, the corps camped near the Potomac. Captain Colter helped Joe and Jon build a fire before they all settled down to a practically tasteless meal of hardtack, bacon, and coffee. Then the boys took advantage of a peaceful evening to write some letters. Joe wrote to his family, telling them most especially of the unfortunate incident involving Jon's father. While Joe was concentrating on his letter, Jon sat down with his back right up against Joe's, also using the light from the campfire to help him write to both his father and Sarah.

Once again they were forced to bed down without benefit of a tent, since many of the regimental supplies still had not caught up to them; and after the difficult time they had experienced the night before, Joe asked both the captain and Chaplain Stewart if they would set up camp beside them. The men's presence, as well as the return of some singing and banjo and fiddle music around some of the nearby campfires, all had their calming effect; and the boys were quick to fall asleep, Captain Colter and two other drummers taking care of tattoo and taps.

After their march the next day, several regiments pitched their tents at the foot of Maryland Heights near Harpers Ferry. While they camped in this area, the men found time to reassemble their drilling unit, though some were absent and would never march again. Jon especially missed his father being at the practice sessions and hoped he would be back one day. However, men from other depleted regiments helped fill in the ranks of the 125th; and several new members volunteered for Captain Colter's special squad.

The captain had contrived all sorts of clever formations and movements for the men to perform when Joe and Jon simultaneously tapped certain drum beats as signals. Everyone practiced fervently in order to attain split-second timing; and after hours of dedicated effort over a period of several days, their precision and snappy moves began to bring men from the entire brigade to the edges of the field, where they watched as the unit performed its intricate, well-timed maneuvers.

Joe could tell that Jon was in the doldrums and still considerably worried. He knew that Monday would be Jon's fifteenth birthday; so along with the captain and Manny, they planned some special treats for him after the evening practice. However, even those efforts did very little to cheer him. Unfortunately, not having his father with him on his birthday for the first time in his life, actually made it a somewhat sad occasion for the young drummer boy.

On Wednesday evening, exactly a week after the battle at Antietam Creek, Captain Colter called to the boys as soon as their drill session was finished. Joe had noticed that his commanding officer was exceptionally quiet that evening, and was wearing an extremely somber expression, as he said in a rather strange tone of voice, "How 'bout gettin' your bedrolls an' personal things, an' comin' along with me? Leave your drums here with the orderly."

After the boys handed their instruments to the corporal, they looked at the captain and then at one another rather inquisitively for a few moments, but did as he suggested without asking any questions. Several minutes later, the captain insisted on taking their bedrolls from them, as the boys slung their haversacks over their backs; and then they began strolling leisurely through the camp together. All the while, the captain's strange, uncustomary quietness was beginning to upset Joe to some degree, as his usually active mind was endeavoring to determine what was happening.

Eventually they approached Chaplain Stewart's quarters. When Joe realized where the captain was leading them, he suddenly felt a strong, foreboding sensation come over him, and instantly glanced sideways at Jon. As they came nearer the chaplain's large Sibley tent, they could see him sitting at his small desk, looking toward them through the open flap.

Suddenly, Jon stopped. When Joe and the captain did likewise, the youngster slowly turned his head to look his commanding officer directly in the eye.

"Why are we comin' to see the chaplain?" he asked in a hushed tone. Then, in the next moment, an extremely frightened look flashed across his young face. "It's about my pa, ain't it?" he nearly shouted, profound fear inflected in his voice.

The look on Captain Colter's face answered Jon's question immediately, as the officer merely stared in somewhat of a daze into Jon's brilliantly blue eyes for several moments, totally unable to utter even one word. Finally, with tears beginning to cloud his vision, the captain closed his eyes momentarily, as he simply began to nod his head.

By this time Chaplain Stewart had come from his tent to meet them, and easily overheard Jon's last words. Fully realizing that it was his place to respond, he faced the lad squarely, put his hands on his slender shoulders and said, "Let's go inside and talk, shall we?"

But Jon never moved. His lips were already quivering; and even as his eyes began to fill with tears, he said with choking words, "Pa died in the hospital, didn't he?"

Chaplain Stewart's arms dropped to his sides like heavy weights. Laboriously, he heaved an exceptionally long sigh and said, "Yes, Jon. It's been awfully difficult for us even to think of having to share this with you. We just received a dispatch late this afternoon informing us of what happened!"

Almost instinctively, Jon suddenly lunged toward Joe, wrapped his arms around him, and buried his head against his chest, sobbing heavily. As Joe looked helplessly through his own tears, across Jon's shoulder at the chaplain and Captain Colter, he embraced his friend with the tightest hug he had ever offered anyone.

"Go ahead an' cry, little brother!" he whispered. "I'll join you!" And they wept together unashamedly in one another's arms, as both officers stepped toward them and tenderly placed their hands on the boys' shoulders.

It was a difficult evening to say the least. Chaplain Stewart spent quite a while sharing comforting words and various passages of the Bible, especially with young Jon.

As he finished, he said, "It's probably difficult to see it now, Jon; but . . . God has the strangest ways of bringing something good out of even the darkest situations!"

"That's right, Jon," Joe agreed, throwing an arm around his shoulders. "That's the way it works! You'll see!"

Then Captain Colter read a letter that Jon's father had written just before his death, giving permission for Jon to remain with the regiment and even extend his enlistment, if he eventually wished to make the army his career. However, he made it clear that all decisions were to be his son's, although both the captain and the chaplain were requested to advise him in any way they felt necessary.

"Now," the chaplain remarked when the captain finished, "Colonel Higgins wants the two of you to sleep here at least for the next several nights. Captain Colter and I'll be right here with you till things begin to settle down to normal again."

By the end of September, time was beginning to heal the boys mentally and emotionally, and Jon gradually showed signs of becoming more like his impish self. Joe, meanwhile, had been certain to write to his family to tell them of his friend's great misfortune.

During those days supply wagons rolled into camp with food, tents, blankets, overcoats, knapsacks, and the most popular items of all - bags of mail. There were packages containing anything from pickles and broma to stockings and round-headed nails for shoes. However, the boys were especially grateful for the letters the company clerks passed their way.

Not long after receiving them, they were together in their own tent once more, and sat down to enjoy their mail.

"So you heard from my sister again!" Joe teased, as he watched Jon open the envelope. "Boy! This is gettin' pretty serious, I'd say!"

Jon gave him a playful punch on the arm. "Just you hush and take care o' your own mail, sonny!" he said in a strained, squeaky voice, trying to imitate a stern, almost grandmother-like expression.

Joe grinned, happy to see his friend acting more like himself once more, and pretended to read his own letter while actually watching Jon out of the corner of his eye for a few moments. His buddy was obviously just as totally engrossed in the contents of this letter as he was with the other he had received. Then, just as he had done before, when he was finished reading, he tucked the letter carefully away with the one that was already in his jacket pocket.

After Joe read his own letter, he looked at Jon and said, "Ma wrote to the Murphys just like I thought she would. I figured she'd appreciate what they did for us. She says she's gonna write to Cap'n Colter too."

"What for? Or shouldn't I ask?" Jon inquired.

"Who knows? You know what mothers are like . . ." Then, catching himself in a blunder, Joe apologized. "I'm sorry, Jon. I didn't mean . . ."

Jon just shook his head and smiled. "Don't worry about it!" he said. "I'm use' to it."

The fresh supplies of government food brought a welcome change in diet. The meat, bread, canned milk, and tea especially went a long way toward lifting the regiment's morale.

The day after the new supplies were received, Joe and Jon were seated near the fire, where Manny Welles was faithfully stirring a huge kettle of soup.

"Just wait'll you Jay Birds let this roll over yer gums!" Manny chirped in his squeaky voice, and adding a shake of his head for emphasis. "You'll think you was back home ag'in!" And he laughed his gleeful chuckle.

Jon grinned and reached into a carton for a cracker to satisfy his hunger until the soup was ready. However, after taking a bite, he stared in wide-eyed amazement at the piece he held in his hand. With a gasp he spit out what he was chewing; for slowly curling through an opening in the cracker, came a small, ugly, brownish worm!

Manny and Joe both turned to see what was causing all the commotion, while Jon looked at Manny in disgust!

"Thunder an' tarnation, Manny!" he complained. "I like crackers an' I like meat; but when I get 'em both together an' the meat's still alive, then things're pretty bad, I'd say!"

"What in thunderation you talkin' 'bout, Little Jay Bird?" demanded Manny, stepping toward the lad. The cook was still confusing the two boys' names; and since both begin with the same letter of the alphabet, he had recently solved his identification problem by beginning to call Joe "Big Jay Bird" and Jon "Little Jay Bird."

Jon held out the cracker and waved it gently before Manny's unbelieving eyes for a few seconds, before the cook angrily snatched it from Jon's hand. Then the boys shook with laughter as Manny raced excitedly through the camp, warning everyone not to touch the shipment of crackers unless they wanted to catch the *hydrophobee*!

For the next several days, the 125th's quartermaster did his best to keep out of the men's sight, since he was responsible for all their supplies. Everyone was jokingly accusing him of trying to "poison" the regiment, swearing that they were going to send the boys out with the wagons to forage for food once more.

Pay day finally arrived and was rapidly followed by another rash of petty thefts. Most of the men took measures to safeguard their pay after what had happened previously, but some of the less careful were soon parted with their earnings. Several sutlers continued to travel with the regiment, carrying all sorts of goods in their wagons; and now that the men had some money to purchase tobacco, pies, cakes, biscuits and other items, they looked forward to buying some of these goods. Once again Company A suffered the most losses, and those whose money had disappeared were understandably angry.

The men were becoming suspicious of one another; and after Slade King had lost all eleven dollars for yet a second time, he convinced some of the others that the company officers should again be told of the thefts. However, as had happened in August, even though another inspection and search resulted, once again nothing was found.

"I sure am glad Cap'n Colter's keepin' *our* money!" Jon remarked as they returned to their tent. "This place ain't exactly as safe as the Columbia Bank!"

The following Saturday the boys asked the captain for some of their funds and received permission to go to Harpers Ferry. Even before they left camp, they were offered a ride in one of the wagons headed for town to pick up supplies. Several weeks earlier the area had been hit heavily by Confederate artillery, and Joe was fearful that no stores would be open for business. The boys knew that the next day was Captain Colter's birthday, and they wanted to surprise him with a gift.

Fortunately, they came upon a store which had escaped damage; and they decided to browse a while. After considering a number of articles, they decided to purchase a leather tobacco pouch. As Jon waited at the counter for the clerk to wrap their gift with some brown paper, Joe was looking at the display in the front window.

While he was admiring a hunting knife, he happened to look across the street and saw a soldier scurrying from an alleyway. By his build and the manner in which he moved, Joe was certain it was Slade King. He was carrying some type of bundle under his left arm; and apparently he must've been running for quite a while, for he appeared to be wiping perspiration with a kerchief that he held to his face.

As soon as he left the alleyway, he abruptly slowed his pace to a walk but still moved rather briskly, constantly casting wary glances over his shoulder. Then, still hurrying, he entered a small hotel only a short distance down the street.

At that moment, Jon appeared with the package. "It's all

wrapped," he called, walking toward the door. "Let's go."

"Wait a minute," Joe replied, not taking his eyes from the hotel. "There's somethin' strange goin' on!"

"What?" inquired Jon, following his friend's gaze toward the street.

"I don't know, but I'd swear I just saw Slade King go into that hotel over there; and for some reason he seemed to be in an awful big hurry!"

After nearly ten minutes, Jon was becoming restless; but Joe insisted that they wait a while longer. At last the hotel door opened, and the boys swiftly pressed forward in an attempt to gain a clearer view. However, the man who walked from the building was a civilian.

"C'mon!" Jon pleaded. "What if you did see Slade King goin' into a hotel in a big hurry! That's no reason to . . . "

"Hey!" Joe interrupted. "Look at that man who just came out!"

Jon leaned forward and stared. Then in disbelief he exclaimed, "Thunder an' tarnation! That's Slade King! What's he doin' in civilian clothes?"

"That's what I'd like to know! He musta had 'em in that bundle I saw him carryin'," Joe reasoned.

"Let's follow him!" Jon whispered excitedly.

But Joe quickly placed a restraining hand on his friend's shoulder. "Hold on a minute! He's liable to see us!" the older lad cautioned. "Wait'll he gets a little farther down the street."

When King nearly reached the corner, the boys began to slip through the doorway just as he stopped to peer over his shoulder. In an instant they scrambled backward, hoping he hadn't seen them. Joe took off his kepi and peered cautiously around the woodwork. Evidently King hadn't spied them, for he continued across the intersection and entered another building.

With Jon at his heels, Joe descended the steps. Together they walked slowly down the street and then stopped just before they reached the corner.

"Let's stand in this little alleyway between these two buildings," Joe suggested. "We can easily watch for him from here."

"Looks like the place he went into's a bank," Jon observed, stepping into the shadows.

They waited impatiently for quite a while before King finally reappeared. Pressing themselves against the wall and crouching behind an old rain barrel, they watched him casually retrace his steps to the hotel, as though he were an ordinary citizen out for a weekend stroll.

After King disappeared from their sight, the two boys slowly stood up and simply looked bewilderedly at one another, completely baffled by all they had seen.

Jon looked quizzically at his friend and said, "This is weird!"

"Boy! I'll say!" Joe acknowledged.

Then, at a loss as to what to do next, the boys let the sound of an approaching wagon help make their decision. Fortunately, it turned out to be the same one that had brought them to town. Quickly stepping from the alleyway, they hailed the wagoner, who gladly offered them a return trip to camp.

They had time to help at the hospital, and to feed, curry and exercise the colonel's mare. Then in the late afternoon, as they were preparing to sound *Roast Beef*, they saw a civilian talking and gesturing rather animatedly to a group of officers.

"What's all the fuss?" Jon wondered; but Joe merely shrugged his shoulders.

However, right after the evening meal, the drummers were ordered to sound *Assembly*. As the men formed ranks, Joe saw the same civilian walking with Colonel Higgins to a central position in front of the regiment. The company clerks gave roll call, and then the officers directed all men who had received permission to leave camp during the afternoon to step forward.

Feeling that they were probably both included, Joe and Jon advanced a few paces and joined approximately fifty men who were in the process of forming a single line. Joe felt uncomfortable when he realized that Slade King was standing directly to his left.

Moments later, the civilian began at the far end of the line and walked along, looking closely at the men who had stepped forward, Colonel Higgins following in his footsteps. Pausing briefly to study certain faces, he gradually moved toward Joe's end of the line, where at last he hardly noticed Joe at all, but knitted his brow and gazed extremely carefully at Slade King. He was about to turn away when he paused for a moment and looked a second time at King, squinting somewhat as if in an effort to see him more clearly.

Then, turning to Colonel Higgins, he inquired, "May I ask this man a question?"

"By all means," the colonel replied with a gesture of his hand.

Looking at King, the man inquired, "Were you in my clothing

store today while you were in town?"

"No, sir!" King replied both firmly and instantly.

Shrugging his shoulders in resignation, the tailor turned to Colonel Higgins and said, "There's something familiar about this man; but the one who robbed my store today had a massive scar that could never be mistaken, and . . . I was sure I saw the number "125" on his sleeve. So he *must* be in this regiment!"

"Well, sir, these numbers *are* fairly small; and perhaps you misread them," the colonel remarked as they walked away.

The word *scar* had pierced Joe's mind like a pistol shot; and he reflected abruptly upon the scar-faced thief of only a few weeks ago, wondering if it could possibly have been the same man.

After taps the boys lay in their tent discussing the series of thefts which had involved their regiment. Joe couldn't dismiss from his mind how the tailor had returned to give Slade King a second close look and thought he should tell the captain of the soldier's strange behavior in town. However, remembering that the man involved in the thefts bore a scar upon his cheek, he dismissed the idea totally, concluding that it could get him into trouble; and he didn't want any more problems with Slade King than he already had.

All thoughts of the robbery were shattered completely the following morning, when Captain Colter called the boys to his tent as soon as they finished sounding reveille. "I've got a surprise for you; one I think you'll like!" he said.

"Good!" exclaimed Joe. "But yours'll hafta wait, sir; 'cause we've got one of our own. Don't we, Jon?"

Without answering, Jon produced their package and extended it toward the captain.

"Happy birthday, sir!" the boys chorused.

Surprised, the head musician graciously accepted the package with a smile. "How'd you know it was my birthday?" he wondered.

"You just happened to mention it one day 'bout a month ago, an' we sorta put it in our memory bank," Joe explained, casting a glance in Jon's direction and feeling happy that they had surprised their commanding officer.

Without hesitating, the captain opened their gift right away. "Well! That's something I can really use!" he admitted, inspecting the pouch carefully before tucking it into a jacket pocket. "Thank you, men!"

It was the first time he had ever called them *men*, and the boys beamed.

"All right, *now* it's *my* turn." The captain threw his arms around their shoulders and asked, "How'd you like to drum for a very special guest?"

"All right, I suppose," Jon acknowledged, though not especially excited about the idea.

"What's up, sir?" Joe asked. "Who is it?"

The captain scratched his head as if in deep thought. "Now let me see . . . Colonel Higgins mentioned his name just last night." He seemed to concentrate deeply for a few seconds, then suddenly snapping his fingers, he said, "Oh, yes, now I remember! I think he said his name's . . . *Lincoln* . . . Abraham Lincoln!"

Both boys practically flew out from under Captain Colter's arms!

"*Lincoln!* " Joe gasped unbelievingly, as he spun to look the officer squarely in the eyes.

"Thunder an' tarnation! *President* Lincoln? From *Washington*?" Jon asked, his eyes almost popping from his head.

"I *think* that's where the colonel said he's livin' at the moment," Captain Colter answered, grinning for all he was worth.

"Cap'n . . . you're jokin' with us!" Joe chided.

Stepping with them through the tent flaps, Captain Colter struck a more serious attitude. "No, I'm not, Joe. The president's scheduled to arrive in camp on Tuesday, an' the entire brigade'll stand review. Colonel Higgins knows our unit's been workin' pretty hard, an' he requested permission for us to perform for Mr. Lincoln."

The boys could hardly contain their enthusiasm. "Good grief!" piped Joe. "That only gives us one more day to practice! We'd better work all day tomorrow, don't you think, sir?"

"As a matter of fact, I've already asked permission for special practice today as well. Right after church services," he informed them.

The unit practiced feverishly Sunday afternoon, and then morning, afternoon and evening on Monday, smoothing every noticeable flaw.

Then, when the important day arrived, the boys set to work brushing their uniforms. Joe was feeling surprisingly calm about the whole affair, but Jon was becoming more fidgety with every passing minute.

"Thunder an' tarnation! I'll be *glad* when *this* is over!" Jon murmured nervously while carefully cleaning his trousers.

"Relax!" Joe urged. "Once we're on the field, just pretend it's another practice session. Our timing's been almost perfect lately; an' we've done our routines so often, I don't think we could forget 'em even if we tried!"

Jon stopped brushing and looked at his friend in absolute wonder. "Ain't you even the *least bit nervous?*" he asked in half surprise.

"Not nervous . . . but anxious maybe . . . an' just a little bit scared!" Joe admitted with a smile.

For a few moments Jon looked at Joe with a far away expression in his eyes. Finally, he said solemnly, "I want this to be somethin' *real* special!" And then, as a smile began to crease his face, he added, "I hope my pa's watchin'!"

"If he can . . . he will!" Joe said with a nod and a grin.

Light, balmy afternoon breezes drifted through the valley as the brigade began to assemble. One by one the regiments paraded onto the field in front of a temporary reviewing stand, which was graced by rippling red, white and blue bunting that gave the freshly hewn timbers an official, colorful appearance. The 125th marched to one of the forward positions, then waited more than half an hour for the entire brigade to assemble.

Finally the drums ceased. Joe stood beside Sergeant Abbott, thrilled at the sight of so many fighting men. Then the shouts of officers broke the quietness, bringing the men to attention; for the president and his party were arriving.

After the honored guest and his officials took their places on the reviewing stand with General McClellan and other officers and dignitaries, Captain Colter struck up the 125th Regimental Band, lending an air of importance to the occasion and making it unnecessary for the drummers to sound cadence. Joe wasn't disappointed, for he wanted to conserve all his energy for the special unit's performance.

It took at least an hour for all the regiments to parade past the reviewing stand; and when they returned to their original places, the long-awaited moment arrived. As the band played its final number, the squad formed briskly in a space between regiments, where they were completely out of sight of the reviewing stand.

No sooner were they in formation than Captain Colter was standing before them. "You boys give me a head start, then let 'er roll," he directed. "I'll be to your left beside the reviewing stand. As soon as I give the signal, start the drills."

Then looking at the men, he added, "An' stay alert, everybody! This is what we've been practicin' for!"

Before long the boys began drumming. In perfect unison and without spoken command, they led the 32-man unit between two Ohio regiments and paraded into the open area in front of the reviewing stand, where they halted side by side, while the men formed two ranks behind them. When the boys saluted and the men presented arms, the president and General McClellan were the first to their feet to acknowledge the gesture.

After the general and the other officers returned the salute and all sat down once more, the boys briskly raised their hands above their head, crossed their sticks in the form of an "X" and fixed their eyes on Captain Colter. The moment he signaled they sprang into action, starting with a roll which increased in speed until they seemed to be grasping a dozen hickories in each hand. Then with some flams and ruffs as a cue, the men commenced their drills.

First they trooped forward in their two ranks. However, each time the boys tapped a burl and staccato, the men kept pivoting and dividing into smaller and smaller groups, all marching in different directions in intricate patterns every time Joe and Jon drummed a new signal, until eventually, each man was marching by himself, executing turns or maneuvering his rifle in perfect timing with all the others.

Even as the boys sounded their beats, they also paraded in and out among the squad members, managing at times to pass only inches in front of the men's stamping feet or swirling rifles, which at times were thrown into the air or even between riflemen as, from moment to moment, they tossed them briskly back and forth to one another.

Then they reversed the procedure. Again responding to the beats, the men formed larger and larger groups until eventually, they returned to their original pair of ranks. All the maneuvers were executed flawlessly, but the boys knew this was only the beginning.

For nearly twenty minutes they drummed and marched with the men who pivoted, exchanged rifles, shifted them from shoulder to shoulder, and twirled them in front or to either side at the exact moment the boys tapped the proper drum beats. Their lightning-like movements were almost unbelievable to watch; but the precision with which each man moved in perfect unison with all the others, was obviously the most eye-catching feature of the drills.

At length, they broke once more into smaller and smaller groups, only to eventually re-form their twin ranks. Then, at the exact moment the two lines were completed, Joe and Jon came from opposite directions and faced each other, standing drum to drum, centered directly in front of their unit.

The final touch was to be theirs, and they agilely flared into the unique drumming routine that Captain Colter had prepared especially for them. Playing nearly every type of rhythm they knew, they changed from one to another with intricate smoothness, always keeping the strengths of their strokes, both loud and soft, identical to one another. At the same time, in the background the men continued marching in place, as they manipulated their weapons with a heavy slap, slap of their hands against the stocks and barrels of their rifles.

As they reached the climax of their performance, the boys gradually moved into a roll that constantly became faster and louder, faster and louder. Then abruptly, they stopped drumming on the vellum heads and began playing a catchy rhythm on the rims of their drums and even on one another's sticks, going back and forth from the rims to the sticks at an almost dizzying rate of speed, as they remained standing face to face.

Suddenly, they closed with a sharp flam, pivoted to face the reviewing stand and once more fired a snappy salute as the men simultaneously presented arms and shouted in unison, "Union Forever!" and then remained absolutely motionless.

Again, everyone on the reviewing stand arose promptly, either to recognize or return the squad's formal salute; and for a few brief seconds, there was absolutely nothing but awe-filled silence! Then, President Lincoln began to applaud, and was immediately joined by General McClellan and the other officers, as well as all the civilians who were with them.

Joe and Jon could hardly restrain their emotions! Each turned his head just enough to catch the other's eye, before breaking into a broad grin.

"Yes!" Jon exclaimed. "We did it!" Then, as Jon slowly lifted his eyes skyward, a shiver ran down Joe's spine as he heard his friend say, "Were you watchin', Pa?"

Seconds later, at Captain Colter's signal, the boys led the unit from the field, proud of the way everyone had performed. After bringing the men to a halt beside the reviewing stand, they heard the captain give the order for parade rest. Then they all watched and listened as the band struck up a march, and the regiments began to leave the field and return to their assigned locations in the encampment.

Within a few moments, the squad heard Captain Colter's voice once more. "Attention! Left face!" he ordered.

The unit executed the maneuvers, and the men found themselves looking directly into the eyes of the President of the United States. Mr. Lincoln had walked to the railing at the side of the stand, General McClellan near his side but standing slightly behind him.

Captain Colter ordered, "Present . . . arms!"

Once more, as the men saluted with their rifles, the boys greeted the president and the general with a hand salute. After it was again returned, the president said, "At ease, men."

Then for more than a minute, he said absolutely nothing, as he continually glanced from one man to another, making eye-to-eye contact with almost every rifleman in the entire unit. Slowly nodding his head in obvious approval of what he had just seen, he said, "That was an *excellent* performance, men!" Then looking directly at Captain Colter, he added, "You're certainly to be congratulated, sir!"

"Thank you, Mr. President!" the captain answered, a touch of unmistakable pride in his voice.

Then, maintaining his calm, dignified, but easy-going manner, and followed closely by General McClellan, the president walked exceedingly slowly down the steps. But even as he descended, his head was turned toward the boys, his eyes continually moving back and forth between them. When he reached the ground, he walked directly in front of them and stopped, still gazing from one to the other.

The boys' hearts began racing like the final roll they had played only minutes previously. Gradually, the president began to beam a broad smile, while simply shaking his head in disbelief at what he had just witnessed on the parade grounds. Then turning to the captain, he inquired, "May I ask their names, captain?"

These are drummers Joseph Shelley and Jonathan Cooper, sir, from York and Lancaster Counties, Pennsylvania."

To the boys' surprise, the president reached out and shook hands with both of them!

"What a magnificent routine you performed!" he said with obvious delight in his voice. "I'm sure that not only the captain and the men in this unit, but the entire brigade must be proud of you!"

"Thank you, sir," the boys chorused, blushing somewhat, but returning his smile.

Then, before walking away with General McClellan, he winked and said in slightly more than a whisper, "And thank you for reminding me of my own two sons today!"

Again, two extremely excited drummer boys caught one another's eye and shared a smile of deep satisfaction over all that had happened.

After the president, General McClellan, and the dignitaries with them had departed, the captain added his own words of praise to everyone before marching with them to the regimental camp site.

Joe and Jon drummed and paraded as though they were marching on clouds; and as their unit passed through the camp grounds, the men from almost the entire brigade lined the way to cheer and applaud as they passed.

When they reached their own regiment's area, goose bumps ran up and down the boys' spines when they received a thunderous ovation from the men of the 125th. Hardly did Captain Colter give the signal to break ranks, before the boys found themselves surrounded, everyone shouting excitedly or pounding someone else's back; but most of the acclaim was heaped upon the regiment's two deliriously happy drummer boys.

"You guys were *great!* " someone shouted.

"We've got the two best drummers in this man's army!" yelled another.

"Somebody git the blankets!" cried Manny; and before Joe or Jon could even make any effort to escape the clutches of the men, they found themselves being cradled in blankets and then tossed into the air three, five, eight, a dozen times, with Jon making the occasion all the more eventful by kicking his legs as though he were running through the air, bringing roars of laughter with his usual impishness.

At last, somewhat dizzy as usual from their escapade, the boys walked along happily with Captain Colter, as the men finally began to scatter toward their tents.

"Well, I'm sure that'll be a day the two of you'll never forget!" the captain declared.

"Thunder an' tarnation! You can count on it, sir! I ain't had this much fun since the day our school burned down!" Jon jested, taking both drumsticks in his right hand and giving Joe a playful swat across the seat of his pants.

Chapter 13

The Portrait

October seemed to pass exceedingly slowly; and autumn, cleverly mixing her colors, was gradually painting the surrounding hills. By this time the men were becoming anxious to follow the Confederates into Virginia rather than set up camp and simply wait for winter to halt the war temporarily, as had happened the previous year.

As the end of the month and still another pay day approached, more than a few campfire discussions centered around the topic of the thefts. This time everyone seemed determined to protect his precious earnings; and when the day finally arrived and passed without incident, Joe was somewhat surprised, though relieved.

On the Saturday after pay day, hundreds of military personnel flocked to Harpers Ferry. Joe and Jon roamed through the town, purchased a few articles, and then returned to camp.

However, the next day, immediately after morning worship services, the 125th and several other regiments received orders to assemble. Then, there followed nearly an exact repetition of what had happened the previous month. A civilian, this time accompanied by a local constable as well as Colonel Higgins, walked among the ranks, looking carefully at several soldiers. But at length, when it was evident that the search had been unsuccessful, Colonel Higgins strode to the front of the regiment and informed everyone of what had happened.

On Saturday, the man who stood with the colonel had made numerous daguerreotypes of military personnel, most of whom wished to send the pictures to their wives, families or sweethearts. However, at the end of the day, someone entered his shop in Harpers Ferry to attack and rob him of nearly a hundred dollars. Then came the words for which Joe had been listening so intently.

"For the third time," the colonel announced in a loud and somewhat irritated voice, "a scar-faced soldier has thrown suspicion upon our regiment. The man was wearing the insignia of the Pennsylvania 46th, and we have several of those men as transfers in our regiment; but we've been unable to identify him. If anyone knows anything about this man, he's to report it to his commanding officer at once!"

However, nearly a week passed and nothing more could be learned about the thief; and once more, as the days wore on, the men discussed the subject less and less.

As the boys were exercising Colonel Higgins' mount one brisk November afternoon, Jon was riding under Joe's watchful eye.

"You're doin' great!" the latter observed after his pal reined in. "You'd better be careful, or you're liable to wind up in the cavalry!" he warned jestingly.

"Yes, an' I need drummers too badly!" Captain Colter called, overhearing Joe's remark, as he came walking along with Chaplain Stewart by his side. Then he asked, "How'd you boys like to take a break? I've got some news."

"Mr. Lincoln's not comin' again, is he?" Jon asked in a mischievous sort of way.

"No," chuckled the captain. "But I got a letter from your folks, Joe. They'd like to know if it's possible for their son to come home for his birthday, which just happens to fall on the day when most folks'll prob'ly celebrate Thanksgivin' this year."

"It does?" Joe responded, half surprised. "I didn't even realize it! But then I haven't seen a calendar for so long, I forget what one looks like!" he laughed.

"Well, Chaplain Stewart an' I spoke with Colonel Higgins at staff meetin' this mornin'; an' since it looks like the regiment's gonna be here indefinitely, he granted permission right away."

"That's great!" Joe beamed. But then, suddenly realizing Jon's situation, he looked at his friend for a brief moment and then turned to the captain once more.

"Sir . . . do you think there's any chance that Jon . . ."

"Don't even worry about askin'," the captain interrupted, even as Chaplain Stewart began to chuckle. "Your parents beat you to the draw, Joe; 'cause they even requested that you bring Jon along!"

"Yes," Chaplain Stewart confirmed, "and everything's already taken care of. You boys have earned some furlough time!"

As both boys were in the midst of congratulating one another, a sudden thought struck Joe. "But wait a minute; how'll we get home an' back, sir?" he inquired.

"Well . . . Chaplain Stewart an' I already milled that over," Captain Colter responded thoughtfully.

Looking at Jon, he said in a concerned tone of voice, "We thought maybe you'd like to see where your father's buried, Jon. Is that a possibility?"

Jon lowered his head and gazed thoughtfully at the ground for a few moments. Then, slowly looking up again, he nodded his head and managed a slight smile. "Yes, sir; I think I'd really like that!"

"Well, then," interjected the chaplain, "the Tuesday before Thanksgiving, the captain and I'll take the two of you by wagon to Frederick. We'll do our best to see if we can learn where your pa was buried and take you there, if everything works out."

"Then afterwards," the captain added, "we can go to the railroad station in Frederick, an' you boys can catch a train to Baltimore, an' then home to Pennsylvania. It's really less than a hundred miles away; an' if you get good train connections, you may even make it in one day."

"Now, just keep your fingers crossed that the Rebs don't start anything and force us to move out of here unexpectedly," the chaplain remarked.

It was obvious that the plans picked up the boys' spirits tremendously; and after thanking the officers for their kindness and thoughtfulness, they returned to the corral and spent the remainder of the day working there, as well as at the hospital.

A week later, the day before they were to leave for Pennsylvania, something happened to set Joe's mind astir. Colonel Higgins had ordered an inspection of all men and equipment, and during the morning hours everyone was preparing for the ordeal. As Joe and Jon were walking among the countless tents, they passed a number of men who were beginning to display their equipment. Along the way they saw Slade King unpacking his haversack and carefully laying his bayonet sheath, belt, cartridge boxes, and other gear on his blankets.

As he was going about his task, his tent partner reached for a small, box-like, metal container which King had earlier laid aside. "What's this?" the soldier asked, bewildered by what he was seeing.

King turned and glared for one brief moment and then snatched it roughly from the man's hand. "Keep your hands to yourself!" he snarled, quickly stuffing the object of the soldier's curiosity inside his haversack once more.

"Why so much fuss about a little box?" his partner grunted.

"None o' your business!" King sneered, returning to his work.

Almost instinctively, and practically without realizing it, Joe and Jon had stopped, out of complete curiosity, to watch the brief rumpus.

When King happened to look up and saw them staring, he blurted, "Well, what're *you* two lookin' at? Get outta here before I stick your heads in your drums!" Then, taking a step in Joe's direction, he barked, "Especially *you!* "

But before he could take another stride, men came charging from every direction.

"You touch either one o' those boys an' you'll have the whole regiment on your back before you know what happened!" Dan Hicks harped, giving King a sharp shove backward.

"Yeah, an' I'll be the first one there!" barked another.

At the sight of so many men streaming menacingly toward him, King grudgingly retreated several steps. After glaring again at Joe, he mumbled something under his breath and returned to his blankets, as the boys, somewhat embarrassed by the episode, headed for their tent.

All the while, Joe was deep in thought, pondering over and over why King had used the words: *"Especially you!"* He kept wondering, *what* could've been inside the container to make him so angry when the other soldier had picked it up? For the next several hours, even with the excitement of departing for home, Joe couldn't dismiss thoughts of Slade King from his mind.

After the evening meal, the boys decided to speak with Captain Colter concerning plans for the following morning. As they stepped into his tent, they realized that he was having a meeting with Lieutenant Stewart and Sergeant Abbott. Excusing themselves for having interrupted, the lads were about to turn and leave when the captain stopped them.

"Come in, boys. We're just makin' plans for some kind o' entertainment for the men in another week or so. What can I do for you?" he asked.

While Joe and Jon were speaking with the captain about their plans for leaving on furlough, Sergeant Abbott interrupted them momentarily.

"Excuse me, cap'n, but I thought you'd like to see this," he said, extending a sheet of paper in the officer's direction. "I was just lookin' through some o' the company records to see who might be able to help out with this entertainment program, an' look what it says here 'bout Slade King!"

The captain reached for the paper; and after a few moments he read aloud in a somewhat incredulous tone of voice: "Was employed as an apprentice tailor and performed on stage in theatrical productions in New York, Philadelphia, Lancaster and Baltimore?"

The captain looked up, dumbfounded. Then, glancing at the sergeant and Lieutenant Stewart, he said slightly laughingly, "Slade King? . . . In the theater?" After shaking his head and smiling to himself, he added, as he returned the paper to the sergeant, "Now *who* in his right *mind* would've ever thought *that* . . . *even* for a moment?"

Joe looked first at Jon and then at the captain with a completely mystified expression, but letting what he had just heard, filter through his alert mind.

The captain shook his head wonderingly, chuckled to himself once more and shrugged his shoulders. Then, turning again to the boys, he completed his plans with them for the next morning, insisting that they be at his tent by seven o'clock sharp.

Early the next day, Manny served his "Jay Birds," the captain and the chaplain a wholesome breakfast; and then all four climbed aboard their wagon. The captain was happy to see that the boys remembered to take along their bedrolls as he had suggested, in case they would need to sleep overnight in a railroad station or some other unexpected place. Then, before reaching for the reins, he turned and handed them the pay he had been keeping safe for them.

The trip to Frederick took little more than an hour; and as

they approached the town, they inquired as to where the nearest military hospital might be. Fortunately, it was only a short distance ahead, along the main road as they approached the southwest part of town.

When they arrived, the chaplain entered to make inquiries and returned within minutes, carrying a small piece of paper. "His name's not on their records, but the lady in charge said that if we stop at this address in Frederick, they should have a complete listing of who was assigned to every hospital in the area."

The captain took the paper, glanced at it momentarily and placed it in his pocket. Then, chucking to the horses, he continued their journey. After arriving at their destination, the chaplain again went inside; and within another ten minutes he returned smiling.

"We hit it right this time," he acknowledged. "Bear left at the next corner, and Mount Olivet Cemetery's less than a mile away."

Then, instead of returning to the front seat, where earlier he had been sitting with the captain, he climbed in back and sat beside Jon, placing his arm around his shoulders. During the remainder of the trip, no one said a word; but it was obvious that the chaplain's presence was an extreme comfort to the young Columbian.

Finally, they arrived. It was a beautiful brisk autumn day with a scattering of billowy, white clouds dotting the crystal-blue skies. The foursome got out of the wagon and walked a short distance with some leaves that were blowing their way.

"According to the man who spoke to me, it should be somewhere in this southeast corner," said the chaplain, slowly waving his arm in that general direction. "Let's spread out. With four of us looking, we ought to be able to find it," he suggested. "Hopefully, they'll all be marked."

Each one went in a slightly different path, looking carefully at the headboards, many of which were just beginning to show the wear and tear of the effects of the weather. They were looking for only a few minutes before Joe happened to glance down the long rows of grave markers to his right, and noticed Jon taking off his kepi and slowly falling to one knee. Hastily, Joe turned and called in a loud whisper to the officers and then pointed toward Jon.

With a nod of their heads, they turned and walked with Joe to his friend's side. For a while they stood in silence beside him until he eventually raised himself once more, standing tall. The

headboard read simply: *Pvt. William J. Cooper, 125th Pa. Vol., Columbia, Pa., Died Sept. 22, 1862.*

"Sir!" Jon remarked, swallowing hard and turning toward the chaplain, tears forming for the first time. Then, chokingly he said, "Pa died . . . on my birthday!"

The chaplain wrapped his right arm around Jon's waist, bowed his head, and began offering a most comforting prayer. After he finished, Jon stared blankly at his father's grave for quite a while; but at length the chaplain slowly put his hand under the young man's chin, and gave it a gentle nudge upward.

"Now look up, Jon. Look at the heavens," he said with a smile, as all four gazed at the beauty of autumn above them. "Because he's not really *down there.*" And pointing into the skies that matched the brilliant blue of the young lad's eyes, he reminded him, "You see, because your father believes that Christ died for him, he's right up *there!* And God promises that you *will* see him again some day!"

Then he paused for a few moments, turned and looked directly into Jon's eyes. "Don't *ever* forget that, Jon! He'll be waiting for you with open arms one day!"

Jon looked at Joe and caught his steadfast friend's smile and nod of assurance, and then turned again to the chaplain. "I won't, sir," he said, adding a smile of his own, even through his tears. "An' thanks for bein' with me today, an' for all you've done for Pa and me."

The officers accompanied them to the railroad station and refused to return to Maryland Heights until Joe and Jon boarded the train. By early afternoon the boys were already in Baltimore, where they were happy to learn that their next train was to depart for York in less than an hour.

Then, by late afternoon they were walking through the York square and found a farmer who was heading east with his wagon. When they explained their situation, the kindly gentleman gladly offered them a ride. The trip over the York Turnpike was long and rough; and darkness had nearly settled by the time they scrambled to the roadside in Wrightsville, where they bid farewell to the generous driver.

The boys practically ran the remaining distance to the Shelley farm; then crept noislessly onto the porch where Joe leaned against the heavy oaken door, pushing gently. His mother and sister were so engrossed in laying fresh bread, pies and other baked goods on a sparkling white tablecloth, that the boys were almost completely inside the kitchen when Sarah finally saw them. Before Joe had a chance to make another move, his mother and sister practically knocked him off his feet, as Mr. Shelley, hearing all the commotion, rushed from the parlor.

While Joe and his family enjoyed these special happy moments, Jon quietly closed the door and stood almost motionless, kepi in hand, secretly admiring the closeness they so obviously shared with one another.

After finally being released from all the family hugs, Joe asked, "What's the latest news about Dan?"

"The last we heard he's in the cavalry now, an' his division's still somewhere southwest o' Washington," his father informed him.

Then, after looking over his shoulder at Jon, Joe stepped back and started to unstrap his friend's bedroll. "I guess I don't hafta tell you who this is!" he said.

Mrs. Shelley instantly stepped forward and hugged Jon just as fervently as she had embraced her own son only moments before. "Welcome, Jon!" she whispered. "I've got a feeling that in a very short time you'll be just like another son!"

"Thank you, ma'am," Jon replied.

Mr. Shelley reached to shake his hand. "Joe's written so much about you, we feel as though we've known you a long time already," he confessed.

Jon laughed. "An' I've heard pretty much about all o' you too!"

Then, looking rather shyly at Joe's sister, Jon smiled and said, "I guess you gotta be Sarah."

Sarah nodded and smiled, her face flushing slightly. "I'm glad you could come home with Joe! I've been hopin' I'd get to meet you some day!"

"An' the same goes for me too," Jon replied somewhat timidly. "Thanks for your letters. You'll never know how much they meant to me!" he admitted, looking down and fidgeting with the visor of his kepi, as he held it in his hands.

"I'll say!" Joe teased. "An' he still has 'em . . . right here!" he added, patting Jon's coat pocket. "He won't let 'em get away, Sarah! He's got 'em practically memorized!"

Sarah blushed, looking at her brother disapprovingly, but then quickly changed the subject. Looking at her parents, she asked, "Can we have the surprise now?"

They both smiled and nodded. "I guess so," said Mr. Shelley. "Now's as good a time as any!"

Since Joe's birthday was only two days away, he thought that perhaps they had planned something special for him; but he was confounded somewhat when his sister reached out and took his buddy by the hand.

"Are you ready, Jon?" she asked.

At first, Jon simply looked at her, mystified. "I . . . guess so," he stammered, giving Joe a questioning look; but his friend simply gave him the old shrugged-shoulders routine.

"Well, come along to the parlor," Sarah said mysteriously. "But you gotta close your eyes till we tell you to open 'em!"

Jon did as he was told; and as Sarah led him around the kitchen table, Mrs. Shelley walked toward her son and put her arm around his waist. After giving him a smile, she motioned with her head that they all should follow.

"Now keep your eyes closed, Jon!" Sarah reminded him as they stepped into the living room.

Then, as Joe and his mother strolled behind them, Mrs. Shelley caught Joe's attention once more and pointed to a large, homemade sign fastened to the door which led to another room on the east side of the parlor. In bold letters were written just two words: *Jon's Room.*

Sarah stepped behind Jon, placed one hand on each shoulder and gradually turned him toward the sign. "Now look!" she directed.

Jon slowly opened his eyes, stared at the sign, and then turned with a smile. "Is this where I'm to stay for the week?" he asked.

"Yes," Mrs. Shelley answered, taking his arm and leading him to the door before opening it. Then, lighting a lamp so Jon could get a better look at the spacious room, she said, "But not just for the week, Jon . . . But for as *long* as you wish!"

Jon knitted his eyebrows and simply stared at her, mystified, for several seconds. Then his gaze shifted to Mr. Shelley, to Joe and Sarah, and then back to their mother once more.

Finally, it was Mr. Shelley who broke the silence. "I'll explain, Jon." He paused for a few moments; then, with a slight catch in his voice, he continued. "After we learned about your father, we wrote to Captain Colter an' asked if there was any way we could possibly adopt you; an' he . . . "

But before he could finish, the look of astonishment on Jon's face stifled Mr. Shelley's words completely; and Joe, hardly believing his ears, rushed to his mother, wrapped his arms around her waist and spun her in a complete circle!

Jon, utterly speechless, suddenly sank into a nearby chair, covering his face with his hands. At first, they couldn't tell if he was laughing or crying; and as it turned out, it was probably a mixture of the two.

Then Joe stepped to his side, placed his hand on his companion's shoulder and said, "Didn't Chaplain Stewart *say* . . . God would bring somethin' *good* outta all this?"

Gradually Jon looked up; first at Joe and then at each member of the family, tears trickling slowly down his cheeks for the second time that day.

"Pardon me," he apologized, obviously somewhat embarrassed. "But this has been an emotion-packed day! An' really," he said hastily, "these ain't tears o' sadness; believe me! They're tears o' *real* happiness! An' I got a feelin' they're the best kind!" he added, beginning to laugh. And then as he stood up and wiped his hand across his tear-stained face, he licked still another tear from the corner of his lips, grinned and said, "An' this kind even *tastes* better!"

Mrs. Shelley reached forward and drew him close, her heart filled with love and compassion. Holding him in her arms, she reminded him, "Remember . . . you were hardly inside the door before I *said* . . . you'd be just like another son!"

"Well, Jon, as I was sayin'," Mr. Shelley continued while they returned to the parlor, "Captain Colter an' Colonel Higgins see no problem with it, but they felt as though we should talk it over with you during your furlough. Then, if you're agreeable, we'll gladly get to work on it!"

"Agreeable?" Jon echoed instantly. "How can I ever possibly thank you even for just thinkin' of it?"

Mrs. Shelley again took him by the arm as she led him toward the kitchen. "We know by Joe's letters that you're a wonderful young man, and we realize that you've been through a great deal lately. This is our way of saying that we love you, and we're opening our home to you. So you think about it while you're with us and let us know some day what you decide. And it doesn't have to be this week!"

Jon looked at Joe and flashed the customary grin that was his trademark. "You *know* that's gonna be a tough decision, don't you, buddy-boy?" he laughed.

Then turning to Mr. and Mrs. Shelley, he said, "Whenever Joe would read me the letters you wrote, I'd think to myself that you must be wonderful people . . . an' now I know it firsthand!"

"And by Joey's letters, *we* know he has a great friend away from home; and that's important to us!" Mrs. Shelley responded.

Then, suddenly scurrying impulsively toward the back door, Joe said, "Please excuse me, but there's somebody else I just gotta see!"

Reaching for a lantern, he looked at Jon and said, "Wanna come along?"

Quickly the pair headed for the stable, Joe handing the lantern to Jon. After opening one of the doors and calling softly through the darkness to Swift, they heard the stallion begin to prance on the hoof-hardened surface and snort and whinny excitedly. Moments later, Joe was carefully backing him out of his stall and patting his solid neck firmly.

"Thunder an' tarnation! He's beautiful!" Jon remarked, as he held the lantern up high to get a better glimpse.

"Sure is!" Joe agreed. "An' wait'll you ride him tomorrow!"

Then, placing his shoulder under Swift's strong neck and patting him lightly once more, he said, "Sure missed you, boy! Are we ever gonna make up for lost time the next couple o' days!"

The following morning Joe and Jon were awake early. Since his mother wanted to wash their uniforms, Joe found suitable clothing for both of them; and soon they were ready for breakfast. Joe was really anxious to see his friends, Dave and Ted; but since it was his first day home, he thought it would be better to wait. He and Jon spent the entire day with the family, helping with many chores, most of which involved repair work of one kind or another.

However, as Joe had promised, late in the afternoon they spent more than an hour taking turns riding Swift, an adventure that almost took Jon's breath away.

The next day was not only Thanksgiving, but Joe's birthday besides; and as he came down the steps, he was greeted accordingly, Sarah not being able to resist pulling his ears sixteen times, the last one bringing a slight wince of pain and Sarah's quick retreat to the other side of the table!

The boys had a quick breakfast. Then, while the women were

bustling about the kitchen making preparations for the Thanksgiving Day meal, the boys helped Mr. Shelley with the farm work, Joe getting special enjoyment from watching Jon do some milking for the first time in his life.

Later, when the boys were in the kitchen once more, Joe asked his mother if he and Jon could visit with Dave and Ted during the late afternoon.

"I think that'd be a fine idea," she answered. Then, slyly catching Sarah's attention, she added, "They'll be surprised to know you're here. We didn't get a chance to tell them. And they'll probably be home, because both of them said their families aren't going to celebrate Thanksgiving until next week."

Upon hearing this comment, Jon shook his head in consternation. "Why can't this country set aside one special day for Thanksgiving like we do for Christmas?" he wondered. "I'm gonna hafta write Mr. Lincoln a letter about that! He's a friend o' mine, you know," he added, flashing the Cooper grin.

Sarah laughed, but Joe was lost in thought. Somewhat mystified, he looked at his mother and asked, "Did Dave an' Ted stop comin' to ride Swift an' help with chores like they promised?"

"Oh, no! They come often! Dave even keeps Swift at their farm for days at a time if we don't need him. But your last letter, telling us for certain that you'd be home, must've gotten lost in the mail, because we just received it a couple of days ago; and we haven't seen Dave or Ted since then."

At noon the boys knew they were in store for a treat, as they sat down to what appeared to be a real feast.

Jon caught Joe's eye; and with a look of near disbelief he said, "Thunder an' tarnation! This looks like the Murphy's place all over again!"

"An' then some!" added Joe. "An' thanks for writin' to them, Ma," he said, giving her a hug around the shoulder. "They were really nice people! What a weekend that was! You'd really like Mrs. Murphy!"

More than an hour later, after everyone felt as stuffed as the duck had been, Mr. Shelley insisted that everyone help with the dishes. They sailed at their task with a will, just enjoying being in one another's company.

After the work was done, Joe was about to announce their intentions of leaving to visit Dave and Ted, when he heard some scuffling sounds on the porch, followed by some slightly suppressed laughter. He looked at his father and mother questioningly, but received only blank expressions in return. However, the grin on Sarah's face let him know that something strange was afoot; and he quickly made a dash for the door.

"Hi, Joey! Happy birthday!" shouted Dave.

"Welcome home!" called Ted, and simultaneously nearly a dozen other voices called from behind them, echoing their words of greeting.

After recovering from his initial shock, Joe introduced Jon to his neighbors and schoolmates; and that afternoon and evening were the happiest hours the boys spent in several months. The surprise party featured games, singing, and dancing in the parlor, where the walls echoed the voices and laughter of the youthful gathering. However, for much of the time, Ted sat calmly, enjoying his favorite pastime of drawing anyone's portrait who would sit still long enough to pose for him.

By early evening most of the group had departed. Only Ted and Dave remained, and at their request Joe and Jon spent nearly another hour telling about some of the things they had seen and done since leaving home. Everyone listened intently while they talked most especially about the battle at Antietam Creek and of the day Captain Colter's unit performed for President Lincoln.

"Sounds as though you guys really had some exciting times, Joey!" Dave commented. "But I guess we shouldn't be surprised. It follows you wherever you go!"

"I'll say!" exclaimed Ted. "Remember the time we went huntin' for Indian relics, an' that man tried to steal Swift?"

"Remember?" piped Dave. "How could we ever forget? He was the *ugliest* man I ever saw!" Then with his finger, Dave traced an imaginary line along his face. "That *big scar* he had across his right cheek was enough to scare the devil himsel . . ."

Dave suddenly stopped and stared when he saw the strange expression on Joe's face. "What's wrong, Joey?" he inquired. "You look like you just saw a ghost!"

"That man!" Joe murmured, his face slowly brightening. "Yeah! That *man* !" he repeated. "An' the *scar* ! I thought about him once, but I never really made the connection till now!"

Joe closed his eyes a few seconds, deep in thought, while everyone else merely exchanged puzzled glances.

"The scar," he muttered to himself once more and became quiet yet again for several moments. Then, suddenly opening his eyes, he looked toward Jon and exclaimed, "Sure! That's it! Sergeant Abbott said just the other day that Slade King was a professional actor! Remember, Jon?" he asked, looking at his drumming partner.

Jon nodded. "Yeah," he responded; but then, shrugging his shoulders he simply inquired, "So?"

"An' who's Slade King?" Mr. Shelley wanted to know. But Joe was in such deep concentration that his father's question escaped him completely.

Then, snapping his fingers he almost shouted. "Ted! Get your drawin' pad, will you? Some *strange* ideas are flyin' through my head, an' I'll bet you can help!"

"Sure! But what in Sam Hill are you talkin' about anyhow?" his friend asked, totally baffled, while reaching for his pad which lay nearby.

"Think you remember that fellow well enough to be able to draw a picture of him?" Joe asked. "I know it's been a long while."

"Well . . . it's been a couple o' months, I'll admit; but I *should* have every feature practically memorized. I was close enough to him!" Ted laughed, rubbing his jaw and recalling their tussle with the man.

"All right," Joe replied. "Now we'll find out just how good an artist you really are!" he said in a challenging voice.

"I'll be glad to try, but why do you want a picture of him?" Ted wondered aloud, fumbling for his stick of charcoal.

"I'll tell you after you're finished . . . if my hunch is right," Joe answered. "But do me a favor."

"What's that?"

"If I remember right, he had a mustache, didn't he?" Joe said pensively.

"Yeah, a small one," Ted acknowledged.

"I don't remember a mustache," Dave interrupted. "All I remember was that big, *ugly* scar!"

"Yeah, an' that's the problem," Joe responded. "It stands out so *much*, that's practically the *only* thing *anybody* ever remembers about him!"

Then turning to Ted again, he said, "So draw every detail you can remember, but don't include either the scar *or* the mustache."

"All right," Ted answered, shrugging his shoulders. "Here goes."

Everyone crowded around, watching intently as Ted's talented fingers went to work. He paused from time to time, closing his eyes in an effort to shut out anything that might distract his attention. First he drew a mere outline, but gradually some facial features began to appear, then the hair. Next came the eyes and a pair of bushy eyebrows.

"I don't remember thick eyebrows like that!" commented Dave.

"I think I remember vaguely, but I'm not sure either," Joe said. "But don't you see, Dave? Ted's interested in drawin' people's faces; we're not. What's just about the only thing you an' I can really count on rememberin' about him?"

"The scar . . . an' at least you thought o' the mustache," Dave replied.

"Exactly!" Joe harped. "But Ted's in the habit o' seein' every last detail of a person's facial features, an' it's obvious already that he saw much more'n anyone *else* did! Even after the man escaped from the Columbia lock-up, do you know what was practically the only bit o' description they printed in the news article?"

"Well, I didn't read it; but prob'ly it said he had a scar on his cheek," Dave guessed.

"Right again! An' somethin' tells me . . . the scar wasn't even real!" Joe added, causing a few puzzled looks and raised eyebrows.

Finally, Ted put the finishing touches on the nose, eyes and mouth. "There! That's about as good as I can remember him," he announced. "That's everything but the scar an' mustache, like you asked."

Joe took the drawing and held it close to the table lamp, slowly nodding his head. "Take a *real* close look, Jon. I hope my imagination's not runnin' away with me, but who does that look like to you?"

Jon leaned over beside him and peered intently at the portrait for a few seconds. "Thunder an' tarnation!" he drawled, astonished by what he was seeing. "The hair's a lot longer . . . but if that ain't Slade King, I don't know who else it would be!"

"You mean you guys know him?" Dave inquired in amazement, glancing over Jon's shoulder.

"I didn't know him early last summer, but I do now! He's in my company an' goes by the name o' Slade King. I'm sure it's him!" Joe said emphatically.

Then, walking leisurely around the table, he said, "When I first saw him at camp, I thought there was *somethin'* familiar about him; but I couldn't remember where I saw him. You see, he shaved his mustache an' cut his hair a *lot* shorter. An' without the scar, I didn't know him at all!"

"But what happened to it?" Ted asked in a puzzled tone. "That's what *I* don't understand!"

"That's the whole point!" Joe exclaimed. "I don't believe he ever *had* one! Not a *real* one, anyway. Look! It's like I said a while ago. Our sergeant found in the company records just the other day, that King use' to be on stage before he joined the army. Involved in theater productions in places like Lancaster, Baltimore, Philadelphia . . . an' even New York; an' undoubtedly, as an actor, he *had* to learn how to use make-up!"

Ted's eyes brightened. "Hey! *Maybe* that explains why his scar was so reddish an' appeared to be such a fresh one, as though he just recently got it!" the young artist commented thoughtfully, recalling their unfortunate encounter with the man.

Then Joe told them of the robberies which had occurred near Rockville and in Harpers Ferry, and of the scar-faced thief who could never be found. "It's my guess," he added, "that whenever he wants to pull off a robbery, he puts on some make-up to form a huge, eye-catchin' scar. Then, if anyone sees him commit a crime, it's so noticeable that no one pays much attention to any of his other features. Afterwards, he just removes his scar; and no one recognizes him without it!"

"Do you think he stopped at the Shultz's that day to steal somethin' from them, an' then decided to go for Swift instead?" Dave asked.

"Gosh! That's possible," Joe replied. "I never thought o' that."

Even as Joe mulled over all these thoughts, his face began to light up. "An' just maybe that's what he was doin' the day I saw him in Harpers Ferry, Jon. Remember? When we were in that store I saw him comin' outta that alleyway pretty fast, an' he looked like he was holdin' a kerchief to his face. I thought he was wipin' away some sweat because he was runnin'. But I'll bet he was either tryin' to *remove* as much of his scar as he could, or else he was just hidin' it till he could get rid of it in the hotel; one or the other. An' the day Colonel Higgins made the whole regiment assemble, that tailor who was robbed looked at King for an *awful* long time, an' even came back for a *second* look!"

"Well, it all sounds pretty clever, but . . . can you be sure?"

Dave cautioned.

"That's what I hope to find out just as soon as we get back to camp!" Joe declared, carefully folding Ted's portrait. "But it looks to me as though Slade King made just *one little* mistake."

"What's that?" Ted asked.

Joe put his hand on his redheaded friend's shoulder. "He just happened to try to steal somethin' one day, when somebody was around who sees more in a face than just the average person does. A *whole* lot more!"

Ted smiled. "I hope you're right, Joey! If you are, then all the drawin' I've been doin' for the past couple o' years'll be worth *somethin'* anyhow!"

"Well, I have a suggestion," Mr. Shelley interrupted, after listening carefully to everything that had transpired.

"What's that, Pa?" Joe asked.

"Since Saturday's market day, why don't we drop in at the Columbia lock-up an' see if we can find out anything else about this . . . *Slade King* . . . if that's really his name, by the way. Because the day I went with Mr. Shultz to press charges, that man not only wouldn't give his name, but he had no identification with him whatsoever. An' I remember the constable sayin' that's typical o' men who desert from the army."

"Good idea, Pa!" Joe said thoughtfully. "Why don't we do that?"

With the hour getting late, Dave and Ted decided to leave; and for the remainder of the evening, the Shelleys and young Jon spent more time getting better acquainted. It was approaching midnight before all went to bed, after spending a most pleasant holiday and birthday celebration combined.

Later, as Joe lay awake restlessly in his room, his mind racing a mile a minute, he was wondering if he had jumped to some hasty conclusions, when Slade King's words: *"I hate that kid!"* and *"Especially you!"* suddenly struck him! As though he had been startled by a nightmare, Joe sat straight up in bed, thinking to himself that Slade King must've recognized him back in August, as one of the persons responsible for his having been arrested!

<No wonder he shoved me into the bushes that day when he was on picket duty!> Joe thought to himself. Then, slumping back on his pillow, he was more certain than ever that his conclusions were warranted.

After a night of much tossing and turning, Joe spent a great part of the next day working side by side with Jon and his father doing all kinds of chores and more repair work. Later, the boys took turns riding Swift once again before taking a long stroll with Sarah, who frequently walked between them, interlocking her arms around theirs, and very obviously enjoying Jon's company more and more.

On Saturday all five rode by wagon and horseback to Columbia for what probably would be the family's last market day of the season. While Sarah and her mother worked at the market stand, Mr. Shelley and the boys headed for the town lock-up. As Joe's father had suspected, the report of the attempted horse theft was still on record, along with some interesting information that had been noted about the culprit. According to the constable's files, he was missing the first two molars in the lower left jaw, and the front molar in the upper right. Aside from that, the report also indicated that the man had a large, one-inch mole at the base of the left shoulder blade and two smaller moles approximately an inch apart just above the left elbow.

Mr. Shelley explained all that Joe and Jon had shared about Slade King, and requested that the constable put the identifying information regarding the moles and missing teeth in writing. Then he asked him to sign the paper in order that the boys would have something official to present to the military personnel when they returned to Maryland.

Since Sunday would be their last day at home, Joe wanted to spend as much time with his family as he could. They attended church, where Joe introduced Jon to Pastor Jackson; and the boys later bid farewell to Ted and Dave. Then, during the afternoon, all the Shelleys rode together with Jon by wagon and horseback in the proximity of the farm, enjoying one another's fellowship.

While they were seated around the supper table that evening, Jon said, "Well, I guess this really won't come as a shock to anybody, but . . . " He paused a few moments as he flashed a smile toward Mr. and Mrs. Shelley. "Well, I guess all I wanna say is . . . I sure would be happy to call you 'Ma' and 'Pa' . . . if you're *sure* that's what you'd *really* like!"

There was spontaneous applause accompanied by a happy shriek from Sarah, as Mrs. Shelley quickly arose, walked behind their young guest and gave him a strong hug. Then, kissing him on the cheek, she said, "Wonderful! I always wanted another son!"

Sarah, seated beside him, grabbed his right arm and added her contribution to the same right cheek, as both Joe and his father extended their hands for a firm shake.

"How about that!" Joe chimed. "I really am gonna have a little brother!"

Jon smiled and nodded, suddenly recalling his father's words as he lay in the ambulance that day near the Antietam Creek.

Obviously very delighted by Jon's decision, Mr. Shelley said, "Well, young man, we thank you for puttin' your confidence in us; an' you can be sure we'll get started on the proper legal procedures, just as soon as we find out how we're to go about it."

The following morning the boys stood outside the house, looking sharp in their clean uniforms, Jon checking carefully to be certain he had replaced Sarah's letters in the pocket where he kept them. Then after adjusting one another's bedrolls on their backs, they were ready to leave.

It was another of those extremely difficult times of parting. There were the usual hugs and kisses, handshakes and tears; but Joe would always remember how Sarah suddenly ran up to Jon, threw her arms around his neck, kissed him on the cheek, and then covered her face and ran crying toward the house.

Joe wrapped his arm around his stunned friend's shoulders. "You know . . . I sorta get the feelin' my sister kinda likes you, little brother! C'mon! Let's go!" he said, as he helped Jon climb onto the wagon.

Then, after the boys waved a final farewell to Mrs. Shelley, and to Sarah who was now waving from the parlor window, Joe's father drove them to the York Railroad Station. This time their train connections were poor, however; and they had difficulty finding transportation to Maryland Heights. Consequently, they didn't reach camp until shortly before noon the following morning.

No sooner did they arrive, before they were walking briskly to Captain Colter's tent, where Jon couldn't wait to tell him excitedly all about the Shelley's plans to adopt him.

The captain smiled. "That's great news, Jon! Actually, most o' the officers really knew all about it, an' we could hardly keep from sharin' it with you before you left! But we managed somehow," he laughed, beaming his approval and assuring him that the army would do everything it could to help with the proceedings.

Joe waited patiently while Jon shared his good news, before turning to the rather serious matter of Slade King, relating everything the boys knew about him, including the time they had seen him dressed in civilian clothing in Harpers Ferry. After mentioning the Columbia constable's report and Ted's drawing, Joe withdrew them both from his coat pocket.

"Say! That *does* look like King!" the captain agreed after studying the portrait carefully. "But I'm sure we'll need much more evidence than this. Besides, King also had pay stolen, you'll remember; though, of course, that coulda been just a bluff," he added.

The officer sat on his camp stool diligently scrutinizing the constable's report and staring at the drawing for several more minutes. Then as he was about to dismiss the boys, he said, "I'll tell Lieutenant Stewart an' the colonel about this; but in the meantime, I'd advise the two o' you to keep this thing *absolutely quiet.* Understand? Don't say even one word to *anybody* about it!"

"We won't, sir!" Joe promised fervently, as Jon nodded in agreement.

However, when pay day passed and Captain Colter made no mention of the matter again, Joe couldn't help feeling somewhat disappointed.

The following Saturday the boys had an opportunity to go into town; but they chose to remain at camp in order to help the new regimental surgeon, Dr. Davidson, with some of the work at the hospital.

By early evening the camp was teeming with soldiers once more. Joe and Jon were seated by a campfire tapping some catchy rhythms on Manny's kettles, while one of the men was accompanying their beats by doing a clog dance on an empty hardtack box. Before long a large group assembled around the crackling fire; and while some of the men played banjos and others were singing some of their campfire favorites, an orderly came through the area.

"Has anyone seen drummers Shelley an' Cooper?" he cried.

"Over here!" piped Jon.

"You're to report to Colonel Higgins' tent," he directed. "Right away!"

The boys looked at one another in half surprise for a few seconds; then hurried through the darkness with the jeers and laughter of the men ringing in their ears.

"Now you're in for it!" one of them shouted.

"Looks like they finally decided to give you two Jay Birds picket duty!" Manny shrilled gleefully, rubbing his hands together as he giggled.

The boys saw several sentries outside the colonel's quarters and heard voices from within; but when the orderly ushered them inside, everything suddenly became quiet. Seeing the colonel, Captain Colter, Lieutenant Stewart, the Harpers Ferry constable and Doctor Davidson, the boys saluted; but Joe's gaze was quickly drawn to the face of a bare-chested soldier with a long, reddish scar on his right cheek. Goose bumps ran down Joe's spine when a closer look revealed that it was Slade King!

"Well, boys," the colonel began, "we've finally gotten to the bottom o' these thefts; an' I understand much o' the credit belongs to you, Shelley."

Joe was somewhat surprised by this remark, but said nothing.

"When Cap'n Colter came to me with your information," the colonel continued, "we decided to have this man watched when he went to town today, since the robberies always occur directly after pay day."

Joe and Jon looked at King, who simply stared continually at the ground.

"Not only did some of our officers have a scuffle with him while he was attemptin' another robbery," the colonel continued; "but they took him to the bank you boys saw him enter, an' learned that he's been depositin' fairly large sums o' money there under another name. So you're to be commended for the part the two o' you played in this man's arrest."

When the colonel finished, Captain Colter handed Joe a metal container. "I thought you'd like to see this. We found it in the room he booked in the same hotel you told us about."

"Why, it's the metal box he was so concerned about right before I went home," Joe observed.

"Look inside!" the captain insisted.

Opening it, Joe found several small packets of powder, as well as a set of printed instructions which explained how to mix them in order to prepare make-up.

"Turn around, King," the captain ordered, and then pointed out the large mole on the thief's back and the two smaller ones near his elbow.

BOT RODA

"And Doctor Davidson confirms that the exact three teeth are missing that were mentioned in this report you brought back from the constable in Columbia," the colonel announced.

Joe and Jon exchanged satisfied glances. Then, turning to the captain, Joe said, "Looks like we can thank my pa for that. It was his idea to go to the Columbia lock-up an' check out everything they had on record."

Before the boys were dismissed, further questioning revealed that King was also guilty of the thefts of the men's pay. Previous searches had been unsuccessful in recovering it, for he had carefully sewn it inside some of his clothing and his haversack, as well as his bedroll. Probably he never would've admitted it, if some of the money hadn't been discovered when his jacket was torn during the scuffle with Captain Colter and the other officers. It became evident that he had pretended his own money was stolen, merely to throw suspicion from himself.

Finally, when the colonel began to pursue his line of questioning even further, King eventually admitted to a charge of desertion as well, having at one time belonged to another Pennsylvania regiment.

"That musta been about the time he tried to steal my brother's horse last summer," Joe commented.

King glared at Joe momentarily but offered nothing further.

"You'll be held for both civil and military courts, King," the colonel announced at length. "An' you could even be held for a second charge o' desertion for leavin' camp without permission in order to rob that elderly gentleman while the regiment was camped near Rockville."

At these words Joe recalled having heard someone moving through the brush that night, remembering that he thought it was a picket going on duty; but probably it had been King leaving the camp to undertake his crime.

Later, as the boys were returning to the campfire with Captain Colter, Jon said, "There's somethin' that don't make sense, cap'n!"

"What's that?" his commanding officer asked.

"If Slade King deserted the army a couple o' months ago, then why'd he volunteer all over again?"

"Well, Jon, in some places men are offered as much as a thousand dollars to volunteer," the captain informed him. "More'n one man's deserted only to join a second an' even a third time, just to make some easy money. This guy was a real schemer!"

"Thunder an' tarnation! What a crazy way to try an' get rich!"

"Cap'n, I have a question too," Joe admitted. "Last month Colonel Higgins said that a soldier wearin' the insignia of the Pennsylvania 46th was involved in that robbery. Remember?"

"Well," the captain replied, "Slade King was pretty good with a needle an' thread, don't forget! He use' to be a tailor. Remember? All he hadda do was get his hands on somebody's shirt or jacket, rip off the insignia, an' then sew it on his own uniform to try to confuse people. Or maybe he even swiped somebody else's clothing that day; there's no way o' tellin'. The important thing is . . . thanks to you guys, we nailed him!"

By this time they arrived at the campfire, where Captain Colter began to tell everyone about what had happened, and informed the men that those who had lost their pay would probably have most or possibly all of it returned soon. Within a matter of minutes the entire regiment was celebrating the good news, slapping the boys' backs and shaking their hands in the process, for their part in bringing the unsavory episode to a welcome close.

Chapter 14

Final Drum Call

With the arrival of December and cold weather, the men prepared more durable winter quarters, digging small cellars, raising log stockades from two to five feet high, and pitching their tents over top of them. With these changes completed, it seemed certain that the 125th would spend the entire winter at Maryland Heights; and Joe and Jon began to talk of possibly spending Christmas at home. Their hopes were shattered one snowy morning, however, when Captain Colter called them to his tent to give them some disappointing news.

"Boys," he said, "I've got somethin' to say that you may not like to hear . . . but orders are orders!"

The expression on the captain's face had them worried; and after hesitating a few moments, he said, "You an' I have been transferred to another division, an' we're to leave immediately!"

For a few seconds the boys were speechless, looking at one another in total disbelief. Then when Joe found his voice, he asked, "But why, Cap'n Colter? I don't understand!"

"I'm not sure I do either, Joe; but I can guess, since General Burnside has replaced General McClellan. No one knows what his plans are, o' course; but some divisions have been ordered into Virginia, an' there may be action. A number o' their regiments lost some drummers at the Antietam and in other battles, but haven't received replacements yet. That's prob'ly why we're bein' transferred."

"But will we be allowed to come back?" Jon wanted to know.

"I would expect so," Captain Colter responded. "At least that's what I've requested. I'm hopin' it's only temporary, an' most likely we'll be returned; but I can't promise you that! Do you understand?" he asked, as he walked between them and threw his arms around their shoulders.

"Yes, sir!" the boys chorused dejectedly.

"Now come along with me to the colonel's tent," he directed. "Both he an' Chaplain Stewart wanna talk to you before we leave."

At the colonel's quarters, the boys had many words of praise heaped upon them; and the pair found it difficult to part from these extremely caring officers who had come to mean so much to them. Then, rather downhearted after all that had occurred so quickly, they returned to their camp site, where they dolefully packed their belongings.

The news that the captain and the boys were being transferred traveled quickly; and as they rode from the camp in one of the supply wagons, Lieutenant Stewart rode up to them and shook their hand, bidding farewell and wishing them luck. Then Manny Welles came running alongside to hand them some of his *special* biscuits and snatch a final handshake. "It ain't gonna be the same without my two Jay Birds!" he yelled, as hundreds of other men from the regiment began to line the road on both sides to give all three a rousing parting cheer.

As they rocked forlornly along the trail toward Harpers Ferry, neither boy spoke for a long time, both feeling an absolutely agonizing sensation, much as though they were leaving home once more.

Within a few hours, they joined other wagons; and for the next two days they were part of a vast train making its way through northern Virginia. Tumbling temperatures and cloudy skies produced more snow, and before long the horses and wagons had the roads packed nearly to solid ice in many places.

Late in the day on December 10th, the wagons reached Falmouth, Virginia, where the captain and the boys were assigned to the 106th Pennsylvania Volunteers. Their new regiment had seen action not only at the Antietam, but also in nearly a dozen other major battles. In that time they had lost the services of three of their drummers, and their head musician had been mortally wounded at the battle of Fair Oaks.

Shortly after their arrival, Captain Colter placed the boys in the hands of two drummers only slightly older than Joe, and soon the lads were on the way to their new living quarters. The air was damp and chilly; and the smoke from the campfires refused to rise, stinging their eyes and making breathing difficult.

Before they fell asleep that night, they learned that the Union forces might at any moment strike at a town called Fredericksburg. Therefore, the boys would be expected to learn all the regimental drum calls in short order. The name Fredericksburg brought back sad memories of Frederick, Maryland; and both boys experienced a strange foreboding at the mere sound of it.

The following morning Captain Colter energetically took charge of the drummers, and the boys were assigned to Companies C and D. Then the captain put them under the care of Jed McCollister, Company F's youthful drummer, who spent several hours working on the new drum calls with Joe and Jon. Fortunately, many of them were identical to those they already knew; and since several others were similar, they learned them quickly.

Later, while they were practicing with all the drummers, an artillery unit passed the camp, escorting a dozen 20-pound Parrot guns.

"That makes nearly a hundred o' those since we came here," commented Jed. "Somethin's bound to break loose soon!"

Then, less than half an hour later, wagonloads of strange-looking wooden structures also skirted the camp and traveled down the road along the Rappahannock River. Even Captain Colter was curious, and everyone stopped drumming to watch.

"They look like canoes!" Jon exclaimed.

"Yeah, but they're pontoons," Jed replied. "Looks like the engineers might build some bridges, since the Johnny Rebs burned 'em all down. Now we'll see how long it takes to cross over to Fredericksburg!"

The name again sent a shudder down Joe's spine.

As they lay awake that night, the boys discussed the possibilities of a battle. Jed said in a somewhat worried tone of voice, "The only thing that bothers me is that we've been waitin' here for nearly a month to get across the Rappahannock. That means every regiment in the whole Confederacy's had plenty o' time to get ready for us!"

Early in the morning hours, Joe was awakened by the sound of big guns in the distance. As he lay listening to them, an orderly suddenly threw open the door to their quarters.

"Get those drums!" he shouted. "The regiment's been ordered under arms!"

With their instruments flaring away, the camp suddenly became a wintry hornets' nest. Men groped in the dark for their equipment, and officers tried desperately to form their companies. While the quartermaster's corps hurriedly doled out rations and ammunition, the soldiers stamped the ground and thrashed their arms in an effort to keep warm, listening all the while for the signal to advance.

While they waited, a steady roar of gunfire burst from the Union batteries ranging through the hills right in front of the regiment. As the flashing tongues of flame spit deadly missiles toward Fredericksburg, excitement reached fever pitch. At last they began moving; but because of dense fog near the river, progress was exceptionally slow.

After a two-mile march, they were ordered to stack rifles and take cover in some pines clustered between the river and the hills concealing the Union batteries, which only recently had become silent. By the time dawn broke, most of the fog had dispersed, revealing a partially completed pontoon bridge. However, it appeared that the work soon would be finished, and that the 106th and her sister regiments would be able to cross the river. Joe and Jon sat together on the trunk of a fallen tree and watched the engineers quietly slide the pontoons into their canvas cases, then carry them from the wagons to the water. Others strung them together with cables and guy ropes while still a third group laid planks across them to form a roadbed.

Suddenly, a rifle shot pierced the silence; and through the slight mist which was still hovering over the waters, the boys saw one of the engineers pitch forward into the swirling Rappahannock.

"Sharpshooters!" someone shouted.

When other shots followed in rapid succession, the engineers began scrambling for the shore. Within seconds the Union guns resumed their clamor; and one by one, the buildings near the Fredericksburg shore were shattered into crumbling, smoking heaps of wood and brick. Joe wondered how anyone could remain in them and still be alive; but before another hour passed, volunteers needed to cross the river in pontoons in order to dislodge the last of the sharpshooters.

Noon passed before work on the bridge could be continued, and it was nightfall by the time the 106th crossed the river and finally entered the town. Joe's company was promptly detailed as skirmishers to help drive out the last remnants of the Confederates; but since this action didn't require a drummer, Joe remained with Jon and the main body of the regiment near the river bank.

The next day General Hooker's Fifth Corps and the rest of General Sumner's Grand Division crossed the river; but except for short exchanges of artillery fire, there was no major engagement with the enemy.

During the afternoon, Joe and Jon walked to a section of the town where they were able to see a long ridge rising beyond the outskirts of Fredericksburg, and stretching for more than five miles.

Jon whistled. "I'll bet plenty o' Johnny Rebs are on the other side o' those hills!" he ventured.

"An' if we hafta fight on those snow-covered ridges, we're gonna be in for a hard time!" Joe pointed out.

The following morning, when the regiment was supplied with ammunition in excess of the usual amount, Joe was more certain than ever that the day of the long-awaited struggle had finally arrived; and it was less than a half hour later, when sounds of battle arose from below the town. While the 106th stacked rifles, Joe and Jon fidgeted uncomfortably with a small group of drummers, awaiting Captain Colter's command to sound *Assembly*. While they huddled together nervously, trying to keep warm, they looked down a rubble-strewn side street, and saw one of their sister brigades heading in the direction of the heights beyond the town.

"We'll prob'ly be next," Jed McCollister observed; and upon hearing these words, Joe and Jon exchanged concerned glances.

As Jed suspected, they soon received the order to march; and Captain Colter was beside them barking orders excitedly. "To your companies, men! Hurry!" he shouted. Then looking at Joe and Jon for an instant, he said, "Stay alert, boys!"

Suddenly, an unexplainable sensation of fear ran rampant throughout Joe's body. Reaching out impulsively, he grasped his friend by the elbow. "Jon!" he said anxiously. "Be careful!"

Jon returned an equally nervous glance. "Good luck, Joe!" he said in a low voice. Then, forcing a slight smile, he said, "We've been through this before. We'll be all right!" And pivoting quickly, he ran toward Company D.

Within a quarter of an hour they were marching toward the hills. Already the din of musket and cannon indicated that the center of the enemy's position had very likely been engaged; and moments later, Confederate artillery fire began striking dangerously near the 106th.

A short distance beyond the town, they came to a halt and assumed attack formation. As they carried out their officers' commands, the men watched the progress of the battle taking place on the slopes ahead of them. The gently rolling ground was broken here and there by low ridges and shallow ravines. There were even a few fences, and halfway up the heights, the Confederates had constructed rifle pits and earthworks.

Joe's attention was momentarily attracted to the top of the hill where a solitary mansion stood like a mighty fortress. Running along the ridge in front of it was a high stone wall; and as the Union forces attempted to fight their way up the hillsides, practically a solid sheet of rifle flame poured from behind it.

This concentrated fire stunned the attacking units; and Joe watched with horror as men in blue toppled by the scores, causing the thinned Union lines to falter for a few moments before bravely surging ahead once more. Nevertheless, a second deadly volley from the blazing wall stopped it abruptly; and finally, the survivors were mercifully ordered to retreat.

As Joe watched the pitiful scene before him, he shivered, noticing for the first time how cold the day really was. His hands were almost numb, and his face felt nearly frozen. There was no relief from the wintry weather as they waited in the frigid ravine, watching the second and third unsuccessful Union attempts to gain the heights. Although most of the Confederates were finally routed from the earthworks, the gallant waves of blue still could not reach the wall.

Then, without warning, cannon balls and canister began coming down like hail upon the ravine; and Joe dived for cover with the rest of the regiment. A quarter of an hour later, when the barrage finally ceased, he rose to his knees just as a fourth Federal assault was launched. However, his thoughts suddenly centered upon the wounded who lay upon the snow-crested slopes. In this kind of weather he was certain they could easily freeze to death before help could reach them!

Turning his attention to the latest attack, he watched hopefully as it surged past the now unmanned earthworks and streamed closer to the top of the slope and the seemingly invincible wall. This time, musket fire came from the windows and balconies of the mansion, as well as from behind the stone breastwork; and under this withering barrage, the attack collapsed just yards short of its goal.

As the battered lines of blue retreated over their fallen comrades, men in gray suddenly began leaping across the fortification. At first they appeared to be giving chase, but Joe was shocked to see them stop to remove a warm coat or a pair of boots from one of their victims, and then return to the safety of their stronghold.

When the pillaging ceased, something occurred which Joe would never forget. An unarmed Confederate jumped over the wall; and at first, Joe thought that he too was searching for much-needed clothing. However, to his surprise, the man began picking his way among the wounded Federals, giving them drinks of water from the many canteens slung around his shoulders. Upon witnessing this incredible act of bravery, the Union troops raised their weapons on high, and sang out a prolonged shout of praise! Then for nearly half an hour, as if in tribute to such mercy, even the artillery ceased firing, as this courageous Confederate soldier returned to the wall time and again for more canteens.

Some time later, as daylight was fading rapidly, Joe hoped that possibly he would hear an order for the troops to fall back; but it never came. Instead, the call to advance came running down the line; and Joe wasn't ashamed to feel his body suddenly tremble. His numb fingers barely responded, and his hickories felt like lead!

Looking fearfully along the ranks, he caught a brief glimpse of Jon, who also chose that very instant to look in Joe's direction. Their eyes met for one brief second, just before the regiment moved out of the ravine and gradually spread far to either side. As the drummers sounded the long roll, the regiment picked up momentum; and only seconds later, they reached the blood-soaked arena, where the pitiful cries of the wounded fell excruciatingly upon their ears. As they ran, Joe kept his eyes on the ground, not wishing to cast even one glance toward the now-despised wall.

Without realizing it, he felt himself trying to run ever faster, even though his feet were continually slipping on the slick surface. Somehow he managed to keep his mind on his drumming, while leaping across those who had already fallen during the previous attacks. To his surprise, during this maddening dash up the slope, he seemed to have lost all concern for safety, and actually felt as though he were burning with fever in spite of the coldness.

Then, suddenly, Company C's ranks seemed to be cut to shreds as a result of the first deafening roar of muskets that issued from behind the stone barricade; and one brief instant later, a deafening explosion, accompanied by a tremendous concussion, sent Joe hurling violently backward and down the slope!

Joe lay unconscious for a long time; and when he opened his eyes, he was staring into a partially starlit sky. Shaking his head slightly, he tried to collect his senses in an effort to determine where he was, gradually becoming aware that he was shivering almost uncontrollably and could barely move his fingers.

Then, he remembered. Realizing that he was lying on the frozen slopes outside Fredericksburg, he determined to struggle to his feet in an effort to move and get warm; but just as he began to raise himself on one elbow, he heard someone walking nearby. A moment later, he felt strong arms lift him to his feet, as piercingly sharp pain seared its way along his outer left thigh.

"You all right?" came a whisper.

In a flash, Joe's senses pricked up, as he thought he recognized the voice. "Is that you, Jed?" he asked, both surprised and elated at hearing a familiar voice.

"Yeah, but not so loud! No truce has been called yet!" he warned. "Boy! I'm glad I found you, Joe! I've been lookin' for you an' Jon for almost . . ."

"Jon?" Joe interrupted instantly, frightened by Jed's words.

"Yeah! When neither o' you answered roll call, me an' three o' the other drummers came back to look for you. They're around here somewhere," he said, squinting his eyes as if trying to penetrate the darkness. "The bunch of us stick together like flies."

Again Joe felt cutting pain and reached instinctively toward his thigh, while setting his drum on the frozen slope. He could tell his trousers were badly torn; and when they felt wet to the touch, he wondered if it was blood or melted snow.

"I think I got hit with either a musket ball or some shrapnel," Joe remarked, wincing because of the throbbing in his thigh.

Jed saw him looking intently at his leg and leaned forward to see what he could determine in the pale glow offered by a shrouded moon.

"Good grief! Your leg's a mess!" he exclaimed. "C'mon! We gotta get you back to the hospital area fast!"

"I'm not leavin' without Jon!" Joe blurted. "I can walk! Let's look for him! If he's on this slope, he'll freeze to death! Don't you understand, Jed? I can't leave him here!"

"All right! All right! But be quiet!" Jed cautioned a second time while shaking his head in admiration of Joe's staunch loyalty to his friend.

"The last time I saw him, he was up that way," Joe said, motioning to their left.

"Well, let's take a look; but if we don't find him in short order, you're goin' back, if I hafta carry you back!" Jed insisted.

As they began their search, Joe asked, "Did we get over the wall at the top o' the hill?"

"No! Tried seven times, but never made it!" Jed replied disgustedly.

His companion's words did little to comfort Joe, as he both limped and slid across the snow-covered landscape. By the muffled sounds around them, he could tell that others were also in the process of searching for fallen comrades. Stopping for a few moments and looking at the silhouettes about him, he tried to get his bearings.

"If he's on this slope, he should be somewhere in this area," Joe indicated with a sweep of his left arm. "You move out in that direction, an' I'll go this way," he whispered.

They separated and gradually ascended the snow-glazed ridge. The moon fought the clouds for control of the skies, and most of the time it was too dark to see even relatively clearly for more than just a few yards. Fortunately, the chill of the night was no longer unbearable; for a balmy wind had begun to blow softly out of the south.

From time to time the boys were distracted by other searchers stumbling through the darkness; and when anyone inadvertently made any kind of loud noise, Joe winced and cringed when a rifle shot would whine through the still of the night, sending its piercing echo reverberating across the hills.

Becoming more and more discouraged with each passing moment, Joe crouched and practically crawled, looking for just one object - a drum. As he groped in the darkness, he could hear the faint moans of some of the wounded and felt a twinge of conscience as he passed; but realizing that the litter-bearers probably would soon find them, he continued onward.

Joe was thinking about changing his area of search, when two men came near him, struggling to carry a comrade down the hillside. As they labored to keep their footing, one of them stumbled upon something which slid a short distance and stopped. Joe's heart nearly leaped to his throat, for it had the familiar sound of a drum!

As he limped painfully toward it, his heart beats quickened. "Jon?" he called out hopefully. "Are you there?"

"Quiet!" barked the soldier who had nearly tripped over the instrument. "You want every Reb on the hill after our hides?"

Joe had only one thought on his mind and paid little attention to the gruff warning, as he hastened painfully toward the drum. Then, when he found it, he carefully removed its strap which was still draped around the slight, motionless figure lying face-down in the heavily trampled snow, and suddenly found himself wishing he had never discovered it! Desperately hoping that it wasn't Jon, he knelt beside the drum and paused for one fearful moment before reaching forward and tugging at the right shoulder. As Joe very gingerly turned the figure, the faint light of the moon fell upon a very familiar face, streaked with blood.

"Jon!" he gasped, attempting to choke back his emotions but failing, as tears almost instantaneously began coursing down his face. Cupping the back of Jon's head in his left hand, he reached around him and put his right palm in the middle of the lad's back, jostling him very gently and half-whispering his name again . . . "Jon!" . . . hoping desperately to see his eyes flicker open. But there was no response, as his "little brother" lay completely limp, cradled in his arms.

Then, his heart churning within him, he gently pulled his fallen comrade almost effortlessly to his chest, and totally enveloped him in a strong embrace as his warm tears flowed steadily.

For several long minutes, Joe simply let his emotions overflow; and as he gradually came to grips with reality, he lapsed into an anguished prayer that God would help him understand!

At last, in a barely audible whisper, he said tearfully, "I don't know why He's taken you, Jon . . . but I know we'll meet again sometime! . . . Your friendship was the greatest gift I ever had!"

As he tenderly laid his unforgettable companion against the snow, he happened to glance at Jon's right hand. By the faint moonlight he could see he was clenching something white in his fist. Mystified, he took Jon's cold, stiff hand into his own and realized he was clutching Sarah's letters! Tugging firmly, he pulled them loose and slid them into his own pocket.

Joe could barely see through the tears, as, for a few moments, he again tenderly embraced Jon's lifeless body. Then, placing his arms under his back and knees, he gathered all the strength he could muster and somehow managed to lift him, pain shooting relentlessly now along his leg. But before he had taken a dozen steps, he came upon Jed.

"Is it Jon?" Jed asked. "Is he . . . " But there was sufficient moonlight to answer his question even before he finished.

The walk back to Fredericksburg was heart-wrenching. Twice Joe refused Jed's offer to help carry Jon, even though the agonizing, searing sting in his leg seemed to become more excruciating with each halting step. But neither the burden nor the pain could even begin to compare with his grief!

When Jed offered a third time, Joe blurted almost angrily, "No, Jed! Don't you understand? He's practically my little brother! I wanna take him back myself!"

Finally, after trudging laboriously the entire distance through mud and snow, they entered the torch-lit hospital area near the river front, where the sight of so many injured and dying men lying in the straw or on countless litters, sent a sickening feeling throughout Joe's system. Finding one of the few vacant spots remaining, he slowly sank to his knees, delicately laying his comrade in the straw that had been strewn on the ground.

By now the pain in his thigh had become totally unbearable; and he seemed to have to strain to be able to see Jed, who had also knelt with him.

At that moment, one of the surgeons stooped beside them, checking for Jon's vital signs; but a shake of his head merely confirmed what Joe already knew.

Quickly seizing the opportunity, Jed informed the officer of Joe's wound; and the doctor snappily called for litter-bearers.

Realizing that he was completely exhausted, Joe reached for Jed's arm. With his eyes now only half open, he whispered weakly, "Would you find Cap'n Colter . . . an' some o' the

other drummers?"

His eyes began to blur; and he closed them for a few seconds, shaking his head in an effort to clear his mind before continuing.

"Would you . . . bury Jon?" he asked.

"Sure!" Jed answered. "We'll take care . . . "

But before Jed could finish, Joe interrupted him. "Please . . . if you can get my bedroll . . . wrap him in it," he pleaded.

Then, before Jed could catch him, Joe suddenly lost consciousness and slumped forward, his head coming to rest directly upon Jon's chest.

Nearly a day later, when Joe's cyes finally fluttered open, they focused somewhat hazily upon rough-hewn rafters high above him. Then he realized that someone was sitting on the floor beside him.

"Well, it's about time!" Jed remarked, forcing a smile. I thought you were gonna sleep all day!"

Then turning aside, Jed called out, "Cap'n Colter! He's awake!"

Within seconds the captain was kneeling beside him. "How're you feelin', Joe?" he asked.

Joe managed a slight smile. "All right, I guess. But I'm cold!" he admitted, as he felt himself shivering.

"I'll see if I can find another blanket," Jed offered, scurrying away.

Joe began looking from side to side, and realized he was lying in a main aisle among church pews. Then, suddenly remembering what had happened, he blurted, "Jon! Did you . . . "

"Yes, Joe. Just relax an' take it easy," the captain advised. "Everything's taken care of. They've made a temporary hospital outta this church, an' Jed an' three other drummers helped me dig a grave right out back in the cemetery, not three minutes from here. We buried Jon this morning!" he said with an obvious huskiness in his voice. "Wrapped in your bedroll."

"Then I've gotta . . . " But as he tried to sit up, the pain quickly dropped him to a prone position just as Jed returned not only carrying a blanket, but with the surgeon as well.

"Easy, son! That was a good-sized piece o' shrapnel I dug out o' that muscle last night, an' it'll take at least six weeks to heal properly," the doctor informed him.

"Can I walk?" Joe inquired hopefully.

"If you feel strong enough, but with crutches for a while," he advised. "That wound has to continue to drain, an' the bandages must be changed regularly. You can go home if you have a good doctor nearby who can take care of you."

"The best!" Joe assured him. "Old Doc Taylor has fixed me up many a time!"

"Good! A train of ambulances leaves here in about an hour," the surgeon informed him.

Then looking at Captain Colter, he said, "I suppose this is the young man you were asking me about?"

"Yes, sir," responded the captain. Then looking at Joe, he said with a smile, "The best drummer I've ever had!"

"Well," responded the surgeon. "You make sure he's in an ambulance when that wagon train pulls out."

"You can count on it, sir!" the captain replied.

Then as the doctor was about to leave, Joe asked, "Sir, could I go with Jed an' the cap'n to the cemetery in back o' the church?"

Catching a concerned glance and a nod from the captain, the surgeon replied as he walked hurriedly away, "By all means! But get some o' that hot broth in your system that those ladies are preparin' over there, an' don't miss that ambulance train," he repeated firmly.

Jed quickly brought his new friend a tinful of hot broth, some crackers and a piece of bread. Then he and Captain Colter helped him into a nearby pew.

"How far is it to the camp, Jed?" Joe inquired between sips of strengthening broth.

"Just across the road. Why?"

"While I finish this, could you get your drum an' bring my haversack an' some heavy twine or cord?"

"Sure! . . . But what's the cord for?" Jed asked with a strange look.

"You'll see. But please hurry! An' if any o' the other drummers can come along, I'd really appreciate it!" Joe called, even as Jed was scurrying away.

The captain sat and chatted with him as he finished eating. Before long, Jed returned with everything Joe had requested, and brought along four other drummers as well. "We even have extra drums for you an' Cap'n Colter," Jed said solemnly. "I think I know what you've got in mind."

Then, looking at Joe, somewhat uncertain as to his physical state, he asked, "Do you think you're strong enough to play it?"

"I hope so," Joe replied. "Can someone get me a pair o' those crutches outta that stack against the wall?" he asked, pointing to a spot near the main door.

Moments later, taking a deep breath, Joe set his empty tin on the pew and pulled his Bible out of the haversack. After reaching for the crutches that one of the drummers handed him, he began walking toward the front of the church. His leg still hurt, but thankfully the piercingly sharp pain of the previous day was gone.

Soon they were outdoors, walking toward Jon's grave. It was a cool, damp afternoon with light snow still clinging tenaciously to the grassy areas and shrubs. Near by, burying details were laboring feverishly to lay to rest countless others who had died in the ill-fated battle.

When they arrived at the sight of Jon's freshly covered final resting place, Jed pointed to the headboard and said, "This is sort of a special place we picked out, Joe."

Captain Colter wrapped his arm around Joe's shoulders. "We intentionally chose a spot under a hickory tree, an' from here you can look across the Rappahannock an' see the ridge where he played his drum for the last time."

Tears began to cloud Joe's eyes, as he looked off to the still snow-covered ridges. Then he asked Jed to drape the drum around his shoulders for him. After pausing a few moments in an effort to settle his emotions, he realized it was futile. Looking at the Bible, he said, "I was gonna read . . . the 23rd Psalm . . . but I don't think I can make it!"

He paused and swallowed hard before looking to his commanding officer. "Would you read it, please, Cap'n Colter?"

"Well, Joe . . . I'd really like to . . . " He began to clear his throat. "But I'm sorta . . . havin' a little trouble seein' very well right now," he admitted, looking at Joe through tear-dimmed eyes. "Maybe we'd better let Jed read it."

"I'd be glad to!" Jed responded. Then, after finding the passage, he read it slowly and extremely solemnly. When he reached *the valley of the shadow of death*, Joe glanced heavenward and managed a grateful smile.

After Jed finished, Joe asked everyone to drum along with him as he called out the various signals he and Jon had learned together over the past four months, Jed and the captain nodding their admiration when they noticed that Joe began with *Retreat*, but ended with *Advance.*

Then, after a few moments of silence, Joe said, "Now, just give me a slow, quiet roll, an' keep it goin' while I play somethin' that was really special to both of us."

Captain Colter began the roll and the others joined him. By this time, all the various burial details around them had temporarily ceased their own grim task; and they stood, kepis in hand, watching and listening intently to what they realized was a tremendously somber occasion for this small band of truly devoted drummers.

Joe took a deep breath and uttered a silent prayer to ask for strength. Then, slowly at first, he began a hushed, gentle roll that became faster and louder; and then he swung into the final routine that he and Jon had performed together for President Lincoln, even going through the motions of striking Jon's now invisible sticks, as, in his very mind, he could picture his young friend standing in spirit before him, striking Joe's sticks rhythmically, and all the while flashing his impish grin. Then, another roll, a sharp flam, and sudden silence, as Joe bowed his head in a final prayer for his unforgettable pal, tears streaming down his cheeks.

Joe stood quietly for several minutes, praying fervently. At last, looking up he said, "Hand me the twine, please, Jed."

His tall friend pulled the fairly lengthy strand from his pocket, then watched curiously as Joe took it and fumbled for a few moments with his drumsticks. Then a smile creased Jed's face as he saw Jon's extremely devoted friend form them into the shape of a cross, and begin to bind the twine about them where they intersected, in order to hold them in position.

"I guess you'd better tie the knot really tight for me, Cap'n. I'm not feelin' too strong," Joe confessed, beginning to sense a slight dizziness after the sudden expenditure of effort that his drumming routine had required.

After the captain readily complied, Joe handed Jed his drum, took his crutches in one hand, and sank to his right knee. Taking the hickories, he began to bury the tip of his hand-fashioned, drumstick cross into the fresh earth, directly in front of Jon's headboard. Then, standing erect, he heaved a heavy sigh, replaced his crutches under his arms, saluted and said in a very confident voice, "Now, little brother . . . you play for *Him* . . . till He lets *us* play together again sometime!"

Back at the church, before the drummers returned to their

camp site, Joe thanked them for all they had done. However, Jed stayed for a few extra moments to see if there was anything else he could do for Joe, realizing that he had been enduring an extremely emotional situation at a time when he was severely wounded besides.

"I'll be all right," Joe assured him. "The cap'n's here with me, an' I'll be on my way home soon. That'll help make me feel better in a hurry, I'm sure!"

Then, looking very appreciatively at his new acquaintance, Joe added, "I only met you a couple o' days ago, Jed; but I already feel like I've known you all my life!"

"Yep! War'll do that to you!" Jed admitted with a slight smile. "An' after seein' how you an' Jon got along, it's sorta obvious that when *you* make a friend, it's for life!" he said solemnly. "I'm glad I got to know you two, even if it was for only a few days. An' don't forget. If you ever get to Williamsport, look me up. An' I hope you make it home for Christmas!" he added, reaching to shake Joe's hand.

After watching Jed disappear through the church doors, Joe saw the pastor of the church talking with some of the wounded nearby. Unobtrusively, he asked the clergyman if he could supply him with the necessary materials to write a letter to his family.

Obligingly, the preacher quickly fulfilled his request; and since Joe had very little time, he shared with his parents and Sarah only the barest details of Jon's death and even less about his own wound, not wishing to worry them unnecessarily. He closed by informing them that he hoped to be home by Christmas, if travel conditions and army processing would permit. Then, after accepting Captain Colter's offer to mail his letter for him, he walked with his commanding officer toward the ambulance wagons.

The captain and two orderlies helped him into the soft bed of straw, where he settled himself comfortably.

Looking at the head musician who had been like a father away from home, he said, "Sir, I can't imagine what my enlistment would've been like without you. You just made everything *so* easy! An' even though this seems to be endin' in the saddest way possible, I don't think I'd've wanted to miss these last couple o' months for anything in the world! So thanks for all you've done for me an' Jon! I'll just never forget it!"

The captain patted his youthful shoulder before reaching to shake his hand firmly. Tears began to cloud his eyes one more time as he said, "Well, young man . . . I feel as though I'm losin' *two sons!* That's how much you've both meant to me! You've practically been my life these past four months, an' I wouldn't trade 'em for any I've ever lived; so we're even. As a matter of fact . . . if I knew your parents wouldn't complain so much, I'd prob'ly kidnap you an' take you home with *my* family!"

Joe smiled. "Thank you, sir. I'll take that as one o' the greatest compliments o' my life!"

Then, as both smiled through tear-stained eyes, they clasped hands firmly for the last time, just as the wagon got underway.

Chapter 15

Trapped in the Flames

Throughout his trip home, an agonizing war of emotions was being fought on the battlefields of Joe's heart and mind, as the sad remembrances of Jon kept vying with the joyful anticipation of being with his family once more, especially with Christmas approaching. He knew that he desperately needed their presence to help him through the turmoil that suddenly had been thrust into his life at such a young age.

After more than a week of riding in ambulances and hospital railway cars, Joe finally arrived on Penn Common in the city of York, late in the morning the day before Christmas. There, aides herded him along, with dozens of others who were to be processed or cared for at the city's military hospital. Several civilian volunteers were helping the wounded; and Joe's attention was suddenly attracted to one of them, an elderly Negro man. Stopping to look carefully, he was certain it was Cato Jourdon; and Joe kept watching him until eventually, the man walked his way.

"Mr. Jourdon!" he called.

Old Cato stopped and looked at Joe curiously. "Yes, suh. An' how does you know me?" he asked.

Joe motioned for him to step away from the others who were busily milling about, and explained in a low voice who he was and how he had been present the day Cato's wagon overturned.

Stepping back and looking at him in astonishment, Cato said, "Oh, Mastuh Shelley! How *much* you an' yoah fathuh an' sistuh has done foh me! . . . An' Dr. Tayloh too!" he added.

Joe smiled. "An' you've done a lot for other folks yourself, Mr. Jourdon!"

"But what is you doin' heah, son?" Cato asked.

"Well, I was wounded at the Battle of Fredericksburg. Now I'm just tryin' to get home for Christmas, an' my folks have no idea where I am!" Joe explained.

"Then you is as good as home, young man!" Cato announced. "Ah's finished as soon as these men is registehed. You come with me; Ah'll take you to the right folks, an' we'll be on the road *real* quick like!"

"But it's the day before Christmas!" Joe exclaimed, completely astonished by the man's generous offer. "What about your *own* family?"

Cato just looked at him for a few seconds, smiled and shook his head. "Ah ain't got no family, Mastuh Shelley. An' 'sides," he added, "this is what Christmas is really all about, now ain't it, son? An' Ah can jus' 'magine how much yoah folks wants to have *you* home right away!"

An hour later they were both wrapped in blankets in Cato's wagon, heading east on the York turnpike under a threatening sky. Eventually, as they neared Wrightsville and passed the very place where Cato's wagon had overturned, the two merely looked at one another with knowing glances.

Joe's attention focused on the fields to their right, as he mentally pictured himself scurrying through the tall weeds with the runaway; and quickly he closed his eyes for a few moments, remembering Nat in prayer once more.

Snow began to fall in the late afternoon, as they headed down the road toward the Shelley Farm. In the distance Joe saw Sarah walking from the barn; and as she stepped onto the porch, she turned to see who was in the approaching wagon. She put up her hand to shield her eyes from the hard-flying snowflakes and kept staring until the rig swung through the gate. When she saw her brother, she gasped in amazement, quickly set the milk pail on the porch and ran toward him as fast as she could.

"Stop the wagon, please, Cato!" Joe said, and immediately lowered himself cautiously to the ground.

"Joey! Joey!" Sarah shouted as she ran; and rushing headlong into his outstretched arms, she burst into tears and cried, "Hold me, Joey! Just hold me!"

Gathering his sister into his arms, he realized without question that the family had received his letter concerning Jon. Then, as Sarah sobbed heavily upon his chest, he looked over her shoulder at Cato and said, "This could be a rough Christmas, Mr. Jourdon!"

"Ah's sorry, Mastuh Shelley!" Cato replied, sensing the sudden atmosphere of sadness. Then looking to the skies, he said, "But Ah thinks Ah had bes' be leavin' right away! This don' look good!"

"No, Cato! Please! If I let you leave, my ma and pa'll skin me alive! Besides, there's no way o' knowin' how bad this storm's gonna be. Please . . . put your wagon right there in the barn; an' you'll find plenty to feed your horse."

Cato shrugged his shoulders in surrender. "Yes, suh, if you insists," he replied, handing Joe his crutches before heading for shelter.

Still comforting his sister, Joe looked toward the house and saw his parents and Pastor Jackson rushing toward them, and together they had a highly emotional reunion. No one mentioned a word about Jon; but Joe could tell by the looks on their faces and the hugs, kisses and handshakes, that his young friend was very much on *their* minds too.

"Excuse the tears, please, pastor," Joe said with clouded eyes, reaching to shake the clergyman's hand. "But these past couple o' weeks've been a little on the emotional side! I've been away from home only four months, but I feel like I've aged thirty years!"

Pastor Jackson placed a comforting hand on his shoulder. "The best words I can offer at a time like this is . . . the Bible says that Jesus wept. And if He can weep . . . so can you, my young friend!"

"Then I guess . . . I'm in pretty good company!" Joe admitted, smiling through his tears.

"Well, I was visiting some of the members of the congregation this afternoon," the pastor informed him, "and thought I'd stop by to see if you got home. It turns out I picked the perfect time! But I'd better be leaving now; Marge'll be expecting me soon. I'm sure I'll see you all at church tonight. Looks as if it might be a great time to break out the family sleigh!" he added, as they all bid farewell.

Mr. Shelley departed to help Cato, and Joe walked cautiously with his mother and sister toward the house over the already slick ground. But even as he gazed at the flakes swirling heavily before him, the sight of snow made his mind suddenly flash back to Fredericksburg . . . and the snowy hillside . . . and fallen men . . . the explosion . . . and Jon!

"Joey Shelley!" his mother called loudly, shaking him from his momentary flashback into the worst day of his life. "Didn't you hear me?"

"Uh . . . Did you say somethin', Ma?" Joe asked. "I'm sorry; I guess I was daydreamin'!" he apologized, somewhat embarrassed.

"I asked you how long you'll need the crutches," she repeated.

"Not long. I'm gettin' stronger every day, but I'm supposed to see Doc Taylor the day after Christmas. He has to inform the military hospital when I'm completely recovered."

Though he had to walk into the house on crutches, he was never happier to see home. Joe took off his coat and hung it over the back of a parlor chair. Slowly, he turned toward Sarah and just stared at her for a few moments. Finally, he said, "I don't have any presents I can offer anyone this year . . . but I think I have somethin' very special . . . for a really *great* sister!"

"Havin' at least one o' my brothers home for Christmas is special enough!" Sara replied, showing her first smile since her brother had arrived.

Joe reached carefully inside his jacket pocket and removed her letters. He found it almost impossible to talk for a few moments. Then, swallowing hard, he said, "When I found Jon on the battlefield . . . believe it or not . . . he had your letters clenched in his hand! I've been keepin' 'em for you . . . An' in case you're wonderin' . . . I haven't read 'em. Honest!"

Sarah reached out and hugged her brother. "It wouldn't've mattered even if you did," she insisted; and she kissed him on the forehead.

Taking her wrist into his hand, Joe gently placed the letters in hers and said, "You keep 'em as somethin' really special to always remember him by!"

Sadly, Sarah unfolded two of them; but when she looked at a third, she glanced up with a look of surprise. "I didn't write this one! It's . . . written to me! . . . But it's not finished!"

Then, stifling some tears, she grasped her skirt, dashed to the kitchen and ran up the stairs to her room, Joe staring blankly after her.

Then, turning his head slightly, his gaze fell upon the little sign saying *Jon's Room,* still hanging in its place.

"We decided not to take it down," his mother smiled weakly.

Joe nodded slowly. "I'd *love* to have him here, but at least I know he's in heaven; an' the Bible says . . . that's far, far better! So we'll just have to take that on faith!"

Mrs. Shelley put a comforting arm around her son's shoulders and said, "You'll meet again one day, Joey; but in the meantime, he'll always be here in our hearts and minds!"

At that moment Mr. Shelley entered with Cato and introduced him to his wife. After making him welcome, and then learning that he had no family, Joe's parents insisted that he wait out the storm and share Christmas with them, especially since he had brought the Shelleys a gift that was truly beyond their ability to express their gratitude.

The men remained in the parlor, and Mrs. Shelley stepped into the kitchen. Sarah's door opened; and she appeared at the top of the stairs. Her mother looked up, but as a parent, knew it was one of those times for silence. Slowly, Sarah descended, gazing constantly at her, but with a faraway expression in her eyes. When she reached the last step and stood facing her, she suddenly threw her arms around her; and they hugged one another.

"He was *so nice,* Ma! I'm really glad I got to meet him at least once!"

During supper, their spirits gradually seemed to attain a much higher level, probably because they were entertaining someone for whom the family held extremely high respect. And later, when they began to trim a handsome tree in the parlor, the feeling of Christmas truly began to pervade the atmosphere. The Shelleys secretly enjoyed watching Cato, for he declared it was the first time in his life that he had ever helped trim a tree.

When they finished, Mr. Shelley hitched Swift to the family sleigh; and soon the five of them were enjoying a refreshing ride through the still-falling snow, heading for church and the traditional Christmas Eve service. Almost unwittingly the cheerful jingling of the bells helped soothe the churning thoughts of Jon that kept coursing through Joe's heart and mind from time to time.

After the many carols and an extremely uplifting worship service, Joe asked his family to wait until everyone left; and once more, as on previous occasions, it was Pastor Jackson who took time to sit with him in the front pew and bring special comfort and prayer in an hour of real spiritual need.

"Thank you, pastor!" Joe said when he finished. "It's so beautiful to *know* where he is, an' that I'll see him again one day!"

"That's what the Christmas story's really all about, Joey, isn't it? That's why He came!" And then, throwing a strong arm around the lad's shoulders, he added, "Now . . . my advice is to go home with your family and enjoy this very special time of the year in the way it was really *meant* to be celebrated; and just keep in mind that Jon . . . and his father . . . are celebrating it too! Only in heaven . . . and with Him!"

"That's just the greatest news in the world!" Joe said with a smile.

As he walked back the aisle on his crutches to join his family and Cato, who were waiting patiently at the rear of the church, he was smiling and feeling much more exhilarated.

The ride home was a light-hearted trip over the beautiful snow-covered York County landscape; and even old Cato joined them as they sang Christmas carols all along the way.

After the holidays, the Shelleys prepared to settle down for the winter siege; and since work around the farm was rather limited, with the schoolmaster's gracious permisson, Joe returned to school. This decision made Dave and Ted especially happy, for to them it seemed like old times once more.

The shrapnel wound was healing rather slowly, but nevertheless, to Doctor Taylor's satisfaction; and Joe soon discarded his crutches. It was slightly more than three weeks after the holidays, when the ageless physician decided that perhaps Joe should return to the military unit at the York Hospital for the army's opinion as to his recovery.

However, that very day Joe received an envelope bearing a Harrisburg postmark. Curious, he tore it open and found a number of papers. One in particular caught his attention quickly. Near the top was a large, blue eagle; and in the center in bold print was the word *Discharged.*

Hastily, he read through all the documents. One was a letter congratulating him for the part he had played in his country's efforts to preserve the Union, and others verified his having served with both the 125th and 106th Regiments.

Joe was taken by surprise, though he suddenly realized that

actually, only several more weeks would've remained on his enlistment. Regardless, his parents were obviously happy that their son would not have to return!

Joe continued to pay regular visits to Doctor Taylor. Most of the smaller wounds eventually healed completely, and the largest lesion was showing excellent progress. However, it wasn't until the middle of February that the country physician was completely satisfied, though there were still signs of a slight limp.

One day at school in early March, Dave asked, "Why don't we start workin' on our Indian collection again? I'm soon ready for another trip to the graveyards!"

"Are you forgettin' what Mr. Loney said about takin' Beauty on long rides?" Ted asked.

Joe was somewhat mystified when he saw Dave cast what appeared to be a warning glance in Ted's direction. "What's wrong with Beauty, Dave?" he asked. "Good weather'll be here before we know it, an' I thought we'd be ridin' to school together again."

Dave hesitated a few moments. "Well, uh . . . I-I'm really not sure," he stammered, looking out of the corner of his eye at Ted for help.

"The other day when I was visitin' Dave, Mr. Loney was over at their farm to have a look at some o' the animals," Ted offered. "An' he said it'd be best to take it easy with 'er for a spell, that's all," he added in an off-handed way, as Dave rolled his eyes in obvious relief.

"Well, Dave, if we decide to do any searchin', we can ride double on Swift," Joe suggested.

During the following weeks, farm work kept Joe busy; but he managed to make a daily trip to Wrightsville in quest of a letter from Dan, or to buy a news sheet in order to follow the latest accounts of the war. However, most of the news concerned the fighting which raged along the Mississippi.

Then, on the third of May, he purchased a copy of the *Columbia Spy* and read of a major battle developing near Chancellorsville, Virginia, not far from Fredericksburg. News from that area sent a cold shiver down his spine and brought back unpleasant memories, especially when he thought of the irony involved as Mr. Cooper had been buried at Frederick, and his son at Fredericksburg!

Each day he carefully checked the progress of the struggle, reading with particular interest anything that concerned the 125th or the 106th Regiments. It was not until the 6th of the month when he read that the issue had been settled. The Union forces were in retreat, and some reports indicated that the Confederate Army was heading north again!

With the passing of another month, school closed and Joe was concerned with the ever-increasing farm work and the news accounts which told of the gradual northerly movement of General Lee's army; for by the middle of June, there were frightening rumors that it was approaching the Pennsylvania border.

One warm day during the third week of June, as Joe rode into Wrightsville, he noticed that there was an excessively long line of traffic headed down the main road toward the bridge. A farmer and his two young sons were driving a small herd of cattle, trying desperately to keep them under control, as they became fidgety among the many wagons loaded with all kinds of personal belongings.

"What's goin' on?" Joe shouted at the driver of a nearby wagon.

"Ain't you heard?" the man asked, hardly believing his ears. "The Confederate Army's just on the other side o' York!"

This news was disturbing enough, but at that very moment Joe was surprised to see a company of militia come marching off the bridge and head up the hill in the direction of York itself. Before entering the general store, he stopped to watch them pass. Then later, as he was returning home, he saw those same men working in the fields just west of Wrightsville. Curious, he rode toward them and discovered that they were constructing earthworks. After riding home as quickly as he could, he found his father working near the barn and told him what he had seen.

His father shook his head. "That doesn't sound good, Joey!" he commented with a worried look.

"I know, Pa. An' if the Rebs pass through here, they'll take everything they can get their hands on! Their supplies've prob'ly been cut off for a long time, an' they've gotta live off the land!"

The two decided to hide various implements, food, and other important possessions in secluded places, but worked in such a manner as not to frighten Sarah or her mother unnecessarily.

The following day Joe again rode to the main trail, where he discovered that the original company had been joined by more than five hundred other militiamen. As he watched them, he also saw an unending stream of people on foot, on horseback and in wagons coming along the York Turnpike and going in the direction of the bridge.

When a farmer passed by, attempting with little success to keep his cattle moving along, Joe shouted, "Where you headin', mister?"

"Anywhere!" was the surprising answer. "Just so's I get across that confounded bridge!"

"What's the latest on the Rebs?" Joe inquired.

"They say they've got western York an' all of Adams County pretty well in hand, an' who knows where they're headin' next?" came the reply, as the gentleman farmer went along his way.

Joe wasn't certain how accurate the man's information was; but during the course of the next few days, news articles seemed to confirm the farmer's statement. Daily, Joe observed cattle, droves of sheep, and many more people in wagons of every description, as they continued fleeing eastward, raising clouds of dust as they approached the covered bridge.

On Saturday, June 27th, the family decided not to go to market in Columbia because of the tense situation; and around ten-thirty in the morning, Joe was returning to the farm after still another venture into Wrightsville. When he rode into the yard, he found his parents sitting dejectedly on the back porch.

"What's wrong?" he asked as he walked up the steps.

"I don't know whether it's a good thing you had Swift with you or not!" his father answered dolefully.

"Why?"

Mr. Shelley held out a slip of paper. "Here's a receipt for our animals. Some military men were here to get 'em out o' the way o' the Confederates, they said. They didn't ask if we had any other animals, an' I didn't offer the information."

Although Joe was concerned about this turn of events, he was somewhat relieved that he and Swift had been away. "I think you did right, Pa," Joe murmured. "I'd sooner take our chances o' keepin' Swift ourselves."

Through all that had been happening, Joe especially admired his mother's courage. Even when one of their neighbors brought news late in the day that York was about to fall completely into Confederate hands, she refused to be taken to the relative safety of Columbia.

When Sunday, the 28th of June, dawned, the sky was ominously overcast. A neighbor came to inform the Shelleys that church worship services were canceled and that many of the parishioners were fleeing town. Chagrined by this news, the family bustled about, hiding everything that could be of any possible use to the Confederates, and then sat down to a late mid-day meal. Only Sarah seemed to be overly disturbed, as she glanced nervously at Joe and her parents from time to time.

After their father prayed for courage and protection, besides giving thanks, Joe's mind was everywhere but on his food.

"I've been thinkin'," he mused. "If the Rebs get across that bridge, they'll have *no* trouble at all takin' Lancaster an' Harrisburg . . . an' maybe even Philadelphia!"

His father nodded in agreement. "You're right, Joey. They've gotta be stopped somehow, or there's no tellin' how far they'll go!"

Hardly had Mr. Shelley spoken when there came a rumble like that of distant thunder. Joe dropped his fork and sat perfectly upright, a momentary shiver running through his body. He realized it was a gloomy day, and a storm could be coming; but he recalled how he had been mistaken by similar sounds once before, as the 125th was marching through Maryland.

Hurrying to the window, he looked to make certain the sky wasn't stormy. Then, his convictions confirmed, without saying a word he raced to his room and seized the musket, powder and bag of shot he had secretly hidden earlier in the week.

Moments later he dashed down the steps. "They're here, Pa! I'm goin' to the earthworks!"

Before anyone had even a moment to react, Joe bolted through the doorway and down the path to the stable. In a matter of minutes, he and Swift left the yard, the sounds of cannon growing nearer. When he arrived at the fortifications, he saw that two emergency regiments, as well as a number of makeshift civilian companies, had been thrown into position in an attempt to thwart the Confederate advance. It didn't take Joe long, however, to realize that this brave but inexperienced band of probably less than a thousand men, would be no match for possibly an entire brigade of soldiers seasoned in battle.

Hopelessly, he looked about him. After tying Swift in a small thicket near the earthworks, he walked to the edge of the trees where he paused to scan the surroundings. He was certain that it would be impossible for the militia to hold back an approaching army, for the defenders were too few and would be totally unable to protect the heights on both their flanks.

Scurrying to the earthworks, he joined both military and civilian riflemen waiting side by side, one company being an entire unit of Negroes from Columbia. After a while the enemy artillery ceased; and an ominous silence followed, which mysteriously lasted for several hours.

While they waited apprehensively in the pits, Joe learned that there were other companies of militia made up of college students from the Normal School in Millerstown, located not too far away, as well as another group of students from Franklin and Marshall College in Lancaster. As he looked across his shoulders in both directions, he shook his head in admiration of these men who had courageously volunteered to take their stand against an oncoming, well-trained army.

As he kept his eye on the western horizon, twice he saw a gray-clad horseman ride along one of the rolling Piedmont hills, well out of the range of accurate rifle fire. Joe felt reasonably certain that their positions and strength were being scouted, and that probably it would be only a matter of time before the army was upon them. But as they waited, he couldn't cease from wondering where the Union forces were, totally puzzled by their absence.

It was nearly five o'clock when Joe's stomach began demanding food, and he yearned for some of the things he had left on his plate earlier that afternoon. Then, suddenly, he had other things to think about; for at that moment a vanguard of Confederates crested the hill directly in front of them. All along the slope, almost as far as the eye could see, troops in butternut and gray were advancing steadily.

First one shot rang out, then another; and quickly Joe found himself engaged in a full-scale conflict. It seemed strange not having his drum with him, and to be firing a musket instead. It was almost bizarre to realize that he had participated in two major battles of the war without ever firing a shot, and now lay practically at his very own doorstep fighting the same army he had previously traveled hundreds of miles to engage!

It didn't take long for the Confederates to show their superior strength. Within minutes their heavy artillery opened fire, pouring several thunderous explosions directly into the vicinity of the earthworks. The colonel in charge of the militia realized quickly that his small forces couldn't possibly deter for very long the massive army advancing toward them, and it was probably less than a quarter of an hour later that Joe heard his command to retreat to the bridge.

It was a wise decision; for if they waited much longer, they easily would be outflanked and quickly surrounded. As Joe scrambled from the earthworks, he wondered if he had taken a human life; but recalling how he had run through these very same fields with Nat on his heels just one year previously, he had no twinge of conscience whatsoever.

Quickly vaulting into the saddle, he glanced over his shoulder, admiring the courage of some of the wounded who continued, even at that moment, to fire upon the advancing Confederate skirmishers.

Swift galloped at full speed to the bridge, and Joe hastily led him a short distance to the south of the structure to tether him. Then he ran back toward the entrance, where he encountered a contingent of men who were refugees from the York Military Hospital. He quickly joined them as they pushed railroad ore cars in front of the bridge to serve as a barricade, overturning them by sheer force of numbers. Just as they successfully toppled the third car, Joe felt a tap on his shoulder.

"Hi, Joey!" came a familiar voice.

"Dave! . . . An' Ted! How'd you guys get here?" Joe asked, surprised to see his friends. "An' I thought Beauty was still sick, Dave!"

"We doubled-up on Ted's nag!" Dave grinned, giving his red-headed companion a jab in the rib cage. "Ted only got here a foot ahead o' me!"

"We sorta decided you're not the only one who's gonna see some action in this war!" Ted added.

"Stick around!" Joe smiled somewhat nervously. "You'll prob'ly get your money's worth! Like my pa says, this ain't gonna be no picnic! Rebs by the thousands are headed this way!"

At that moment Joe looked toward the bridge, where he saw a swarm of men working feverishly to do all that they could to weaken the fourth span, by sawing as many of the timbers as possible.

"Looks like they're gettin' ready to surprise the Rebs if they try to cross the bridge!" Joe observed, pointing toward the crew of carpenters.

He had hardly spoken, when a Confederate artillery shell burst deafeningly almost directly overhead, sending everyone scurrying for cover and instinctively throwing their arms about their heads for protection.

"Jumpin' catfish!" Dave gulped, looking at Joe wide-eyed. "It ain't the Fourth o' July yet, is it?"

"Like I said," Joe reminded him. "This ain't gonna be *no* picnic!"

While the bewhiskered colonel issued orders to place as many timbers near the entrance as possible, the small band of rapidly retreating defenders arrived at the bridge and was directed to head for Columbia without delay, along with several late-fleeing citizens who were running for their lives.

All at once, more cannonading began to rock the streets of Wrightsville; and as the militia approached the mammoth, wooden structure, the colonel shouted to one of his junior officers, "We'll probably have to destroy one of the sections of the bridge!"

When Joe overheard that remark, he looked at Dave and Ted. "What'll we do? Head for Columbia or stay here?"

Dave just looked at him and grinned. "Well, buddy-boy, now we know how the Minute Men musta felt at Lexington an' Concord," he said in a surprisingly calm manner. Then, brandishing an old firearm, he said, "I swiped my pa's musket, an' I aim to plunk me a Reb!" he announced. "I stay!"

"Me too!" piped Ted with a nod of his head.

"Then we all stay!" Joe agreed. "But let's get down to the canal where there's plenty o' protection! We can shoot from there; an' when things get too hot, we can jump on the horses an' head down the towpath lickety-split!"

While the militia retreated across the bridge, only a few volunteers remained. Within moments, the area seemed almost completely deserted, as a mere handful of men hid behind the railroad cars and at various places close to the bridge, in an effort to conceal their positions.

Meanwhile, the boys leaped to their horses and dashed for the canal. After they tied their mounts to some tall bushes, they hid behind the canal embankment, their feet at the water's edge and their rifles, primed and loaded, lying across the towpath.

Joe felt his heart beating at a tremendous rate, and his mind flashed back to the night when he and Nat had crept along that very path. In the midst of his thoughts, he recalled how his heart had gone wild on that occasion too.

Slowly he turned his head toward the amazingly long covered bridge, which had practically become the centerpiece of his life. Then, even as he was gazing at the huge structure, a sharp explosion sent fragments of the fourth span hurtling through the air!

"They're blowin' up the bridge!" Dave yelled.

"I hope they've got more powder!" Joe observed, as the last of the shingles, splinters of wood and other flying debris splashed into the Susquehanna. Along the fourth span, parts of the side of the structure had been blown away, but the roadbed was obviously still intact.

"That charge didn't do a very good job!" Ted observed. "The Rebs can still get across easy!"

The boys watched for several minutes but saw no one, and nothing else seemed to be happening. "Maybe they don't realize they haven't completely destroyed the span!" Joe blurted. "I'm goin' up there!"

"Count me in!" Dave cried.

"You stay, Ted! Two's enough!" Joe shouted as he leaped to the saddle, reaching to grab Dave's arm and helping him swing into position right behind him. Swift, seeming to sense the urgency of the situation, galloped at top speed. When they reached the crest of the slope, Joe reined the stallion's head hard to the right, signaling his chestnut mount to dash toward the ramp, where a militiaman suddenly rushed from the shadows of the bridge, holding his rifle above his head in an effort to stop them. At the sight of him, Swift reared unexpectedly, causing Dave to lose his grasp and go sprawling to the ground.

"You can't cross!" the man shouted, thinking the span had been destroyed. "Part of it's been blown to bits!"

"No, it ain't!" Dave yelled, scrambling to his feet. "That's what we came to tell you!"

Realizing there was no time for explanations, and without hesitating another second, Joe urged Swift forward and brushed past the astonished militiaman, riding desperately toward the damaged span. Light filtering through some holes in the roof and several gaps in the walls proved that Joe's fears were not unfounded - no one was near!

He rode as fast as he could under the circumstances; but when he reached the span where the charges had been set, there were so many splintered boards, shingles and other debris on the roadbed, that he was forced to dismount. Then, from force of habit, he tied Swift's reins to a section of the handrail that people on foot used when they walked across the bridge.

After picking his way through the rubble and eventually leaping to better footing along the fifth span of the bridge floor, he raced ahead through the semi-darkness in an effort to overtake the retreating men who were, by now, more than a hundred yards ahead of him, and evidently totally unaware that their plans had gone awry.

In the subdued light he nearly bumped into some heavy casks, but fortunately managed to side-step them without incident. As he ran, he shouted at the top of his voice, at last catching the men's attention. When they turned, they simply stared at Joe in disbelief.

"Where'd you come from, young man?" demanded the colonel he had seen earlier.

"From Wrightsville!" Joe blurted. "The explosives didn't destroy the roadbed! All the Rebs hafta do is clear the debris, an' they can still get across!"

In the obscure light the men exchanged worried glances. "Colonel Frick! For as much powder as we used, it should've blown that span to bits!" a burly civilian exclaimed.

"Well, if it had, Mr. Rich, this young man wouldn't be here!" the colonel stated emphatically.

Looking at another gentleman, the colonel said hurriedly, "Mr. Denney, it looks as if we'll have to fall back on our other plans!"

At that moment echoes of rifle shots sounded along the trestlework. Turning to look anxiously toward Wrightsville, they could barely see some of the rear guard firing from behind the overturned railroad cars.

"Quick! The casks!" Colonel Frick shouted to Mr. Denney, who already had sized up the situation and started to run. "It's our only chance!"

"But we're liable to burn the whole bridge down!" another civilian shouted fearfully.

"We don't have any choice, Mr. Lockard!" Colonel Frick pointed out in sheer desperation.

Terrified by these words, Joe turned to race for Swift; but even before he could take a stride, the colonel grasped him strongly by the arm. "Hold on, son! You can't go back there!" he bellowed.

"But my horse is on the bridge, an' I got him tied!" Joe shrieked.

At that moment, a group of young militiamen also rushed toward the casks which Joe had passed earlier, for they contained crude oil and were placed there just in the event of such an emergency.

"Let me go!" Joe pleaded with the colonel, still struggling to free himself from the officer's grasp. "Please!"

"Don't you understand, son? I can't *possibly* let you go back there!" the colonel repeated.

Turning to two of the civilians who evidently were members of the party in charge of setting the explosives, he called in a firm voice, "Mr. Miller an' Mr. Lockard, take this boy to the other side o' the bridge with you before he gets hurt! An' be firm if you must!"

"Grab his other arm, John!" said one of the men, as he took Joe forcefully by his left elbow.

Then looking at the lad somewhat sympathetically, Mr. Lockard said, "There's nothin' you can do for your horse now anyway, son!"

As Joe looked over his shoulder, he saw that the men had already knocked in the heads of the barrels and were hastily spilling their contents, drenching the floor of the bridge. Joe made one last desperate effort to escape the clutches of the two well-meaning Columbia cititzens, but was unable to break away, their vice-like grips revealing that they were fully committed to the carrying out of Colonel Frick's orders.

Totally sickened by this incredible turn of events, Joe looked back again and caught a brief glimpse of Swift in the distance, still firmly tied and pacing nervously in the light that was coming through the damaged area of the fourth span. Then his heart felt as though it were being wrenched from his body when he saw the men throw blazing torches onto the oil-soaked boards, which instantaneously mushroomed into a vast wall of flame and dense, black smoke!

Chapter 16

Surprises for Joe

For several hours Joe sat dejectedly upon the platform of the Philadelphia and Columbia Railroad Station, watching the roaring mass of flames across the Susquehanna, nearly a mile-long conflagration which now cast a deep reddish-purple glow through the sky, and dancing reflections across the relatively placid surface of the gently-flowing river. The angry sounds of the snapping, crackling flames seemed to be growing louder by the minute as the scorching blaze reached an almost deafening pitch, spreading eastward toward Columbia.

A loud, clanging noise suddenly caught Joe's attention; and he turned to see fire wagons accompanied by countless firemen, as they began to take up strategic positions along Front Street to protect the structures there, as well as those nearer the shore. Several people appeared to be on the verge of panic, and one hotel owner in particular was shouting nervously to the firemen to stay as close to his business establishment as possible.

Even though many in the huge throng milling all about him were spreading rumors about the Rebels having taken Harrisburg, and even that they had crossed the river just a few miles upstream at Marietta, Joe took it all as mere hearsay. He remembered very well how false rumors often ran rampant while he was serving with the 125th Pennsylvania.

Joe was certain that the Confederate advance, at the very least, had been temporarily halted. <This far an' not one step farther!

Printed by permission of the Columbia Historical Preservation Society - Sketched by A. Berghaus, 1863

Printed by permission of the Columbia Historical Preservation Society - Sketched by a correspondent, 1863.

They're *not* takin' Lancaster an' Philadelphia!>Joe thought to himself, as he gazed at the far end of the bridge at Wrightsville and pictured the frustrated Confederate Army cooling its heels on the other side of the river.

But despite this seeming triumph, the loss of Swift thoroughly dampened his spirits and was almost too much to bear, as several times throughout the evening he fought desperately with himself to choke back tears of bitter anguish, as he sat and simply shook his head in dismay each time his mind's eye stirred up visions of the chestnut stallion prancing nervously on the bridge.

The previously overcast sky had finally dissipated somewhat, and the moon's silvery disk was now gliding serenely amid a cluster of dark, bluish and purplish-red clouds; but nature's beauty and the awe-inspiring scene which lay before him, seemed to be practically ignored by the thousands of spectators, who obviously had flocked to the shores of the Susquehanna in the mere quest for excitement. The almost picnic-like gaiety of the crowd did nothing to soothe Joe's feelings. For some unknown reason, everyone seemed to be acting as though he were witnessing the final act of a grand circus, rather than a dangerous and costly action of the war.

Becoming more and more upset and angry with each passing moment, Joe suddenly wished he were far away. Rising slowly, he felt a slight breeze as it bore the searing heat from the blazing, crackling flames. Then he watched in awe, as suddenly an entire bridge span collapsed not far from shore, timbers and arches falling with a steaming hiss, plunging heavily into the foaming waters. However, not all the flames were extinguished, and some of the loose timbers floated down the river like great fiery rafts, almost giving the appearance of an entire flotilla of burning ships.

Now extremely hungry and totally at a loss as to what he should do or where he should go, Joe was about to turn and walk away, when he saw an elderly gentleman in the throng whose face he recognized; and his spirits soared immediately!

"Excuse me, sir!" he called. "Mr. Wright!"

Upon hearing his name, the kindly stationmaster turned and smiled when he realized who had called him. As the two acquaintances reached to shake hands, they were about to strike up a conversation, when they heard a loud, unexpected rumble, even above the tumult of the crowd and the roar of the constantly approaching flames. Terrified screams followed, and people began scattering in all directions before Joe could fully comprehend what was happening.

The disturbance was coming from the direction of Wrightsville, and a glance across the river revealed short flashes that accompanied the distant but loud rumbling. Joe recognized instantly that the Confederates had evidently swung artillery pieces into position and were directing their missiles toward the eastern shore.

"The Rebs are firin' cannon!" Joe shouted to Mr. Wright. "We better get outta here!"

Though Joe was concerned for Mr. Wright's safety and welfare, he felt no regrets at the sudden dispersal of some of the ridiculous mob of sight-seers who had descended upon the scene more for the express purpose of being entertained than for any other reason.

Turning hurriedly to leave, Mr. Wright asked in a concerned tone of voice, "Are you with anyone else, young man?"

Joe simply looked at the gentleman for a few moments. Then, shaking his head he replied, "Mr. Wright . . . you're not gonna believe this, but I'm in a mess again!"

"Not another runaway!" his elderly companion exclaimed, eyes opening wide.

"No, sir!" Joe assured him with a slight chuckle. "But it's been every bit as hair-raisin'; believe me!"

"Then why don't you come with me to my home, and you can explain along the way. Besides, I was looking for you or your folks at the market just yesterday; but with all the ruckus lately, I'm sure that's why you weren't there."

"Yes, sir," Joe replied. "Otherwise we'd've been there; you can be sure."

"Well, you come to the house; and I'll show you why I was hunting you," Mr. Wright responded, courteously extending a second invitation.

They walked quickly, but Joe gradually felt less concerned; for since there were no shattering explosions anywhere around them, it was fairly evident that the enemy probably had only light artillery with them, incapable of firing entirely across the broad Susquehanna. Then when they reached the foot of Locust Street, as Joe was hoping, the guns ceased their futile cries altogether.

At that point, Joe stopped and looked back toward the incredible mass of flames across the Susquehanna one more time, and saw that the blaze had just reached the very extreme end of the Columbia side of the bridge.

"Do you happen to know the hour, sir?" Joe asked.

Mr. Wright fumbled for his pocket watch and held it in the dim light of a nearby lamp. "It's just about twenty-five minutes past midnight, young man."

"That's almost unbelievable!" Joe said in an awe-filled tone. "Do you realize that bridge has been burnin' for almost five hours?" he questioned incredulously.

"Yes," nodded Mr. Wright. "It's been a most eventful day, to say the least!"

They continued talking as they walked up the hill toward Second Street, where Mr. Wright lived. As they trudged along somewhat disconsolately, the stationmaster shook his head and said, "You know, the entire time I was watching this amazing catastrophe tonight, I kept wondering to myself what this will do to the canal and railroad traffic. It's bound to have an incredible impact on the people of Columbia and Wrightsville!"

He said these words just as they reached the corner of Second and Locust Streets. There he stopped and simply stared at the building that stood on the southwest corner. "Especially this place!" he continued, pointing with the knob of his walking stick. "The Columbia Bank!" And he shook his head once more before adding, "They owned the bridge, you know."

Then, still shaking his head despondently, he took his young friend by the arm and continued their early-morning journey.

By the time the pair arrived at Mr. Wright's home, situated beside the unforgettable old mansion, Joe had informed his acquaintance of the events which brought him to Columbia on this occasion.

"For a young man, you've certainly had your share of harrowing experiences!" Mr. Wright remarked as he opened the front door. "And it sounds as though you haven't had anything to eat for quite a while; so let's get out to the kitchen and see what we can find."

After lighting a candle, he took Joe's musket and placed it in a corner. Then he called to his wife who was standing at a window near the top of the stairs, completely enthralled by the awesome, spectacular sight upon the river.

After she descended, Mr. Wright introduced her to Joe, before leading him to the kitchen. There the lad continued talking with the elderly gentleman and his wife, while Mrs. Wright provided him with something to eat, as well as a large mug of cool, refreshing meadow tea.

When Joe's appetite was finally satisfied, Mr. Wright said, "Now, I suggest you stay here and try to get some rest. But first, there's something I'd like you to see."

Walking with the lad into the parlor and stepping to his desk, he reached for a letter and handed it to Joe.

"This is what I took to the market for you yesterday," he said, pointing to the front of the envelope. "You notice it's merely addressed to 'The Wright Family, Columbia, Pa.' It's written by a woman from a place called Islington, Canada, by the name of . . . Ann Woomert, if I recall correctly; and she has some wonderful news about Nat, the boy you brought to the mansion. Remember?"

"Really?" Joe asked, pleasantly surprised and his face beaming, as he withdrew the letter from the envelope.

"Nat can't read or write too well yet, but she says he's going to school and learning more every day; and he talks about you so much, that she just felt she had to try to write to you about him. But since she didn't know your address, she wrote it to us, hoping we could get in touch with you."

"Great!" Joe remarked, as he anxiously sat down at Mr. Wright's desk to read. The next few minutes were a real delight, as Joe learned how Nat was progressing and had obviously found a home where he was truly loved, and given the kind of care and attention he really needed. However, what touched Joe's heart and mind most of all, was that Mrs. Woomert wanted Joe to know that Nat was attending church with her family, and had begun to read short portions of the Bible.

When he finished and began folding the letter, Joe looked up and said, "Thank you, Mr. Wright! That sure helps take some o' the sting outta today's nightmare!"

Mr. Wright began to realize that this had been such an emotional day for Joe, that he was extremely stirred up and evidently not at all sleepy. Sympathetically sensing the lad's restlessness, he suggested he find a more comfortable chair where he could relax a while, and encouraged him to tell more details about what had transpired in Wrightsville prior to the destruction of the bridge. Then, in the course of their conversation, he eventually led him to relate some of the highlights of his days as a drummer boy.

Mr. Wright was truly one of Joe's favorite people in the world, and he enjoyed talking with him, almost endlessly. Consequently, it was nearly three o'clock in the morning before weariness finally began to make it's mark. When at length he began to yawn from time to time, his extremely amiable and understanding host led him upstairs, to a room where he could spend the night.

However, even before lying down, Joe gazed rather dejectedly out the window facing west; and far into the distance, for nearly another quarter of an hour, he stared almost as though he were hypnotized, watching remorsefully the dying embers of the smoldering bridge.

Later, still lying awake in the Wright's guest room, he knew that his parents were probably once again extremely worried about where he might be; and at once he turned to prayer for them. Then, concern for his mother and father subsequently led him to petitions on Dan's behalf, praying that his Heavenly Father would place a hedge of protection about his brother, and bring him home safely one day.

More often than not, a time of prayer would have a restful, calming effect upon Joe; but the horrendous events of the day, and constantly returning thoughts of Swift, preyed almost incessantly upon his mind, causing him to roll and toss far into the morning hours. However, at last he fell fitfully asleep, and never awakened until nearly one o'clock in the afternoon.

"I thought I'd let you rest," Mr. Wright said when Joe came downstairs at last. "You had quite a day yesterday, young man! Come out to the kitchen, and we'll find you something to eat."

Mrs. Wright graciously offered him a bowl of soup, some freshly baked bread, and a cup of tea. After the kindly woman excused herself to take care of some of her household chores, Joe chatted at length once more with his host, being certain to thank him again for the letter as well as for his customary generosity.

Then, after bidding the Wrights farewell, he gathered his letter and musket and was soon hurrying toward the river front where he hoped to learn the latest news regarding the Confederates. It was nearly two o'clock when he approached the foot of Locust Street. Once there, he saw that quite a large crowd had assembled once more. He expected that everyone had come to view the ruins of the once magnificent bridge, but he noticed that the people's attention was drawn more to the river itself.

Even standing on tiptoe he was unable to see what was demanding the throng's concern. Then, by overhearing bits and snatches of

several conversations going on all at one time, he determined that a boat of some kind was evidently approaching from Wrightsville.

Suddenly, the level of the voices in the huge crowd began to rise almost like a wave, as incredibly wonderful news was being passed along from one group to another! Whoever had rowed the boat from Wrightsville informed the spectators along the shore, that although many of the Confederates had begun their retreat early the preceding evening, the last of General Gordon's troops hadn't pulled out of the town until around ten o'clock in the morning. When several citizens had ridden west to check their movement, they learned that the rear guard of the Confederates was well on its way toward York.

As this news was happily exchanged, general pandemonium began to break loose; and people started running to homes where folks from the west shore had gone to seek shelter with friends or relatives.

Within less than an hour, the river was teeming with rafts and nearly every kind of boat imaginable, as the people of the two sister communities were engaged in thoughtful acts of generosity, ferrying people, animals and possessions back to York County once more. It was almost as though the specter of the original Wright's Ferry had come alive again.

As Joe roamed aimlessly around the Front Street area, he was feeling extremely proud of his two favorite towns, witnessing genuine neighborliness being extended to one and all.

But eventually, his eyes settled sadly upon the mile-long mass of smoking bridge ruins, tilted down in some places with the ends of the timbers plunged into the waters, a sight of utter, heart-rending destruction! Joe found himself expelling a heavy sigh of nearly complete despair! Staring in dismay, he thought to himself: <Without that bridge, how would I ever have gotten Nat to safety?>

It was almost as though he had lost still another great friend to the war. Then, after gradually turning, he stood looking directly up Walnut Street, where he could see the very area where Jon had lived. A knot came instantly into his throat. He felt a strong churning sensation in his mid-section, as highly treasured reflections of his wonderful friend began to stream through his mind; and he longed for his companionship once more.

At last, for some unknown reason, a portion of Scripture that his mother had suggested he memorize, started to weave its way into his thought patterns. The words came almost as though they were a healing balm to a troubled mind: <...but this one thing I do, forgetting those things which are behind, and reaching forth unto those things which are before.>

As Joe recalled these words, he smiled to himself and looked upward gratefully. Then, quickly shaking himself from his temporary doldrums, he decided resolutely to get on with life.

Spiritedly he began searching for someone who might offer him a ride to Wrightsville, and before long he was helping a generous Columbian to row a mother and her three children across the river.

As he pulled on the oars for the next half hour, his brown eyes could do little more than constantly scan the heaps of charred timbers which still clung tenaciously to their stone piers.

When they reached the other side, Joe exchanged thanks with those whom he had accompanied; and then, before heading home, he cast a mournful glance at the burned buildings and the bridge ruins that lay before him on the Wrightsville side of the Susquehanna, and suddenly remembered Dave and Ted. He had been so engrossed with concern for his family and Swift, that thoughts regarding his buddies had eluded him entirely. Feeling somewhat ashamed of himself, he momentarily feared for their safety; but with a quick smile and a shake of his head, he made a private wager that his wily companions had somehow managed to elude the Confederates.

Joe's arms were tired from rowing, but his legs willingly carried him up the long hill. When he reached the top, a strong drive from deep within caused him to turn and look back just one last time. He never wanted to forget June 28th, 1863. As he gazed at the long, smoking, topsy-turvy heap of ruins, and the lonely stone bridge piers standing like faithful sentinels across the waters of the Susquehanna, he knew unquestioningly that he would never be able to erase that day from his memory. The unbelievable view of the remnants of the bridge, as seen from the hilltop in Wrightsville, would be implanted indelibly in his mind forever!

Then, a quarter of an hour later, musket in hand, he was approaching his barnyard gate with mixed emotions. Everything looked safe and sound, but he wondered how to present his own sad news about Swift to his parents. Then, just as the gate creaked shut behind him, he heard a familiar whinny! With a shivering thrill he would always remember, he turned to see Swift leaning over the top half of the stable door, whinnying and tossing his head excitedly as he greeted his young master.

"Swift!" Joe shouted, almost too shocked to believe his eyes; and in his haste to run to the stable, he nearly tripped over his own feet. As he was running, he heard the back door slam; but he was so happy to see Swift, that he didn't turn even for a moment to see who was there. Then a few moments later, as he was affectionately hugging and stroking the stallion's strong neck, he turned to see who was playfully jabbing him in the ribs.

"Dave!" he shouted upon seeing his devilish buddy. "What're *you* doin' here in the middle o' the afternoon?"

"Afternoon? Hey! My pa brought me over in the wagon first thing this mornin', an' I've been here ever since! I just *had* to see if you got home!" Dave explained.

"Is Ted all right?" Joe asked quickly.

"Oh, sure," Dave guaranteed him as off-handedly as though the preceding day had been nothing but another hunt for Indian relics.

"Well, how'd you guys get outta that mess anyhow? I just *knew* you would!" Joe laughed.

"How could I help it?" Dave remarked with a prolonged shrug of his shoulders. "I was ridin' the fastest horse this side o' the Mississippi!"

"Swift?" Joe asked, finding Dave's words hard to believe.

"Who else?" Dave grinned. "I was just inside the bridge entrance, when all at once it looked like the whole *world* went up in flames! From where I was standin' it wasn't hard to see Swift against *that* background! But when I didn't see you anywhere, I thought I'd better get movin'! I know I never in my life beat you in a foot race, but I'll bet even *you* woulda had a dandy time tryin' to out-run me then! But by the time I got to Swift, I thought I was in an oven! An' there I was, thinkin' I'm a big hero or somethin'; an' guess what *he* does?" Dave asked, pointing an accusing finger at Swift.

"What?" Joe said, cocking his head and waiting for an explanation.

"First he tries his level best to kick my teeth right down my throat, jumpin' around like he's just been attacked by a swarm o' horse flies or somethin'!"

"Well, you can hardly blame him!" Joe laughed, at the same time that Swift gave Dave a playful nudge with his muzzle and snorted as though he understood every word Joe's friend was saying.

"But wait a minute!" Dave continued. "I didn't even get to the excitin' part yet! When I finally *do* get him loose, then he tries to leave without me! *Fine* friend he turns out to be! Anyhow, I manage to get into the saddle an' ride off the ramp just as the Rebs make their rush for the bridge!"

"Boy! That was close!" Joe acknowledged. "Did you get a chance to use your pa's musket?"

Dave's eyes nearly bulged from his head. "Do you know what you're askin'? When I saw 'bout a thousand Rebs come swarmin' down that road screamin' them Rebel yells, me an' Swift lit out for the towpath like a streak o' lightnin'! An' you know *me!* I can't even shoot straight when I'm standin' on my own two feet let alone tryin' it when I'm in the saddle! Especially one that's tied to *his* back!"

As Dave related his story, Joe kept laughing at his excitable friend's gestures and facial expressions. "Some cavalryman you turned out to be, Dave! If you're ever gonna wind up in this war, you'd better take up drummin' like me!"

"Yeah, I guess that showed me what war's all about," Dave admitted. "As a matter o' fact, I'd hafta say that's the scaredest I've ever been in my life! Anyhow, Ted saw us comin' an' jumped on his horse; an' thanks to Swift . . . good grief! He put about five miles between me and them Johnny Rebs lickety-split! Joey, there ain't no musket ball on the face o' this whole earth coulda caught up to us! I'll tell you somethin'! If he'da been tied up to one o' them canal barge ropes, them people woulda thought they were on the fastest trip *they* ever took through the canal!"

By this time, hearing Swift's whinnying, Dave's banter and Joe's laughter, the rest of the Shelleys came from the house, all rejoicing over one another's safety, Joe being especially happy to hear that not one Confederate had even come near the farm.

As they were talking, Bob Loney drove his rig through the main gate, on the way home from Wrightsville. "Did you hear what the Rebs did in town?" he called.

"No, what happened?" Mr. Shelley asked.

"They say that when the bridge started to burn, the Rebs tried to get buckets from the townspeople to put out the fire, but could hardly find any. Seems like nearly everybody in town hid their buckets some place!" Mr. Loney chuckled. "But later, when the flames spread to some buildings near the bridge, buckets came outta nowhere; an' General Gordon actually ordered two Reb regiments to form a bucket brigade down to the river an' help fight the fires!"

Joe just shook his head in amazement! "Well, can you beat that?" he remarked, suddenly recalling the generous act of the Confederate soldier who had leaped over the wall with the canteens on the frozen slopes of Fredericksburg. "War's absolutely crazy!"

Mr. Loney nodded his head in agreement and chuckled slightly. "I've never heard of a war yet that made any sense, young man. They're all ridiculous! Man's his own worst enemy!"

Then, after clucking to his horse, he said, "Gotta be headin' home to tell the Mrs. that everything's safc an' sound. See you again sometime."

As the family waved, Dave tugged on Joe's sleeve and said, "Uh . . . by the way, Joey . . . you'd better go along home with me. I sorta got somethin' to show you."

"Jumpin' grasshoppers! Can't it wait, Dave?" Joe asked. "I just got home!"

"Afraid not," Mr. Shelley interrupted, flashing a mysterious smile in Dave's direction. "It's been weeks since we've had anything nice happen around here! C'mon, everybody; I'll hitch up the wagon an' we'll all go!"

Joe couldn't understand why they were making the trip; and no one would tell him, though it was easy to see that everyone was excited about something. But what really needled Joe was the way Sarah kept looking at him and laughing to herself.

"What's goin' on anyhow?" Joe asked, mystified, as he looked from one to the other while they rode in the back of the wagon.

"You'll see," his mother said with her usual smile and a matter-of-fact tone of voice. "Just be patient."

Joe simply shrugged his shoulders and then asked, "What's the latest news on the Rebs, by the way? Has anyone heard anything 'bout where they are or where they're headed?"

"Pastor Jackson stopped by shortly before you got home and told us that word got through that they're clear on the other side of York, heading west toward a place called Gettysburg," his mother informed him.

"Gettysburg?" Joe echoed. He lowered his eyes and thought hard for a few moments before shaking his head. "Don't think I ever heard of it before," he admitted.

"Neither did I," Dave remarked. "An' we'll prob'ly never hear of it again either. I guess it's in the next county somewhere."

When they finally arrived at Dave's farm, Mr. Shelley drove directly to the stable.

"Have a look inside!" Dave said to Joe, leading the way, and unable to suppress a big smile.

When they reached the stable door, Dave swung it open and allowed Joe to enter first, whose initial reaction was to squint his eyes in an effort to adjust to the sudden change in light. Then, as he gradually became accustomed to the semi-darkness, he glanced into a large stall area, a broad grin slowly streaming across his face.

"So! . . . That's why you haven't been ridin' Beauty!" he exclaimed.

At the mare's feet lay a solid chestnut colt; and near the stall boards a slightly dappled filly, with white stockings on her forelegs, was struggling to her feet.

"The chestnut's a stallion, an' the filly's really frisky!" Dave informed them. Then, looking at his close friend, he said, "An' guess what?"

Joe merely answered his question with a blank stare.

"They're yours, Joey!" Dave informed him, flashing a broad grin.

Joe looked first at Dave and then at his parents in disbelief!

"Swift's their sire!" Dave explained. "An' among the whole bunch of us, your brother Dan included, we decided that the foal would be yours; but ol' Beauty worked overtime an' delivered *two* instead o' one!" he laughed.

Before Joe had a chance to recover from his state of surprised shock, his father interrupted. "Hold on, Dave! Mrs. Shelley an' I already decided that one o' them's to be yours. An' after what happened on the bridge yesterday, we're *sure* Dan would insist on it too!"

"I'll say!" Joe agreed.

Now it was Dave's turn to be surprised. "Gosh! Thanks!"

But then his eyes fell upon Sarah, who had knelt to pet the newborn colt. After thinking carefully for a few moments, he said, "But really, on second thought, we have two other mares that are about to foal real soon; an' I just *know* I'm gonna have my hands full!" Dave admitted.

Then, looking at Joe's sister again, he said, "Why don't we just keep it in the family . . . an' let Sarah have one of 'em?"

"Do you mean it?" Sarah almost shrieked, looking up first at

Dave, and then at Joe and her parents with a look that almost begged their permission to accept such a gift.

"Sure! Why not? We never planned on twins anyhow!" Dave remarked.

Mr. and Mrs. Shelley looked at one another and smiled. "Well . . . if that's your wish, Dave, that's fine with all of us, I'm sure," Mr. Shelley announced.

Joe looked at his delighted sister and laughed. "You really deserve that just for keepin' this a secret for so long! I don't know how you ever did it, Sarah!"

His sister looked up with a satisfied smile from where she was kneeling and giving the colt a fond hug. Then looking at Dave, she asked, "What're their names, Dave? Did you give 'em one yet?"

"Well, no; not really," Dave answered. Then, looking slightly embarrassed, he added, "After they were born last night, the first thing my ma insisted on was that somebody else name 'em besides me. She says I always give such dumb names to all our animals! I guess she just don't appreciate my creativity an' sense o' humor!"

"You mean . . . like your duck, Mortimer?" Joe asked.

"You got the idea exactly!" Dave shot back with a beady-eyed glance.

"Well, Joey," Mrs. Shelley laughed, as she gently stroked the filly. "Why don't you and Sarah name them then?"

"You do it, Joey," Sarah insisted vigorously. "Whatever you pick'll be fine with me."

"Are you sure?" her brother asked.

After Sarah nodded quite emphatically, Joe smiled and slowly walked toward the open stable door, deep in thought. "Well, let me give this a *good* think," he mused, stroking his chin and staring off into space.

He stopped and leaned against the stable door jamb, looking out across the meadows and eventually, far over the river toward Columbia.

In the distance, he could distinguish the most remote sections of the destroyed bridge; and then his gaze moved slowly farther eastward toward the middle of the little town, to the area where he knew that Jon had lived. Immediately his thoughts centered on his unforgettable young friend, and he slowly glanced into the skies above Columbia. Clusters of small, white and wispy clouds floated through the beautiful blue heavens, reminding him of

Jon's brilliant eyes and that day when they had stood together at his father's grave in Frederick, Maryland, under an equally blue sky.

Then, gradually, there among the clouds, in his mind's eye, he began to catch a vision of a blonde-haired, blue-eyed Union drummer boy staring down at him; and he was sure his ears could even pick up the faint sound of distant, muffled drum beats.

At that moment, Dave approached, looking wonderingly at his friend, and detecting the solemn, faraway look in his eyes.

Then Joe started to nod his head, as a broad, beaming smile gradually began to fill his face.

"I can tell you're cookin' up somethin'!" Dave surmised. "Now what're these names gonna be?"

"Well . . ." Joe drawled, still smiling and gazing into the heavens, "I guess we're gonna call that colt *Thunder*, and the filly's gonna be . . . *Tarnation*!"

Dave thought for a few moments. "Hmmm. *Thunder* . . . an' *Tarnation*," he repeated. "*Thunder* an' *Tarnation*! Yeah! I *like* that!" he said, nodding his head and looking at the Shelleys as he announced his approval, while Sarah dashed toward Joe, threw her arms around her brother's neck and kissed him on the cheek.

But all the while, as Joe put his arm around his sister, he continued looking into the skies; and as his vision of Jon slowly diminished, he was sure he could detect . . . a very . . . impish . . . grin, even as the drum beats began to fade.

RAT-A-PLAN, PLAN, PLAN, RAT-A-PLAN
RAT-A-PLAN, PLAN, PLAN, RAT-A-PLAN
RAT-A-PLAN, PLAN, PLAN, RAT-A-PLAN
RAT-A-PLAN, PLAN, PLAN, RAT-A-PLAN
RAT-A-PLAN, PLAN, PLAN, RAT-A-PLAN
RAT-A-PLAN, PLAN, PLAN, RAT-A-PLAN
RAT-A-PLAN, PLAN, PLAN, RAT-A-PLAN
RAT-A-PLAN, PLAN, PLAN, RAT-A-PLAN
RAT-A-PLAN, PLAN, PLAN, RAT-A-PLAN

EPILOGUE

Perhaps it may be of interest to the reader to know that Bob Loney, William Goodrich and Cato Jourdon were real people who were actually listed among the participants of those involved with the operations of the Underground Railroad. Cato was a black man who helped his people escape and frequently transported them from York to both Wrightsville and Columbia.

Mary and Susan Wright really were the two descendants of John Wright who were living in the Wright Mansion during the era in which this novel takes place. According to Mr. Willis Shirk, native of Columbia and a member of the Columbia Historic Preservation Society, William Wright, who did live next door to the family mansion for many years, actually died in December of 1846.

The accounts of the movements of the 125th and 106th regiments are based on historical fact. For instance, the travel and prolonged marching from Harrisburg all the way to the Antietam Creek; feeding the regiment right in the streets of Baltimore; the worship service in the warehouse at Washington, D. C.; the dogs howling as the men marched; the "razzing" by the New Englanders; the search for food among the Maryland homesteaders; the Confederates searching for their mortally wounded general; the Confederate band playing in the distance; the ambulance trains passing through the night; General McClellan riding past the 125th and actually waving his hat to them; the death of General Mansfield, and every military maneuver performed by the regiment at Antietam is recorded in the annals of the 125th's diary, from the woods to the corn field to the sunken road and back to the line of artillery that saved their lives; the careening gun limber that crippled several members of the regiment; working right alongside Confederate burying details; the cremation of the horses, and the bodies of the Confederates on the lawns and porches at Sharpsburg; and even the worms in the crackers and Manny's concern about catching the *hydrophobee*! All these things actually happened to the 125th Pennsylvania Volunteers.

The long wagon train to Virginia through the snow was also factual, as were all the events surrounding the building of the pontoon bridges, the snipers and cannonading of Fredericksburg; and, of course, the famous scene of the Confederate soldier bringing canteens of water to the wounded Union soldiers, is well documented in our country's history books.

The two drummer boys, Jon's father, Captain Colter and Slade King are the only military characters whose names were not included on the actual roster of the 125th Regiment Pennsylvania Volunteers. Sergeant Abbott was the leading enlisted man in Company A, and Manny Welles really was the head cook. And, as fate would have it, there really were two men named Stewart, who served in the exact capacities mentioned in the novel. However, they probably were not related in actual life.

Admittedly, the author himself was surprised to learn during his research that some regiments actually formed special drill units; and since one of the purposes of the novel was to pay tribute to the drummer boys, often unsung heroes of the Civil War, a special effort was made to include one of those units in order to showcase this special duty of at least some of the war's drummers. Of course, history records that President Lincoln actually did visit the military encampments on several occasions. However, both the date and place of his visit to the 125th's brigade were changed at the discretion of the author.

Finally, realizing that it is all too simple to write in error concerning any period of time more than a century after its occurrence, and despite the fact that much careful research has been done, sincere apologies are offered for any unintentional misrepresentations of any nature that may be found in this novel. Hopefully there are none! My heartfelt desire is that the reader enjoyed himself following the adventures of Joey Shelley, as much as the author did while writing about him!

Glenn S. Banner
October 8, 1993

ACKNOWLEDGEMENTS

The author wishes to extend his gratitude to Randy Kusel for helping conquer the greatest handicap in writing this book: finding information concerning the drummer boys of the Civil War. It follows, then, that Olive Dean Hormel also deserves much credit since it was her excellent book, ***With Sherman to the Sea***, which acquainted me with many other duties of the drummers. Through the efforts of these people I learned of the drummers' work in the hospital and the corrals; searching for straw, fuel and water; and preparing headboards for grave markers.

Susan Mumper, Tom Sultzbach, Blanche and Win Davis III, Ronald Bramhall, Doris Wertz and Paul Kaseman also provided material which contributed to the writing, as did Faith Delaney, the extremely helpful librarian at Wheatland Junior High School in Lancaster, Pennsylvania.

Dr. John Price of Franklin and Marshall College graciously provided information concerning Susquehannock Indian lore.

Special thanks is given to Dr. John Denney and Mr. Emmett Rasbridge. I will long remember the extremely informative personal interview with Dr. Denney, whose grandfather actually helped set the charges to blow up the fourth span of the covered bridge. I am certain that it was on the evening of that particular interview that I determined to write this story!

Mr. Rasbridge provided me with a most enlightening tour of the Wright Mansion, personally showing or telling me of all the unique features mentioned in the chapters dealing with that famous landmark, which still stands proudly at the juncture of Second and Cherry Streets in Columbia, Pennsylvania, to this day. The evening spent with these two gentlemen was truly one of the most eventful of my life!

Veterinarians Dr. George Nylin and Dr. Richard Smith helped with knowledge regarding horses; and Dr. David Fuchs not only rendered information which aided with the writing of some of the historical phases of the novel, but provided considerable insight concerning wounds and their treatment during the Civil War era. It was also through Dr. Fuchs' efforts that the best drawing of the old, wooden bridge was made available, helping immeasurably with the writing of the runaway slave scene across the bridge, as well as with plans for illustrations.

Special kudos are in order for Edna Clark, Columbia's "living history book!" Her wealth of knowledge concerning the author's home town history was a treasure chest to which I needed to turn on several occasions.

I sincerely wish to thank Jim Weaver, Carla Snyder, Byron Wright, Noel Kegerise, Kim Redcay and all the dedicated people involved with Brookshire Printing and Publications, Inc., of Lancaster, Pennsylvania, for their untiring efforts to put this novel into print.

Still another area which demands recognition is that of the illustrator, John "Bot" Roda, who became involved only weeks before the book was to be published. I appreciate his endeavors at a time when he was extremely busy! I also wish to thank Rosemary Robinson for the use of her very noteworthy sketch on the dedication page honoring the Civil War drummer boys.

Both Charles Hauer and my wife Dorothy were especially helpful in keeping me from falling into traps regarding the proper times of the year for certain crops to be gathered; and, I must add, that nothing would probably have ever come to fruition insofar as the publication of this book is concerned, if my wife hadn't continued to nag, nag, nag in order to get it into print more than thirty years after its inception! The fundamental plot for the book was written in the early 1960's, just prior to the centennial year of the burning of the bridge.

Finally, and with much heartfelt gratitude, I express my very special thanks to Mr. Wayne Von Stetten and all the wonderful people who make the Columbia Historical Preservation Society what it is today. Without Wayne's help and encouragement in many areas, and the society's incredible enthusiasm to see the "story of the bridge" finally be recognized in some tangible way, I probably still would be working on chapter one! These people truly spurred me on!

To all whose names are listed above, and probably to some whose names I've unfortunately neglected to mention, I express a very warm *THANK YOU*!

Glenn S. Banner

SOURCES

Allen, Richard Sanders. ***Covered Bridges of the Middle Atlantic States.*** Brattleboro, Vermont: The Stephen Greene Press, 1959.
Billett, Glenn E. "The Department of the Susquehanna." ***Journal of the Lancaster County Historical Society.*** Vol. 66, #1, 1962.
Bitts, Carole. "The Gem of the Susquehanna." ***Lancaster County Magazine.*** Lancaster, Pennsylvania: Brookshire Publications, July, 1993.
Carter, W. C. and A. J. Glossbrenner. ***History of York County.*** Harrisburg, Pennsylvania: The Aurand Press, 1932.
Catton, Bruce. ***This Hallowed Ground.*** New York: Doubleday and Company, Inc., 1956.
Coakley, Lt. Col. Robert J., ed. ***The Lesson and the Legacy.*** Washington, D. C.: The United States of America War Office, 1961.
The Columbia Civil War Centennial. 1963.
The Columbia News. (various articles and editions)
Cornell and Altland. ***Our Pennsylvania Heritage.*** State College, Pennsylvania: Penns Valley Publishers, Inc., 1887.
Dedication Program and History of Lancaster-York Intercounty Bridge.
Ellis, Franklin and Samuel Evans. ***History of Lancaster County.*** Philadelphia, Pensylvania: Everts and Peck, 1883.
Gibson, John, Historical Ed. ***History of York County, Pennsylvania.*** F. A. Battey Publishing Company, 1886.
History of the One Hundred Twenty-fifth Regiment Pennsylvania Volunteers by the Regimental Committee. Philadelphia, Pennsylvania: J. B. Lippincott Co., 1906.
History of the Twenty-third Pennsylvania Volunteer Infantry compiled by the survivors. Published by the State of Pennsylvania, 1904.
Hormel, Olive Dean. ***With Sherman to the Sea.*** New York: The John Day Co., 1960.
The Lancaster Intelligencer-Journal. (Various articles and editions)
Lossing, Benson J. ***A History of the Civil War.*** New York: The War Memorial Association, 1912.
Mandel, Paul. ***Great Battles of the Civil War.*** New York: Life Magazine editors, Time Inc., 1961.
Palfrey, Francis Winthrop. ***The Antietam and Fredericksburg.*** New York: Chas. Scribner's Sons, 1882.
Rupp, J. Daniel. ***History of Lancaster County.*** Gilbert Hills, Publishers, 1844.
Self, Margaret. ***The Horseman's Encyclopedia.*** New York: A. S. Barnes and Co., 1946.
Smedley, R. C. ***History of the Underground Railroad.*** Lancaster, Pennsylvania: Office of the Journal, 1883.

Tilberg, Frederick. ***Antietam.*** Washington, D. C.: National Park Service Historical Handbook Series #31, 1961.
Under the Maltese Cross - Antietam to Appomattox compiled by the rank and file of the 155th Pennsylvania Regiment. Pittsburgh, Pennsylvania: The 155th Regimental Association, 1910.
U. S. Army Publication Services (Various articles)
Ward, Joseph R. C. ***History of the One Hundred Sixth Regiment Pennsylvania Volunteers.*** Philadelphia, Pennsylvania: F. McManus, Jr. and Co., 1906.
Werstein, Irving. ***1861-1865.*** Paterson, N. J.: Pageant Books, Inc., 1960.
The York Gazette, Centennial Edition. 1963.

AFTERWORD

As long as I can remember, there has always been concern, doubt, consternation and even downright disbelief involving the "tunnels" which may or may not have been associated with the construction of the old Wright Mansion. It's a subject which I am certain will never truly be put to rest, and probably no one will ever know the exact story.

When I visited the mansion and spoke with Mr. Rasbridge, I never doubted for a moment his convictions that the tunnels existed; and although I did not accept his invitation to crawl through the rear of the fireplace and see for myself the sealed entryway which he declared emphatically was there, I felt absolutely certain that it was! And he was equally convincing when he referred to the other tunnel which once led toward the river.

My own thoughts on the matter are that quite likely there really were two tunnels leading from the basement of the mansion, but I hardly believe that they were as long as what most people surmise. For instance, I find it nearly impossible to believe that a tunnel could have been dug in that era, nearly the length of three modern-day city blocks, most especially given the topography of the land between the mansion and the Blunston homestead!

However, I will be the first to admit that even stranger things have occurred in the history of mankind; and I am thoroughly convinced that all the quandary revolving around the tunnels is what has given rise to the charm and mystery that have always enshrouded the *charisma* of the old Wright Mansion of Columbia, Pennsylvania!